D1053323

Mercury

ALSO BY

CARY HOLLADAY

•   •   •

THE PEOPLE DOWN SOUTH

THE PALACE OF WASTED FOOTSTEPS

Mercury

A NOVEL

CARY HOLLADAY

SHAYE AREHEART BOOKS
NEW YORK

This is a work of fiction, with no intended resemblance
to actual persons or events.

•　　•　　•

Published by Shaye Areheart Books, New York, New York.
Member of the Crown Publishing Group, a division of Random House, Inc.
www.randomhouse.com

Shaye Areheart Books and colophon are trademarks of Random House, Inc.

Printed in the United States of America

DESIGN BY LYNNE AMFT

Library of Congress Cataloging-in-Publication Data
Holladay, Cary C., 1958–
Mercury : a novel / Cary Holladay.—1st ed.
I. Title.
PS3558.O347777 M47   2002
813'.54—dc21   2002016347

ISBN 0-609-60814-2

10 9 8 7 6 5 4 3 2 1

First Edition

For John

Mercury

PART I

*K*ATELYNN'S ROOM IS MADE OF

glass. At least, three sides of it are glass, and with the curtains pulled

back, she has a spectacular view of Hawk Lake. Her house occupies

a point jutting into the lake. As the tour boat slides into view, right on

time, Katelynn sits up in bed and reaches for her binoculars, glad to

set aside her homework. She can't concentrate anyway. Only her his-

tory teacher, Mr. Stiles, is keeping up even a pretense of assigning

work to her. He leaves books with her mother. Pokes his head into her

room sometimes to say hi. She's too weak to talk to him for long or to

do the work that will allow her to get a diploma. Back in the spring,

she was too sick to do any homework or take any tests, too sick to

graduate, and she doesn't feel much better now. She's thinner and weaker than she's been in her life, has no appetite for anything except candy corn and Tootsie Rolls, and has hardly been out of the house for weeks. For her, Dr. McKellar makes house calls. Her parents are rich enough to warrant that. He takes samples of her hair, blood, and urine, and packs them off to his lab.

She did go to the lakeside convenience store one day with her mother. The store was too dazzling, with the bright boxes of cat food and the bags of potato chips. Katelynn picked out a blue lipstick that promised it would turn pink on her lips. Her mother talked it up and paid for it ("You could do with a little color in your face"), but Katelynn just brought it home and threw it in a drawer, for she is through with makeup now, she who used to slather hundred-dollar lotions on her skin. She hardly even washes her face, and she has cut off her hair.

It's a Saturday in late September, ten o'clock in the morning. If she's lucky, she might see the boat three or even four times today, before twilight settles in, as it does earlier every day. The tourist business was good all summer. One day, the boat made a record seven trips, laden with sight-seers. The white-haired guide, Captain Louisa, must have made big money that day. By this time of year, though, the tourist trade is dropping off. Visitors come to the town of Hawk Lake to enjoy the warm-springs spa, shop at the craft fairs, and drop in on the occasional music festival, often just a few fiddles, banjos, and harmonicas on somebody's front porch. Also popular is the nearby diamond mine, not a cave but a plowed-up dirt field where you use your own tools and keep a sharp eye out. Just this summer, a boy found a big yellow gem worth some real money. The boy's photo is everywhere now, on posters in the windows of restaurants, inns, and shops. Katelynn has memorized his face: all buckteeth and sunshine, with the soft jaw of a preteen. The caption reads: "I found a diamond! So can you!"

Of course, the best way to see the lake itself, with its two sides, rich and poor, is by taking a cruise on the *Arkansas Belle*. The tour boat—a duck boat, salvaged from World War II and refashioned—can't go very fast, but it is amphibious. It putters through the town's narrow streets, tooting along as Captain Louisa points out land-marks—museum, old-fashioned ice-cream parlor, bathhouse and spa—and then, its wheels retracting, its land-self transforming into a sea-self, it noses into the lake and glides on a long circuit, slow and sturdy if not graceful. A yellow-and-white-striped canvas top stretches across it, making a sort of roof to shield passengers from the sun. At the back end of the boat, the canvas top is open. Railings surround the passengers. It would be hard to fall out.

Hawk Lake is wide, deep, and complicated by coves. Fishermen love it. The rich side—Katelynn's side—has mansions made of glass and tile and stone, with gardens of magnolia trees, crape myrtle, foun-tains, and sculptures. Katelynn's family has not been rich forever, only for a few years, since she was in middle school. It still felt natural to her to go into the convenience store and buy the cheap blue lipstick.

The appearance of the boat is the high point of Katelynn's days. It reminds her of a get-well card, the tiny figures on deck alert in their stance as they gaze at the fancy lakeside houses. Captain Louisa has been around as long as Katelynn can remember, her trademark scarlet cap a beacon as she moves around on deck. This season, as in most years, the *Arkansas Belle* is the only tour boat. Most of the time, Captain Louisa has a monopoly. There are plenty of other boats, at times, private little sailboats and flat-bottomed fishing boats, but no permanent competition for the *Belle. That's what I want to do with my life,* Katelynn decides, unwrapping a Tootsie Roll and putting it in her mouth, savoring the familiar, elastic texture. *I want to sail a boat on a pretty lake and tell stories to people. I want to be the best part of their vacation.* Already, she has lived many lives, has been a cheerleader, a lifeguard.

Gazing at the boat, she feels connected to it. She will get her mother to take her out on it, on a day when she is feeling better. Of course she has been out on the lake, plenty. Till recently, her parents had a little boat. You operated it with a key; it was simpler than a car or even a golf cart, just a floating platform. Its motor gave out; they will get another boat. Every Fourth of July, there's a small fireworks show at the lake, and everybody goes out on boats or just watches from their windows. But Katelynn has never ridden aboard the *Belle*. It has a peculiarly beautiful wake for a slow-moving craft, like a line of whipped cream. Seen from the *Belle*, her house will look glassier and more majestic than it does when she's seen it from other boats, reflecting in the water like a thunderhead.

During her sickness, she's had time to look up subjects that interest her. Mr. Stiles has helped. Knowing how she waits for the duck boat, he brought her a library book about amphibious craft, and from it she learned that twenty thousand of these vessels were manufactured during World War II. The design is just a truck chassis with boat features. The same type of front-wheel drive is still used today on GMC trucks such as the Chevy Blazer. A duck boat's top speed is only six miles per hour in the water and thirty-five on land. Katelynn has read all this and stored it away, finding satisfaction in knowing that these vehicles have had such long careers. Duck boats have air compressors, and their six tires, she has learned, can be inflated or deflated by controls on the dashboard. During the war, the duck boats were used to transport guns, vehicles, and other cargo from ship to shore—valiant, tough little voyagers, duck boats are, the quick-change artists of the transportation world.

Katelynn admires the *Belle*. It's not enough just to be sturdy in this world. You need an extra identity, a whole other self for the separate challenges of land and water.

The boat disappears predictably into a cove and then rounds the bend and edges toward Katelynn as if it's going to sail right into her house. She loves this moment, when the boat comes close enough for her to wave and see people smiling and waving back, as friendly and excited as if they're each other's long-lost family. Any second, they will look up and see her. She feels certain Captain Louisa tells every boatload of passengers her story ("That poor girl smoked mercury-covered cigarettes, can you believe it, and a friend of hers died") and explains that she might be sick for a long time.

Katelynn knows a lot about mercury now, for she has not only survived mercury poisoning but, thanks to Mr. Stiles, has read about it. The devoted history teacher brings her stacks of photocopied articles from medical journals and tells her the good parts. She has learned that President Andrew Jackson, for example, may have died of mercury poisoning. His doctor kept prescribing calomel—mercurous chloride—a favorite remedy back then, and poor Andrew Jackson got sicker and sicker. The article didn't say what calomel looked like. Katelynn pictures Pepto-Bismol. Mr. Stiles was excited about that article, going on about Andrew Jackson's tooth loss, kidney problems, tremors, constant salivation, and suspicion. In some weird way, Katelynn's illness excites him, and this embarrasses her. Yet Mr. Stiles is a relief from her mother, who doesn't want to talk about the mercury, who hates to even say the word. When Katelynn told her mother about Andrew Jackson's drooling, her mother held up her hand: stop. Her mother almost hates her for what she did, most of all for the fact that she played with the mercury and smoked it on three different occasions, she and her friends did, she and Jenelle and Harvey.

Mercury poisoning has its own vocabulary: *erethism*, which means great and terrible excitement; *cachexia*—emaciation; *acrodynia*—redness of the hands and feet. The words are beautiful. Katelynn loves to say them, but they wear her out. Dr. McKellar has been clear and severe about what she is and is not supposed to do. *Avoid sugar, caffeine, and alcohol.* The alcohol part is easy. The thought of it turns her stomach. But she can't give up candy or Pepsi and in fact craves them. Exasperated, her mother keeps this a secret from Dr. McKellar. *Eat two eggs and up to a quarter of a pound of butter a day.* "That's a whole stick!" she'd told the doctor, horrified. Occasionally, she's hungry enough to eat an egg. She can't imagine ever eating a stick of butter per day, or wanting to. "When can I drive again? How will I know when I'm well again?" she asked Dr. McKellar, and he said, "Driving is the least of your worries right now. And you'll know when you're well."

So she's practically grounded. Her BMW gathers dust in the garage.

The articles that Mr. Stiles brings her talk about low body temperature as a result of mercury poisoning. She certainly has that. Then she'll spring a wildfire fever that ends in a soaking sweat. Electric currents are another side effect, one article states. This puzzles her. She wonders if she has become magnetic, if she'll shock people with the touch of a fingertip or mess up the microwave when she stands near it. She feels contagious, though she is not.

Yes, for just a moment, the people on the boat will focus on her, no doubt knowing by now about the mercury-covered cigarettes, maybe feeling sorry for her or satisfied that she was punished, that this is what you come to when you break the law: skinny, bedridden, pitiful. At least she doesn't drool. Her first symptoms developed just days after she smoked the cigarettes—cough, chills, fever, upset stomach. She passed it off as flu, staying home from school, getting together with Harvey and Jenelle in the evening, to smoke the mercury-doused cigarettes twice more, but the novelty was wearing off. The pinkness on her hands and feet took longer to develop than the other symptoms. They're better now, not so red. "Acrodynia is more common in children," Dr. McKellar said, his mouth tight. He's disgusted with her. Once was bad enough, but the serial usage, as he calls it, *that . . .* and he doesn't have to say out loud, *that is a sin.* With his high, heavy brow and fierce blue eyes, Dr. McKellar might be an old-timey preacher. Her shame about everything connected with the mercury grows each time she sees him. The hair loss, the rapid heartbeat, high blood pressure, diarrhea, oh, all of that is still with her. She'd really believed she had the flu, a lingering, weird flu, until she had a seizure. That's what made her tell Dr. McKellar about the mercury.

It happened when she was alone in her bathroom, leaning over the sink to brush her teeth. It felt like she'd stuck her whole body into an electrical socket, like a dozen people were dancing with different parts of her, roughly and all at once. She'd found herself on her back, on the floor, her head sore from being banged against the toilet, her arms and legs twisted into shapes goofier than anything she'd ever tried in cheerleading, her mouth all foamy, but it was just toothpaste. She can laugh about that now.

Now the boat is close enough for her to wave.

Her mother has told her not to wave from her bed, that it's tacky, but Katelynn doesn't care. She's been waiting all morning for the boat. She waves to it in big broad motions as if washing windows. Instead of college, where she is supposed to be by now, seducing professors and figuring out ways to keep ants out of packaged food in a dorm room, she has these daily visits from the *Arkansas Belle*. She loves the little craft and feels proud of it and of the lake.

What's happening? Katelynn waves, but the passengers don't seem to notice her. Not one of them waves back. She feels invisible. She waits for Captain Louisa to make her usual gesture toward the house, which has more glass than any other on the lake: glass patio doors, skylights, even a glass turret. The house was featured in a famous magazine just last month, its architecture and gardens splashed across eight glossy pages. Pictures showed how, from the street, the house looks just like any old gorgeous Tudor mansion built of Arkansas field-stone, but then go around to the lake side, and *ta-dah,* it's a glass house, with plenty of screens and windows and doors and louvers built in. Katelynn can't help but be proud of it.

She wonders if Captain Louisa saw the magazine article. The duck boat itself appears in a corner of one of the pictures, though it is not mentioned in the article, which goes on at length about the rainbow of colored marble in the floor of the foyer, the view from the glass tur-ret, and the many varieties of crape myrtle in the garden.

Through the dark spectacles Katelynn must wear, which make using the binoculars hard, the boat gives off a coppery gleam in the September sun. She lies there, loving its company. Her father's at work, her mother's off getting her hair done. Her father will leave this evening for another trip to Burma—Myanmar, it's called now. Such a pretty sound. Myanmar. Her father has been there many times. When he gets back, and she asks him how it was—*Was it fun, Dad? Was it scary? What's it like over there?*—he just shakes his head. Her father has always seemed boyish, even vulnerable. He's tall but stooped. With his short hair standing up on his head, he reminds her of a newly hatched chick. But the newly hatched chick must be clever and tough to grow as rich as he has become, to travel as he does in a country she understands to be dangerous. She imagines him riding a water buffalo across a shallow brown river and running his fingers through piles of golden, foreign coins.

She has postcards he has sent her, a whole slew of them. They take such a long time to come, but they have beautiful stamps, and her father always writes "Love, Dad" in capital letters. And she has a little statuette he brought to her, a temple maiden, smiling with her eyes closed. "Nothing valuable," her father said. "They make 'em for tourists." Katelynn loves the carved statue with its slim arms and faint odor of incense. She lays down the binoculars to check it: there it is on the shelf above her desk, smiling its shut-eyed smile. She eats another Tootsie Roll, then some candy corn, picks up the binoculars again, stares out at the lake, and waves again.

No response.

Something's wrong with the boat. Sitting up within her sweaty sheets, Katelynn leans forward. The boat's about a hundred feet from her. She doesn't need the binoculars anymore. The boat's gone lopsided, tilting to the side. A fat man stands on the low side, toward the front. Captain Louisa approaches him, and he moves to the other side of the boat. Katelynn wishes Jenelle were here to see this. They'd say, "So fat he almost sank the boat!" And they'd roar with laughter.

But Jenelle is dead. The mercury killed her. She had all of Katelynn's symptoms and more: irreversible kidney damage, paralysis, coma, death. Katelynn never saw Jenelle once Jenelle got sick. They'd just talked on the phone. But Katelynn's getting better. She takes her medication twice a day, a synthetic resin, the doctor calls it, which enables her body to excrete the mercury instead of retain it. "The mercury is so dangerous because it binds to body proteins," Dr. McKellar has explained.

Katelynn focuses the binoculars on the boat again and counts heads: seven or eight on board, maybe more. But the big man's changing positions hasn't helped. The boat's lower than before, as if it's plowing the water with its back end. As Katelynn watches, the front end slants upward, with a couple of people falling—or jumping?—out the sides into the water. She hears a scream, muted to tininess by the glass walls and the water. She doesn't breathe. The boat points straight out of the lake, its striped canvas top gone vertical.

It's sinking.

Passengers are thrashing and struggling in the water, but not many, maybe two or three. One breaks away and swims toward shore, toward Katelynn's house. For a moment, the rounded end of the striped canvas top is visible, like an egg yolk floating in the water, and then the boat vanishes as if yanked below by a giant hand.

As Katelynn reaches across the bed for her phone, laughter escapes from her lips, first in bubbles, then in whoops. It's an effect of the poisoning, laughing at the wrong time. Her lifeguard instincts would have her running out and diving into the lake, but she'd never make it now, with her muscles turned to string. She dials but is laughing too hard to speak, plus her mouth is dry from all the candy she has eaten. The operator answers immediately and asks questions.

At last Katelynn chokes out, "The boat sank. The duck boat."

The emergency operator asks for her name, but Katelynn is too convulsed to give it. She prays the operator won't think she's playing on the phone and hang up on her.

"I don't mean to sound like this is funny," Katelynn says, "but the boat sank."

At last the operator—she thinks it's a man's voice but she's not sure—says, "You mean the boat on the lake? The tour boat?"

"Just now," Katelynn whispers. She hangs up.

A woman has made it to shore and is sprinting, screaming, toward Katelynn's glass walls. She'll burst through them, Katelynn thinks, staring at the woman, she'll splinter the glass and kill herself. Blood will be all over the glass.

The woman's bathing-suit top has gone crosswise so that one breast is exposed. Spotting Katelynn, who is still in her bed, frozen in place, the woman yells, "Help, help!"

Katelynn hates it that the woman sees her laughing. Hates that those who drowned might have observed, as their last earthly sight, a girl in black glasses cackling at them, uproarious as she reached for the phone. *I didn't mean it.* Haunted by it even though she's still in the moment. The woman reaches the glass walls and beats on them so hard the house shakes.

There's a sliding glass panel in the glass wall, but Katelynn's too weak to open it. She jerks her thumb toward the door on the side of the house, meaning: *Go around that way.* The woman locks eyes with her and just screams. Katelynn will have to go let her in. She has to, though she doesn't have the strength. She pushes her legs out of the sheets, stands up, and falls onto the floor.

DEEP IN THE LAKE, descending, her ears and eyes sealed with water as if with clear plastic, Louisa sees him go past her—the fat man, sinking at about the same speed as a person might climb down a ladder, deliberately, not all that slow, yet not too fast. She's keeping a grip on herself. Careful. She reaches out to touch the fat man, to apologize that way, to say: "You sank the boat, but I know you didn't mean to and I didn't mean to hurt your feelings." The man slips just beyond her reach, as if now he has stepped on an elevator and is plummeting faster. She thinks of her father. The years fall away and she hears his voice, ringing with its Ozark inflection: "G'awn up that ladder!" So that she could help him on the roof, a small, slight child, scared of heights but scareder of him. She's on the ladder all right, but going the wrong way. Her father needs her, up on the roof.

She's falling through the water gracefully, losing sight of the fat man. Too dark in the water and her shoes are heavy.

She'd lasted about five minutes on that roof with her father fussing at her. She picked up nails and loose shingles like he told her to.

She's back there, with the sun beating down, the nails hot as blazes in her fingers so that she pitches them off the house, and her father shouts at her, "Don't just throw 'em in the grass, Louisa!" That was back at their old house in Yellville. She was a small, slight girl, when her father had hoped for a boy. She'd beefed up in high school. The sequence of her life reels out before her, as she's always heard it does: a review offered up to her as if for her approval. As if she could change a thing.

But she pays attention. There she is in the high school hallways, braving her unpopularity with broad shoulders, her hair bumpy from the rollers and bobby pins her mother insists she use every night. Her daddy'd go off for weeks on jobs, painting, handyman stuff. Twenty years he's been dead. Even though she's drowning, she still can't believe she's so old—officially a senior citizen.

The movie reel pauses, and she hears her daddy's voice again, late in his life, long after her mother died. He'd been on a job down in Little Rock for months and was back home in Yellville: "Gone so long, the 'lectric company cut off my lights." How is it he sounds so satisfied to be back in his trailer in the dark, burning candles till the lights come on again? Telling any story from his life, he would sigh and say, "Hit's the truth, porely explained," and now, underwater, Louisa wants to say that herself, to peg this awful mishap for what it is, whatever it is.

Her daddy's voice comes loud as a bullfrog's through the water, disgusted, powerful: "Louisa, g'awn up that ladder."

There it is, the splintery old paint-splashed wooden one, leaning against the side of the house, warm from the sun, rough and familiar beneath her hands. She gathers her strength and climbs. She climbs the ladder up to the roof, through the lake, into air.

WHEN JERRY FIVEASH comes out of the bathroom, he finds Glo at the window, wrapped in a curtain so that she's naked only from the back. He snaps his towel at her bare behind, gently, so that it just whispers across the white cheeks. Still, it leaves a pink flush. Her skin's that soft.

She doesn't move. Just stands like a statue in the curtain, gripping handfuls of the fabric in bunches around her hips. He puts a hand on her shoulder and kisses her neck. Her skin tastes salty, like potato chips.

"It sank," she says. Her head spins around. Her eyes—her eyes remind him of something, but he can't think what. "The boat sank, the tour boat," she says and points to the water.

He thinks she's joking. He doesn't even look out the window. If he's going to get any painting done today, he better get started.

"Jerry," she says, "it really did sink. Just now. I think I'm going to be sick."

"Jesus," he says and steps to the window.

"Way out there," Glo says and points across the big lake.

He squints to focus three-quarters of a mile across the bright water and sees dots that must be people thrashing, circling out there. He says, "We have to help 'em. Call for help."

"I can't do it," Glo says in a whisper. "Nobody can know I'm here. I said I was going to get my hair done. I can't ever say I saw."

Jerry yanks the cordless phone off his dresser and punches 911. It's the first time in his life he's needed to dial that number. The operator tells him to go out and keep an eye on the people, on the spot where it happened. Does he have a long rope? To throw to them? "Call out to them. Tell them help is on the way," the operator says.

"I got a rope," he says into the phone.

Glo's at the mirror with scissors in her hand. She grabs a fistful of her shoulder-length hair and hacks it off at chin level. Grabs the other side and saws at that. The hair slides down her chest to the floor in beautiful, wine-red clumps. To Jerry, she says, as if pleading for her life: "Get the rest of it, around back. I missed some."

Her eyes are so panicky he's afraid she's going into shock. He won't argue with her, just throws the phone on the bed, grabs the scissors, and whacks off the back of her hair, then takes off running. He jumps in his truck. There's a rope in the back. As he bumps and jounces along the shore road, he tries to keep his eyes on the people in the water. Looks like one of 'em made it to land already. The house closest to them is Glo's—the house where she lives with her husband and daughter. Her husband's often away for months at a time. The boat sank practically in Glo's front yard.

Even so, he won't park in her driveway. He leaves the truck near the house next door—the Johnsons' house—throws the rope over his shoulder, and races to the lake.

Up at the house, there's a woman screaming. He dashes out on the point, ready to throw the rope, but the water's empty. Then somebody breaks up to the surface, a person gray-faced and choking, water streaming, arms clawing at air.

"I got you," Jerry yells.

Forget the rope. He rips off his shirt and dives into the water, chops through it, stops to look around. Damn, there's nobody: they sank. No, there's the person, a woman, farther out than she was a minute ago. He makes fast for her and grabs her by the shoulder. She goes nuts, flailing, crawling on top of him, sinking him. He has to fight her so they won't both drown, and it feels like a desperate, crazy game—her hands on his face, her knee on his shoulder, his palm pushing her head away. At last he gets hold of her elbow and half-pushes, half-tows her along. She goes limp, which is better than the crawling. By the time they get to shore, he's winded. He stumbles up on the bank and drags the woman with him, stretching her out on the grass. She sits up, and water gushes out of her mouth, so much that Jerry expects a fish or two to come with it. He slaps her on her back.

He knows her. It's Louisa Shepherd. Captain Louisa. He's known her all his life. Catching his breath, wheezing, he calls her name. "Louisa? You okay?"

Another woman—the screamer—is hurrying toward them, soaked and wild. She has on jeans with a bathing-suit top, and the top's half off so that one breast is covered and the other is bare. She's crying out, "My husband's down there. Save him."

Someone—a skeletal young girl—is following this woman, creeping slowly as if in pain. She's wearing dark glasses and a long T-shirt, and she's barefoot. She's dry, but something's wrong.

Before he realizes that he knows who this is, Jerry says, "Were you on the boat, too?"

The girl starts laughing, her face contorting beneath the dark glasses.

"What's so funny," screams the bare-breasted woman. "What's so goddam funny."

"It's how I cry," the girl says. She asks Jerry, "Who are you?"

The bare-breasted woman saves him from having to answer. She leans down to the woman lying on the bank and hits her across the face, screaming, "You killed my husband. You made him move. You bitch, bitch."

Jerry pulls her off Louisa. Behind him, the girl's laughing hard. So this is Glo's kid that almost died. He's only seen her at a distance, and that was months ago, before she got sick. He has never spoken to her before. She's not supposed to be out in the sun. Glo told him that. It's an effect of mercury poisoning: photo-something or other. Photosensitivity.

He stares at the lake but can't see anybody else out there. Far off, he hears sirens. A motorboat with a couple of fishermen in it is sputtering through the water toward them, the men yelling.

To the girl, Jerry says, "You go on inside. Get out of this, this bright light."

The girl turns and goes, stiff-legged, slow.

"What? What do you mean?" The bare-breasted woman is shrieking at him. "Save my husband," she says. "Oh God. I'll get him. I'll get him myself."

She unzips her jeans and shimmies out of them. Her underpants are plaid. She kicks her way into the lake, furiously, and swims a few yards until Jerry goes out and drags her back in.

• • •

FOR ONCE, Katelynn's glad to see Mr. Stiles, the history teacher, even lets him come into her room and sit on a chair beside the bed. She's desperate for somebody to talk to, can't bear to watch the reports on TV with her mother in the living room. Her father left for the airport in Memphis several hours ago. From there, he'll fly to Denver, then to L.A., then to Hong Kong, and then somehow he will reach Burma—Myanmar—though whether that is accomplished by rickshaw, rental car, or roller skates, she isn't sure. He hugged her hard before he left, so hard she had to hold her breath, and she wished for his sake she had not seen what she saw. She's a disaster magnet, a lightning rod for badness. All he took with him was a black leather duffel bag with his running shoes tied onto the strap, as if he's going no farther than the gym.

An only child, she has always wished for a brother or sister. She doesn't understand sibling rivalry, swears she wouldn't resent her siblings if she had any. Why begrudge them, when the world's own forces would probably crush them before they were even grown?

The twilight stretches, holds, as if to give the rescuers time to work.

They are bringing up the bodies, her mother has told her, the bodies of all those people who drowned. Katelynn said, "Why watch it on TV when you can just look out the window or go out in the yard?" But she can't bear to watch it either way, not on TV and not in real life. The curtains in her room are drawn so she won't see what's going on in the lake, and she has her CD player on, very low, so she won't hear much of anything, either.

"Did they find anybody else alive?" she asks Mr. Stiles.

He shakes his head and says, "People are singing out there, out in your yard, on that little point of land. They're singing hymns. Would it comfort you to hear them?"

"No," Katelynn says, but she is curious. If she were well, she'd be singing with them. "Who are they? Anybody you know? Or are they relatives of—of the people on the boat?"

Mr. Stiles shrugs, still looking out, his shoulders rounded, his bald spot a small wan moon. "Just people. They're holding candles and singing and praying." He snaps off her CD player, and she covers her ears. After a moment, she takes her hands away, and the voices reach her through the glass, faint and eerie, weaving a melody she knows from church:

Fairest Lord Jesus, Ruler of all nature . . .

Dr. McKellar has already visited, bringing tranquilizers. Katelynn didn't want any, but her mother did, dumping the bottle into her hand and pawing at the pills the way Katelynn goes after candy corn. Katelynn's been lying in bed for hours with songs on her mind, oldies. That's a weird symptom that she keeps forgetting to tell the doctor about. Songs stay on her mind for hours, no matter how hard she hums "Jingle Bells" to drive them away. It'll be any old song, insisting she listen, popping out of some crevice of her brain, the brain she pictures as luxurious, crumpled black velvet, with drops of mercury hidden in its creases like diamonds in a black velvet box.

She could tell Mr. Stiles about this, the music in her head. He's actually a better listener than Dr. McKellar is about her symptoms. Mr. Stiles probably goes home and writes them down in a creepy little notebook: irritability, insomnia, decreased hearing, jerky gait, stiffness.

Mr. Stiles says, "I brought you a picture and a book."

"Let's see." She takes the picture from his hand. It's an arty-looking photograph of silver branches shining through fog. "Pretty," she says. "What is it, trees in the wintertime?"

"It's lungs," says Mr. Stiles, nodding with satisfaction, "an X ray of lungs belonging to a dental assistant in California who tried to commit suicide by giving herself a mercury injection."

Katelynn thrusts the picture back at him. "Who is she? Do you know why she was so unhappy?"

"Who knows? The good thing is, she's now perfectly all right. I xeroxed the whole article. It took her only ten months to recover," he says, folding the picture and tucking it into his pocket.

"Give me the book," she says. She is allowed to treat him this way, now that she is sick. She would never have been so brusque with a teacher before.

It's a big hardback, with lustrous pictures. "The world's fair," she says, propping it up on her chest and paging through it, though it's uncomfortably heavy across her body. "All the world's fairs. Thank you," she says.

"I wanted to bring you a present, after what you've been through, and I didn't even know about today," Mr. Stiles says, sounding defensive. Jenelle would have laughed at that. She made relentless fun of him behind his back. Katelynn can almost hear Jenelle's low, snorting laugh. The thought flashes across her mind that the book is a suitor's gift. Nobody ever uses that word anymore. She wants a suitor, but not him. She wants Harvey, Jenelle's boyfriend, but Harvey is gone, and nobody seems to know where he is. When the three of them got sick, separately, Katelynn went to Dr. McKellar, Jenelle to the emergency room, and Harvey vanished. The uncle he used to stay with said he packed up his car and just drove away.

"Do they still have them? World's fairs?" Katelynn asks Mr. Stiles.

"I think so," he says, biting his lip. "They call them expos now."

"I want to go to one."

Mr. Stiles blinks. Seated stiffly in a leather chair he lugged in from the living room, he reminds her of some creature, a swamp turtle maybe, something quiet and mysterious that bites. Besides teaching history, he's the high school track coach. He had coached Harvey, pole-vaulting Harvey, all the way to a regional championship. Coaches are supposed to be popular, to tell jokes, have glamorous wives, and give parties for the athletes and their girlfriends, but Mr. Stiles is shy, unmarried, awkward, ugly. When Jenelle made fun of him, Harvey and Katelynn defended him. "Throw your heart over the bar, and your body will follow," Harvey used to say, quoting Mr. Stiles. Harvey and other boys had gotten scholarships from colleges. The other track stars are there now—in college. Not Harvey. For Katelynn, the worst part of the mercury episode is not knowing where Harvey is.

With a conspiratorial smile, Mr. Stiles says, "I bet you didn't study world's fairs at the academy, did you? Maybe then you'd have stayed."

"Nothing," she says, "would have made me stay there."

The fall of her senior year, at Glo's insistence, Katelynn had enrolled at a private, all-girls academy in Memphis, a famous, small, very expensive school with a walled boxwood garden, a formal dining room, and whispery corridors. Biology, French, ballet lessons, Roman history, and horseback riding at a suburban stable filled her days, but evenings and weekends were torture. "It's just homesickness. You'll get over it. Come home for a weekend, and it'll pass," said Glo on the phone, but visits home only made Katelynn more eager to get back to her old life. She hated the privileged, competitive girls and the sibilant, patronizing teachers. She lay awake wondering what was wrong. Did she just miss boys? Cheerleading? She was rich, as her classmates were. She was free; like most of the other girls, she had a car; she could have explored, taken as lovers men she met in the city, as the others did, sneaking out for weekends at hotels. She must still be a child, a failed grown-up, her metamorphosis stalled so that she is stuck in her chrysalis, one wing out, one in. She still believes she'll like college, if she ever gets there. It will be different.

At the academy, her grades were terrible because she was trying to flunk out. She sought injury, sliding off her horse and lying sprawled in the muddy rink, but the riding instructor just snapped, "Stand up, Miss Troy, and get back on that horse." She missed her parents, even though her father was gone most of the time. She missed her glass house, Jenelle, her old school. At last she hit on a way to get expelled. Stealing. She swiped a girl's backpack from the dining hall, stole her roommate's wallet, and nabbed a rake that a groundskeeper had left in the boxwood garden. All these things she kept in her room, in full view, so that when she was swiftly determined to be the culprit, she was able to keep silent as events reached a satisfactory conclusion: she was sent home.

Her first day back, she saw Harvey, the new guy. She stopped right there in the hallway to gaze at him, and he grinned at her, seeing right into her heart. He was so tall, and his eyes looked smart, sleepy, sexy; his hair curled just right. He'd moved to Hawk Lake from Colorado, he said, and everybody had accepted that. Girls asked him was Colorado beautiful like they'd always heard it was, and he said gorgeous, that there was always snow on the mountaintops. In Hawk Lake, he lived with an uncle who worked the night shift at the bottling plant—the same uncle who once worked at a neon factory, now abandoned, the building where Harvey had found the mercury. The part about the uncle, at least, was true. And Harvey's genius with the pole vault: that was real, too. When girls asked him was Colorado beautiful, they were saying with their eyes, with the tilt of their heads, with the cadence of their voices, that they wanted him. They asked about snow and mountains, and what they meant was, *You can have me.* Katelynn saw it, everybody did; it was part of the game. But he belonged to Jenelle. He had leaned against her locker and claimed her, reaching out to put his hands around her waist and pull her to him. Katelynn was en route from gym class to Mr. Stiles's history class, upset because the curl had come out of her hair, knowing she smelled bad because you always did stink after P.E. Showering just made it worse because the showers had a moldy smell and the towels stayed damp in the lockers and even a fresh towel caught that locker-room reek, and no deodorant or perfume could cover it up. She was worrying about smelling bad when she saw Harvey pull Jenelle toward him lightly, as if they were dancing. In the open locker beside them, she saw Jenelle's cheerleader uniform hanging from its hook and her cartons of cigarettes jumbled in the bottom, never mind that it was illegal to have them at school; you couldn't have cigarettes or Midol or even aspirin. Oh, she'd felt how hopeless it was to be second prettiest. What an old, tired feeling that was. In that moment, she'd felt all the striving and despair of others who had walked those hallways and curled their hair, curled their eyelashes, and sucked in their stomachs to fit into the next-size-smaller cheerleading outfit.

Now she can rest. Now she's done with it, with all the hair spray and volumizer, eye shadow and blusher, all the practicing in the mirror to achieve the right expression. All those hairdos! Jenelle had tried to help her. Side braids, bangs, low ponytails, clip it up here, tuck it back there, perm it, blond-streak it, tease it, gel it, smooth it up, down, fluff it out, for long beautiful hair was power, and hers would never be as beautiful as Jenelle's, Jenelle who wore her coal-black hair straight down her back like an Indian maiden, and it looked good whether she washed it or not. Katelynn's blond hair was debilitated even before the mercury, soaked in chemicals and tortured by hot curls. What a relief to give it up. What is left is soft as one of the herbs her mother cultivates, the one called lamb's ear that grows in a sunny spot next to the verbena and the lemon balm, a short, brief sigh of hair that is sick and wants to be well, hair that doesn't care about being pretty anymore and the same with her eyes; she wore so much makeup all those years of competing with Jenelle, that it's lovely now to stop. Jenelle's eyes were gas-flame blue, like jewels in a setting of kohl and mascara, with so much going on in them, more drama than a whole multiplex of movies. Katelynn's own eyes, brown and round, look so obvious. She was even jealous of Jenelle's voice, a voice ruined by too much cheerleading, so that its low huskiness had a way of disappearing entirely in the middle of a word or a sentence, leaving split-second gaps and silences. Everybody used to lean close to Jenelle, to catch what she was saying. Katelynn used to want a glamorous, ruined voice, too, used to yell extra loud on cold nights at football games, but her vocal cords held out.

Mercury has freed her from all of that. She remembers a weekend she spent obsessing over what she thought was an age spot on her hand. Jenelle had dismissed it as a freckle, but that was just as bad. Through with all that. She laughs, and Mr. Stiles shoots her a worried look. He knows about the mixed-up-with-tears laughter and seems to understand it.

She's been daydreaming so long, she's almost forgotten he is here.

"So you want to go to a world's fair," says Mr. Stiles, in the voice he used in class to move a discussion along. She remembers his using that tone of voice to talk about war: a pompous tone, but he's smart, she has to give him that, and there's always something more behind what he's saying. Even when other students dozed off, she'd stayed resentfully tuned in, her cheek mashed against her hand, doodling Harvey's initials in the margin of her history book in a complicated pattern, so if asked, she could deny that they were his initials at all. Mr. Stiles says, as if it's a line he has rehearsed, "You will have to get well, then, Katelynn."

The world's fair book is too heavy. Katelynn closes it, slides it off her chest onto the bed. The TV in the living room is turned up too loud. An announcer is describing duck boats: "Thousands of these crafts were manufactured during World War II to land troops in shallow European bays. Many were converted to tourist vehicles after the war. Powered by gasoline engines, they are neither fast nor easy to maneuver. The *Arkansas Belle* was typical, with a metal hull attached to wheels, and a canvas top stretched across a metal frame."

Mr. Stiles closes the door, comes back to his chair, and says, "Guess what. I'm living at the school."

"That's what people always say, when they work hard," she says, feeling impatient with him. *He doesn't count,* she hears Jenelle say, and she wants to answer back, *I'm not counting him. I'm waiting for Harvey.* Or if not Harvey, somebody else who will take her out of this glass house and into the world. It's too much to fight with Jenelle, with Jenelle's ghost that lives in this room, mimicking, criticizing, blowing smoke out of the corner of her mouth.

"I mean actually living there. Living at the school," Mr. Stiles says. Katelynn blinks at him, and he nods once, deliberately, grandly. "I moved out of my apartment and sold my car. I have to be careful nobody catches me, the janitors early in the morning or the students who stay late for club meetings and such. I'll have to be extra careful when track practice starts. I only wonder why I didn't do this a long time ago."

"Where do you sleep?"

"In the nurse's office, on the cot. I shower in the locker room and keep food in the refrigerator of the home ec room. I've lived there almost two weeks."

"And nobody knows?"

"Only you. Will it be a hard secret to keep?"

She shakes her head no, suddenly tired, but she has so many questions for him. She asks them all at once, before her strength gives out: "Do you ever get scared? What does the school sound like, in the middle of the night? Where do you keep your clothes?"

He takes his time answering, almost preening, running a hand through his thin, ragged hair. "I use five or six different lockers for my clothes and stuff, but I gave most of what I owned to the Salvation Army. I don't need furniture anymore, or mirrors or pictures or lamps. I'm always scared, but that's part of the pleasure. One night I heard what I thought was a bowling ball going down the hall, but it was only a pencil rolling off a desk, echoing. It was louder than you would believe."

"Why are you doing this? To save money?"

He looks at her with shy, shining eyes. "It makes me happy. I feel powerful, living there, not leaving at the end of the day after I've taught my last class. I walk past the ballot box for homecoming queen in the hallway, and knowing I could stuff it with anybody's name I want—that makes me very happy. I'll do it, too. I'll choose the queen. It could be you. You haven't graduated, so technically, you're eligible." He leans forward and asks, "Katelynn, would you like to be queen? You were runner-up last year, when Jenelle was queen. You should have won. This year, I'll make you queen. I'll stay up all night writing your name on ballots, using different pens and different handwriting. Who's to know?"

"No, don't do that." She hesitates and then says, "It's kind of a relief not to be pretty anymore. I used to worry about it so much. I'd never have been as pretty as Jenelle, anyway."

As soon as she's said this, she wishes she hadn't told him. The person she'd like to tell is her mother, who was always so proud of Katelynn's almost-prettiness. It is a comfort to have whacked off her hair and to dress like a slob, if she gets dressed at all—in stained moccasins without socks, in shorts and T-shirts that have been balled up in the bottom of her closet for months. As if she had the energy to do otherwise. But Mr. Stiles's expression doesn't change. He's still a turtle, eyes hooded. His eyebrows are small, thick triangles of fur.

"You're still pretty, Katelynn. You're beautiful," he says, but he doesn't insist on stuffing the ballot box, and she's glad about that. She's about to ring the bell on her nightstand, the bell that will summon her mother, but as if reading her mind, he rises to leave. He says, "I wouldn't have told you my secret except for what happened today. That boat sinking—that changed everything. I had to tell you."

She says, "How do you get around, without your car?"

"I have a bicycle. I can take it inside the school and store it in a closet, and nobody thinks a thing about it. I rode it out here. It was hard, balancing the book on the handlebars. I need to get a backpack or something."

"Somebody'll see you," she says. "They'll see you going into the school. You don't have eyes in the back of your head. I bet somebody's already seen you."

"I like the home ec suite the best," he says. "I like having my supper there, when everything is quiet. I set the table for one, cook my food, and take my time eating. Then I clean up and put everything away. It's the best home I've ever had. It's odd to think that boys cook there, too. When I was your age, only girls took home ec."

Katelynn holds up her hand, where a thin scar runs almost invisibly across her palm. "Well, I took shop one semester and cut my hand on a saw, but I did learn how to make a bookcase," she says, exhausted now, wishing he would leave. She'll picture him at the school and worry about him.

"Katelynn," comes her mother's voice, and Glo pushes the door open. "I brought you some orange juice." To Mr. Stiles, she says, "Would you like some, too?"

Her mother's face is ashen. Katelynn feels so bad, for making her mother worry all the time. Glo's new haircut looks awful, as if her hairdresser were drunk and used pruning shears. Glo sets the juice on the nightstand. "They seem to think they found all the bodies," she says. To Mr. Stiles, she says, "I don't want those people out there, singing in my yard. It won't do any good. They're worse than the TV people. It's dark now, and they should just go home."

Mr. Stiles says, "Would you like me to ask them to leave?" He goes to the curtains, peeks outside, and says, "The TV vans are gone, but yep, the singers are still here. They're reading their hymnbooks by flashlight and candlelight."

Glo seems to wilt. "Oh, I guess they can stay, but I'm not letting any of them in to use the bathroom."

"Mom!" says Katelynn. Why is her mother so hateful? "Have they been asking to use it?"

"No," admits Glo, "but they're trespassing. They damn well better not pee in my yard or mess up the flowers or set the house on fire with those candles."

"I don't think they'll do that," says Mr. Stiles doubtfully, and Katelynn thinks her mother looks, finally, abashed. Mr. Stiles says good night and steps out of Katelynn's room, into the living room, where the TV is showing footage of the duck boat in its operative days, clumsy and buslike as it rolls through the streets. Katelynn sees that in the instant before he closes her door.

"Did you have anything to eat yet, Mom?" Katelynn asks.

"Your father and I had an early supper. He doesn't eat much before he gets on a plane. All I wanted was applesauce. Do you want anything?"

"No."

Glo turns off the light and goes out. Katelynn turns up her CD player and puts her headphones on so she won't hear the hymn singers out her window. If she were well, she'd have dived into the lake herself, when the boat went down, and she would have pulled the people out. Yes, she'd have saved as many as she could, and then she'd have sung for those who died, joining the hymn singers at the water's edge, where the wet reeds spring up so slippery beneath their feet.

From bed, she stares at her heavy curtains, but no light peeks around the edges. She turns up the volume on her CD player.

There was only one thing at the private academy that she liked: the boxwood maze. Walled in, the garden made a secret world. The maze was hard. She had to work to find her way to the center, where a stone sundial kept time. She used to spend hours in the riddling center of that maze, waiting for the perfect silence that came when all the teachers went home for the day and the girls were in the dining hall, having their supper. Once she'd spent the night there and went to class the next day in her same clothes. Nobody seemed even to have noticed she was gone, not even her roommate, a debutante from St. Louis with a habit of knitting her eyebrows whenever Katelynn spoke to her.

More than family or school or friends, she had missed the lake.

She had never, really, thought of anybody losing their life in the lake. To her knowledge, nobody had ever drowned there. She curls deeply in her bed, trying not to think how it would feel to drown. Pulling the headphones from her ears, she sets the CD player on the floor, on top of the world's fair book. She used to be able to swim from one end of a pool to the other on one deep breath of air. But the lake is so deep, deeper than any pool.

Faintly, the singers' voices reach her through the glass.

She misses the boat the way she'd miss a person. The lake's empty without it. She won't see it again. Unless she watches them haul it up. She falls asleep agitated, frowning, her dry lips twitching with laughter.

LOUISA WISHES her neighbor would go home and take her noisy twins with her. The neighbor, whose name is Barbie, had one course in psychology and one course in nursing about ten years ago and thinks she is an expert in all things physical, emotional, and mental.

"You can expect to feel very fragile in the next few days," Barbie instructs Louisa, who is lying on the sofa with a cold cloth on her head. Louisa feels fine. She accepted the cold cloth only to give Barbie something to do. It smells sour. There are fresh cloths in the bathroom closet, but she won't bother to tell Barbie that. Barbie is the most persistent of all the visitors who have come by. Most of them have stayed only a few minutes, wringing their hands and glancing furtively at Louisa. There is a stigma, she realizes, in being the captain of a boat that sinks, and in surviving when most of your passengers die. She was at the hospital only a few hours. They couldn't think of anything to do except take her temperature and give her hot tea and Tylenol, that useless stuff. She'd said, "At least give me some real aspirin, for heaven's sake," but they wouldn't.

Two of Hawk Lake's six policemen got to the hospital fast, and from her bed she talked to them, telling them all she knew, all she could remember. "I'm fine," she kept insisting when they asked her if she wanted to wait till tomorrow to talk. They had already contacted the Coast Guard, they said, and the National Transportation Safety Board. The officers were young, bug-eyed with excitement.

How did she manage to talk with them?

She has questions for them, things she didn't think to ask them at the time. Namely, how will they identify the people on the boat? From her hospital bed, she gave them descriptions of people, which they wrote down. They asked, "Do you have insurance?" and she said yes.

Disaster insurance seems beside the point, when people drown.

It was Barbie who came to the hospital and got her, remembering to bring dry clothes—a clean sweat suit—and brought her home, Barbie who fixed a meal of fish sticks and Tater Tots while the twins, Madison and Fairley, screamed underfoot. The jeans and blouse Louisa had almost drowned in are still sopping wet in a plastic bag by the door. She'll ask Barbie to throw them in the washing machine. Better yet, just throw them out.

She has got to thank Jerry Fiveash for saving her life. She has known him ever since he was a little tiny baby and she was working as a practical nurse for his grandfather, oh, years and years ago. But he's what, about thirty years old by now, and his hair's gotten so long she hardly recognized him. And today was the first time she got a good look at the mercury girl, that little gal who almost died and who's been waving at the boat from her bed all these months, a thin pale person hovering there while the fat man's wife beat Louisa up. *Wham. Pow.* Who knows, that might have helped knock the lake water out of her lungs.

She couldn't eat the fish sticks Barbie fixed earlier, but now she's hungry.

She craves bacon, but not the regular kind. She wants bear bacon. Bear bacon, hominy, and biscuits, like her grandmother in the Ozarks used to fix, with a cup of hot sassafras tea, sweetened with sorghum pressed out of canes on the iron roller mill in the backyard, the mill powered by a mule-drawn sweep. All of it fascinated Louisa when she visited. Her grandparents died so long ago, died at home in their log cabin way up in the mountains during a winter of deep snow.

Almost drowning has jarred loose her memories. She sees again the raccoon skins stretched out on the wall of the cabin, legs splayed out and striped tails hanging down, and the slices of dried pumpkin strung on rope across the beams of the kitchen ceiling. Oh, her grandparents were old, and they would not live in the modern world. Yellville, where their son had moved, was a big city to them and they never bothered to visit, though back then it still had some unpaved roads with stumps in the middle of them. Louisa used to count the rings on those stumps, imagining the trees were a million years old. Her grandparents were suspicious of Louisa's mother, Violet, their daughter-in-law, because she was from far-off Maine. Whenever they pronounced her name, it sounded like *Violent*. Louisa loved to hear them say it. "Here in the Ozarks, we stomp our own snakes," her granddaddy used to say, growling about outsiders moving in. Louisa loved his voice and laughed and laughed from a corner of the room where her grandma had bedposted her—had stuck the tail of her dress under a bedpost so the weight of the bed would keep the little child from wandering out of the cabin and pitching down the steep ravine that led to a creek where, at night, panthers drank. You could hear them screeching, sometimes, at dusk or in the early morning.

The ravine had already claimed one child—Louisa's two-year-old brother, who went rolling and bouncing down the slope a few months before Louisa was born. Her father found his son lying on the rocky creek bank beneath the scarlet sumac and the sycamores. The coonhounds had raced after the child, yipping, fast but not fast enough to grab him. Louisa was born in the midst of her mother's long grief.

Clear as day, Louisa sees the walls of that battered cabin, chinked with clay that was mixed with moss and hog hair to make it stick. Often on visits, her grandmother would be making sausage, speckled hands flying, as the old woman smacked a layer of lard around the meat and slapped some into gourds, some into cornshucks, then smoked it over an open fire. Louisa smells the fire now: spicewood, pawpaw, dogwood. Gum and ash smell sweeter when they burn. She can tell the difference. She will close her eyes and breathe in the smoke. By the time Louisa was about five or six, Violet had refused to go to the mountains at all, so the visits became fewer than ever. Standing on the edge of the ravine, Louisa used to think how it would hurt to slip, fall, and roll down so far, how steep the slope was and how bristly with the tangle of vines and sharp rocks picking and poking at your skin, at a little child's soft body moving fast as a rocket, the flat places of the stones like slaps and kicks. The thicket was too massed and deep to permit a view of the creek down below. You had to listen close to hear the distant stream. She had stood there and thought about her brother, about her mother's face, twisted with sorrow and with wrinkles like stars at the corners of her eyes. What did her brother hear as he fell?

Now, on the sofa with the cold cloth on her face, she closes her eyes and thinks what it's like to fall. You probably wouldn't hear anything, not creek nor dogs. Did he cry out or was he too surprised? Did he make his flight in silence? She never asked her mother or her father, either one. Her grandmother might have told her. Louisa wishes she'd asked.

The noise of Barbie and the twins fades away, and Louisa's suddenly six years old, poised on the edge of the ravine. She loves marbles. Back in Yellville, she's a champ, never mind that she is so young, beating the pants off boys and older girls. For luck, she always keeps a marble in her pocket, a hefty heavy one, round as a grape through the cloth of her dress. She has deadly aim, immense power in her thumb, and a weapon all her own—a throaty exclamation of "Hunh!" as she shoots, a war cry that unnerves opponents and sends the sissy boys running to the teacher.

"Hunh!" she shouts into the ravine, and her echo booms back at her, over and over, like hide-and-seekers popping up from their hidey-holes.

Fire pink clusters at six-year-old Louisa's feet, and adder's-tongue, bloodroot, violets, phlox. Her grandfather's hammer drowns out the sound of the creek. He's a blacksmith, a chairmaker (he calls them "cheers"), a coffinmaker, likes to talk about the old days when he was the local bonesetter and tooth-puller too. He made his grandson's casket. Louisa has never seen any pictures of the little boy; she doesn't know what he looked like or what games he liked to play. Only a few of his things are left: a tiny chair his grandfather made for him. Once, when nobody was looking, Louisa smelled the chair's slatted seat. Nothing. No human scent. Just wood and smoke.

There's a still, too, which her grandparents tend, thinking it is their secret. Louisa found it one day when she was following a rabbit through the woods, and since then she has sometimes seen her grandparents returning from it, furtive and proud. She hadn't known grown-ups could have secrets, too. It will be years before she knows the name of what she found. It's just something else her grandparents do, along with raising goats, tending strawberries, and growing tomatoes, cane, tobacco. Both smoke corncob pipes. During the war, they had not signed up for rations of meat or butter or sugar but had used parched sweet potatoes for a coffee substitute and lived as they always have on small game, nuts, berries, and goat milk. Her father has told her this, proud. Up in the loft of the cabin are a loom and a spinning wheel, cobwebbed and dusty. Louisa both hopes and fears that her old granny will try to teach her how to use them.

She hears the hammer and tastes on the back of her tongue the tang of the wild bee honey and alum her grandmother fed her as a cure for a cold. If her brother were alive, it'd be fun to pull a wishbone with him—and wish for what? For their old black cat to have orange kittens, for her grades in school to be good. She's teetering on the edge of that Ozark ravine, oh it's tempting to lean far over, loose from bedposting, older now, hearing the hammer that her own daddy will inherit for his handyman jobs, the hammer ringing out its rhythm in the hills. She loves her grandparents. Her grandmother is a tough, leathery mystery in a flour-sack dress with buttons cut from mussel shells, her feet shod in men's button-style boots, which must be hooked with a buttonhook. For dress-up, she wears a calico dress and a clean apron. She survived a copperhead bite and that is the only thing that will get her talking, the memory of it and the story of the coal-oil rubs that saved her life. "I lived," Louisa hears the old woman declare, holding out her arm to show the puncture-pattern scar of the bite, "and I'm plum-nelly proud I did."

A babbling child, either Madison or Fairley, falls backward against Louisa, its sharp elbow digging into her side. "Ouch! Y'all watch out," Louisa cries. The child sneezes, rights itself, and spins away toward its double. Her memories vanish, and instead of feeling a lucky marble in her pocket, she tweaks her painful side and finds where the kid bruised her rib. Hasn't she been pummeled enough for one day?

Stretched out on the sofa, gazing out from beneath the folded wet cloth on her face, Louisa eyes the ketchup-spattered twins as they push and shove each other, communicating in some unintelligible, manic language of their own making. Twins have always unnerved her; there is something mistaken about them, like a genetic glitch. What will these grow up to be? All she knows is, they're bound to turn into something extreme, if only in reaction to their bossy mother. Missionaries, killers. Or just nuts. Just this morning, before setting out on the *Belle,* she read an article in the paper about a crazy man in Sweden who ate an electric drill, swallowing it part by part until the entire thing was in his stomach. The article did not say he was crazy, but that was obvious. How could anybody eat a drill? You can't believe everything you read. It can't be true, she decides, as Madison and Fairley hurtle gibbering into the sofa, knocking her feet askew. "Watch out," she says, picturing the Swede's guts packed with motor, cord, and drill bits, poking out every which-a-way through his skin. These kids oughta be bedposted but good, their long, dirty T-shirts stuck beneath the sofa legs so they'll stay in one place. One of them keeps on sneezing. Louisa hopes she doesn't catch its cold.

From the kitchen, Barbie calls into the living room: "Kids? What are you doing in there?"

"Stomping their own snakes," Louisa says, but it comes out as a gurgle, as jumbled as the twins' voices.

Barbie is acting as hostess, accepting gifts of food shoved into her hands at the front door, explaining to visitors, "Louisa can't really see anybody right now. I'm sure you understand." She says the same thing into the telephone, which rings constantly, and for Barbie's help in deflecting these calls, Louisa is grateful.

"That was Channel 13," Barbie announces, sticking her head into the living room. "Before that, it was the Memphis paper and some woman who says she's a lawyer and wants to represent you. Are you sure you don't want to say anything to the reporters, like get it on record it wasn't your fault, even if it was?"

"Take the phone off the hook, Barbie," Louisa says, "right now."

"Oh," says Barbie, sounding disappointed, but apparently she does, because the phone quits ringing.

Louisa hears a man's voice in the kitchen and recognizes it as the sheriff's.

"Louisa isn't up to having visitors right now. I'm sure you understand," Barbie repeats to the sheriff, who promises he'll come back the next day. From the sofa, Louisa hears his deep voice go even deeper in tones of respect, as if somebody has died. Somebody did die, she reminds herself. Her brother. He has always seemed like a little brother, because he was so young when he died. It's hard to think of him as an older brother. Oh, and all those passengers. She's trying to remember them, account for them. She had them all sign in on her yellow plastic clipboard, using the red pen on a coil, on lined paper with a yellow duck printed at the top—their names and where they were from. At the end of a day, she used to file away the lists in a big box in her closet and mull over how many different states were represented. People write so differently. She has thousands of signatures, printed neatly in block letters or scrawled illegibly, so the names look like smashed bugs on the paper.

She still has the lists in her closet. But that clipboard is at the bottom of the lake.

She's surprised she didn't lose a few teeth from the way the fat man's wife hit her so hard, when she was lying on the bank. *Pow, pow, pow.* If she hadn't been so waterlogged, she'd have given that woman a punch or two in return. But she, Louisa, told the fat man to move.

These thoughts do not register on her as facts, not yet. They are pieces of information in search of other pieces—solutions, salvation, contradiction.

"—to keep looking until they find all the bodies," comes Barbie's voice, authoritative and so irritating Louisa wants to sit up and scream at her, "Get lost." She hears Barbie add ingratiatingly, "Here, have some cake."

The sheriff says something, and Barbie repeats in a scandalized shriek: "No life jackets on? What was she thinking?"

The sheriff steps into Louisa's living room just long enough to tip his cap to her. He's chewing on a slice of yellow cake. She can smell its lemon icing. He doesn't speak, just blinks at her and glides back into the kitchen. How can there be such things as lemon cake in this world, after a boat sinks and so many die?

But she just had the boat checked yesterday. Her mechanic, who everybody calls Raggedy Andy, had smiled his sweet, gappy smile, and said, "She's A-OK, even if she's gettin' older. Your bilge alarm came in, Louisa. Want me to install it today?"

"The Coast Guard has to approve it first," she said. "It'll have to wait."

The bilge alarm: if it had been on board, it would have let her know how deep the water was, alerted her that something was really wrong. And nobody ever wears life jackets, even though she always points them out, stored in the overhead bins. She knows the law, and the law says all she has to do is make sure her passengers know the life jackets are there.

"—planning to stay here with her overnight," comes Barbie's voice again, self-assured, smug even, the voice of a young busybody thriving on somebody else's tragedy. "Best if she's not left by herself . . . the children and I will manage . . . my husband's traveling, not due back till Monday."

Who said you could stay? Louisa wants to bark. But her powers of speech have deserted her. How dare Barbie waltz in and make herself at home, with her two brats. Madison and Fairley indeed. They ought to be called Dot and Dash, Pete and Repeat, Tweedle-dee and Tweedle-dum. Traveling indeed. Her husband's a truck driver. Why does he come home at all to this woman who is such a know-it-all, with a repulsive habit of pausing, as if about to say something important, and then belching, chin held high and prim? Barbie is always claiming that men are looking at her in inappropriate ways. Louisa doesn't know why this is so annoying; it just is. Nobody looks at Barbie funny; she is just bossy and ordinary. Why do her children obey her? Louisa has rarely felt such antipathy toward children as she does toward these six-year-olds. Runty and backward, they look and act about four. One is a girl, the other a boy, is all she knows or cares to know. She honestly can't tell which is which. She avoids looking at them; they're loud nuisances at the corner of her eye, a tornado touching down beside her, then swooping into the other room. Yet, dadburn it, she feels sorry for them, because they've got Barbie as a mother. What was it that Louisa's mother used to call people like Barbie— pushy, nosy people? Nosey Parkers, that's what. Mama. Violet. *Violent.* Mama, help me.

In the kitchen, Barbie and the sheriff are still conferring. "She has no kin whatsoever," Louisa hears Barbie say, in tones of utter triumph and finality, as if Louisa is dead in her coffin and they're wondering where to put her.

Mumble, mumble, comes from the cake-eating officer.

"Her parents must be dead. She's no spring chicken herself," Barbie replies. "No, I'm sure she's never been married."

"How do you know?" Louisa yells, furious that Barbie is right— she's never been married.

The two heads peer into the living room and vanish again, like prairie dogs poking up from a hole. "You don't know anything," Louisa cries, so loud the twins start wailing in the other room. Louisa whispers, "And I do so have kin. I have a son."

THE BOY WAS A SHATFORD. That was all that had mattered to Louisa's mother. He was a Shatford, and the Shatfords owned land all around the cove. That was the year her parents had separated, and she and her mother had gone to stay with her mother's mother in the little Maine village where her mother had grown up. Teddy Shatford had asked Louisa to the prom, which would be held at a place called the

Shore Club. Violet sang while she sewed and ironed a new dress for Louisa, blue with pink buttons: a baby dress. Louisa dreaded the prom, yet she didn't want to ruin her mother's happiness.

Like Louisa's house in Yellville, the house in Maine had only cold running water. It was just so much colder in Maine. Shampooing was so much trouble, her mother and grandmother rarely bothered. Use cornstarch, they said, a trick they had learned during the war. Louisa tried the cornstarch method and hated the way it left her hair greasy, full of bits of meal. Yet her mother had a delicate beauty, like the violets she was named after, and the cornstarch left her hair with the patina of old silk. Next to her mother, Louisa felt increasingly hulking and plain. She wouldn't have cared except that it mattered to her mother.

Her mother and grandmother talked all the time about the war, so fast Louisa couldn't keep up with them. You would almost think they missed it. It had been such a time of upheaval in their lives, glorious trouble and change. That was when Violet had met the man from Arkansas that she married. The war had been a happy time for her, Louisa gathered, before the time of sorrow that started when her baby son rolled down the cliff. Louisa's grandmother, widowed for decades, worked year-round at a fish-packing plant. Violet found work there too, and mother and daughter walked to the plant together in the morning and walked home for lunch and at day's end, tired and contented. They drank coffee at all their meals and let Louisa drink it too, something Violet would never have allowed in Arkansas. From her grandmother, Louisa learned how to make thick chowders and fish pies. They were a whole houseful of women working. Chopping cod and halibut, onions and potatoes, Louisa longed to ask her grandmother about her husband who died at sea and her mother who had died young, working at a valentine factory, painting silk and satin flowers on cards, licking her paintbrush with her tongue, dying of lead poisoning. But Nana, dressed all in black and wearing black shoes, was even quieter and more distant than the Arkansas granny. Waiting for just the right time, Louisa found she couldn't ask her anything. To be a fisherman's wife and watch the fog settle in at night, to have his boat never come back, to learn he was lost at sea: she could not imagine that.

Teddy Shatford was not the catch her mother thought he was. Working as a clerk in a tourist motel that was just gearing up for the season, Louisa had summoned the local doctor more than once for unwary visitors sickened by the dead lobsters Teddy's father cooked up in his backyard shack. Louisa didn't tell her mother this. Her mother worked so hard and dreamed so desperately that Louisa would have a happy life. The blue dress with its pink buttons had ruffles around the neckline—"To make your shoulders look smaller," her mother said apologetically as she fluffed the ruffles. Louisa had to fight the urge to grab her mother's hand and say, "Don't hope. Don't pin your hopes on Teddy Shatford!"

"You can wear some of my rouge and paint your nails. To think you're going to the Shore Club," her mother said and beamed. "To the Shore Club with the Shatford boy! Dinner and dancing—oh my, Louisa! And to think, you're only a junior, and he's a senior. How did you get his attention?" And her mother fluffed the ruffles, beaming, dreaming, so that Louisa held on to the moment even through her dread. Teddy asked her only because every other girl in the junior class and the senior class had turned him down. Louisa, a new girl, and plain, had been dead last on Teddy's list. She'd watched other girls refuse him outright and then elbow each other, giggling, as he'd relentlessly gone on to ask others. The Shatford magic had run out several generations ago, in the eyes of all but Louisa's mother. The whole Shatford family—Teddy, his two older sisters, their mama and papa— had short necks and bad posture, as if their heads were on backward, Louisa thought, and they had a tendency to get sties in their eyes. Why were they ever local royalty? She said yes to Teddy only because she was surprised to be asked out by any boy, and saying yes had seemed the only polite response. He was her first official date (though she had already had a romance that her mother knew nothing about, on a visit to her grandparents in the Ozarks before the move to Maine. She had met a boy at a pie supper, danced with him, kissed him on the lips, and even felt superior to him because in bidding on her pie, he was declaring himself, pledging himself to her). By the time of the date with Teddy Shatford, she had been in Maine exactly one month. She was sixteen.

She loved Maine, even though most of her waking hours were spent at school or at work at the motel. The village overlooked a small bay, its harbor crammed with sturdy fishing boats. In summertime, her mother predicted gleefully, the town would come alive with tourists, ice-cream stands, lobster bakes, and even a yacht race. Early-bird vacationers zipped around the bay in slim speedboats. A few times, Louisa and her mother took long walks beyond the town, out to the wild edge of the ocean. Why was it she loved wild places best—the sea and the Ozark Mountains? Wading in cold surf up to her knees, she thought about the ravine in her grandparents' yard. "Don't go too far, Louisa," her mother implored, and obediently, Louisa plodded back to shore. It was only May, after all, and the water was cold as snow. The horizon wasn't a flat line but instead had an uneven look, from the high waves far out at sea.

She knew she wasn't pretty, with her wide shoulders. Other girls had hairdos; she just had bumpy hair. With her widow's peak and down-turning eyes, she thought she resembled a sad owl. At the Shore Club, sitting across the table from Teddy, she wondered if the whole thing was a joke he was playing on her. She was unbearably nervous as they waited for their meal to arrive, a set menu of steamed mussels, salad, lobster, rolls, and coconut cream pie.

As Teddy cracked open his lobster, he spoke proudly of his father's cleverness at selling dead lobsters to unsuspecting tourists. "Cooks up his deadies at the end of the day and sells 'em to those stupes," Teddy bragged. "Sold one that'd been dead in the tank for so long, the others had eaten off all its legs and most of the tail. It was one ragged son of a bitch."

Teddy hooted. How small his features were. Tiny eyes (with a sty twinkling redly on one lid; Louisa thought of Mars in her science book), pursed-up lips, little bitty chip of a nose. A photographer had snapped their picture as soon as they arrived. The picture would look unflattering and accurate—Teddy smirking, herself with shoulders hunched to appear slimmer. Teddy had laid one sweaty hand on her arm, clumsily, almost as if he were pushing her away.

He went on, "That lobster musta weighed four pounds. That's a lotta dead lobster, and it had a big burn from the pot. Dad sold it to this couple from the South who ate it on our picnic table out back and never knew the difference. I'd seen that big 'un in the pound myself, with the others eating on it."

"And you think that's funny?" Louisa asked, thinking she could never eat lobster again, including the one on her plate that had looked delicious moments earlier. The image of the huge lobster with the others attacking it: horrible. She hated Teddy for making fun of southerners, too. She felt like a teacher with an incorrigible student on her hands. Surely this was not what a date was supposed to feel like.

Teddy whirled a toothpick between his teeth. "Sure it's funny." He jerked his chin toward a raised platform beyond the dining area. "Look," he said, in a voice tinged with awe. "That's Sam Moon. You heard him sing before?"

A man stepped to the mike and opened his mouth, and out poured the most beautiful sound Louisa had ever heard: a voice so easy, so rich and honeyed, deep and wooing, that she laid down her fork, pushed her plate aside, and leaned on her elbows. She was dimly aware that girls and women all over the restaurant were doing the same thing, their escorts forgotten. Sam Moon. She had heard of him, of course, had seen his face on a life-sized cardboard stand-up sign in the motel lobby where she worked, had studied the pasteboard rendition of his suntanned skin, glossy black hair, and perfect teeth. Musical notes were painted around his face, a cardboard face, yet so good-looking you could feel the presence of a person there.

And there was Sam Moon up on stage, Sam Moon who had sung at the Shore Club since it was built, in the early 1950s. Now Sam Moon was famous, surely, all over the world, sending his sweet deep voice out from this little stage in Maine. She imagined the Shore Club as a clamshell opening and closing as his music poured out. The passion she'd heard at the Ozark mountain pie supper, the ringing promise of reel and jig, of leather drum and wild fiddle, found its human voice in Sam Moon, though his melodies were modern ones.

"You never heard him sing?" Teddy said in evident disgust. "Not even on the radio? He's famous."

"I know who he is. I just don't listen to the radio." She wished Teddy would go away. She realized that he'd never spoken her name, not when he'd asked her out and not all evening.

Other couples were moving onto the dance floor, their arms wrapped around each other. Louisa didn't want to dance with Teddy Shatford. She only wanted to listen to Sam Moon sing for the rest of her life. To her relief, Teddy didn't ask her to dance. He sat, lumpen, for a while, picking at his sty, then leaned over to say, "Going outside."

She nodded. He vanished, weaving among the dancing couples and disappearing out the door. Spellbound, she watched Sam Moon. The waiter brought two slices of pie and asked did she want her lobster wrapped up to take home? "No thank you," she said, and he took it away. Louisa ate her pie, which was marvelous, and considered eating the other piece. But Teddy might come back for it. The waiter returned with a coffeepot and offered her a cup. "Yes," she said, and he poured. The waiter's eyes looked sympathetic, and she wanted to tell him sympathy wasn't necessary. She was, in fact, enjoying her prom, now that Teddy was gone.

Sam Moon took a break, bowing to applause and stepping off the stage, his black hair gleaming. Louisa asked the waiter, "Could I work here?"

In the blaze of Sam Moon's presence and his glorious voice, she had seen the shape her life might take if she could be near him. She saw that you could have romance in your life even if all you had was nearness. The waiter said, "Just ask the manager. But why not wait till Monday, miss? This is your prom, after all."

Sam Moon was standing at her table. Sam Moon was plopping down into Teddy Shatford's chair, grinning at her, and saying to the waiter, "I'll have the usual, Charlie." To Louisa, Sam Moon said, "I still remember my own prom. I love proms. Are you having a good time?"

She heard herself say, "I love your voice."

Sam Moon picked up a fork and cut into Teddy's slice of pie. "What's your name?"

She told him, certain she was dreaming.

"You're not from here," he said, and she said no, she was from Arkansas.

"My grandpa plays the fiddle. I was at a dance in the mountains," she was proud to say, for it sounded as if she went to dances all the time, "and they were playing jigs and reels on fiddles and jawbones. It was great. Your voice would go with those sounds."

He didn't laugh about fiddles and jawbones. "I wish I could hear that," he said. "I can't keep on doing this stuff forever. Cocktail-lounge songs. I've started writing my own. Those last couple songs were both new ones," he said. "What did you think?"

"They were beautiful." Had she turned into a movie star, saying lines rehearsed for this scene? "They're perfect." She heard her father's voice in her head: *Hit's the truth, porely explained.* "I mean it. I wish I had more words to say so, Mr. Moon."

"Call me Sam." When the waiter brought his drink, which was some smoky liquid in a glass, he said, "Charlie, bring this table another piece of pie. I ate her boyfriend's dessert. Would you like another piece, Louisa?"

"I sure would," she said, "and he's not my boyfriend. I think he left. I hope he left."

"I have more songs to sing than I can ever write down," Sam Moon said as he sipped the smoky drink. "Every time I stroll along the beach,

I think of another one." He paused and said, "Louisa, I'll think of you, and I'll write songs."

She caught her breath. It was too much to take in.

A girl came up to the table, dressed in a black cashmere sweater, her blond hair a perfect pageboy. She didn't bother to speak to Louisa, though her eyes met Louisa's for an instant and showed how mystified, how impressed she was that Sam Moon was sitting there. The girl pushed a record album toward him and cooed, "May I have your autograph?"

He signed it for her. Then the table was surrounded by boys and girls all wanting autographs, and Louisa could safely stare at Sam Moon's profile, so handsome it hurt to look at him. She thought of the cardboard advertisement back at the motel lobby, how people would actually go around to the back of it, it looked so real, never mind the musical notes painted around his head.

Sam Moon stood up, leaned across the table, and shook Louisa's hand. "It's been a pleasure, Louisa Shepherd," he said. Then he was back onstage, the mike in his hand, his voice sailing out over the room, and couples were swirling onto the dance floor again. Louisa watched in ecstasy, imagining telling her mother: "I had dessert with Sam Moon."

Teddy was back, sliding into his chair, grinning. "You thought I'd left, didn't ya? I just went out for a drink. I got some whiskey in the car."

He gobbled his pie. "Let's go," he said.

"Can't we stay and listen to the music?" Louisa asked.

"I'm ready to leave," he said, his face going sour. "Come on."

He drove too fast. The whiskey sloshed around in a big rectangular bottle on the floor of the car. Teddy kept uncapping it and swigging from it. He drove inland, away from the shore, pulled into a patch of woods, and switched off the engine.

"I want to go home," Louisa said, thinking: *Afraid. I'm afraid of him.*

He jumped her. She was too shocked to fight him off. There was just his sharp-as-pee whiskey smell and that face with the tiny features eating her own face up, so that she thought of the giant, dying lobster attacked by other lobsters. She thought of her mother and decided, I'll tell her the truth, all of it, so she won't be fooled anymore. She struck out at Teddy, her knuckles scraping against his teeth, but he grabbed her arm and pinned her down. While he raped her, she tried to keep her head averted, in hopes at least of warding off the germs from his sty.

She got pregnant, never mind that it was the first time. Her mother sent her to her Aunt Patsy's, in Boston, to hide away and have it. Aunt Patsy had been a WAVE during the war. She was tough and stylish and took Louisa all over Boston, to museums and restaurants and movie theaters. Louisa was allowed to listen while Aunt Patsy talked with her boyfriends on the phone, rolling her eyes, winking at Louisa, saying, "Okay, buster, who died and made you king?" She'd tell Louisa, "They love that. You gotta dish it right back to 'em."

After Louisa had the baby and gave it up for adoption, she and her mother went back to Yellville, Arkansas. Her parents reconciled. Why had they separated, and why did they get back together? They weren't the kind of people who explained that, at least not to their daughter. But from then on, they stayed together. That much was good, even though Violet spent most of her time reading romance novels; when Louisa or her father said anything to her, she would look up from the sofa and roar, "Lemme read!" Such a tiny little person to be roaring so loud. "Fine, Violet," Louisa's father would say. *Violent.* She roared and read, and there were no more ruffly-necked dresses. Louisa went back to school, steeling herself for questions about what she had done during her time in Maine, but nobody asked. She never told Teddy Shatford about the baby. She never wanted to see him again in her life and was glad that he lived so far away.

Months later the fact registered on her, that she had given birth. She was between classes at the big new countywide high school that had been finished during the time she was away. In the hallway with dozens of other students flowing past her, she stopped short, dizzy with a sense of having forgotten something, her heart suddenly dancing. It took her a full five minutes, standing there until the bell stopped ringing and the hallway was empty and silent, to realize that what she felt was love for her baby, a useless emotion now that she'd given the baby away. She'd never even seen it, for it had been taken from her as soon as she'd had it, and some stranger, presumably, had gotten to hold it and feed it. "A boy," Aunt Patsy had said, patting Louisa's hand. "Now just forget about it." Aunt Patsy had brought presents to the hospital and urged Louisa to open them: a pale silk scarf, a new pocketbook with a shoulder strap.

It was Aunt Patsy who'd inspired Louisa to study nursing. After high school, Louisa enrolled in a practical nursing program and then worked in an old folks' home in Little Rock. The good thing was, the old folks rarely asked her about herself. They were taken up with their own troubles. The longer an old person was in the home, the less likely their family was to fool with them. It hurt to see.

One day, an ad in the paper caught her eye: "Private nurse wanted for individual in Hawk Lake area." On her lunch hour, she dialed the number. An old man gave her directions in a shaky voice. Screeches on the old man's end of the line filled the background so that Louisa had to hold one hand over her ear to make out his words. That weekend, she caught a bus to Hawk Lake and walked two miles to the address she'd been given. The lake back then was smaller, and the old man was Jerry Fiveash's grandfather, a compact, arthritic gentleman sporting a navy blue beret, like a French painter.

Of course, that was before Jerry was born. The screeches Louisa had heard over the phone came from a parrot that the old man said was a hundred years old. The parrot screamed and cursed during Louisa's interview with Mr. Fiveash, which took place in a damp sunroom where moss grew in cracks between the floor tiles. The parrot's companion was a giant tortoise that sat unmoving in a corner of the sunroom, like a table.

"They're the same age," Mr. Fiveash declared. "I got them in Tahiti, during my young bohemian artist phase." The parrot shrieked at the turtle, a few feathers shaking loose.

"They hate each other," Louisa said and was filled with sorrow for the critters, locked in a battle of who could outlive the other.

"You're right," the old man murmured, his beret slipping sideways as he looked up at her, his eyes going wide as ponds behind his glasses. "How insightful."

"Do you still paint?" she asked him, intrigued by all of it—the tortoise, the parrot, the old man in the beret, the sunroom where light had savagely faded the curtains—intrigued by anybody who had been to Tahiti, wherever that was.

The old man let loose a mirthful bellow. "No, I don't paint anymore," he said. "I was never all that good."

She liked him for that. So few people were really honest about what they could and could not do. She knew she was a good nurse, not the best but able, yet she felt she was waiting for something, had been waiting ever since she heard Sam Moon's voice sailing out across the dance floor of the Shore Club. As Mr. Fiveash offered her the job of taking care of him—he was the patient, the only one—and as she accepted, she was aching for Sam Moon, longing to hear his voice, realizing that all these years she could have bought his records and played them, but she had never had any money to spare for luxuries like that. *Wake up, Louisa, and live your life.* She scuffed her dusty white shoes over the moss in the sunroom and said yes, she would be glad to work for Mr. Fiveash.

Would this be better or worse than the old folks' home? She would have a room in the house and a salary in exchange for fixing his meals, giving him his medicine, recording his blood pressure, listening to his heart, and making sure he saw his doctor on schedule. He'd had two massive heart attacks. "I won't be much trouble," he said.

And he wasn't. She brought him trays in the sunroom. She poured seeds in a dish for the parrot and put out fresh cabbage leaves for the tortoise. Both the animals liked fruit, so when she shopped for Mr.

Fiveash and herself, she bought melons and apples. She did the cleaning and the cooking, answered the telephone, and drove Mr. Fiveash
to the doctor and to various houses that he owned around Hawk Lake
so that he could collect rent from tenants. Often, he asked her just to
drive him around the lake, so he could look at it.

When she had two days off in a row, she'd go and visit her parents.
Violet worried that Louisa had no social life. With Mr. Fiveash's
encouragement, Louisa started giving talks at a nearby elementary
school on health and hygiene. That wasn't really a social life, but it
was enough to get her mother off her back. She hadn't had a date
since Teddy Shatford. She liked visiting with Mr. Fiveash's son and
daughter-in-law, a laughing couple who talked about enlarging the
lake and building more houses on it, beautiful houses.

Her career with the duck boat was thanks to the old man's only
son, a kind-faced man who lived nearby with his sweet wife and their
little baby, Jerry. Jerry was such a tiny baby. His parents and his grandfather doted on him. He used to reach out his small hands to grab hold
of his grandfather's beret, to the old man's delight.

Mr. Fiveash's son had plans for the lake. With money his father
gave him, he was buying land all around, having the lake deepened,
and building houses on its shores. "Hawk Lake will be a premier
attraction," he said. For a long time, Louisa thought he had invented
that phrase. He bought the duck boat, an ex–war craft, and refur-
bished it, mapping out a route for a driver to take, calculating what
percentage of ticket sales the driver should keep. He hired a retired
school bus driver to operate the boat.

Before Louisa's eyes, the lake was developing, growing, becoming
a tourist mecca. A worn-out diamond mine was opened as a try-your-
luck attraction for tourists. The oldest bathhouse was renovated and
turned into a museum displaying nineteenth-century artifacts. Bed-
and-breakfast establishments sprang up. The Fiveashes created a
lakeside campground, complete with barbecue grills, hot showers, and
a fishing dock.

"We are doing this for different reasons," the old man surprised Louisa by saying one day. "Do you see? I do it because of a dream. My son, fine man that he is, he does it for the money."

"He has to think about that," Louisa said, startled. "He has a wife and family to support."

"Yes," said old Mr. Fiveash testily, "and if that's his dream, it'll come true before mine ever does."

"What do you mean?" asked Louisa. She was sweeping leaves off the front porch of his house while he sat in a chair beneath an afghan. If she didn't ask him right then, she'd wonder about his remark her whole life.

"I mean this." The old man gestured toward the lake, which was empty, because it was a cold day in late fall. "This lake is a money dream for him. That's his genius. But I, well, I always wanted this lake to love me back." His beret slipped to his shoulder, and he clapped it back on his head. "A lake won't love you, Louisa. I wish I'd known that when my wife was alive. I wish I'd spent more time with her. She's gone now, and the lake I worked so hard on all those years, well, it doesn't hug and kiss me. It doesn't ask me how I'm feeling, or what I think."

"I understand," said Louisa, pausing in her sweeping. The winter wind lifted the leaves like a rug at her feet. She did understand.

"You can have love and the lake, too, and not realize it," he said. "My little grandson, he's like me. The money won't mean that much to him, and he'll wonder why."

Mr. Fiveash enjoyed good health for most of the ten years that Louisa worked for him; then one night, he died in his sleep. When his will was read, she learned he had left her one of his properties, a modest little house a couple of miles from the lake, vacant and in need of minor repairs. The will even paid for those repairs.

It was around this time that the duck boat operator said that he was ready to stop giving tours. Mr. Fiveash's son said, "Louisa, I want you to train with him. Learn how to operate the *Belle*. Get your master marine license from the Coast Guard, and then you'll be allowed to give tours in certain parts of the lake. You'll be set."

Before Louisa knew it, she had a new career. Every morning, she'd wake up and get the keys from her nightstand, holding them in her lap while she ate breakfast. She was that eager to start her day. She'd start up the duck boat in its garage and drive to a little bandstand in town, a pointy-roofed gazebo built over a clear-spring drinking fountain, which served as the ticket booth and where people were always waiting.

The first time she'd eased the duck boat into the water and heard that delighted "Ohhh!" from her passengers, she was hooked. This was it, what she'd been waiting for. What she'd heard in Sam Moon's voice she found again at the helm of the *Arkansas Belle.* "Ohhh!" the passengers exclaimed, sounding elated and yet relaxed, as if they were all getting their necks rubbed.

She was in love with all of it: the boat, the tours, the lake. She would stay up late in her own house, counting up the money she made, tallying the number of passengers she'd had in a day, a week, a summer. All she had to do was pick them up and drive them around and ease them into the lake. "Ohhh!" they chorused, and she would point out the big houses owned by wealthy folks and bring her passengers back again to the dock, after that trip to other worlds: land, lake, waterfront mansions. More big, beautiful homes were going up, and old Mr. Fiveash's son—Jerry's father—was the developer. All around the lake, rich people moved into houses of glass and pink brick designed by famous architects and landscapers, and lived their lives almost close enough to touch.

Then as now, swans lived on the lake, and dozens of ducks and geese. She always thrilled with pride when her passengers exclaimed over the platoons of ducklings and goslings swimming out from shore behind their mothers. Dragonflies, turtles, snakes, frogs, and fish— bass, crappie, catfish, redhorse: there is so much life in and on and around Hawk Lake, thriving, secretive and furtive, teeming among the water lilies and cypress knees and out in the open water. When the lake turns over, fall and spring, there's occasionally a fish kill, from the oxygen levels changing. It hurts to see the dead fish floating, to know they ran out of air. Hawk Lake has a community association—homeowners with boats who clean up the dead fish.

She loved to point out flora and fauna to passengers. Floating plants might look ordinary, but they have wonderful names: frogbit, smartweed, mare's tail, sundew, pickerelweed. Kids love the little newts and salamanders and things like that, which live at the water's edge. Once she saw a funny-looking critter a yard and a half long, not really a lizard, not a snake. She looked it up in her guidebook and found out it was a hellbender, a crayfish eater that mostly lives in the Ohio Valley and had somehow strayed this far. She loves the name, but since she's never seen another one, she never gets a chance to say it.

Passengers often asked if there were alligators in Hawk Lake, and they were disappointed when she said no. She kept her trusty, well-thumbed guidebook on board, with its pictures and descriptions of native plants and animals. Of course, the birds and animals in the guidebook tended to have brighter colors than in real life. Most everything in the book she has seen in or around Hawk Lake, except a king rail, "a shy marsh bird, elusive and hard to see," said the guidebook. She wants to see a king rail. That has been her goal for some years.

The guidebook, of course, went down with the boat.

All that can't be over. She has to get up from this sofa, get up and get ready for tomorrow, for more tours. The weather will be fair. Clouds over the lake and planes flying above it will cast sudden shadows, and when they lift, the passengers will exclaim about that, too. Over the years, there was slight competition in the form of other tour boats, just enough so that she never took her good fortune for granted. Another boat operator might stay in business for a season or two, but Louisa and the *Belle* were fixtures. The *Belle* was the only duck boat in Hawk Lake, the first tour boat out in the spring and the last to turn in, in the winter.

And now, all these years later, on the evening of the day when all those people drowned on her boat, she's thinking about her baby and wanting to find the man he has become. Why, if he's still alive, he's more than forty years old.

Pressing the cold cloth over her eyes, she shifts her weight on the sofa, feeling heavy, bruised, and still waterlogged, though only the cloth on her face is wet. She is indebted to three generations of the Fiveash family: the old gentleman who employed her all those years and left her a good house with a garage; his kind son, who set her up in business with the *Belle*; and grandson Jerry, who saved her life today.

Louisa hears somebody gabbling at her and jerks the cloth from her head to see a strange young woman standing over her in her living room. It takes her a moment to realize it's just Barbie, who is asking, "Want more tea, Louisa? Or some soup? Maybe some of that lemon cake? The sheriff ate two pieces of that, so it must be pretty good."

"I want you to leave me alone," Louisa says. "I have a lot to do."

Barbie nods. "Did you see the way the sheriff kept looking at me? Like he was trying to stare right through my clothes. I'm glad my husband wasn't here to see that. Is there any special guy in your life, Louisa?"

Somehow, Louisa just can't answer no. Barbie clearly expects her to say no. Over the years, there's been the occasional male passenger who has shown an interest in her. Very few. Years ago, she went out for coffee with an older man after a tour, saw the wedding ring on his hand, and thought, *This will never do.*

Barbie sighs. "I try to dress modestly, but the way some guys look at me, I may as well be naked."

"Oh, shut up, Barbie. I don't believe the sheriff even noticed you." She hasn't said *shut up* to anybody in years, not since she was a child. Her mother used to say, "We may be poor, but we won't talk like trash," and her father would agree, "That's abs'lutely right, Violet." *Violent.*

Barbie pauses for a long moment, then belches softly, with an expression of great patience. "Just stay here and be comfy. I've got the kids settled in your bed, and we'll keep you company tonight. You ought not to be alone. I can't stop thinking about it. You and that fat guy's wife are the only ones who didn't drown. God, Louisa! What was it like?"

"I'll tell you sometime," Louisa says. She closes her eyes. She's back in the high school hallway, a plain, broad-shouldered girl unnoticed by the students who career around her, with her heart filling up, filling up with love for her baby.

KATELYNN HEARS a voice ask: "Would you like to move into the guest room?"

She startles awake. It's only her mother, standing over the bed. The curtains are pulled back, and in the darkness outside, Katelynn sees the glimmering lights of houses dotting the lakeshore. She's surprised to see the curtains pulled back. Hadn't her mother drawn them, earlier? Her memory is so bad now. Ruined. Shot. Glo is a silhouette against the big glass walls.

Her mother says, "In the guest room, you wouldn't have to look at the lake and be reminded. Come on. Bring your pillow."

"I was asleep," Katelynn says. "Besides," she fumbles, "the bad part was mostly underwater. I didn't see that. I mean, once the people were down there, I couldn't see them."

Her mother's face twists. "Oh, it was horrible."

Katelynn flinches. Everything Glo says is criticism. Horrible that Katelynn saw it, her fault for seeing it. Katelynn feels again that sense of contagion, of carrying plague. She could make her mother happy, could pick up the pillow and crawl out of bed to the guest room, but she says, "I want to stay here."

Her mother's silence has a concentrated quality, steady. When she doesn't answer, Katelynn says, "Are you mad, Mom?"

"Yes," her mother says in a hiss, taking a step toward the bed. "You were so damn dumb, Katelynn, pouring that mercury all over the ground. You and your idiot friends, poisoning the water supply so we're still drinking bottled water!"

"I know that was a dumb thing to do. We didn't know it would get into the water. But it's safe now. The EPA guy said so. Remember? That was a few weeks ago."

"I don't believe it," her mother says. "I'm going to keep on drinking bottled water. I, for one, don't want to end up like you. Or Harvey. He'll probably have mutant kids. God knows where he is. I feel sorry for *his* mother, whoever she is."

"Stop!"

"Do you intend to finish school, Katelynn?"

"I'm working on it. Mr. Stiles—"

"Just try and get better. Eat more, for heaven's sake. I won't have you brooding all day, thinking about that damn boat."

They're both quiet then. The clock on the nightstand, half buried beneath bags of candy, says 3:00 A.M. At last Glo says, "Your check came today, your prize money from the D.A.R., the check and the certificate you were supposed to pick up that night. They mailed it to you with a get-well note. It's a wonder they sent it. They had every right not to."

Katelynn stares with fury at her mother until she realizes that Glo has left the room and she's gazing at a column of blackness that might be glass or lake water beyond the glass. "That night" was the night Katelynn and Jenelle and Harvey had their first mercury party, dipping cigarettes into the vat of silver liquid and smoking them. Katelynn had won an essay contest sponsored by the local chapter of the D.A.R. and was scheduled to have dinner that evening with the old ladies and read her essay to them. When Harvey invited her to go with him and Jenelle, to break into the crumbling warehouse, an abandoned neon factory where the mercury was stored, all plans to attend the D.A.R. dinner went right out of her head. She knew what they were doing wasn't right, but when she was clowning around with Jenelle and Harvey, she would always think, *This is the happiest I've ever been*—even though it looked, then, as if Jenelle would be with Harvey forever. Katelynn's happiness hurt. She used to write poems about joy and pain, or try to, and this was what she'd meant.

Dunking his arms up to the elbows in the vat of mercury, Harvey said, "My uncle used to work in this factory. He said if there's anything you need to scratch before you start bending hot glass—well, you'd better scratch first."

Harvey pulled his hands out of the vat and flung them out wide, so that the slippery, silvery mercury pellets pinged off the walls and the floor.

Katelynn was aware of the strange pungency of their mercury-coated cigarettes, a smell that made her think of volcanoes. The air had developed a sheen, as if the vapors were shadows, or a wash of water, rather than smoke. Leaning over the vat of quicksilver, she found her reflection wavering there, as if she were gazing into the lake or a well or the sea, only this was darker, less familiar, as if she were watching herself drown.

"Look, there's my soul," she said, and Jenelle and Harvey laughed.

"You're high," Harvey said. "Enjoy."

"It's the ocean. We've got the ocean in a bucket," Katelynn said. She dipped her finger in it and imagined painting the whole world with mercury, painting with her hand: a silver world, painting her house, the sky, the trees. The mercury pooled in her palm and she let it fall gently to the floor, as if releasing a creature, something small and alive. Pot had never made her feel like this—glorious, exposed, yet frightened, as if all her pretenses had been burned away. This wasn't just being high.

She *had* seen her soul.

She wanted to look again, but Harvey and Jenelle crowded around the vat, dipping their lit cigarettes and relighting them with matches.

"This reminds me of a poem," Katelynn said, "a poem called 'Silver,' by Walter de la Mare. I remember reading it in the fourth grade and falling in love with it. Everything in the poem is silver. Remember it, Jenelle? Oh, I can almost recite it!"

Absorbed in their play, Harvey and Jenelle weren't paying her any attention. She had an inkling then of danger (she'd had chemistry in tenth grade; she should have known). Stubbing out her cigarette, she stood up so fast her head spun. She would go to the D.A.R. supper after all. She was late, yes, but maybe the old ladies would forgive that. Maybe she'd have to curtsy as she apologized. When she was two or three, she used to curtsy till she was dizzy, dipping her head, holding up her skirt with her fingertips, sliding one foot out in front, delicately, a movement both elegant and deferential, so different from cheerleading, which is all bravado and acrobatics.

Will she ever be strong enough to do splits again? How proud she'd been when her legs were suddenly long enough, supple enough, to slide all the way forward, all the way back.

Loving Harvey was her secret. Jenelle must have known. It was March then, and to have loved anybody since fall, since getting back from the walled academy, seemed like a long time. She went to every one of his track meets and cheered while he raced with his pole and vaulted into the sun, his body torquing. She'd clench her hands till he was safe again, standing on the rubber mat with his arms flung above his head and the announcer crying out how high he'd gone.

"Should we tell her?" Jenelle was asking Harvey. "She'll find out sooner or later. Everybody will. It'll probably be in the paper."

"Tell me what?" Katelynn said. She shook her head, trying to clear her thoughts.

Harvey blurted, "Coach Stiles found out I'm not nineteen. I'm a little older than that." Harvey looked at Jenelle. She nodded, and he said, "I'm twenty-four."

"No you're not," said Katelynn, thinking that their jokes were usually better than this.

"It's true, Katelynn. Listen. Coach Stiles found my old yearbook," Harvey said. "I graduated from a different high school already, a few years ago."

Was his face aging, even as she stared at him? "You went back to school? Why?"

"That's what I keep asking him," Jenelle said, smiling her distinctive smile: her upper lip rolled back from her teeth so that her teeth made a white square.

"To improve my grades," Harvey said, and they all laughed, nervously. The walls of the warehouse echoed.

"But really, why," Katelynn said, almost whispering.

"To get it right," Harvey said, "because I'd missed out the first time around. Back then, I was just a runt. Couldn't vault worth a dern. Plus, I wanted to meet the right girl." He pulled Jenelle close to him. For the first time, Katelynn heard Arkansas in his voice and wondered how he'd fooled her. She didn't know what a Colorado accent sounded like, but he didn't have one.

"So he's not from Colorado," Jenelle said, "but I still love him."

"No snow-covered mountains?" Katelynn said. She tried to grin but couldn't.

"Never been there," Harvey said.

"Are you going to graduate? Again?" asked Katelynn. The word *floored* occurred to her. Yes, she was floored. From Walter de la Mare to this—she didn't know what to call this turn of events. "Does the principal know?" The yearbooks were already out. Harvey had been voted Best Athlete and Most Likely to Succeed. "You don't look old," she said, searching his face. You could see the years on him; it was part of why he was so good-looking. Yes, she still loved him. If she'd been high moments earlier, she wasn't anymore.

"I think it's pretty funny," Jenelle said, as if she had accepted all this and it was old news. "He can still go to college. He's just too old to get a track scholarship."

"What were you doing the last few years?" Katelynn asked, but Jenelle broke in to say, "Leave him alone now. We were having fun. This is a party, right?"

"It doesn't matter," said Katelynn loyally, flustered, scared for him now, for what he might have done during those lost, mystery years. Had he committed a crime? Would he go to jail? Already she was defending him in her head against—who? her mother?—saying, Why is it so wrong to want to be younger? Jenelle was watching Katelynn's face. She looked so smug and proud. *She* knew what he'd been doing. Harvey would have told her. Katelynn vowed to get it out of Jenelle, even if she had to beg.

"Look," Jenelle said, holding a drop of mercury high on one finger. "Isn't it beautiful?"

Even as Jenelle flicked the drop, Katelynn said, "Don't. Oh Jenelle, don't."

The silver drop fell from Jenelle's finger to the back of her other hand, the hands with broken nails, a ring on her thumb, and chipped cranberry-colored polish—pretty, trashy hands. One drop to the back of her hand, seeking out the blue vein beneath the skin. That drop took so long to fall. Katelynn knew she should reach out and catch it, snatch it out of the air, break its heavy arc.

But she hadn't.

THE HOUSE IS IN Mississippi, just over the Arkansas state line, which of course is formed by the river itself. Like Hawk Lake, this part of Mississippi is in the Delta, the flat, low-lying river land that stretches from New Orleans to Memphis. Jerry has brought his crowbar, but the door to the old house is already open, the padlock busted off by somebody else. He got the property in a tax sale. If you pay the back taxes two years in a row and confirm it in court, you've got it. He doesn't have to do this kind of work. His parents left him their fortune plus the lakeside house.

Jerry just enjoys going to the tax sales at county courthouses and sitting in a circle with weathered farmers ("Stop by that pecan grove on the way out of town, young fella," one old man always tells him, "and pick you a few sacks full") and a couple of lacquer-haired real-estate ladies, bidding through pursed lips. It's the best-kept secret to earning money. Of course, you can lose your shirt. You might wind up with a chemical dump, a lot in a slum (for small Mississippi towns have their slums, too), or a bankrupt funeral parlor; these properties are tough to get rid of. So far, he's been lucky. He's claimed oddly shaped parcels with road frontage, a few patches of timber, and the occasional abandoned house on a forgotten lot.

This property is the best of all.

He'll clean the place up and sell it. Even as he stands on the threshold with his hand on the door, he smells a skunky odor. He's not put off. The thing is to be grateful for what you get.

No matter that this house is a solid hour from Hawk Lake. He likes to drive. It's relaxing. Usually while he drives, he thinks about his paintings. They're not that good. He knows that. But he wants to get better and believes he can, if he just observes closely enough. His grandfather was a fantastic painter. Jerry has a few of his canvases.

The house is a small one-story foursquare, common in the Delta countryside, with no basement and a crudely added-on front stoop. Beside the stoop, a dozen chipped pots hold the frizzled remnants of geraniums. He pushes open the door and steps inside.

"Whoa," he says, under his breath. Are people still living here, among the few pieces of cheap furniture and the fussy knickknacks? A card game is spread out on the rug, cartoon-character cards fanned out in a circle, as if the players are coming back any second. He explores a short, narrow hallway, finding balls of lint and broken pecan shells in a trail from kitchen to bathroom to bedroom. That means mice and squirrels. He pulls open a kitchen drawer. It's full of fluff, but he doesn't see any baby mice. The pecan shells mean squirrels got in during the wintertime, bringing the nuts inside to crack open and savor. A spice rack hangs on the kitchen wall with spices still in it, the jars coated evenly in dust. New beer bottles sit on the counter beside the sink, and there's an open bag of Fritos that the critters haven't gotten to yet.

Kids: that's what this means. The local sheriff has told him that kids rove in bands at night, breaking into empty houses and doing mischief, sometimes building a fire in an old living room on a cold night and dancing to music provided by a boom box. Cards and corn chips: pretty tame party. He thinks of Glo's daughter, that pale, sick girl, and wonders if she'll really recover. Glo has forbidden him to talk about Katelynn unless she mentions her first. "My baby could still die," Glo will say, tears spurting from her eyes. Glo will lie around at Jerry's house all afternoon, then spring up and rush out the door without kissing him good-bye, crying out that her daughter might be starting to die at that very moment. Glo has figured out that while Katelynn was playing with mercury, she herself was with Jerry, and she torments herself about it.

It bothers him that Glo is married, that she is betraying not only her husband but her sick daughter. Jerry pictures himself married to Glo. To leave her family, all she would have to do is pack a few suitcases and drive the graveled semicircle of road around the lake to his house. Of course she always takes another route when she visits him, long and circuitous. Their affair has lasted six months. He's surprised they're getting away with it. They are neighbors, after all, with only a part of the lake between them. He never has enough time with her, just scraps of hours here and there. Unlike other women he has known, even loved, he knows little about Glo's background. Practically all she has ever told him about her childhood is how she enjoyed an old metal merry-go-round on the playground of her elementary school in Indiana, the dangerous, limitless kind of centrifuge that you never see anymore, the kind you had to power with your own legs. "The boys used to push the girls off," she has said, "but I always got right back on."

He pictures her clinging to a metal bar while the merry-go-round spins and whirls, the ground beneath it churned to mud, her mind all white noise and wildness, full of Glo-thoughts, even then.

Outside, it's a brilliant September day, but the tax-sale house is shaded by giant pecan trees. Inside, it's twilight.

In the bedroom, in the watery circle of mirror attached to a musty vanity, he stares at his sunburned cheeks and bleached-out hair, almost whitened by sunlight. He surveys the room reflected in the mirror. Must have been an elderly lady living here, judging from the piles of curlers and stacks of embroidered housedresses piled on an ironing board. He feels claustrophobic under the low ceiling. He pulls on a shade, which rolls up with a screech. The window behind it is cracked as if from a fist, and mimosa branches press against it. Mimosa, privet, creeper—takeover plants, as fast-growing as kudzu. The skunk smell is strongest in this room. He stays away from the dark, lumpy bed, heavy with stained comforters. Not everybody dies in the hospital. Some die at home. Anyway, it was her room, the old lady's bedroom. He will not disturb it. He spies a Whitman's Sampler box and lifts the top off, holding his breath—always a chance for treasure. The box yields letters, cards, and bills, which he holds up to the thin light from the window. The most recent postmark on the letters is five years ago. Mother's Day cards, birthday cards, and a hospital release form ("Activity as tolerated") are crammed into the candy box.

Beneath the box is a small, thick photo album, which he tucks under his arm.

"Why do you fool with those old houses?" Glo has asked him. She knows about his inheritance.

"I like 'em," he always says, "and someday I might be poor. I might be living in one of 'em." He doesn't tell her it's other people's lives that attract him, the randomness of claiming a house and finding whatever has fallen through the cracks of a life that otherwise would never have touched his. There's another reason, too: if he concentrates hard enough, he can imagine what the people looked like who used to own the land or live in the houses, and then, using the same palette his grandfather used, he paints them.

Growing up, he'd always thought his family was rich just because his mother bought drinking straws and boxes of Popsicles every time she went to the store. His father was proud that he'd expanded the lake to its present size. Though nature had created it as one of the Mississippi's countless oxbows, he'd deepened it and designed its inlets and tiny bays. Jerry remembers his father sketching maps with crayons, marking with an exclamation point the lots and the houses he had sold, crowing, "They're selling like hotcakes!" He used to lift Jerry's mother up off the ground and swing her around every time he sold another house. He hired Louisa to give tours on the *Arkansas Belle* and eventually allowed her to buy the serviceable old duck boat over a period of years.

Louisa and the boat have been a fixture on the lake all of Jerry's life. Yesterday, when he'd pulled her from the lake, it had taken him a moment to realize who she was. Sopping wet, gasping, she hadn't looked like herself. To think she'd been his granddaddy's nurse, all those years. The old gentleman had died when Jerry was about five. His huge house, the screaming parrot, and the massive, silent turtle on its leathery legs were extensions of himself. It still hurts to think that the house was torn down, his father having decided the termites had gone too far with it. The old man had encouraged Jerry, at age three, four, five, to draw, to paint, to play with modeling clay. Together, they would examine a sprig of clover, a cloud, the marks on the turtle's shell.

One of Jerry's earliest memories is of Louisa telling him, "I wish those critters got along. They want to outlive each other just from spite." The parrot died first. The turtle won. Who would have predicted that? At the end, it was just his grandfather and the old tortoise, one snoozing in a Mission oak chair, one frozen in place as it had been for decades, proving its vitality only by the gouges it left in melons during the night. And, of course, there was Louisa, who must have been young then, or sort of young. She ran his grandfather's errands, bought his groceries and medicine, and played Chinese checkers with Jerry.

When the turtle and the parrot were gone, his grandfather commissioned an art student to make statues of them. Jerry wishes his grandfather had sculpted the animals himself. The statues, of painted plaster, turned out clownish and crude, resembling hybrid creatures, a penguin crossed with a buzzard, a mollusk with the feet of a deer.

The statues stood on the edge of the lake until his grandfather died, reminding Jerry of gods not quite evil, yet not benign, guarding the lake and its small, unremarkable tides. Now they occupy his garage, their bright paint chipped, their expressions baleful.

Jerry is thirty. His parents had him late, their only child, long before they perished together in a car wreck on the casino road just three weeks before his twenty-third birthday. He inherited everything his parents had when they died. They had no business on that road. Gambling was not in their natures; it was just a lark, something to do. Such a narrow road, not built for heavy traffic; it was a country road back then.

His work now, on these old houses, is for them. His dad's work on the lake, and on the developments around it, is finished. But buying these old properties, some of their titles stretching back to the days of the Indians, gives Jerry enjoyment. They're up for another go-round, giving up their stories if only you listen to the wind blowing through the broken windows and look a little harder at the things left behind, clues for lives gone awry, gone missing. Somebody lives alone, dies without a will, and there you go. A recluse passes on, and the heirs are unknown or can't be found. Aging siblings rent out their late mother's house to a tenant, who moves on, and the siblings quarrel for a while about who should go over and cut the grass and clean the trash out of the barn, fuss so hard they quit speaking to each other, forget about the place for long stretches of time, and stick the tax notice in a drawer.

This house has a sweet feeling, from being lived in so long. Once, it was a nice little farm where you could work all day, year-round except Christmas, and get something back: corn, hay, cotton, vegetables, pecans from those trees. In December, when the nuts are ripe, he'll spread a sheet below the trees and shake the branches so the pecans fall off. All up and down the Delta roads, in wintertime, you see that: sheets and rugs spread out, eager arms shaking the limbs of pecan trees, faces all lit up, anticipating pies. He is thrilled to have his own pecan trees. He'll get Glo to come with him, to jiggle the trees with him.

Horses and cows, chickens and pigs, they had a place here, too. With the album in his hand, he steps outside, explores the yard, and circles the barn, where he smells the faintest, lingering odors of pigs and chickens. A woodpecker drums in a pecan tree. The barn door gives easily, and inside, he finds exactly what he expected—an oil-stained concrete floor, rusty farming implements, and a few bales of hay. The air smells greasy, cidery, leathery, all good smells. Near the house, a yucca plant stretches its spines toward the sky. He wonders if yuccas were a fad back in the twenties or thirties. They're not a native species.

He'll confirm this property in court; it will officially belong to him.

Sitting in his truck, he eats the lunch he brought, a fast-food chicken sandwich, just spicy fried leather between two buns. Flipping open the album, he finds black-and-white photos taped inside. Something for Glo. She loves old pictures. She'd seemed crazy yesterday. He's felt for a while as if something he'd suspected was being verified. Of course, what she saw—that boat sinking—wouldn't that unhinge anybody? She's from the part of Indiana that doesn't have daylight saving time, and he always sees a stubbornness, a refusal, in her face that he connects with that, as if she's holding on to that hour, not giving it up, just as she will hold on to the image of the sunken boat.

He sits in his truck in the yard and feels the oldness all around him. The house is on a gravel road, far from any town. The tips of weeping willows graze the top of the truck. The faces that confront him from the album have a dogged, hardscrabble quality. A few were taken here, at this house. He recognizes a corner of it, back when it was new. An exhausted-looking young couple sits in tall grass, expressionless, the man's arm around the woman's shoulders. One page has pictures of schoolboys, their shirt-collars askew. One face repeats itself, and the words *3rd grade, 4th grade, 5th grade* are written beneath the pictures. An enlarged photo shows a kind of celebration, or picnic: three old ladies at a table beneath a tree, a rug spread out on the grass beneath them. Nearby is the yucca plant, a tiny version of itself. One woman holds a baby, her head ducked to nuzzle its face. Do people still do that, set up tables under backyard trees and have little picnics? He wants to paint that scene—the liveliness of the woman nuzzling the baby.

The last photo shows a grave covered in floral wreaths, mounds of white blossoms, their white ribbons incandescent with light. The gravediggers are nearby, working on another. Jerry counts seven men, or parts of seven men. The photographer caught a pair of hands with a shovel, here, and the side of a sunburned face at the bottom, there. The way the sunlight hits the funeral wreaths looks like late afternoon.

It's beautiful, and he's a sucker for beauty. Glo is the most beautiful woman he's ever seen, even though she's getting self-conscious about her age, claims her bottom is sagging and her hair's going gray. He can't believe she bothers with him. He puts the little album in the glove compartment. No need to show it to her just yet. Too much death, right now, to be studying funeral pictures.

"TELL ME WHAT you saw," says the voice on the telephone.

"Jenelle?" Katelynn says into the receiver. "Is that you?"

A sigh. "No, honey," says the voice, and Katelynn realizes it's an old person.

"I was dreaming," she says. She looks at her bedside clock: four in the afternoon, silence in the house. She'd picked up the phone before fully waking up. She hasn't felt really awake since she saw the boat sink yesterday.

"Who's Jenelle?" the voice asks. "A friend of yours?"

"She died," Katelynn says.

"On the boat? On my boat?"

"Who is this?" Katelynn says.

The person sighs again and says, "Louisa Shepherd. The captain. I was in your front yard yesterday, after Jerry Fiveash rescued me. His hair's gotten so long, I didn't recognize him at first. I just called him and thanked him for saving my life. There really aren't words for that, are there? I've known him all his life, ever since he was a little bitty baby and I was working for his granddaddy. His daddy sold me the boat. Are you up to talking? I know you've been sick."

"What did he say, when you thanked him?" Katelynn stretches her legs deep into her bed. She pictures little pools of mercury in her muscles, gathering while she sleeps. She has to get rid of it, every bit. She is fascinated to get a call from Captain Louisa, whom she has seen only at a distance. Now Louisa is right here, in her ear.

"Oh, he just said, 'You're welcome,' like it was no big deal. Said it had been a long time since he took a swim in the lake." Captain Louisa pauses. "I usually tell my passengers about you, just that you're under the weather. I don't give any details. But I don't think they remember half of what I say, anyway."

"You could make up stories," Katelynn says, sitting up in bed. "I would! I'd make up all kinds of things about the people who live around here, just to see how much I could get people to believe."

"How many people were on my boat yesterday? Did you count them?"

"I've been trying to remember how many I saw," Katelynn says. "I didn't like that woman who hit you. Does your face hurt?"

"It sure does. What if they can never figure out who-all, exactly, was on that boat with me? I told the police what I could remember, but the names were on my clipboard, and it sank." The voice suddenly sounds frail and faint.

"The Internet," says Katelynn. "That's how they'll find them."

"So that's what the Internet is for, huh, finding lost people? Are you good on it? Using computers, I mean?"

"Pretty good," Katelynn says. "I used to be, before I got sick. We have computers at school, and I have one here. I'm not supposed to look at it for long. I can't watch TV either. The light hurts my eyes."

Captain Louisa asks, "What if somebody needed to find a baby they gave up?"

"Oh, it would be so easy. That happens all the time now," Katelynn says. Pain sweeps through her stomach. That's how hunger feels. "I wasn't laughing yesterday, not for real."

"How easy? Like using the phone book?"

"Better. Satellites can put lost people in touch with other people. You don't have to understand it for it to work," Katelynn says.

She suddenly looks through her glass walls to the lake and notices elaborate activity there: a gunmetal gray craft has arrived, unmistakably peopled with divers poised to jump from its deck. "Hey," she says, as if Louisa is watching it with her. "They're out there on the water—searchers. They've got wet suits on and flippers and goggles, and oxygen tanks on their backs. I thought they found all the people yesterday. Maybe there are more. People were out here last evening praying and singing hymns."

"Well, I hope they can find them all and haul them back up, though I'd as soon have gone down to Davy Jones's locker, as the saying goes, than endure all of this. What about you? How are you feeling?"

"Okay," Katelynn says, holding her binoculars to her eyes and following the balletlike movement of a diver, a man-fish, as he launches over the side of the boat. "Splash!" Katelynn says, and Louisa laughs as if watching with Katelynn or even through Katelynn's eyes. "My doctor says I should be well by now or else dead, instead of just in limbo, where I kind of am. Oh, look. The boat has all this equipment on it and something like a hook."

"Probably a navy salvage boat," Louisa offers.

"There's another type of boat out there, too. A barge. Can you see it?"

"Oh gosh no, I'm at home," Louisa says. "I live a few miles from the lake. Can't see a thing from here. I keep thinking about my mother, though. She had such dreams for me. Yours must, too. Mama used to talk about cigarette boats, how rich folks with yachts and all kinds of sleek boats started coming to Maine, where she grew up. I was up in Maine for a while, myself. Aren't cigarette boats those skinny little fast ones?"

"They have them in Europe, I think, on the Riviera," says Katelynn, "and in the movies. Did you used to say 'Ahoy' to people on land?"

"No," says Louisa. "Those divers should have taken me out there with them. They must be looking for the *Belle*. I could tell them where to look. They might look all day and not find it. Will you call me if they bring it up? I guess they'll never find my cap, that red one I always wore. I can't tell them to look for it. That would sound awful."

"You'll have to get a new one," Katelynn says, her eye falling on something on the grass just outside her glass walls, a small pile of something that wasn't there before, a heap of stones maybe. "I'll help you look."

"Will you help me look for the lost baby I need to find?"

"Of course," says Katelynn, laughing, unable to tell if it's her old laugh or the weird crying laugh spawned by her illness. Louisa follows her thoughts so well, the way Jenelle used to. Jenelle had let the drop of mercury fall from her finger to the back of her other hand, had looked at Katelynn as it fell, had read in Katelynn's eyes what that drop would do.

Katelynn hangs up the phone and crawls out of bed, taking it slow, navigating across the room to the wall, pressing her nose against the glass. Her mother used to forbid her that, scold her near to screaming: "There's not enough Windex in the world if you mess up these walls. I won't clean up your fingerprints or nosemarks, I won't do it!"

Pignut hickories. That's what's piled there. "Harvey," Katelynn says. She scans the yard and the point of land that leads down to the lake. So he's back. He has been to see her. He must have looked in while she was asleep. Nobody else would leave these. There was a pignut hickory just outside the warehouse where they'd played with the mercury. She and Jenelle and Harvey had collected the nuts after they poured some of the mercury out on the ground (and some they had saved, in bottles and jars from the warehouse). There had been so many nuts lying around, and they were hungry. Harvey had held a few nuts between rocks and cracked them open and they had all eaten them. The memory of that taste springs to Katelynn's tongue, raw and woody and sweet. She'd known the three of them were on borrowed time, even as they idled there with the nuts, old nuts from the previous fall, toeing them into a pile in the yellow dust. Just a few yards away lay the overturned vat where Harvey had poured the mercury onto the ground. It didn't seep into the dirt, just rolled and spread in crazy, quicksilver rivulets.

"We shouldn't have done that," Katelynn had said at the time, thinking, *Why have we done any of this?* and Jenelle, blowing smoke from a regular cigarette, had said, "Too late now. It's still pretty, though, the way it makes a little pool." Jenelle had tossed her handful of pignuts aside and reached up to kiss Harvey, who was gathering up the bottles and jars, saying he could sell them or give them out to friends.

Katelynn had said, "I remember wanting to write a letter to Walter de la Mare, after I read his poem 'Silver.' Suddenly, it was like I was in love with *him*." She'd looked at Harvey as she was saying that, Harvey, who was kissing Jenelle.

"You could still write to him," Jenelle had said, showing that she'd been listening even during the kiss.

Now, out on the lake, the divers look like they're playing, surfacing and gesturing to each other and to those on the rescue boat. Only it can't be a rescue boat. Nobody could still be alive. As Katelynn watches, a bigger craft with a crane on it looms into view, and she understands that the duck boat has been found. She blinks, watching them, happiness rising bubblelike inside her heart. She'll find Louisa's lost baby, too. She will. She turns her gaze toward the pile of nuts and counts them through the glass. Thirty, thirty-five, forty nuts, like guessing the number of jelly beans in a jar. Walter de la Mare had longed to go back to his childhood, her teacher had said, and Katelynn had understood the desire to retrieve that radiant past. He was still around: Harvey, who vanished months ago and didn't leave a note. He might be half dead by now, and the light must be bad for him like it is for her.

Was Katelynn really a lifeguard once? She can hardly believe it now. She worked at the community swimming pool, not here at the lake. You can swim in the lake, but only a few people do. Her next-door neighbors, the Johnsons, a retired couple, occasionally swim out a few dozen yards, slowly, their arms and legs flashing whitely through the water. Katelynn always worries about them, but then they swim back to shore, slip their feet into their flip-flops, and stagger up the short grassy point to their own house. Before she got sick, she could have saved them easily, if they needed saving.

At the pool where she used to work, she held her breath, dove in, and swam an hour every day before her shift started. Then her mind was clear, ready to concentrate. She used to squint across a blazing stretch of turquoise—the surface faintly waxy from suntan lotion in the water—blowing her whistle, settling squabbles among kids who ran alongside the pool no matter how many times she told them not to, their feet slapslapslapping the wet concrete. She'd been strong then, with zinc oxide striping her nose and mirrored sunglasses small as bottlecaps protecting her eyes. Yet she'd never saved a life; she had never had to. She had planned to join a water ballet team, once she got to college.

College. She'll still go, someday. Her mother has promised to give her all of her own nifty college accessories, artifacts from the '80s: vintage clogs, Braemar sweaters, a hot pot, an electric coil that you plunge into water to heat it up for cocoa or ramen or instant soup.

She watches the boats in the water, the arm of the crane swinging wide. It takes a long time for the *Belle* to be hauled to the surface, water and silt streaming off of it, and deposited on the barge. She watches, fascinated. She wonders how the boat can look at all like itself, after what has happened. The canopy is shredded and torn like a candy wrapper, and the chassis looks crumpled and dirty, but it's still the *Belle*. When the salvage operation is over, when the barge holding the *Belle* glides out of view around a curve in the lake, Katelynn stretches, thirsty and stiff, glad Louisa didn't see that. Maybe she'll call Louisa later. Right now, she's too tired.

To think Harvey was here, all shadow and swiftness. How thin his arms might be by now, since he has run away and come home. He might be a ghost, coming for her, bringing her something to eat.

"I HEARD YOU held on to a child's hand for a while, underwater, but then you let go. Can you tell me a little more about that?" The voice belongs to a reporter. Louisa recognizes her name: she's a big-boned woman on Memphis TV, a reporter who covers fires and murders, the one the station sends outside in really bad storms to rant about the weather, while tornadoes whip her hair across her face. Louisa hangs up. Shaken, she stands in her kitchen.

In her mind, she goes over the *Belle,* bow to stern. Its anatomy is simple as a cat's. What went wrong? Every bit of it is known and familiar to her: axles, engine, pumps, propeller, spare wheel. Why, Raggedy Andy had just fixed the bilge pump, because she'd noticed that it was switching on and off.

There were three pumps. The main one, the bilge pump, was so powerful it could shoot water over a house. If more than four inches of water collected in the bottom of the boat, the pumps were supposed to come on. Yet the boat swamped so fast that the pumps couldn't save it.

She is shaking again.

Before the tour, she'd done her customary walk around the *Belle,* had looked underneath it, and all was well. What had she missed?

"She's A-OK," Raggedy Andy had said, yet in the same breath he said what she didn't want to hear, that the *Belle* was getting old.

You should eat something, comes a soft voice she recognizes as her mother's, as if her mother were here in the kitchen, looking after her.

Barbie's twins have ravaged the goodies that people brought.

Gingerbread with a pretty pattern on top—powdered sugar sifted through a doily to make a snowflake design—has been gouged and smeared, its glass plate littered with crumbs. The middle has been eaten out of a lattice-topped blackberry pie.

Did she ever really go to a pie supper up in the Ozarks? Yes, she did, just as sure as she was once sixteen years old. That was during the last visit she'd ever had with her grandparents. Her father took her to see them. She made a blackberry pie with her grandmother's canned blackberries, which smelled like summertime itself, and she put the pie in a box decorated with her hair ribbons. The pie supper was held in a one-room schoolhouse where the potbellied stove was fired up red-hot to chase away the chilly spring air. Men and boys would bid on the boxes and then everybody would pair off so each man could eat his pie with the woman who made it. The money went to buy things for the school. The auctioneer lifted up Louisa's ribbon-covered box, which was lopsided from the heavy pie inside, and bawled out: "Miss Louisa Shepherd, who is kindly visiting with us, made this pretty box with a goody in it. There she is, boys, and she's a pretty one herself. What'm I bid?"

It was the only time in her life she'd been called pretty in public, or by anybody except her parents. She felt beautiful, even though she knew she was as bumpy-haired and plain there in the Ozarks as she was back in Yellville.

The eighteen-year-old youth who stared at her and then bid on her pie was the person she should have married. She knows that now. Tall, with scrubbed, callused hands and eyes that could see a country mile, he paid out his money, took the beribboned box, and smiled at her.

"He's wife-huntin', Louisa, and he's a ketch. His folks are givin' him a good piece-a land," her grandmother whispered encouragingly, her breath sharp with tobacco. When Louisa told the boy she was only visiting her grandparents for a week, she could tell he was crushed. Still, he ate the blackberry pie with gusto, sharing it with her and gallantly not mentioning the burned crust. Later, there was dancing.

How was it that her feet knew what to do, when she'd never danced before? Reels and jigs: her grandfather was one of the fiddlers, and her grandmother beat on the strings with knitting needles. Another man played a jawbone, still another a Jew's harp. Somebody played the pipes, and a young man pounded on a strange leather thing that looked to Louisa like a cross between a drum and a tambourine and gave dark, hollow reverberations that made her want to leap up and cry out.

The boy danced her out the door, into the air, where a fine sleet was falling, and kissed her. As she tasted the blackberries on his lips, she thought, *This could be my life,* and she almost chose it, but she knew her parents were separating, that she and her mother would go to Maine the very next week.

She should have known she was too plain to have many chances. The boy led her back inside and danced the rest of the evening with other girls. No other boys asked her to dance. Her father, morose about the impending separation, sat by the stove all evening and didn't eat, dance, or talk. Every time the boy danced by with another partner, Louisa looked away and told herself, *Maine.* She wondered if this could count as heartbreak, for she really liked him. He probably married one of those other girls that very summer, by the time the new berries were ripe.

She remembers that he'd tucked the ribbons from the decorated pie box into the pocket of his overalls.

Between that blackberry pie and this one, what the hell happened?

Louisa stares at the desecration in her kitchen. Barbie and the twins have departed, but Louisa's heart still pounds from their invasion. Nobody but a monster would really go after the very middle of a pie, leaving a liquid crater of purple juice in the center of the crust. A purple handprint decorates her refrigerator. She wipes it off with a dish towel. More than one full day has passed since the boat sank, and now it's evening. She had called that girl, Katelynn, and eventually the girl had called back, saying they had pulled the *Belle* out of the water.

That's all she did today, talk with Katelynn. It had taken all morning and most of the afternoon just to get rid of Barbie and the twins.

"I'll never have them in my house again," Louisa vows to her kitchen. She ought to eat something, but she can't. How odd it feels to be home this time of day, when she should be out on the *Belle*. She has worked six and seven days a week, eight or nine months of the year, for years on end. She has fought retirement, fearing Tupperware parties, quilting clubs, sewing circles, TV soap operas, dreading that she would be shanghaied into teaching Sunday school. She has oper- ated the boat and the tour business for so long, has kept so hale and strong, that without it, she will have to battle old age. The *Belle* has been her weapon against arthritis and cataracts, osteoporosis and Alzheimer's. You've got to be strong to navigate a boat around a big lake. She has battened down the hatches in sudden storms, when the *Belle* rode three-inch wavelets like a clipper ship in a typhoon. The *Belle* had two identities, bus on land, boat on water, just as Louisa has her two selves, her captain self and her round-shouldered younger self, hidden deep inside her sagging, mostly white-haired older body.

Did her mother, gentle, harsh Violet—*Violent*—have two selves? And Nana in Maine and Granny in the Ozarks? She never understood any of the women in her family, so she will just have to love them, even though they are gone.

What did they think of getting older? Violet was still middle-aged when she died, but Nana and Granny were surely born old. What if they'd lived into this modern age, dressing as she does in colorful sweatsuits and thick athletic shoes, laced with Mickey Mouse shoe- strings? These clothes are modern clichés, saying *little old lady* just as surely as Nana's black dresses and Granny's high-buttoned boots once did, yet Louisa will never feel anything but young.

"I will never," she says to her kitchen, meaning she'll never talk in old folks' clichés, will never say, "I've got snow on the roof" or "I'm having a senior moment" or "My forgetter is working." Such stupid, doomed talk, the things people say in nursing homes, getting ready to die. Even if the day comes when she's plagued by incontinence and all the rest, she will not talk about it. She remembers a story about an aged recluse who died alone and was known to have pulled her own teeth rather than go to a dentist. Louisa can see how you would get that way. Living alone, even if you had to pull your own teeth, might be the easiest way to deal with old age. It will take all her strength, she thinks, to meet it. Her duck boat spiel has warded off aging, the peppy talk with her arm-waving gestures has educated thousands of tourists, and that is the kind of talk she's meant for, not the narrative so many use as their lives wind down. Oh, of course she has aged. Years go by, you can't help it. Years of sun on her skin have coarsened it to almost the texture of cantaloupe rind. The rough skin on the back of her elbows makes funny little faces when she holds her arms out straight. But she has hardly had to look at herself, all these years; every morning she gets up and throws on a sweat suit and she's set to go.

Maybe it's because she used to be a nurse that she knows too much. Working at the nursing home, she had learned such hard, practical things, learning more from the other nurses working there than she had learned in school. She remembers one very large man . . . like the man who sank the boat. But *he* was fairly young. He would have lived for years. She sees him hurrying down the invisible steps of the water, absorbed in his journey, racing as matter-of-factly as he might descend the steps of his own house.

All those people tangled up and trapped in the canvas cover of the duck boat the way you'd be caught in a hammock spun too fast, till it wrapped around you and sealed you in.

Her mind reels away from it all, from the bits of recollection her brain allows her of those passengers: the way one woman hesitated about the cost of a ticket. The woman had dug in her pocketbook for the money, her face serious with the expenditure. Louisa had felt impatient, knowing even then how mean she was to begrudge this woman for wavering, for weighing the price of the ticket against who knows what other demands of her budget. The woman, who was with her husband and son, was the first to sign on for the afternoon's tour. They were still on land then, as Louisa pointed out this landmark and that one. She had to work harder for the land part, regaling passengers with the history of Hawk Lake's old bathhouses and the story of the Fiveash family. She used the word "dynasty." She was proudest of the old man, proud to say she'd worked for him. Once on the water, she concentrated on the rich side of the lake, because that's what people always wanted to see. The poor side was closer to where she herself lived. The reeds were more raggedy, the water a little scummy on top, the houses ramshackle. She always felt bad, avoiding that part of the lake, as if she should sail back by herself and apologize at the end of each day.

That day, as she approached the lake with her cargo of passengers, she'd felt lucky because she saw a hawk perched high in a tree. She spoke into her microphone: "Hawk Lake's named after 'em. Look, folks! There's a red-tail."

The little boy whose mother had hesitated said, "I bet it's a fake one you put up there. A stuffed one," and the child's father said in a heavy Alabama accent, "Quit bein' a smart aleck, Bobby," even as Louisa chuckled and thought it wouldn't be a bad idea, and who would know it, if she stuck a stuffed bird or a painted one up in a tree to point out to tourists.

"I'll tell you something," she said to the little boy. "Hawks are easy to find. There's lots of 'em around, and they don't mind being seen. But the bird I'm after is so hard to spot, I've never seen one."

That got the boy's interest. "What bird?" he cried, hopping up and down.

She told him about the king rail, showed him the picture in the guidebook. She could tell he was disappointed, because the picture looked ordinary, just a brown-and-yellow bird with a long beak. But she felt hopeful, that day, that she just might see one, and she said so.

There were two sisters, black, pretty, in early middle age, who declared they felt lucky, too. They had just had their fortunes told. They were on vacation, they announced to the other passengers, and they were having a wonderful time. "The fortune-telling was an analysis of a kissprint," said the older sister. "The fortune-teller was from Mexico. She got us to put on lipstick and then blot our lips on a Kleenex, and she examined the prints."

"And she predicted all sorts of good things. She gave us our lucky numbers. We're going to Tunica next!" chimed the younger sister, patting her pocketbook. The others chortled. You could get an easy laugh with Tunica. Oh, don't waste your money, Louisa wanted to tell the women.

And there was a young, brainy-looking woman who brought a camera and said she wanted to see "iggles." It had taken Louisa a moment to realize she meant eagles. She heard the little smart-aleck boy say "iggles" under his breath and guffaw.

"I've heard iggles have made a comeback around here," the young woman had said as they neared the lake's edge. "I'm researching them. Best place for iggle-watching is Reelfoot Lake in Tennessee. Any of y'all been there? Oh," she said as if remembering something. "Don't leave yet," and she clambered off the *Belle*—which was still a bus— scooped up some lake water in a small glass tube, stuck a stopper in the tube, and tucked it inside her jacket.

Ever since her first trip out on the *Belle,* the lake has spoken to Louisa with a sure, sounding voice, a loving and approving voice, and now, since the accident, that voice has gone silent. If she tells anybody this, they'll think she's crazy.

Standing blindly in the middle of her kitchen, she realizes that her legs hurt. She's prone to leg cramps, and her muscles always stay sore for a couple days afterward. She's glad to have the ache to focus on, but the faces of the passengers keep zooming in on her: hesitating woman, brainy young iggle-watching gal taking a test tube of water to the lake bottom with her.

When she does fight off the images, her mind is an aching blank. Her gaze sweeps across her cupboards until it registers on her that the kitchen is dirty, filthy even. High up, the cabinets are so covered in dust and grease that it looks like they're wearing coats of mohair. Still in her robe, she fills a bucket with hot water from the faucet and a glug of ammonia, hauls out her stepladder, and scrubs. She hasn't cleaned this hard in years, not since she scoured old Mr. Fiveash's sunroom. He himself was neat as a pin, but those critters, the warring old parrot and the stoic tortoise! Those animals left their mark, all right, with the thick pasty swirls of parrot poop and the dry, curiously dusty turtle droppings. When the parrot died, Mr. Fiveash just shook his head, saved a few feathers, and got Louisa to wrap the light, stiff body in a sheet and bury it in the yard. When the tortoise finally expired, the old man cried, called the vet out to see if it could be revived, and finally ordered it buried at sea. Louisa didn't have the *Belle* then, of course. She summoned some neighbor boys. Luckily the boys were big and strong, but even so she had to help them lift the tortoise into the rowboat. Out in the water, the boat rode low. Grunting with effort, Louisa and the boys hefted the huge dead creature over the side. It sank immediately. What had the tortoise thought about, all those years in the sunroom?

Bottom of the lake. She keeps holding her breath and letting it out in stingy little gasps, as if that would give the passengers more air in their lungs, as if it weren't too late. That woman who pummeled her—that's who should have died. Louisa beats the furry cabinets with her sponge and breathes in tiny sips. She can't believe her mechanic made a mistake: Andy, Raggedy Andy, with his big, sweet eyes, his thin face and little stitched-on smile just like the Raggedy Andy doll she'd had as a child. He has a jerky walk, the way a doll would walk if it came to life. She always wanted to hug him. "She's A-OK," he'd said, wiping the grease from his hands onto a towel, and she'd wanted to hug him then; he was a sweet little pet of a person, like no mechanic she'd seen before, so sweet and scared looking at the same time, his whole heart in his big eyes. Her arm goes numb from holding the sponge up high on the grimy cabinets as she scrubs. A numb arm: the first sign of a stroke, she imagines Barbie saying. Fine. Bring on a stroke, a heart attack. Anything.

The doorbell rings. Why hurry to answer it? How could this be anything but bad news? But she climbs down the ladder and opens the door. Barbie breezes in, plunks down on the sofa, picks up the remote, and clicks on the TV, saying, "Well, they're acting like it's all your fault, Louisa. There's speculation you were on a murder-suicide rampage. There was a woman on TV just a minute ago saying it's your fault for making her husband move," she says. "I came right over. They've gone to a commercial. I bet she'll be back on in a second."

"But that man sank the boat!" cries Louisa. "He weighed too much. I shouldn't have let him on board. Although I've had big folks before. I had him move from port to starboard, to balance the boat better, but it didn't help."

Barbie frowns at her, a focused, narrow frown, taking in Louisa's sweaty robe and the sudsy sponge in her hand. "What are you doing, Louisa?"

"Killing people, I guess," says Louisa, but Barbie has clicked on the sound again. She tries to remember what Katelynn told her. Katelynn had been watching divers. She had said, "Splash!"

The woman who slapped Louisa is on the TV screen, furious. She says to a reporter, "One minute, there was just a little puddle on deck, and then what's-her-face came over and insulted my husband, asking him to move to the other side of the boat. She didn't flat-out accuse him of being fat, but that's what she meant."

Louisa says, "There was nothing wrong with the *Belle*. Andy had checked it over, just the day before." She doesn't say anything about the bilge alarm not being in it. Barbie wouldn't understand, and anyway, the alarm wasn't ready to be installed. The Coast Guard had to inspect it first, didn't they? Louisa's cheek is still sore from where the woman hit her, bruised to the bone.

"Shhh," says Barbie, intent on watching the TV.

"Nobody knows how bad this is, Barbie," Louisa says.

Barbie's head snaps up. "Your guilt, you mean? Is it starting to sink in?"

"Leg cramps." She rubs her legs and takes some pleasure in the horror on Barbie's face.

THE LAKESIDE CONVENIENCE STORE has posters on the door for the diamond mine, showing a picture of the freckle-faced boy who found the big yellow gem last summer. There used to be a poster for the *Arkansas Belle,* but that's been ripped clean off. Ringing up Jerry's purchases, the cashier says, "Did you ever take a tour on that boat?"

"Long time ago, when I was a kid," Jerry says. He doesn't advertise the fact that his father created this lake and the developments all around it. Most people around here probably don't know who he is. He likes it that way, likes his quiet life. To the cashier, he's just a local redneck.

The cashier shakes her head. "I always meant to take a tour, but I never did and now I'm glad," she says with dramatic gloom, fixing Jerry with a frown. "That water out there is sixty feet deep. Cold and dark, too dark to see which way air bubbles are going, so you don't know if you're swimming up to the top, or sideways, or down to the bottom. I'm amazed they got any of those bodies out. In water that deep, they said on TV, bodies can't float back up. They ain't got no booey . . . how do you say that?"

"Buoyancy," says a little boy in line behind Jerry to buy Slim Jims.

"Yeah," the cashier says. "They found a lotta bodies further out from the boat and they say that means they tried to swim but didn't know which way. I hear that boat sank in about thirty seconds. A gal who saw it happen told 'em that."

"Who?" Jerry asks, wondering if anybody besides Katelynn and Glo and a few fishermen saw the sinking.

"That girl, that bad one that ate the poison, ate a thermometer or something," the cashier says, sticking a pen behind her ear. "One of the rich folks. Lives in the glass house. They called her and got that much out of her and then she hung up on them, real rude. You know her?"

"Come *on*," the little boy says in a squeal. "I'm hungry."

"Don't your folks feed you?" the cashier asks the child, giving Jerry his change. "I tell you what," the cashier says, "I'm glad I'm not poor old Captain Louisa. She'll have it on her conscience for the rest of her life."

"But there was something wrong with the boat. Must've been," Jerry says.

"Those people didn't have life jackets on, even though Louisa had 'em on the boat. Why didn't she make 'em put 'em on? You don't guess she was on some rampage, do you? Like, murder-suicide? That's what some people're sayin', that she was tired of her life and took it out on that bunch of strangers."

"Now that," says Jerry, "is really stupid."

"All I'm saying is what I've heard." The cashier rings up the child's Slim Jims.

Jerry takes his groceries out to his truck. The store sits between the rich side of the lake and the poor side, and Jerry has always felt more at home on the poor side, where the houses are cheap prefab jobs, built since his father died. He's a rich boy with a taste for the simple life. In the lot nearest the store, three heavy-set teenage girls are riding an ATV, grinding it across the gravel of their driveway, up a small, steep hill into pine trees and back again toward Jerry. A busted sofa, foam rubber spilling out of its sodden cushions, sits in their yard. There's been no rain in so long, Jerry hates to think why the cushions might be wet. Dogs are eating the sofa, gobbling chunks of foam rubber. He hasn't seen any of them before, not the girls or the dogs. They must be a new family, just moved in.

"Don't let them do that," Jerry yells, sweeping his arm toward the dogs, but the girls' eyes slew away from him. The one steering the ATV shrugs her shoulders defiantly, as if she hears him over the noise of the motor. Her mouth moves angrily.

Jerry sticks the bag of groceries in the truck and goes to the pack of dogs, which are snuffling and chuffing as they chew. A puppy tumbles over to him and licks his shoe. When he scoops it up, it licks his face, and he can smell the foam rubber on its breath, sour and plastic. The puppy's some kind of funny mix, with fur all different colors, small and heavy in his arms.

The girls on the ATV are watching him. The driver revs the engine and comes closer, steering right toward him. The girls' flat, thin hair lifts off their shoulders. They've got dark circles under their eyes and creases of darkness around their mouths, which make them look haggard even though they're probably Katelynn's age or younger. The noise from the ATV drones in Jerry's head as the girls roll toward him, their mouths opening in triple caves of mirth or threat. He stands his ground, holding the puppy, daring them to mow him down. Beetle-browed, the driver bellows something when she sees he's not moving out of the way.

He doesn't know what he's going to do. Why doesn't he step aside?

At the last second, he swings on board, still clutching the puppy, grabbing the driver's shoulder and piling on top of the two girls in the back of the ATV. The girls roar—whether with laughter or outrage, he can't tell. He's right there on them, their broad thighs in jeans, their hot, busy hands working at him. One's pulling him to her, the other is pushing him away. He rolls off them and hops to the ground, to safety, the puppy in his arms. The girls turn as fast as the clumsy vehicle allows, pursuing him, but he hops into his truck. They chase him partway down the shore road, but he goes too fast and gets away from them. They make a buzzing triangle in his rearview mirror.

THE REPORTERS TRY harder than ever to catch up with Louisa. They call day and night, and she hangs up on them. They sit in their cars and vans in her driveway, yelling questions when she walks out-side her house for any reason. She keeps her head down, moving fast when she has to go out to the grocery store, which she eventually does, once she has eaten all the sensible food the neighbors brought as well as all the canned beans and soup she had in her pantry. There are pies and cakes and cookies enough to feed an army, but you can't just eat sweets.

But the reporters get their stories from somebody anyway, stories that say she never offered life jackets to anybody.

It's not true, she wants to tell them. She *always* pointed the life jackets out to people, twenty-eight life jackets stowed in storage compartments. She always suggested they put them on, even if they were good swimmers. "I recommend it," she said. In all those years, hardly anybody put one on. She knows the state law by heart: you only have to wear a life jacket if you are under twelve and the boat is a pleasure boat. But the *Belle* is commercial, and it is regulated by the Coast Guard. Even if the passengers had put the life jackets on, they would probably still have drowned. That's what she hears on the news. The canvas roof stretched across the top and the front end of the boat and cupped people in the taut, wet fabric. There wasn't enough space between the railings and the canvas top for people to get out easily.

That's what her lawyer is telling her, a young woman who has materialized out of thin air, a woman who started calling that first night and who, apparently, believes she has been hired by Louisa. They have talked on the phone; Louisa can't remember quite when. It might have been the middle of the night. She remembers the lawyer saying, "They were ensnared in the canopy, caged by it. Life jackets wouldn't have helped. Do you hear me, Louisa?" as if Louisa is deaf. The fat man's wife has filed a wrongful-death suit against her. "We'll fight it," the lawyer says, and Louisa wonders if the lawyer is crazy or if she is not a lawyer at all but some crank caller. Her voice is a Yankee voice, bright and hard. There's to be a hearing in a few days.

How did *she* get out?

The memory flees even as she tries to hold on to it. She'd warned them all that they were going down, yelling to them to jump and swim for shore. But she didn't have time to jump. Like a diving board reverberating after you leap off it, the boat stuck its nose up toward the sky, out of the water, and bounced her off the deck, into the air, and down into the water.

Those unlucky enough to be closed in by the yellow-and-white-striped canopy never had a chance, unless they were strong enough to kick their way free through the railings. Of all the others, only the big man's wife managed to do that.

Seven dead, each a stone on Louisa's heart: the fat man, the two black sisters, the iggle-watcher, and the hawk-doubting child and his parents. Their faces are everywhere. She hauls her TV off her bedroom dresser and maneuvers it into the back of a closet. She lets the newspapers pile up in the yard, yellowing from the sunshine. Yet the identities are made known to her anyway, as if she's picking up the pulse of their life stories from the air. She hears enough to know, to connect her own brief memories of the people with their official, media-generated identities. Seven dead. As a day passes, two days, three, she remembers more about them. The little boy's mother announced she was hungry and asked if there was any food on board. Louisa had to tell her no. Usually, Louisa had a stash of goodies for sale—Nabs, Milky Ways, and peanut butter fudge she made herself—but ants had gotten into the fudge, and she was out of everything else. The woman marveled that she'd just had a late lunch, how could she be hungry?

"Maybe you're pregnant," another woman had said—the fat man's wife—and the hungry one looked alarmed, saying, "I hope not."

Louisa was just about to tell them all about the Swedish man she'd read about in the paper who ate an electric drill, piece by piece, when the brainy young woman said, "I've got just the thing," and reached into her jacket pocket and pulled something out. "Ham sandwich, with a dab of mustard?" she said, offering it to the hungry woman, who reached out and took it with no protest, no reluctance, just a hearty thanks to the younger woman. Louisa liked her for that.

"What'll you do now?" Louisa asked the iggle-watcher. "If you get hungry yourself with no sandwich left in your pocket? We'll be out on this lake a solid hour."

"I don't need to eat much," the woman said, and Louisa felt embarrassed, as if her joshing had uncovered some closely guarded secret.

Hearts beating beneath such ordinary clothes. In recollection she examines the T-shirts her passengers wore, the rumpled jackets a few had pulled out when they launched. She remembers how the veins on the woman's hand were tiny ropes as she lifted the ham sandwich to her mouth.

Louisa's head is a TV set she can't turn off. The passengers' names, ages, hometowns roll through her brain while she rubs her eyes, unable to eat or sleep, her clean kitchen smelling so sharply of ammonia and bleach it's as if she's got needles up her nose. Their names, it seems, were known immediately to the world, as if the corpses themselves had reeled off their identities to those who pulled them from the water. Beverly Hedgepeth, of Kirkwood, Missouri, and Candace Hairston-Dodd, of Jefferson City, Missouri: the sisters who'd just had their fortunes told. If that's not proof, once and for all, that fortune-tellers are a bunch of phonies, then Louisa doesn't know what is. The sisters collected miniature stuffed animals. They pulled their latest acquisitions out of their pocketbooks to show the other passengers—plush critters in lurid colors, with name tags in their ears. "We've each got a couple hundred," the sisters said happily. So that had been the last day in the lives of Beverly Hedgepeth and Candace Hairston-Dodd.

The fat man: Truman Testa, a barber from Tenafly, New Jersey. His is the name that stabs her the worst, each syllable an ice pick in her heart.

Josephine Lamar: the iggle seeker, an amateur biologist from Lexington, Kentucky. The hawk-doubting child: Bobby Usry, who had just the day before the boat ride survived a fall into a pit at a Jiffy Lube in Little Rock, where his family took their car for an oil change. This according to his older brother, the only family member who never set foot on the *Arkansas Belle,* having spent the afternoon sleeping in the family's trailer, parked in the lakeside campground.

"He, like, just stepped over the edge at the Jiffy Lube and come up all covered in grease. It took two hours to get him cleaned up in the shower at the campground," the teenage brother, Beebe, announces. How does Louisa, without TV or papers, know this? She turns the radio on in snatches. She hears it all. "Them guys at the Jiffy Lube said he oughta be a fireman, popping up out of that hole so fast. He climbed up some pole that they hitch the cars onto. Just fell into the pit and climbed back up the pole, crawled out the pit that way," the brother tells the world. The car and trailer belong to him, now that his mother and father and little brother are dead. He guesses he'll drive back to Arab, Alabama, where they're from.

That boy, alone in the woods, with all his family dead.

Louisa piles some of the cakes and cookies the neighbors have brought into a brown paper sack and drives to Katelynn's house. From all the tours Louisa has given, she knows exactly which room is Katelynn's. She doesn't bother ringing the doorbell, just goes to the glass walls of Katelynn's room and waves to the girl, who is lying in bed with a big book across her knees. Seeing Louisa, Katelynn jumps, a whole-body flinch that makes Louisa think of some critter jumping even though it's already dead. She's seen snakes do that, and chickens. Katelynn's face is so white that Louisa thinks of the pasty paleness of people in nursing homes who will never get out.

"I was hoping you might come with me," Louisa hollers through the glass. Only then does it occur to her that Katelynn might not even recognize her, that Katelynn has previously seen her only as a figure on board the boat or as the drowned-rat version of herself in Katelynn's yard, and now, maybe, won't know who she is.

But Katelynn shoves the book aside with something like a smile. It takes her a long time to crawl out of bed, as if she hurts all over. If you didn't know she was sick, you'd think she was lazy, one of those gals who just lie around all day and get up late to eat lunch at a restaurant. Long time getting her feet on the floor, standing up like she'll keel over. She seems to cast around the room for something and then picks up a coat off a chair and puts it on over her nightgown, scuffing her feet into some kind of shoes. She points to a glass panel in the wall, shakes her head, and makes a motion that Louisa understands to mean *I'll meet you around the other side.*

"I haven't been outside since the other day," Katelynn announces as she pushes the door open and steps out, squinting, fumbling for her dark glasses. "Oh, it's bright out here," she says. "What are we going to do? Are we going somewhere?"

"I thought we might go help that boy out at the campground. I got food for him. Are you up to going out there with me?" The answer, she knows, is no. Katelynn probably ought to be in the hospital.

But Katelynn's face perks up, at least what Louisa can see around the dark sunglasses. "Oh, the brother," Katelynn says, "from that family in Arab." She knows to pronounce it with the long *A*. "Yeah, I'd like to try and help him. Let's go before I run out of steam."

She's too weak to pull the door shut, so Louisa does that, and helps Katelynn into her beat-up orange Datsun.

The campground that Mr. Fiveash created long ago, on the poor side of the lake, has never been used much. Only part of it has any lakefront, and Louisa has never, in all the years of giving tours, seen any campers swimming there, even though the campground is heralded by a faded billboard that says SWIMMING BOATING MINIATURE GOLF. Louisa parks the car in the parking lot and goes around to give Katelynn a hand. The girl's grip is weak, but with Louisa's help she manages to haul herself out of the car and stand up. She reaches into her coat pocket, takes a handful of candy corn, and slings it back into her mouth, reminding Louisa of a baby bird, anxious to be fed.

They find the boy's campsite easily. He's the only one there. The trailer is the old-fashioned metal kind, like a long-lost spaceship, with a small window on each side. It is unhitched from an old car and parked in weedy woods as if it and the car have been there for a long time, the sandy earth around them dry and hard. Louisa tries to remember the last time it rained. She wonders who brought the car back from the little bandstand in town, where the tours started. Maybe the boy hiked over and fetched it or maybe the police gave him a lift.

"Ladies. Beebe Usry, at your service." It's as if he's been waiting for them. He steps out of the trailer, hopping down from its one step onto a carpet of leaves and tipping an imaginary hat. "Hey, I'll take that," he says and lifts the sack of food from Louisa's arms, sniffing it deeply. Is it only the light coming through the woods, or is his hair really gray? How could that be, when he is so young? His face has a sleepy look. His narrow shoulders and long back buckle and sway as he unpacks the food, placing it on a couple of nearby tree stumps as if for a ceremony. He tears into a foil-wrapped package of chocolate cookies and squats on the grass, eating the biggest one. Why, he has holes in his jeans, Louisa sees, crotch holes. She doesn't know where to look. She moves a platter of cake slices off a stump and sits there, holding it in her lap. Katelynn leans against a tree, clutching at her coat.

Beebe Usry addresses them both. "Folks a been coming by, bringing me stuff to eat. This is good timing. I was just about out." He finishes the cookie and reaches for another.

"Want some cake?" Louisa asks, offering him the platter.

He takes a thick slice, folds it over, and eats it as if it's a hot dog. When it's gone, he wipes his mouth on his sleeve and says to Katelynn, "Don't you get any thinner. I know this whole houseful of thin girls back in Arab. Anorectics. They smell like bugs. One of my neighbor-ladies looks after 'em. They're famous singers, The Candles. Ever heard of 'em?"

"Oh yes, The Candles," says Katelynn. "They are famous. They sing about the end of the world."

Beebe motions for Louisa to hand him more cake, and she passes him the whole platter. Eating, he goes on, "My neighbor says if she calls them sweetie and darling, over and over again, they might eat a little tiny bit. All of 'em cut off their hair and bleached it white, and they sing gospel songs. My neighbor sold all of her diamond rings to buy things for 'em."

"What kinds of things did your neighbor buy for them?" Katelynn asks. To Louisa, Katelynn's voice sounds higher and fainter out here in the woods.

"Stuff to exercise with," the boy says, crinkling his eyes, sunlight sparkling off his gray hair. "They do jumping jacks and play on these wheel things, like rats. But they're nice. They like me."

"What'll you do now?" Louisa asks. "I'm the captain, from the boat, by the way."

Beebe nods as if unsurprised. "That guy's wife, the one you made move." He pauses and then says, "She's the one told me what happened to my folks. She'd been talking to 'em on the boat, and they'd told her about this campground, that I was out here, that I didn't go with 'em."

"She came out here?" Louisa can't reconcile the woman's kind concern with those punches across the face.

Beebe flashes her a smile so searing that she draws back. "A little consolation, that's what she mostly wanted," he says. "She talked right bad about her husband. Said he had bad breath and wasn't at all jolly, like she wanted him to be." The boy fixes Louisa with his eyes. "What was it like for you, underwater?"

"I saw my father," Louisa answers, "up on a roof that I helped him fix a long time ago."

"Good," says the boy smoothly, as if she has given a correct answer. Those holes in his jeans, just at the crotch, are really bothering her: she can't look at them, yet she can't look away, and the boy keeps opening and closing his thighs like a hinge. "What did you say to make that guy move?"

"They weren't any special words. I don't even want to remember."

"Tell me," the boy insists.

She hesitates. "I said, '*Sir, could you maybe go around to the other side of the boat, to kinda balance it better?*'"

Beebe slaps his knee as if she has told a joke, though none of them laugh.

"I didn't mean to sound mean to him. I'm no slim thing myself," she says. "It was just that the boat was getting lower in the water, right where he was standing."

"Who'll pay for the funerals of all your family?" Katelynn asks the boy.

"I don't know. They're in the morgue. I told 'em to cremate 'em. I'll do something with the ashes."

All your family. Louisa leans her head down as the truth swims over her once again: all those people dead. She will spend the rest of her existence staggered by this, if people let her live. If they don't hunt her down and kill her.

The *Belle* was never meant to take on water, to sink.

"It was never meant for that," Louisa murmurs, but the young people don't seem to hear her.

Katelynn holds up one finger excitedly. "Wait, wait," she says. "I have some money of my own. I can help you pay for a nice service and some urns. Want me to?"

"I should pay for all the funerals," Louisa says faintly, but Katelynn shakes her head. Louisa says, "Back when my grandma was little, they just laid people out on a cooling board." Her head is whirring, but maybe it's just insects out here in the woods making that noise.

"There's worse things than being dead," Beebe is saying, and Louisa wishes she hadn't brought Katelynn. The girl is too weak and sick to be outside. The boy will sidetrack her so that Katelynn will never help Louisa find her baby. "Lots worse," he says. "I heard of a little girl who sat down on some valve in a swimming pool and had all her bowels sucked right out of her." He looks over at Katelynn. A smile has appeared on her lips. "Why're you laughing?" he asks her.

"She's crying," says Louisa, understanding Katelynn's writhing face.

"You do right to cry," Beebe says. Then he stops, and a look of surprise, even wonder, crosses his face. "Hey, wait a minute," he says. "I think I know who you are."

"You do?" Katelynn asks, still leaning against the tree and rocking slightly, side to side, her dark glasses wide as a car's bumper across her nose. "How?"

"I read the news stories. You're her," he says. "You're the mercury girl. I've heard you laugh sometimes when you're sad. I heard about that and the dark glasses you have to wear."

Louisa hauls herself to her feet and touches Katelynn's elbow. "We'll head on back now, Beebe. We just wanted to check on you."

"I've saved everything ever written about you," he tells Katelynn. "I can't believe you're here with me. I read about you in the paper, down in Arab, and I studied up on mercury. The astronauts took mercury-vapor lights to the moon, did you know that?"

"No," says Katelynn.

Beebe grins. "You might as well have syphilis, 'cuz mercury's the treatment for it, or anyway, it used to be."

"Watch your mouth," Louisa snaps at him.

"It's just the truth," he says. "Mercury's a fine thing. It's in Mercurochrome. It just don't belong in the body, not fillings in your teeth or nothing else. Katelynn," he says, "did you get punished for what you did?"

"Kind of," Katelynn says. "The three of us who went into that warehouse, we got charged with breaking and entering, and with criminal mischief for pouring the mercury out on the ground. My dad paid some fines. The owner of the warehouse lives out of town. He was notified." Katelynn's dark glasses slip down her nose, and she shoves them into place with a pale finger. "A judge sentenced us to do community service. By then, Jenelle had already . . ."

"Died," says the boy.

Louisa hears again the humming of insects, or a roaring in her own head. It seems to her that they're all three silent for a long time, listening, or waiting, and then Beebe says, "I dreamed of this. Don't everybody dream of their family dying and being left alone? It's, like, god-awful, but I feel so free."

Katelynn stares at him, her lips parted.

Louisa tells him, "There's people you can stay with if you want. Church people. Preachers." It's been years since she went to church. She still considers herself a churchgoer; she's just missed a few decades. Last time she checked, preachers were still kind. They did things like take in the poor, the orphaned, the desperate. She should take him in herself.

Who will take *her* in? Nobody. She might wake any night to a brick through her window, a mob with a rope in her yard.

Beebe shakes his gray head. "I'm fine here," he says. "I take showers at the campground shower. Got it all to myself these days. A sign says the water's okay to drink. But I wonder about that. The mercury's still in the ground, not that far away, and it'll be there for a long time."

"I'll bring you water," Louisa tells him, because she doesn't want Katelynn coming out here again, and she can see it: the girl living with this boy, out here in the woods, not eating, giving up even the candy corn, drying out like the pine needles.

Beebe points to the dishes of food spread out around them. "This stuff, it's like prayers," he says. "Every cupcake and every pie, it's somebody's hymn to Jesus, for all of us."

"WE CAN HAVE an oral exam," Mr. Stiles says, "on a topic of your choice. The world's fairs, for instance. If you pass, I'll give you credits toward graduation. You do want to graduate, don't you?"

An oral exam. How Jenelle would sneer at that. Her ghost is here in the room, snickering. Safe behind her dark glasses, Katelynn rolls her eyes. "So what if I never graduate?"

"But you like the book I gave you," Mr. Stiles prompts, and she has to admit she does.

"I like that one of the fairs was called the White City," she says.

Sunshine pours in through the glass walls, making the room too hot. Her mother has set up a card table with pencils, paper, a laptop, and glasses of iced tea with lemon. *Tutoring,* Mr. Stiles calls this meeting. Katelynn hears her mother's car leave the driveway. Her hearing's getting better. For a while, wasn't she deaf as a post? She and Mr. Stiles sit across the card table from each other. His loud breathing annoys her, and the way he cocks his head to watch her—that's annoying, too. She wants to say, "I'll never love you," but that would be rude. He's still her teacher. She likes him for giving her the book. She likes the pageantry in it.

Isn't pageantry in her blood? Her father's grandparents, who died so long ago, long before Katelynn was born, operated an ostrich-cart business in Hawk Lake. When she is stronger, she will find the photographs of the giant birds racing along, pulling those buggies, so impossibly tall, necks so long and heads so tiny, their humpy tail feathers blurred by motion, their naked legs and scaly feet stretched wide. The tourists' faces were shocked beneath their caps and hats. It was the era of the divided beard. Why did men ever wear their beards in those awful, double points reaching far down their chests? Women's hairstyles weren't much better: rows of tight, greasy spit curls decorate the brows of the females in those pictures.

She'll show those pictures to Mr. Stiles. Plus, she has crystals that came from crystal peddlers of long ago—hunks of pink and white and lavender quartz that any New Ager would be proud of. She will find those too and show him. They're relics from the days when mercury was a cure. At the local museum, she has seen an old tub from back then, a deep, scary contraption where people bathed after a mercury rub. From books Mr. Stiles loaned her, she has learned that the rubs involved one-sixth an ounce of mercury mixed with a blue petroleum-based jelly, which was applied to the body. A bath was the next step, to expel the toxins. Instead of a rub, you could choose to have mercury put in a steam cabinet, so that a thin film of mercury collected on your skin and remained there.

She shudders, but Mr. Stiles doesn't notice.

"The White City. Oh yes. The Chicago exposition," he cries, his face coloring, his eyes looking wet. "The World's Columbian Exposition. So beautiful, and it ended so badly. Why, Mayor Harrison was killed on the last night of the fair by a jealous husband who came to his house and shot him. And during the winter of 1893, vagrants moved into the fairgrounds and set fires in the buildings to keep warm. It's not wrong to fall in love with the past."

"No," says Katelynn, listening to the engine of her mother's car as it sinks to a tiny whine, out on the road. To her amazement, she can follow it even through Mr. Stiles's voice, can track it as it blends in with the minor traffic out by the little store and swings onto the state road that goes to the highway. Though she did not hear Harvey when he piled the nuts outside her glass walls, she's following the sound of her mother's car as surely as if she's in a traffic copter, her hearing sharp as a dog's, as if the lingering poison has suddenly enhanced those tiny flexible tools in her middle ear. Isn't one of them called an anvil?

"Shhh," she tells Mr. Stiles, and he frowns but shushes.

Her mother, always going out, always shopping and coming home with one thing, always murmuring, *I was at the bank, I was at the store, I was over at so-and-so's house:* a chant long tuned out by the family, except now Katelynn hears it loud and clear, hears how false it is.

Her mother is having an affair. The knowledge comes to Katelynn as the Doppler effect of her mother's car outdistances the last possible zone of her hearing. She's sure of it. Her mother so bossy yet like a sleepwalker in the house, clucking over her like a hen over a chick, yet with that somewhere-else look in her eyes, and quieter these days, compared with when she used to talk on the phone to her friends all the time, saying everything twice ("Let's have lunch. Yes, let's have lunch tomorrow. Tomorrow at twelve-thirty, is that okay for you? Twelve-thirty"), the words twining through Katelynn's self-absorption like a comforting tune. Now Glo says things only once, and the phone calls with friends have died down to almost nothing.

Who is it?

"Last night I dreamed I heard intruders breaking in," Mr. Stiles is saying, "and I woke myself up by yelling. I was on my feet, shouting, in the nurse's office. Nobody was breaking in. I'm the intruder. And you know what I was saying? *Who? Who?* Like an owl, calling." He hoots the word, and she's embarrassed for him. A forty-year-old geek, yelping like a kid.

"I need to go to my bank and get some money for that boy who lost his family," Katelynn tells him, "and I need to find a grown-up baby. I need your help," she says, thinking Jenelle would be proud of the way her mouth curves as she speaks these words. Jenelle would cackle and pound her fists on her knees as Mr. Stiles melts, saying, "Money? A baby? What's this?"

But she's out of energy, as if the effort of listening to her mother's car has wrung the juice out of her. She doesn't have the strength to tell him about the boy in the woods or about Louisa's search for a now grown-up, lost, given-away infant. She says, "I'm sorry. You'll have to go now."

A chill runs through her whole body. When she points to the blanket on her bed, Mr. Stiles understands and fetches it for her. "Harvey's back," she says.

His eyes widen. "Have you seen him?"

"I haven't seen him. He was here, though. He brought me some hickory nuts."

Mr. Stiles blushes as he says, "Don't mess with him, Katelynn. Remember how he lied about his age. A grown man, claiming to be a kid. You deserve better."

Mr. Stiles will never seem like a coach to her, although she saw him out on the track at so many meets, watched him clock the sprinters, shout at the hurdlers, and crane his neck to follow Harvey's triumphant flight over the vault.

Nobody is what they seem to be, not Harvey and not Mr. Stiles. A real coach wouldn't blush all the time. She lets him see the anger in her eyes.

While Mr. Stiles fumbles for his books and says good-bye, her mind goes back to her mother. Who? Who is her mother's lover? She could figure it out if the mercury hadn't eaten holes in her brain. She naps and dreams she's riding in an ostrich cart, the giant bird racing, pulling the cart so fast she cries out. The bird stops and whips its head around at her. The face is Louisa's. She wakes laughing, crying, with her heart pounding out of her chest.

"HE LIKES YOU," Jerry tells Glo as the puppy scrambles into her arms and licks her face. "Want him? I had to fight three Amazons for him."

"What do you mean?" asks Glo, hugging the puppy, with more light in her eyes than he's seen since the boat sank.

He tells her the story. She doesn't laugh. "They'll come after you," she says. "I've seen those girls, when I've gone to the store. You don't want to rile them. And you did steal him."

"Would it cheer up your daughter to have a puppy around?"

"Don't you understand, that stuff changed her whole personality. She used to laugh a lot and have friends. Of course, her best friend died." Tears start in Glo's eyes.

"Hey." He takes her face in his hands.

"I'm just so mad at her," Glo says, setting the puppy down. He whimpers at her feet. "I can't help her at all. It shook her up bad to see that boat sink. Of course, I saw it, too. I can't tell her that." She looks hysterical again, far gone, the way she looked when she chopped off her hair.

"If you married me, you could still have your daughter. You know I'd never take you away from her."

"Oh, she's almost grown," Glo says. "Once she's well, she won't need me anymore."

"Course she will."

"Jerry, I've never done anything in my whole life that I've really wanted to."

"Except ride that old merry-go-round, as a child," he says.

"I wish you wouldn't remember every little thing I say to you."

He laughs and reaches out for her, but she backs away from him. He says, "I used to like jungle gyms, myself. Those things, you could *climb*. These plastic tower things they've got nowadays, they're no challenge for kids. Why don't we have a kid, Glo?"

She makes a face. "I got married too young, and I'm tired of being a wife and mother. Sick of knowing how selfish I am. I was on the duck boat one time, did I ever tell you that? Craig and I had had a fight, and Katelynn was over at a friend's house, and it was a beautiful summer day. I went into town and boarded at that little gazebo where Louisa always started the tours. I wore sunglasses and a hat to be incognito. She gave a pretty good tour. I wanted to be alone then, on my own."

"When was that?"

"Couple summers ago." She leans down and pets the puppy. "You know, after I'd been married two weeks, I was standing at my kitchen sink, washing a vase. Craig was at work, and I'd been in the house by myself all day. I held up that vase and thought how quiet marriage was."

"How quiet it was?" Jerry says, wanting to understand her, trying to get at the deepest part of her complaint. He's hoping she'll go away with him to New Orleans for a weekend. Maybe they could manage that. He hasn't been there since he was a child and his parents took him on a whim. They'd eaten supper at a restaurant called The Court of Two Sisters. He remembers that meal: for his parents, Rock Cornish game hen baked in gold foil, and for himself, red snapper adorned with sparklers. "You ever eaten fish served with sparklers on top?" he asks her, deciding he can't bear to hear any more about some long-ago vase.

It works. She laughs, sits down on the floor, and tickles the puppy's tummy. "Tell me about it," she says.

⁕ ⁕ ⁕

LOUISA STARTLES AWAKE: there was somebody else, another person not accounted for yet in the papers. Didn't she hear his footsteps climbing aboard and feel a presence behind her? Then he asked her, in a cozy tenor, "Room for one more?" and she held out her hand for his money, the sun in her eyes, distracted—though she had noticed his voice, that beautiful voice. That always did it for her, more than a man's looks or anything else about him. Not that she's had many men pay attention to her. But she always notices when a man has a wonderful voice: she's all ears around a marvelous male voice, whether or not the man sings. She'd heard the grand voice, and she had frozen, holding out her hand for his money, waiting, and for what? She can't remember if he gave her any money. There is no memory in her palm of bills or coins. The last-minute man.

It would be easy to be lost track of. If there's nobody you talk to regularly, nobody you live with or write to, nobody who would look for you or miss you, why then, you could vanish, and nobody would think to search.

It's the middle of the night. Her face hurts only a little bit now from where the fat man's wife hit her. She has talked and talked with the police, talked with them all day after she dropped off Katelynn. She'd found them waiting at her house. She'd told them all she could remember about the passengers, but she'd forgotten about this man until now.

Barbie had come over, excited, as soon as the police had left. "There's going to be a memorial service soon, for the victims' families," she told Louisa. "At the lake. Want to go?"

"They wouldn't want me there," she managed to say.

"You can go with me," Barbie said. "It's been a whole week. They need to do this."

In the dark, Louisa thinks back to the last-minute man. She thinks he was young middle age, about the age her son must be. God wouldn't do that, would He? Reunite her with her son only to kill him off? Once the tour was under way, she had tried to focus on the man, but he'd slipped away from her. She could no more keep him in range than she could keep her sights on a floater in her eye when the sun reflected off the water and made her blink. The man disappeared behind the others, and she hadn't heard him speak again. Had he sensed trouble and leaped off the boat before it sank? Isn't there a way to dive that makes no sound, no splash? She has seen divers do that, as quietly as if leaping into a hole in the water. Teenagers, never. They like to make a big noisy splash. The last-minute man was the mysterious type. He would have jackknifed over the side of the boat, held his breath underwater, and surfaced cool as a cucumber on the shore, strolling out of the lake. He might have shaken himself once, limb by limb, the way a rained-on cat shakes its paws.

Maybe, after he gave her his money, he changed his mind and stepped off the boat, not bothering to ask for his money back, just taking his beautiful voice somewhere else for the afternoon. Maybe, along with that voice, he possessed some sixth sense about danger, and the *Arkansas Belle* was sporting a skull-and-crossbones flag that he alone could see. His light question, "Room for one more?" had been answered by something in his own head that said, *Go back.*

He's dry and safe somewhere, lying low. Maybe he's running from the law or from a bad marriage. A door has opened for him, a side door that offers a way out of his troubles, and he has stepped through it, escaping. He could be spending his time at the diamond mine, paying a dollar to try his luck all day, sifting through soft loose earth with his hands, close, oh so close, to a big beautiful jewel.

Or he might be at the bottom of the lake.

She dials the police station and tells the voice that answers: "This is Captain Louisa. I've remembered another person who was on my boat."

Is she in a movie? Sounding English, the voice says, "Oh, righto. Just let me get a pencil and I'll jot it all down."

She speaks, thinking she must be dreaming, almost drifting back to sleep as she says, "He got on at the last minute. I don't remember him very well, even less than I remember the others."

"Would you be willing to try hypnosis?" asks the voice, cajolingly. "It helps you remember things."

And before she knows it, she has agreed. She never does get back to sleep. Early in the morning, she fills several jars with water, makes BLTs, puts the sandwiches in a sack with some apples, and drives out to the campground. Beebe's camp seems farther back in the woods than before, and he's already up and awake, sitting tailor-fashion on a rock as if expecting her. He's got a fire going, and a coffeepot is suspended over it from a wire.

"I make coffee the good way," he says, pointing to the pot. "You put a raw egg in a sock and mash it up good inside the sock, then boil it with the coffee." He takes a sandwich and bites into it. "You must be good to your grandkids."

She gulps. "I don't know about that."

"You ask Katelynn if she knows where the biggest mercury mine in the world is," Beebe says, chewing. "It's in Spain. I read about it. I'm gunna go there sometime and see it. When the miners get sick from breathing the fumes, they go to this special hospital room where they sweat it out. They just strip naked and walk round and round. It takes 'em months to get well, just like it's taking her."

"I'm not telling Katelynn any such thing," Louisa says.

"And in Japan," the boy goes on, "people saw cats walking in circles and crows falling out of trees. Then a bunch of kids started having fits and couldn't talk. That was a case of it getting into the fish that the cats and the crows and the people was eating. I've seen pictures of a twisted-up Japanese girl who used to be smart and now spends all day lying on a mat, whose handwriting don't make sense anymore. Even her own mother says it's just scrawls going every which way off the page."

"Do you have anybody you want me to call?" Louisa asks. "About your folks."

He puts the sandwich down. "I found one of my mama's eyelashes in the sink this morning. You wouldn't think to look at that trailer that it's got a sink in there, but it does. It's not hooked up. Hasn't been for a long time."

"I'm so sorry." Louisa remembers his mother vividly at that moment, a gap in the side of her teeth flashing blackly when she laughed, the facing of her blouse coming out at the neckline. She'd been so happy to get that ham sandwich given to her by the iggle woman.

Beebe says, "We camped out a lot, my folks and me. There's been times we lived off eating what we found in the wild. They always knew what was okay to eat."

"They must've been smart. Not many people know that kind of thing," Louisa says. Her heart aches.

"Just go. Just lemme be," says Beebe, eyes downcast, waving his hand close to his face as if a fly is bothering him.

"YOU CAN LOOK UP any book in the library," Katelynn says, punching at the keyboard of her computer, "and it can tell you not only if the book is checked in, but also what's next to it on the shelf. It's really smart."

Louisa pulls her chair close to the computer, trying to follow Katelynn's flying fingers. It looks like Katelynn's just typing, but Louisa knows she's doing more than that. Louisa never learned how to type. The year she was away having the baby was the year the other girls learned to type. Some went on to make careers of it. Even if she'd learned how to type, she wouldn't have wanted to be a secretary.

With her dark glasses and very short hair, Katelynn looks like a child as she peers at the screen. "I've tried entering some key words," Katelynn says, "but it's not enough. Unfortunately, the hospital where you had the baby doesn't even seem to exist anymore, and I can't find out what they did with their records. You'll have to give me more to go on."

"I was raped."

Katelynn's hands lift off the keyboard as if it's a hot stove. She stares at Louisa.

"His name was Teddy Shatford. I was sixteen years old, and it was prom night." Louisa names the town, the date it happened.

"Okay. I won't use his name. I'll use the rest. I'll log you in." Katelynn's fingers click at the keys. "First, take a look at this."

Louisa blinks at the screen. "It's want ads. What are they wanting?" She reads the strange messages. "They want eggs? Why don't they just go to the store?"

"People eggs. For babies," Katelynn says carefully. "My friend Jenelle." She pauses. "Jenelle wanted to sell her eggs."

"Why? What for?"

"To make money. There's lots of couples who can't have babies and want one real bad. Jenelle was beautiful, plus she had a high I.Q. She answered one of these ads. Doctors take the eggs and mix 'em with a guy's sperm in a test tube. Then they put all of that into the wife's womb and hope the baby will grow there."

"You wouldn't do that, would you?" Louisa says.

"No." Katelynn's eyes are invisible behind the dark glasses. "Jenelle needed the money. I don't. Besides, nobody would want my eggs now. I've probably warped my genes. And I really don't think it's right, selling them. Jenelle and I used to fight about it. Her boyfriend didn't want her to do it, either."

"I gave a baby away," Louisa says, thinking out loud, "so why does it seem worse to give your eggs away? Or sell them? Maybe that's it. I didn't take any money for the baby."

"Jenelle was planning to do it a bunch of times and put herself through college with the money."

Louisa pictures a cardboard container of chicken eggs nestled in her stomach. But people eggs are tiny, like grains of tapioca. Teddy Shatford made a connection with one of those grains, deep inside of her.

"Now, tell me about your baby," Katelynn says briskly, as if she's an interviewer. "About the baby's father. Everything."

A redheaded woman steps into the room, pulling at her hair in a nervous way. "Katelynn," she says, "you know you're not supposed to be looking at this screen so long."

"Hey there," says Louisa, realizing this is Katelynn's mother. She has seen her at the store a few times, has waved to her from the boat. Louisa puts out her hand, but when Glo doesn't take it, Louisa feels embarrassed and puts her hand awkwardly on top of her head. Close up, Glo looks worn out. She always looked so carefree when she was gardening, with the lake breeze blowing her hair.

"Louisa," Glo says, addressing Louisa but looking at Katelynn's computer, "I don't want her thinking about your boat. I'm sorry for what happened, but I don't want her reminded of it."

"We're just doing research," Katelynn says. "I have a question for you, Mom."

"You do? What?"

"Where were you today? Where'd you go after Mr. Stiles got here?"

"Looking at a puppy that I might get for you," says Glo. Louisa sees panic in her eyes.

Katelynn's face lights up. "A puppy! I'd love that. I want it."

"Now turn it off." Glo raises her chin toward the computer, but Katelynn has swung back to the screen and is typing fast and furious. *Click, click,* and she turns to Louisa with a look of triumph.

"I've registered you," she says.

"What's going on?" Glo demands.

"As somebody who wants to know, if the opportunity should arise," says Katelynn to Louisa, ignoring Glo. "That's what people do. You just put it out there and hope to hear something back. There's a special Web site for that, for finding people. It's a start."

Glo steps forward and punches off the machine. Louisa tries to remember what she knows about Katelynn's father—Glo's husband. He's a rich man, and he's away a lot. Beyond that, she comes up empty.

. • .

THAT NIGHT, Katelynn hears a tapping on the glass. Isn't there an ancient superstition that a knocking on a windowpane means somebody will die soon? She remembers what her driver's education teacher did to dramatize the importance of not drinking and driving. The teacher arranged for half a dozen students to stand up at various times during the day and announce, "I died." They had to do it seriously, not like it was a joke, and then those students had to stay quiet the rest of the day, even at lunch period and in their other classes, so that the others would think about what it really would be like if their classmates had been drinking and driving and had died. Katelynn did it because she liked the teacher and because she thought it would be cool. Wearing a long black dress, pale makeup, and dark eye shadow, she practiced in front of her mirror, saying, "I died." She stood up first thing in the morning to proclaim it, since she had the driver's ed teacher for homeroom. Jenelle teased her and tried to get her to talk the rest of the day, but Katelynn wouldn't. She *couldn't* speak. Saying those words had unleashed terror in her, not the showy sense of tragedy she had anticipated with such pleasure, nor even so much an awareness of her mortality, but something else, a recognition of her own selfishness. She saw her ability to hurt the people who loved her, and it was shame that drove her to hide in a restroom stall, frantic, mute, rubbing her face and her dry eyes, crushing the fabric of her black dress in her fists, while Jenelle knocked on the stall door, saying, "Okay, Drama Queen, you won the Academy Award. Come out now." Even if she could have found the words, she would not have told Jenelle about the permanent sense of isolation descending on her.

The "I died" episode was a couple of years ago, but it seems longer. The teacher got in trouble with some parents who said the whole thing was morbid. Glo was furious when she found out Katelynn had participated.

When Katelynn gazed into the vat of mercury and met her drowning silver face, she felt again the depths of her flawed spirit, only that time there was something marvelous, too, the edge of rapture. *There's my soul.*

Tap, tap. How long has the tapping been going on? The mercury messed up her sense of time. She can't tell a minute from an hour.

It's Harvey. She sits up in bed, sensing this, staring at the dark glass, her short hair electrified, the back of her neck tingling. Through the glass is an outline that could be a person or an animal, and she creeps from her bed to the glass wall and the waving shadow. When she's inches from the wall, he turns on a flashlight and holds it up to his face.

She catches her breath. It's a skeleton of Harvey, smiling. Maybe it's just the effect of the flashlight, the way it turns his eye sockets to holes. He trains the flashlight on her, and the beam refracts through the glass walls. She puts her palm against the glass, and he lays his own hand on the other side, but she doesn't feel any warmth.

She's not strong enough to slide back the glass panel and let him in, any more than she was able to let in the screaming woman who'd crawled up from the lake, or Louisa, the day she came over. But Harvey nods as if he understands. He has been to her house before. He and Jenelle used to come over all the time, "to study," she'd tell her mother, though they just sat in her room, listening to music and smoking.

Still shining the light on his face, Harvey presses his lips against the glass so they turn all rubbery, and she laughs, a real laugh. He steps back and mouths words at her. She shakes her head, and he keeps on, mouthing them slowly, knowing she'll never hear through the glass. She'll have to read his lips.

Come with me.

She nods. She goes to her closet and pulls out the long black dress she wore when she said, "I'm dead." She yanks her T-shirt over her head, sweating with the effort. Naked, she turns so he can see her, not that she's feeling sexy but just hoping that maybe, in a moment, she'll feel that way. He pounds his chest, pantomiming a heavy heartbeat, and she smiles at his dark outline. The black dress feels heavy as she puts it on, and it takes energy to zip it up at the side. Because she's lost so much weight, the dress is far too big. The clock on her night-stand says 11:30 P.M.

She hasn't been outside since a couple of days ago, when Louisa took her out to the campground to visit Beebe. Taking slow, small steps, the soles of her shoes whispering across the carpets and then over the tile in the foyer, she makes her way through the house and out the door.

Harvey's there already. He wraps his arms around her, his face all bony but handsome as she remembers, and he kisses her as he never did when Jenelle was alive. His skin feels cold, though the evening is balmy.

"Oh, Harvey. Where've you been? Why didn't you call?"

"I went to Chicago. I haven't been back for long," he says.

"How do you feel?"

"Okay, most of the time."

"You do? I don't. I get tired so easy, and I have to wear my dark glasses all the time except like now, at night, and I'm never hungry." She talks fast, afraid he'll disappear.

He doesn't respond to this, and she wonders if she's whining. She says, "Mr. Stiles comes over sometimes. Everybody wonders where you are."

"Coach Stiles! How's he doing?"

"He's living at the school. That's a secret. Don't tell anybody." She's sorry she said it, remembering Mr. Stiles's face when he told her.

"Well, that's pretty weird," he says. "What else has been going on?"

How can she bring him up to date on the last six months, when everything and yet nothing has happened? "A little boy found a dia-mond at the diamond mine," she says. "His picture was in the paper. It was big."

But he just says, "Come on, get in the car. There's somebody I want you to meet."

"You're driving again?" she says. "I wish I could. The doctor won't let me."

"My friend's driving, and it's her car."

He propels her around the house to the sidewalk. It's been weeks since she was even out here, this far, after dark. A low roaring starts up in her ears. Friend. Girlfriend? He leads her to a car parked a block away. He says over his shoulder, "I didn't want to wake up your folks by parking too close to your house."

A woman is waiting in the driver's seat. She leans over and opens the passenger door for Harvey, and he motions for Katelynn to get in the back. "Alissa, Katelynn," Harvey says.

Alissa has black hair as short as a teddy bear's, with five or six thin braids that extend from just above one ear all the way down to her waist. She has on a dark, shiny minidress.

"Where are we going?" asks Katelynn.

"How 'bout a Halloween party?" says Harvey.

"Oh! Okay. But it's not Halloween yet."

"A costume party, then. Hey, Katelynn. You still in this world, or what? When was the last time you went to a party?" Harvey reaches back to squeeze her knee.

"Long time," she says, wondering where they are. Alissa drives as if she knows these roads. They're on the main highway for a while, and then Alissa turns off onto one small road and then another, and Katelynn can't see any landmarks, just woods sliding past them. "Where? Whose house?"

"My house. One of mine," Harvey says, and he and Alissa laugh. "There's lots of empty houses around here, perfect for partying. No neighbors to tell you to turn the music down."

"Will you take me back home when it's over?"

"These parties might last a couple days at a time," says Alissa, turning to frown at Katelynn. "You don't want to be back by sunup or anything, do you?"

"Well, yes, it's just that . . . "

Harvey laughs. "She's joking, Katelynn. We'll take you back. You just say when. But I guarantee you'll have fun. You look like you've forgotten how."

She's angry suddenly, wants to say, *I've been sick, remember? And you were the one who found that stuff and got us to use it.* She doesn't think he ever did the forty hours of community service that he is supposed to do, but she doesn't bring it up. It might embarrass him. She'll do hers, though.

They're crossing the river now, the Mississippi, and she wishes she'd stayed home in bed. Harvey and Alissa are laughing in the front seat, and the car's going too fast for the bridge.

And now they're bumping along on a gravel road and pulling up to a little house surrounded by cars and pickup trucks. It's remote, all right—no other houses in sight, and the only light comes from the full moon. But what a moon it is, even at this time of night.

"Is the electricity cut off?" Katelynn asks.

"Yep, and the water too," says Harvey. "There's candles and drinks and stuff inside. We brought everything over earlier."

They park in a field. Katelynn can just make out shapes of people in the dark, streaming toward the house and moving around inside, behind its dusty windows. "It hasn't rained for so long," she says, conscious of the dry dirt beneath her shoes. She thinks of field mice, wonders how they survive a drought. And birds too, but she supposes they can fly to a river or a creek.

"Rain. What, you turning into a farmer?" Harvey says. "This used to be a farm, I guess, a long time back."

He accepts something Alissa hands him: a hat. A cowboy hat. He claps it on his head, takes a bandanna from his pocket, and ties it around his neck.

"I don't have a costume," says Katelynn, thinking Alissa isn't in costume either, and so she feels better about it. Tall and curvy, Alissa wobbles a little on her high heels. She and Harvey walk close beside each other.

In the dim, smoky house, lit by candles and jack-o'-lanterns, Harvey and Alissa vanish. One room—the kitchen—contains a wildly flashing strobe light that makes Katelynn feel sick at her stomach. Something else is bothering her, too, an odor that she places as skunk. She makes her way into the living room. She has forgotten the rhythm of parties, of moving through crowds, of accepting notice, discouraging it, extending delicate antennae of desire and disdain. People she can barely see brush up against her, wearing masks and capes and elaborate disguises.

A clown with oversized, turned-down orange lips and white triangles around his eyes hands her a bottle of beer and says, "You've come as Katelynn Troy."

"Real funny. Who are you?" she says, trying to see past the paint.

"You know me," says the clown, "and you never met anybody like me in your whole life. Last night, I dreamed you paid me to kiss you."

She can almost place the voice, but she can't see past the thick, geometric makeup on his face. Gulping her beer, she realizes she has eaten almost nothing all day, just the Tootsie Rolls and candy corn she can't get enough of. The clown points to somebody behind Katelynn, saying, "Look who's here."

Katelynn turns and sees a woman in a curly white wig and a red cap, with a Styrofoam life ring around her neck, the words *Arkansas Belle* lettered in black marker on the life ring: a caricature of Louisa. Others laugh, forming a circle around the woman, who says, "Come drown with me! Ride my duck boat and see the bottom of beautiful Hawk Lake!" The woman puts her palms together and makes a plunging motion, while the others cry out, "Glub, glub, glub." It's the fat man's wife, Katelynn realizes, the woman who swam to shore and hit Louisa in the face.

The clown isn't laughing. He gazes from Katelynn to the woman, and Katelynn imagines that beneath the paint, he looks somber.

She stares at the woman, then feels a hand on her wrist. It's Harvey, leaning down to say, "Come on. Alissa's going to tell us how it was."

"How what was?" Is it just because she's still sick that she's having trouble making sense of anything?

"You don't know her story," says Harvey as he leads her out the door. She's relieved to be out in the air again, even if it feels warm and sticky rather than fresh. How soon can she ask them to take her home? People are crowding around a small bonfire in the yard. Beyond them stretches a partly harvested field of cotton, the white bolls glowing in the moonlight. She coughs as if breathing the lint deep in her lungs.

"I don't care about Alissa," she says, but Harvey tugs her along. She presses his arm and says, "Harvey. Can we get together, just us?"

He turns around. "You know what, Katelynn? Alissa's good for me in a way Jenelle never was. She's been through things. With Jenelle, it was all cheerleading and cliques."

"Her life was more than that."

He makes a dismissive motion. "I met Alissa in Chicago," he says, as if that explains everything. "She walked in here not knowing anybody, and look." He waves his hand toward the crowd. Alissa is climbing up a tall stepladder, carefully, in her tight dress and heels. She perches herself on top of it.

"Tell us," the crowd cries.

"She survived a massacre," Harvey says. "Lots of people were shot."

"I don't want to hear it," says Katelynn.

"Yes, you do," says Harvey, turning her around by her shoulders so she faces Alissa, who is high up on the ladder.

Alissa calls out to the crowd, "Can you hear me?"

"Yeah!" they cry.

"It happened in McDonald's, in the middle of the afternoon, in Chicago," Alissa says, her voice loud enough to carry over the bonfire. "I was in line buying chicken nuggets. So a guy comes in with a rifle, swings it around, and opens fire, and I end up under a pile of bodies with just my head and my hand sticking out."

"Did you get hit?" calls the clown, his makeup shiny as aluminum foil in the darkness.

"I didn't know if I'd been shot or not. I'm lying there not breathing," Alissa says from atop the ladder, "with my eyes just slits so I can watch him. Something's running down my cheek from the person on top of me, and I don't know if it's blood or ketchup. There's bodies all around the McDonald's, lying on the floor and hanging out of chairs."

The crowd claps. Next to Katelynn, holding her hand, Harvey's shaking (with laughter or some other emotion? Katelynn can't tell). He murmurs, "She's great. Very great. But we're just good friends, Katelynn," he says, as if realizing, only now, that she thinks they are lovers.

"Really?" asks Katelynn. "Harvey?" She reaches up to touch his face, but he's watching Alissa with a rapt expression.

Alissa goes on, "So the gunman takes a mirror out of his pocket and starts going around checking bodies, seeing if there's breath showing up on his mirror. Now and then, he'll shoot somebody again to make sure they're dead. Then he comes toward the pile where I am, and I see that his mirror is in this little green case with *Clinique* written on it. I've got the same kind of mirror in my purse. He holds the mirror up to somebody right above me, and he takes his gun and shoots them. Feels like an earthquake, and the pile of bodies falls apart. Somebody's coffee spills and burns my arm. It hurts like hell, and I want to scream, but I still play dead."

"Tell it all, Alissa. It's sweet as a song," cries Harvey, pulling Katelynn to him again as if to shield himself—from what?—but it feels so good to be held tightly by him, after all her months of dreaming, that she just presses her head against his chest and listens to his heart with one ear and to Alissa's voice with the other.

"Then he's right in front of me, bending down, holding that mirror to my mouth," Alissa says, "for the longest time. But I wouldn't breathe. I could have held my breath forever. I could see his hairy hand. While he was holding that mirror, waiting for me to breathe, he reached out and grabbed some fries off a tray. He'd already killed the guy who was eating them. But I lie there and don't breathe, and then the cops bust in and shoot him."

Silence, then applause for Alissa, who half-bows from her seat on the ladder and spreads out her arms. "One more thing. I sat up and made sure I was okay. I see the bodies and the paramedics all around me, and then I look out into the parking lot, and there's this weird gray cloud. I'd never seen a swarm of bees before, but that's what it was, buzzing around in the parking lot and finally going up into this thin little tree." She pauses. "It was springtime."

More applause for Alissa, and the bonfire is poked so it flames higher. Harvey melts away while Katelynn blinks. Her eyes sting from the smoke. The clown is beside her instead, his huge orange mouth puckering as he says, "See, you ain't the only one beating death," and she knows him, then: Beebe, from the woods. "You won't be famous forever," he says.

Somebody's brought a boom box, cranked it up loud as it will go. The boy seizes her and starts dancing. It's all Katelynn can do to gasp out, "I can't."

She sees Harvey and Alissa up against the side of the house, laughing. She asks Beebe, "Do you have a car?"

"If I don't, what'll you do? You might have to stay here all night, sleep on the cold ground, or sleep in the bed inside there, where critters have been. Or you could start walking that road. We're way off the map."

"There's a house over there," says Katelynn, pointing to blurred lights in the distance, pretending to be sure. "I could go there."

"But you couldn't walk a hundred yards," he says, taking her arm, leading her away from the party, toward the field where his old car is parked. She recognizes it from the campsite.

She imagines the inside of the old metal trailer back in the woods, sees herself bound and gagged, smells the rust of its walls. "You've got to take me home. You're not going to kill me, are you?"

"Why, it never crossed my mind," he says.

MYANMAR, MEANING: a new measurement of distance, longer than miles. Meaning: it can change its name again, erase itself.

"Are all the cats Burmese?" his daughter, Katelynn, had asked him once, as if it were a joke, and he'd said, "Every one."

The outermost kingdom. Land of children and travelers. Land of *I deny you one last picture of me, I turn my head with a sidelong smile.*

The woman he loves now, whom he calls his wife, burns the rice, spills the tea, finds a new mole on his back that she weeps over, predicting it will be his death. Writing out a card, he smudges the ink with his thumb.

"Daughter ate silver?" the woman asks. He cannot make her understand. "Silver, like this?" and her thin rings flash in the moonlight over their bed. He lays down the card. It's too dark in this small apartment to write, anyway.

"Not silver," he says, "but something like it and very dangerous."

The woman is silent a long time, and then she says, "Bad, but not the worst. The worst thing is when people are mean during a war. My husband and my mother and my sisters, all mean during the war. Not just to me. To everybody. As long as that does not happen to her. . . . As long as she is kind . . . "

It's the longest speech he has ever heard her make.

"Katelynn's wonderful," he says. The card is a rectangle of light in the dark. He may never finish writing it, never mail it. Mice will nibble on it or a monkey will swoop through and take it off to the jungle. He's crying.

"Shh," the woman says, covering his face with hers, speaking right into his heart.

HYPNOSIS: nothing like what Louisa expected, not a pocket watch swaying in front of her face or a voice, a magician's conniving voice, crooning, "You're getting *sleeepy*," but instead this businesslike approach to relaxing her wrists, knees, and neck as she sits in a puffy chair in an office with a color scheme of mauve and navy blue. What was that old story about hypnotizing a chicken? Kids talked about that when she was a kid herself—you were supposed to draw a line in the dirt in front of a chicken, real slow, and the motion would put the chicken into a trance. She should have tried that with the chickens her mother kept, back in Yellville. She misses that old house and the countryside around it, with the crows cawing. She used to get homesick when she was living at Mr. Fiveash's house, used to call her parents and say, "Hold the phone out the window so I can hear the crows." If only she could do that now.

She can't relax. "I get leg cramps sometimes, in the middle of the night," she volunteers.

The psychiatrist, Dr. Morton, nods blandly. He's wearing a light blue shirt with just a hint of shine to the cloth, and he manages not to look directly into her eyes. Men like this who rode her boat usually had talkative wives and wanted to pay with credit cards. She'd insisted on cash until just last year. People didn't carry much cash, so she was losing business. That made her cave in. It meant using a gizmo, a little contraption that she never trusted.

"Cash was better," she says.

"What's that?" asks Dr. Morton.

"Can I choose a time to go back to? A time that's earlier than the boat?" Can this person help her retrieve her baby?

Dr. Morton makes eye contact with her for the first time. "I was actually on your boat once, though I doubt you'd remember me. It was a good five or six years ago."

"What was the occasion?" She wants to put off going under. Her fingers grip the armrests, but her knees are weak and rubbery. If he takes her back there, she'll be underwater, never coming up. "I'm afraid I'll quit breathing."

"That won't happen. This does work." He looks just past the side of her face, at the buttons on the back of the overstuffed chair. His eyes are puffy-lidded, dark and mild behind glasses. "It was my wife's birthday, I believe, the day we rode your boat. You gave a very nice tour."

"You really remember it? What I said, and all?"

"I do." He smiles. "You pointed out landmarks—the oldest church, the museum, the spa where my wife gets a facial every week, by the way, and I'm partial to the steam baths, myself. And I remember when the bus turned into a boat, that was really something."

Louisa feels terribly nervous, anxious to get back to why she's here. "I can't remember anything about that man except what I've already told the police. He got on at the last minute." As she says it, he's there, a light step behind her, clearing his throat, creating the faintest motion as the *Belle* registers his weight. She closes her eyes and hears him say, "Room for one more?" She turns toward him, the sun in her eyes, and sees his shadow on the shiny white deck of the *Arkansas Belle*. It was her pride to keep the craft so clean. Nobody ever noticed that enough or even acknowledged it, though her passengers always thanked her at the end of the tours.

Except the last bunch, of course.

"If he lived and swam to shore, we might never know any more about him," somebody says—it's her own voice, and she's blinking awake. "I'm counting him," she says, "even if they didn't find him. He could've lost his memory and be wandering around wondering who he is."

"You made him up, Louisa," says Dr. Morton triumphantly, glancing at his watch. "It's been an hour." She sees a clipboard covered with notes in his hands.

"Did I say all that?" She's sweating freely from both armpits.

"You recalled quite a bit." He flips through the pages. "You talked about your father, about helping him up on that roof. And you've got pretty good recall of your passengers. That last-minute man," he says and pauses, then does a little dance with his upper body. "Sounds like a name of a song, doesn't it: 'Last-Minute Man.' I believe you invented him. Grief is a powerful emotion. There might be more such passengers that you 'remember.' You want somebody to love you, Louisa. I know that sounds blunt and reductionist, but isn't it true, for all of us? You've just done a creative thing with it."

"Did I say anything about the baby?"

"There was no baby on board. Was there?" He consults the clip-board.

"My own baby. The one I had when I was so young. The only one."

"You talked about your Aunt Patsy, a little bit," he says. "She was with you at a crucial time. She must have been quite a card. 'Who died and made you king?'"

"Can you take a person back to any day of their life?" she asks. "A day they choose?"

"It's all there," he says, rising, reaching to take her hand and help her out of the chair, the way she used to help her passengers on and off the boat, if they were real young or real old, or if they just looked like they needed a hand. "Do you feel all right, Louisa?"

"Yes," she says, though she feels weightless, her limbs bouncy and loose.

Dr. Morton's face turns suddenly merry. "A diver popped up right beside the boat, on my tour. Somebody asked was he diving for pearls." How is it he has grown a five o'clock shadow just since she's been here? Has that much time passed? "I wanted to see a mermaid. I half-believed I would."

Louisa steadies herself against the chair, her legs so heavy she wonders if this is how sea legs feel to sailors who have been on ships for months.

"Your rooftop story reminded me of something." Dr. Morton is chatty now, leading her out to the navy-blue-and-mauve foyer, where a receptionist sits behind a glass window. "When I was a child, my family had these great big cherry trees. You had to climb on top of this flat-roofed garage to pick them. One day, our minister was up there picking, and my dad said, 'This may be the closest to heaven you ever get.' The minister didn't think that was funny. Not at all." Dr. Morton laughs so hard he has to wipe away tears, and the receptionist laughs too, her chuckle as tinkly and distant as wind chimes behind her glass cage. Leaning forward, she taps her window, indicating to Louisa a jar full of lollipops, outside the glass, the good kind, two flavors swirled together. Louisa shakes her head, and the receptionist's voice squeaks through the glass: "Aha! Dentures?"

"Crowns," Louisa says, and the receptionist nods dreamily.

So this is psychiatry? The police or the taxpayers are paying for this, Louisa knows. Money will change hands somehow because of this session, and she thinks of the little metal cash box she kept on the *Belle,* the dimes and quarters gathering silt, the folding money turning to paste. She'd clunked down its lid so many times, turned its familiar latch.

JERRY'S FATHER'S MOTTO was "Time is money," and never mind that somebody else had said it first. Still, he had imagination, inherited from his father, whose paintings of the lake, the tortoise, and the parrot Jerry displays in his own house. Jerry's father had invented what their family called The Game, which was a lot like Monopoly except that it was based on Hawk Lake. The game board depicted the lake and the surrounding houses—some mansions, some dilapidated little shacks with chickens in the yard and privies out back, all the product of his father's egalitarian genius—though in real life, all the houses had indoor plumbing. The object of the game was to own as much of the land as possible, plus a boat. You had to avoid a monster, sort of a dragon, which might turn up in any part of the lake. You had to avoid, also, storms and property foreclosures. There were cards with the bad things on them—monster, tornadoes, foreclosures. Prizes included miniature sportfish like blue marlins, though there were no marlins in the lake and never had been.

"What kind of monster is it exactly, Dad?" Jerry asked his father one time, knowing his father rarely thought in terms of the supernatural. That had been more his grandfather's area, his grandfather the painter, who, in Jerry's memories of him, had grown vaguely skeptical of his own success and his son's success, as money poured in from their developments. "What does the monster do?"

"This?" Jerry's father had asked, jabbing the picture of a winged dragon on a card. "It's death. Disaster. A stock market crash. It's failed banks and bad tenants. It's the end of prosperity, Jerry."

"Oh." Jerry was about fifteen at the time. The acne-covered, sulking face he saw in the mirror was at odds with the wonder he often felt in his heart. "What's left for me to do, Dad? Here at the lake, I mean? You've done it all."

It was the only time in his life he'd ever seen his father floored, but his father recovered. "You're to carry on with my work and your grandfather's work. This lake is our diamond mine. That little fake tourist mine, where people go and chip away for gems, that's a child's game, Jerry, but this lake will never play out. I have sowed. You keep on reaping." Tremendously pleased with himself, his father clapped him on the shoulder. Jerry's mother came in then, with a tray of snacks. They played The Game, his father with even more gusto than usual, while Jerry tried to figure out how the hell he could keep on reaping when his father had made more money out of this lake and marshy land than anybody would ever believe.

Rummaging around in his garage, looking for a broom to use at the abandoned house, Jerry finds The Game, just one set perched on a high shelf, greasy with oil and hung with cobwebs. He pictures his father reaching up to put it there. Its cardboard box is a faded red, hardly a color at all in the weak light from the single ceiling bulb. When Jerry shakes the box, the pieces rattle. Inside, the game board, the list of rules, the dice, and the markers look clean and new. He examines a tiny boat with a red body and white sail. When he played The Game with his parents, the two of them grew giddy as they rolled the dice. His father used to rub his hands together in an exaggerated way, while Jerry's mother watched him with shining eyes, hardly paying attention to her own turns.

Jerry holds the game board up to the light. It includes a picture of the *Arkansas Belle*, and he wonders if Louisa ever saw The Game, if his father ever gave her a set. His father had had several dozen made by a manufacturer and was waiting on a patent when he died.

Here's a dragon card, and a foreclosure card. All the booby traps in The Game are real. The monster came out of the lake and got the *Belle*.

"Hey, mister," comes a voice from behind him, and Jerry turns to see a silhouette in the door.

"Who's there?" he calls. Ever since the boat sank, he's felt jumpy.

"I've come for my dog." The figure moves toward him. It's one of the ATV girls—the driver. Even in the gloom, he can see the dark circles under her eyes and the faint mustache above her mouth. "I been watching you awhile. What's that you got?"

He holds the box toward her, and she takes it in grimy hands. "A game?" she asks.

"It's a game about here," he says. "Hawk Lake. My dad made it. It's a real good game. Go ahead and look at it."

She paws through the pieces inside. "I'm good at games. I could beat the crap out of you or anybody. How'd your dad come up with this?"

"He just had lots of ideas. He and my granddad developed this lake."

"What does that mean?"

"They enlarged the lake and built houses around it."

"I thought it was a real lake, like, natural. You mean they dug out more ground and filled it up?"

"Basically. See those statues over there?" He points to the plaster renditions of the turtle and the parrot, side by side in a cramped, gloomy corner they share with yard tools. "They used to stand on the edge of the lake. My granddad had them made in honor of his pets, a tortoise and a parrot."

The girl glances contemptuously at the statues. "They're ugly. I wouldn't want them nowhere near me."

"Look," he says, "you can have that game if you want it, but you can't have the puppy back. You weren't treating him right. You can't let animals eat foam rubber."

The puppy is safe inside his house, asleep. The girl holds the box to the dim lightbulb, examines it, and slips it under her arm. "It don't hurt 'em. They eat all kinds of shit. Them dogs eat better than I do, sometimes." Her gaze is level and fierce. "We ain't even. You got to think up something else."

"What do you want, money?" Impatiently, he reaches in his back pocket, but the girl says, "I'm here for work. I want steady pay, not just to sell a dog. I applied to that damn store, but the lady there told me to get lost."

The abandoned house, his new acquisition, blooms in his mind's eye, dirty and smelly. He usually cleans the houses himself before he sells them. He likes doing the work. But he hears himself offer the work to her, and she says, "Sure. I can scrub and clean." She hitches up her overalls. "My name's Dora. Where is this house?"

"Way out in the country, in Mississippi. Across the river. I'm driving over there today, right now. If you want to go."

"I was at a party last night at a house that sounds a lot like that," Dora says. "There was a girl there talking about how she almost got shot. She was a real slut. She yelled her story from on top of a ladder."

Jerry laughs, but Dora doesn't. He finds the broom he wants and puts it in the truck. Dora hauls herself into the passenger seat.

Out on the road, the engine's so loud they can't talk over it. Glo sometimes asks him why he doesn't buy himself a new truck, and he says it's to remind himself he might not be rich forever. Dora smells like sweat, cheese puffs, and dog hair. She shouts over the noise, "You ever go to the casinos?"

Jerry shakes his head no. He thinks, briefly, about the casino road where his parents' car crashed.

"Good," Dora says. "Those casinos are bad, real bad. I hate 'em. Stealin' people's money, breaking up marriages. My old man got bit by the gambling bug and left my mom."

They pass cotton fields being harvested, with bits of lint clinging to the roadside in puffs. Jerry glances at Dora and remembers his first affair—with a maid who cleaned house for his mother, a maid who had swarthy skin like this girl—swarthy but with a strong, stacked body, not unlike Glo's. He'd been sixteen or seventeen, the woman in her mid-twenties. They'd have sex in his bed when his parents were out, then stand on the bed and bounce on it like it was a trampoline. Somehow, his father found out, then cornered him and said, "You stop that, son," and even then, his father was jolly: "You know what I mean, Jerry," he said, and Jerry stopped. The maid had gone on cleaning their house as if none of it had happened. He'd seemed to be the only one who found the whole thing bizarre.

Once, Jerry asked his mother, "What would you have done if you hadn't married Dad?" She'd been putting groceries away, settling boxes of Popsicles in the freezer. Seen from the side, her smile looked permanent and not quite real, like a cat's. Not missing a beat, she said, "Why, I'd have found somebody else to love. My mind was made up." She handed him a Popsicle.

Why didn't he ask her to explain? He felt amazed; she seemed to think he understood.

Now he has to look sharp to find the way to the house. "Yep, the house is out this way," Dora says as Jerry turns onto the gravel road. "You're lucky they didn't burn it down. That party got pretty dadgum wild." He pulls up in front of the house, and she says in an awestruck tone, "This is it, the very one."

The yard's a mess: beer cans, bottles, potato chip bags. "What'd you do for lights? The electricity's cut off. I wish I'd known. I'd've had every one of you arrested," Jerry says. What worries him most is the liability. If anybody'd been hurt, he, as the nearest thing to an owner, could have been held responsible.

Dora crosses her arms across her big chest and says, "Too late now. Besides, there was people here you'd be scared to arrest, even though they was trespassin' and trashin' the place. Rich kids. Like your girl-friend's kid, that sick one that ate mercury. She didn't have a costume on, just a dumb-looking black dress."

It's the first time anybody has ever spoken to him about Glo. Is their affair common knowledge? Shocked, he can only say, "You don't know a thing about me or anybody I know."

"I ain't telling. I don't think nobody knows but me, and I don't talk." Dora eases herself out of the truck and fumbles in the back for a package of trash bags. "I just see stuff, when I ride around on my ATV."

"What did you go as, last night? What was your disguise?"

"I was a ghost. Being heavy, you know, a sheet's the easiest thing. I been a ghost since I was a little kid. I just cut me some eyeholes." She flaps open a trash bag, which billows in a sudden fresh breeze blowing across the farmland. "You asked what we did for lights. Didn't you notice the moon was full? And there was a bonfire." She points to a charred circle in the dry grass. "My sisters and me, we put it out," she says. "Smothered it with a blanket we found and with my ghost sheet, stomped it out with our boots, poured Pepsi on it, and even spit on it till there was only smoke. I'm still thirsty, from all that spittin'. Them other people, and that woman yelling from up on the ladder, they wouldn'ta cared if it had all burnt up, your house and them trees." She gestures to the tall, rustling pecan trees, their leaves dry and yellow, clustered with nuts still in their fuzzy hulls, too green yet to harvest.

THE CLERK IN THE music shop has so many thin rings of blue-green metal in her nose, upper lip, eyebrow, cheek, and the inner curve of one ear, that Louisa thinks of the Slinky she used to have, that springy metal toy that could flip over itself on TV commercials, going down the steps, except you could never get a Slinky to do that in real life.

"At least, I never could," she says out loud.

The clerk says, "What's that?"

"I'm looking for records by a singer named Sam Moon. Do you have them?" Louisa has to speak loudly over the wild, pounding music that shudders from the ceiling and the floor. Only half an hour ago, she was under hypnosis. She doesn't yet trust her senses. "Sam Moon."

"Sam Moon, oh yeah," says the clerk, fingering the ring in her eyebrow. "He was, like, a Frank Sinatra type guy."

"Was? You mean he's dead?" But she should expect that to be so, should expect people to die, now that she has killed so many in her boat, now that she is getting old. Her heart gives a kick in her chest, and she remembers the baby's kicks deep in her stomach, a shadow-boxing embryo, maybe knowing what she was going to do and striking back at her. What had been wrong with her, that she didn't love him in time? He's out there now, getting on toward middle age, feeling his disappointments and how hard life always is. If only she could know if he has a wife, if his adoptive parents were good to him, if he's had any happiness after the betrayal that was his beginning. To think she had him in Boston and just left him there, where the winters are so cold, where there was snow on the ground the day he was born.

"Oh, I just mean Sam Moon was old-fashioned," the girl says. "My grandma has his records. She used to play 'em all day long, and then she switched over to rock. I guess she's still got those Sam Moon records. She has a lot of yard sales. She mighta sold 'em."

"I'll buy every one of them. Sam Moon's better than Frank Sinatra ever was."

"What about CDs? I might be able to order Sam Moon on CD. Don't you have a CD player?"

"I don't even have a record player."

"So you want records. Platters." The girl's earrings glint. "Gimme your name and number, and I'll get Grandma to call you."

Louisa writes the information on a slip of paper the girl hands to her.

The girl says, "They're those big old 33s and 78s, real thick and hard. She keeps 'em in her attic. One time, when I was little, I starting throwing 'em against the wall, just to see 'em break, but I felt bad, from the waste of it, so I quit."

"From the waste of it," Louisa murmurs, thinking of all of them, all seven.

KATELYNN WAKES UP in her black dress, in her own bed, her mother in midsentence in the chair beside her: ". . . won't try to police you, now that you're almost grown, even though you're still so sick."

Katelynn struggles to sit up. Chills race up and down her arms and legs, and the crying-laughter starts up in her throat, but the sound doesn't make it past her lips. Her face just twists the way a dousing rod wrenched in her hands, when as a little girl she'd taken a peach switch and paced around the backyard looking for water.

Glo picks up a bottle of Pepsi from Katelynn's nightstand and hands it to her. Katelynn takes a swig. It's just what she needs, that friendly brown-sugar fizz. She takes another gulp and her eyes fall on the temple maiden statuette, calm and smiling on the shelf. Her father's never coming home. If her life were a story, the statue would contain a treasure. She would turn its pretty head and rubies would pour out of its neck, or there'd be a letter from her father.

"So if it's okay with you, Katelynn, if you'll be all right for a weekend, I'm going away for a couple of days, to New Orleans. Who would you like to come stay with you?"

"Louisa. I want Louisa to stay with me," Katelynn says.

Glo sighs. "Oh, Katelynn. She's just a poor soul. Make sure she's gone home by Sunday evening. I don't want to deal with her."

Katelynn reaches out to her mother, but Glo's hug feels light, restrained, as if she's already halfway out the door. "You can have the puppy," Glo says. "I'll bring him over before I leave."

THINGS SHE DID differently the day the boat sank: Louisa tallies them up, searching for a cause, a clue. Things she did for the first time. For the first time ever, she used mousse on her hair. It made no difference. The watery, foamy goop just made her hair sticky. She'd found the little spray can left behind on the *Belle*, the day before. Used it once, rubbing it through the white pelt that her hair has become, hair that looks like a duck's back with folded wings, idly wondering who she would meet that afternoon, who would climb aboard. She'd wet a washcloth and gotten the stuff out of her hair as best she could and planned to give the little spray can to Barbie. What a funny word, *mousse*. It's still around the house, somewhere. For the first time in her life, that day, she mixed olives into the egg salad she made for lunch. That's a great advantage of living close to where you work—you can come home for lunch. She'd had a long run of microwaved pizzas, and then, that day, she craved egg salad. The olives, like the mousse, were pure impulse. And, for the first time ever, she'd used the word *obtuse* in conversation, remarking to the iggle woman that it was obtuse of people in general to kill off so many eagles for so many years, obtuse to kill them at all. The woman nodded fiercely, loyally, her eyes swimming with sudden tears that Louisa sensed had less to do with eagles than with something gone wrong in the woman's own life, a secret that, of course, she died with.

In New Orleans, Glo tears the sheets off the bed and hangs them over the windows of the hotel room to block out the light from the street. Every time Jerry wakes up from a static-filled sleep beneath a blanket, he sees her pacing around the room—just barely sees her, because to him, the room is dark. Finally, she puts her hands over her eyes and cries. "Nowhere on earth is it really dark enough to sleep. It's worse here than at home."

He gets out of bed and goes to her, holds her. "You want me to make you a little blindfold out of a bra or something?"

She won't laugh. She feels rigid in his arms. Down below them, on the sidewalk, revelers sing and shout. He says, "The French Quarter isn't the place to come to if you want peace and quiet."

"It's just started bothering me since that boat sank. My room at home gets too much starlight, even with the curtains. A glass house is a bad idea, Jerry. It makes you want to smash the walls. What's glass good for? It gets chipped, like a windshield. It gets flyspecked. I'm amazed it doesn't start fires, like a magnifying glass. And all that damn light."

"Shh," he says, pressing her head against his heart. "You don't have to live in that house if you don't want to."

Raging, she points to the windows. "If I had a gun, I'd shoot out those streetlamps."

LOUISA AND KATELYNN start with plain Pepsi, then spike it with shots of whiskey. It's such a warm, beautiful afternoon that they're in lawn chairs out in Katelynn's yard, the lake stretching before them like a huge, innocent, unblinking eye. Oak leaves and elm leaves float down to the grass, and the new puppy chases them, barking with glee. Katelynn has named him Peppy. The radio's playing a country song. Callers are trying to guess who sings it.

"Is it Alabama?" somebody says.

"No," says the DJ.

"Is it Confederate Railroad?" somebody asks, in a hopeful voice.

"No!" Katelynn tells the radio, and Louisa laughs.

"Is it the Charlie Daniels Band? Hank Williams Jr.?" a voice cries.

"Nooo!" moans the DJ, and Katelynn, laughing now too, fumbles for the dial and turns the radio off. The puppy licks her hand, clambers up beside her on the chaise longue.

"So Louisa, which reporter's been bugging you the worst? There was this lady from a Memphis station, I can't remember which one, who wouldn't let go of the mercury story. She called me all the time. You'd think they'd have something better to do. I wouldn't talk to her." Katelynn is talking fast, already feeling the Pepsi merge with the slow fire of the whiskey. Lightning bolts brew in her lungs. "TV got hold of Harvey's story, but not Harvey. They tried to make out it was a big deal that he'd already graduated from high school, but they ran out of steam quick on that."

"Who's Harvey?" asks Louisa, holding the whiskey bottle by the neck and pouring some into her glass.

"He's the guy I love," says Katelynn.

"Would you be happy with him?"

"Yes! I'm not going to be like my parents," Katelynn declares, wishing Glo could hear her say that. "I won't be like my mother. The happiest I ever saw her was when we had a wasp infestation. They were all over the tops of the curtains in my parents' room, great big clouds of them, all gold and black." She moves her hands, trying to make Louisa understand just how it was. "I was about seven. It happened all of a sudden, first just two or three, then zillions of 'em, loose all over the house. I got stung. Mom took the vacuum cleaner and vacuumed them off the curtains, sucking them up in that hose till they were all gone, and then she cut the vacuum cleaner off, and she had the gladdest expression on her face."

"I may as well've done that with those people," Louisa says, gulping from her glass. "I may as well have shot 'em or held their heads under."

Katelynn rolls to her side and holds up her head with her hand. "You tried to save them."

"I didn't, really. There wasn't time. I asked that man to move, and next thing I knew, we'd sunk." Shading her eyes, Louisa scans the lake. "What did I look like out there? What did the boat look like? Not when it went under, but when it was sailing, all those years."

"It was beautiful," says Katelynn. "I used to watch for your red hat. I used to wait to see the boat and wave to everybody."

"The things I used to say, before I caught myself," Louisa says. "Why, I used to tell my passengers who was on vacation in these big houses around here. 'See that mansion?' I'd say. 'That's the so-and-sos' house, but they've gone to Atlanta for the weekend—or London or San Francisco or wherever—and then one day I realized there might be burglars on my boat who'd break into those houses, and I'd have myself to blame. So I quit saying who was home and who wasn't. But the stories about the people and their houses and history—why, that's what makes my tours! If there was something I wanted to talk about, I just talked. Like Yellville, where I was born and grew up. When somebody asked me where I was from, they'd always say, What a funny name for a town, and then I'd get to tell them about Archibald Yell, who hated banks and got to be governor and died in the Mexican War. If somebody mentioned Stuttgart, you know, where they grow rice and hunt ducks? I'd tell the best Stuttgart story I ever heard—that during a cold spell in 1973, frozen ducks fell right out of the sky. My daddy used to swear he was there to see it. Oh, Katelynn, I had so many good days on that boat, I wish I'd wrote 'em all down."

"Land and sea," says Katelynn, scratching Peppy behind his ears. He's some kind of crazy mix, with big feet and a brindle coat.

"Land and sea. Well, land and lake." Louisa pours herself another drink. "I've got a picture of a duck boat from World War Two. I've always thought it must be the *Belle,* though it might be another one. It's on a beach in Sicily, with these happy-looking fellas on it, these sailors or soldiers, and it's driving across this mesh thing that they rolled out to use as a road."

Louisa pronounces soldiers "sojers." Katelynn says, "Two questions," and she's so drunk by now that lake and sky spin past her, a movie of themselves. "First, do you have a lawyer?"

"For all the people who are going to sue me, you mean. They can have whatever I've got. There's one suit already. Truman Testa's wife filed it. And I do have a lawyer, I guess. Some Yankee gal. We've talked on the phone. She seems right nice."

Katelynn sits up, batting the spinning lake and sky away with her hand. "You don't know what happened, exactly. The boat probably had some kind of mechanical problem. They'll inspect it and find out. You've got to protect yourself. Don't just assume you were responsible."

"Of course I was responsible. What's your other question?" Louisa says. "Good thing I don't have to drive home. I'd never make it."

"What did you tell people about my house? On the tours?"

"Oh! I used to point out all your glass and skylights. They reflect so pretty in the sun. People were always asking, Is that a solar-powered house? I been meaning to find out. Is it?"

"Yes," says Katelynn.

"What if it's cloudy for a long time?"

"Everything still works, even if it's winter." Katelynn pauses. "You were raped, Louisa. You could have had that guy arrested and sent to jail. Why didn't you? Didn't anybody say that word back then? Did you ever tell anybody what really happened?"

"I told my mother." Louisa has hiccups, and Katelynn sees that she's drunk, too.

"How can you love a child of rape? Your baby, I mean. I think I might have hated the baby, because of how it started."

"He was separate from Teddy Shatford. It all comes down to that pink-and-blue dress with ruffles, and that extra slice of pie at the dance, and him signing all those records. Oh, I'm not making sense. You were a cheerleader, weren't you, Katelynn? I remember reading about that when there was all that mercury stuff in the paper."

"That was another life," says Katelynn in a dramatic voice, with a wave of her hand, and they both laugh. "I was a cheerleader in the fall, for football games, and a lifeguard in the summertime."

"And now you're just waiting it out," says Louisa.

"I just don't feel right. I'm never hungry, and my memory's gone."

"You remembered about your mother and the wasps."

"More recent stuff is harder. I can't remember any cheers." She tries to recall the words and rhythms of the cheers she shouted and the shapes she used to make with her body, snapping her head up and down, pushing her blue-and-white pom-poms in and out of the air, spelling out the team's name in letters (H-A-W-K-S: she'd fling out her arms and legs, then curve her back and knees for the S), but it's her mother's laughter that comes back to her and the *whoom* of the vacuum cleaner the day Glo attacked the wasps. She closes her eyes and hears Harvey's rapid footsteps on turf, sees him, pole in hand, charging toward the vault and going airborne, twisting so slowly in the air he might never come down, and she says, "I've seen Harvey."

"What? Who? I was almost asleep." Louisa sounds cross.

"Harvey! He was the one who found the mercury. He used to be Jenelle's boyfriend. You know—Jenelle, my friend who died. I've loved Harvey for so long. The other night, he came over."

"Are you going to have a baby? Oh, honey, I'm not making fun of you, just asking."

"I've never slept with him. Now he's with this other girl, but he says they're just friends. I know he loved Jenelle. I just can't stop thinking about him." She needs more Pepsi. Standing up, wobbling toward the house, she must be balancing weights on her head. The whiskey was a bad idea. Yet she pictures it cleansing her inside out, sweetening the quicksilver. She could be sicker. She does not have tunnel vision; Jenelle had that. They had talked about it on the phone, the last time they talked before Jenelle died, her heart shutting down and her kidneys too. Tunnel vision, "like when you hold up your hands and make goggles for your eyes," Jenelle said, and Katelynn could tell she was smoking, by the puffs and pauses in her voice, smoking in her hospital bed. Jenelle had smoked since fifth grade, when her older brother gave her clove cigarettes.

Katelynn misses smoking. Inside, in the kitchen, she's hungry enough to eat half a bagel before her stomach turns over, as if someone cranked it. Peppy follows her, and she pours some puppy chow into his bowl and watches him scarf it up. Will she ever be as thoroughly hungry again as this little dog? Taped to the side of the refrigerator is the get-well card sent to her by the D.A.R., the note her mother told her about. She reaches out and tears it off, reading the signature of the chapter president: "Mrs. J. T. Connors." Beneath the name is a number. Why not call and thank them? She reaches for the phone.

"Hello, may I speak to Mrs. Connors? This is Katelynn Troy. I want to read my essay to your club. I'm sorry I couldn't do it before. Do you remember me?"

The voice on the other end does not sound like that of an eighty-year-old. Katelynn can't reconcile its musical vigor with her concept of the D.A.R. members as old dragons or tough little terriers. The lilting, energetic voice says, "Why, Katelynn! Of course I know who you are. I know exactly who you are. You can come over this minute. We're having a meeting. Right now."

"I'm not supposed to drive yet, because of the mercury poisoning, and my friend who could drive me is drunk, plus she's asleep. I'm drunk, too."

"So are we, Katelynn. Drunk as can be," says Mrs. J. T. Connors and laughs. "What do you think these meetings are for? The business of the revolution was done a couple centuries ago, hon! Listen. I'll hold out the phone, so you can hear us." Katelynn hears muted, distant hilarity, and then Mrs. J. T. Connors says, "We're playing a game, Katelynn, to see who has ever had the most embarrassing moment."

"What was yours?" Katelynn asks her. She had not meant to get hooked into an actual conversation. She wishes she hadn't called.

"My maid caught me masturbating. But wait, that's not the worst thing. Some of the girls here have had lots worse stuff. You live long enough, it all happens." Mrs. J. T. Connors giggles. "Come by anytime, Katelynn! We all loved your essay. Good-bye."

Stunned, Katelynn hangs up, but the phone rings immediately, right under her hand. "Hello?"

"Hey, Katelynn! It's Dad. How you feeling?" Ten thousand miles of wind and water in the phone line, his voice the light of a star.

Jittery laughter shakes her lungs, tears sharp as vinegar sting her eyes. "Dad! Dad, I miss you. I can't stop thinking about the boat. When are you coming home?"

"Katelynn, I miss you too. I'll be over here for a while." Bursts of static shred his words.

"Dad, can you hear me? I've got a puppy. Mom gave him to me."
She must remember to ask Glo where the puppy came from.

"Katelynn, is your mother there?"

"She went out for a little while. Dad, I had this funny dream. I was
riding in the ostrich cart, going so fast I yelled." Static crackles in her
ear, and her own words sound crazy to her. He might have no idea
what she's talking about. She grips the phone and says, "Give me your
number so I can call you back. So Mom can call you back."

He says numbers, lots of numbers, but his voice is the light from
a star and she's drunk, grabbing for a pencil on the kitchen counter.
She has lied to him for the first time, has said her mother is out for a
little while, when she knows Glo is in New Orleans. "Dad," she says
into the phone, talking loud so he'll hear her, so he'll really listen. She
wants him to know there is more going on than the new puppy or the
dream of the ostrich cart.

In fact, she's furious at him, and she wants him to know that.
"Dad, when the hell are you coming home?"

The pencil rolls away from her, and as she lunges for it, the
receiver slips out of her hand and clunks onto the floor. By the time
she picks it up again, there's just wind in it.

"IS THIS THE ONLY black top you've got?" Barbie yells from within
Louisa's closet. She comes into the kitchen, where Louisa is baby-
sitting the twins, and holds up a black sweatshirt with a lion's head
appliquéd on it. "I can't find a single black dress here. Don't you have
one? I always keep this black dress on hand for funerals, this one I've
got on. I guess if you wear your black slacks and this sweatshirt, plus
something over the sweatshirt, you'll be okay."

"Don't worry so much. It's only a memorial service for all those
people I drowned," Louisa says under her breath. She's volunteered to
trim the twins' hair. Identical bowl haircuts, hideous haircuts: that's
what Barbie wants. Louisa is trimming one of them now. Boy or girl?
Madison or Fairley? She doesn't know. "Hold still," she says to the

squirming, farting person in front of her. Her scissors bite dully at the weak, thin hair. The child sneezes. Is this the one that kept sneezing the other night? Its double is scrabbling in the refrigerator, helping itself to milk, grabbing a cup from the dish rack, dropping it, spilling the milk all over the floor.

"You're done," she says to the twin in front of her, laying down the scissors. Flipping at the ragged ends of its hair, the child turns and gives her a look so intelligent, so sympathetic, that she gasps. This child senses the boulder on her heart. It sees not a terrible old woman but only her grief. She reaches out to touch the pale cheek, but the child sneezes and ducks away from her, eyes downcast, escaping. Its milk-splashed twin hustles over for its hair to be worked on next, the same fine, weak little hair.

Brandishing the sweatshirt, Barbie says, "We could stop by my house and see if my black coat is big enough to fit you. Hey, did you know you're in *People* this week? My copy's out in the car." Barbie returns to Louisa's closet and her voice trails off. "You don't seem to have any black shoes except those sneakers you've got on, and they're really ugly. I've always been able to tell my friends the truth about how their hair looks or clothes or whatever. If something's ugly, I'll say so. It's one of my strengths. And God, you've at least got to put black shoestrings in your shoes. The ones you've got on have Disney characters on 'em. You can't wear Tweety-bird shoestrings to a funeral."

"It doesn't matter, Barbie," Louisa snaps, horrified to hear she's in that magazine. *People.* Her stomach turns over. Drat, she's cut this child's hair too short. She has to even up here, even up there. The back of its neck looks so white and vulnerable. "Quit fooling with my clothes, Barbie. I'll wear what I've got on." There's something she wants to give Barbie. What? The stuff she put in her hair the day the boat sank. She asks the child in front of her, "Does your mother use mousse in her hair?" The child turns and stares at her balefully, and she decides that's the last time she'll ever bother to think about mousse, let alone talk about it.

In Barbie's car, on the way to the lake, Louisa flips through *People*. There she is. Where did this picture come from, of her young self in that ruffly-necked dress? "The only time I wore this was to the prom," she says. "Then how . . . ?" There are her broad shoulders and her anxious face, young, with her too thick lips yolky from dark lipstick. She feels woozy, the way she did from the whiskey-laced Pepsi at Katelynn's the other day. Then she sees the hand on her arm in the picture. Teddy Shatford's hand.

It's raining, which seems to Louisa miraculous after the long spell of dry heat. Barbie peers through the slick windshield and says, "The article explains about that picture. It was your prom picture! The guy who was your date sold it to the magazine but cut himself out of it. Said he didn't want to be seen with you, after what happened with the boat." Barbie leans over and taps the picture. "You can see the jagged line where he cut around you."

"Teddy Shatford." The magazine falls from Louisa's hands.

"Aha! Does an old flame burn bright? I was asked to my prom by three different guys. I could've married any one of 'em, but what did I do? I married stupid Dennis! Now, when I see the way men look at me, I realize I could have had my pick."

"How dare he." Teddy Shatford. "How dare he," Louisa fumes under her breath, but Barbie doesn't seem to hear.

"This is not a funeral, you know, this thing today," Barbie says. "They've had them already, most of them. Those two black women's families had them cremated. Don't you think that's creepy, Louisa? And the others, most of 'em's relatives came and got them and took them back to wherever they were from and buried them."

"What about the family from Arab? That boy's parents and brother?"

"I don't know about them," Barbie says. "I was kind of disappointed that the local funeral parlors didn't get more business. I mean, it would make a difference to our economy. In New Jersey and places like that, it doesn't make a bit of difference."

The twins wail from the backseat. A rich stench boils up in the air. "Mom-mee, Maddy pooped her pants!"

"Madison?" coos Barbie. "Did you do a yuck-o? Fairley says you did a yuck-o. You're not a baby anymore, remember, Maddy?"

"Pull over, Barbie," Louisa says. "I'm getting out."

Barbie's head whips toward her. "You can't get out, Louisa. It's raining and we're almost there." She barks over her shoulder, "Pipe down, kids! Goodness, you do stink."

Louisa opens her door. Cold rain rushes in, and the door makes a heavy whooshing sound as it moves through the air. "I mean it, Barbie. Let me out."

"God, Louisa. Have you gone nuts? All right then, fine." Barbie wrenches the steering wheel and pulls over so hard that one tire goes into a ditch. The car hangs lopsidedly off the road as Louisa swings her legs out the open door. *People* slides from her lap into high, wet grass. Barbie says, "Everybody's been telling me I'll go crazy if I hang around you, Louisa. I've been the soul of kindness, and you kick me in the teeth."

"No good deed goes unpunished," Louisa murmurs. She doesn't mean to hurt Barbie's feelings. She sticks her head in the backseat and speaks to the children. "I'm sorry I gave you-all such bad haircuts." Which one is the sweet one, the one who gave her that gentle gaze? She can't tell. The children swat at each other, fussing in their secret twins' language.

Barbie looks straight ahead, her lips tight. Louisa hauls herself out of the car.

Rain slaps Louisa's face as the car grinds out of the ditch and rolls off. For a moment, she just stands in the road, her hands at her sides, her glasses liquid with rain. The truth is, she intends to go to the memorial ceremony. She just couldn't bear another second with Barbie. The lake's about a mile away. Slowly, feeling old (had she ever been as young as her girl-self in the picture?), with rain and ditch water squishing in her sneakers, she heads down the road, wanting to be late so she can stand in the back of the crowd. If somebody recognizes her and points, she'll just run. Forever.

. . .

"You DIDN'T HAVE to do all this, Mom," Katelynn says, not so much to her mother as to her mother's retreating back and running feet. Glo has been busy with the caterers all day. When she got back from New Orleans, she announced that she would give a reception after the memorial ceremony, "and everybody is invited. Families, relatives, friends." She waved her hands vaguely.

"If I don't do this, Katelynn, who will?" Spinning around, Glo frowns, and Katelynn feels just a little afraid of her. Glo looks like she hasn't slept for a week. Her chopped-off red hair has developed a rusty tinge at the roots, and her eyes peer out from new little nests of wrinkles.

"This is like a wedding," Katelynn says, gazing at tables where caterers have piled platters of gingered shrimp, creamed chicken patties, barbecued lamb chops, and grilled bite-sized pieces of shark paired with watermelon pickle. None of it appeals to Katelynn, at least not the smells, but she can't stop taking an inventory of the artful displays and fancy recipes. A few months ago, she'd have been dipping into everything, tasting and exclaiming. Her mother doesn't seem to want any, either. The caterers are arranging the desserts and coffee on a big mahogany sideboard: silver trays of lemon tarts, almond-topped pastries, meringue shells filled with raspberry puree, a crystal dish of melon balls and strawberries sprinkled with kirsch, chocolate truffles iced in different colors and surrounded by pastel mint wafers.

The puppy is locked in the laundry room with his food and water, clean newspaper spread out on the floor. Katelynn hears him faintly whining. She wishes the party were over.

"Look, they've got a tent set up," her mother says, gesturing across the lake, where the ceremony is taking place at a public dock. Slanting rain makes the lake look frizzly, like there's gravel hitting the surface. Katelynn makes out a dark green canvas tent, in fact several tents, loaned by a funeral home. From this distance, the people are a slowly shifting mass—wasps on top of the curtains. She's heard that four or five ministers will speak, that wreaths of flowers will be tossed into the water, that relatives of the deceased will read poems about their loved ones. She tried to convince Louisa not to go. Press vans are there from TV stations and radio stations in Memphis and Little Rock and others she doesn't recognize.

"What was Jenelle's funeral like?" she asks her mother, and again Glo whirls, looking grim. If she keeps that up, she'll get more wrinkles than she's already got. Katelynn feels a little dart of satisfaction.

"Jenelle's funeral," Glo says, as if it's hard to remember. "You were too sick to go, of course. Harvey was in a wheelchair. He looked terrible. He was reading from the Bible about the maiden who was not dead but sleepeth, and he broke down and couldn't finish. There weren't all that many people there, considering how popular she was supposed to be."

"You are the meanest, most hateful person," Katelynn says, at the same instant that the head caterer chirps, "Mrs. Troy? Could you tell me if you're satisfied with the way we've set up the bar?"

So her mother doesn't hear her, just turns toward the caterer. Katelynn closes her eyes against a sudden, slashing pain in one temple, and when she opens her eyes, there is Mr. Stiles right in front of her, holding a tiny plate piled with food.

"I looked for you there," he says. "It's kind of a zoo. There's a girl selling umbrellas for five bucks each. There was a tamale wagon that the police chased away. I saw Harvey."

"Is he coming?" Katelynn asks. This is what the day means for her: that she might see him.

"Everybody's coming. Your mother should put something over this light-colored carpet." Even as he speaks, the caterers appear with rolls of plastic to cover it.

"Harvey told me you're the one who found out about him," she says. "You found out he'd graduated already."

"I had a hunch. All year I'd had the feeling I'd seen him somewhere before, and I had, of course. I'd seen him a few years ago, before he was any good. He's grown a lot since then." Mr. Stiles sighs. "But I wasn't the one who told the newspaper. I think Harvey himself did that. It's pretty weird, going back to high school when you're in your twenties, masquerading as a teenager."

"You've done more than go back. You're living there."

"Shhh," he says, glancing around them.

"I feel like a clock that's out of whack," Katelynn tells him, transfixed by a dab of barbecue sauce that clings to his upper lip. "I go ticking along for a few hours, and then I race or just stop."

"You're not the talk of the school anymore," Mr. Stiles says.

"As if I'd ever wanted to be!"

"Other things take center stage so rapidly, among the young. I did get a couple of good papers in my history class about mad hatters, using mercury to tan beaver hides for hats and getting sickened from it," he says. He blinks as someone jostles his elbow. "For a few days, it was considered hysterically funny among the college prep kids to pretend they had the Danbury shakes." Deliberately, he shudders and twitches.

She is shocked. Is he making fun of her, or is he just an idiot? She hears Jenelle's voice, speaking one of Jenelle's favorite words. *Immature. He's just so imma-churr.*

"Danbury, Connecticut, was a big hat-making town," he says with naughty glee, while she stares at him. "Tremors and tooth loss and all that good stuff, much of which you escaped."

"Talk about anything else," she says.

People are arriving, mobbing the tables of food and drink. Mr. Stiles seems suddenly safe and reasonable. She forgives him.

"If this gets out of hand," she says, "will you help? I was at a party the other night, and I wasn't ready to be there, around so many people. This was my mother's idea, but I'm not sure it's such a good one."

"I'll do anything you want," he says.

There's Harvey in the doorway, Harvey here in her own house, her own living room. It's the first good look she's had of his face, seeing him in daylight, and he is so tall, the bones of his face sharp in his thin cheeks, his eyes a traveler's eyes, a dreamer's eyes, meeting hers. Alissa's just behind him, but Katelynn doesn't care. She pushes her way through the people to him and puts her arms around him, crying her joy. He pole-vaulted into the sky, he stuck his arms into mercury, he went away and came back, for her.

HALF A MILE down the road, Louisa spies trouble. There's some kind of vehicle in the ditch—a little mustard-yellow truck that says TITO'S TAMALES—and beside it boys are fighting, two boys holding up a third between them so that his legs bicycle in the air. "Put me down!" he cries, and she recognizes Beebe, the gray-haired boy from Arab. "I don't have no money to give you!"

"Then give us the food," the others say. They don't see Louisa, who has strolled up right next to them.

"They didn't turn out so good. They're mostly burnt. Today was the first time I ever made tamales. You're hurtin' my armpits!" Beebe says, and the others drop him, turn toward the truck, and bump into Louisa.

"If you-all have weapons, put 'em away," she says, though she doesn't see any guns or knives. "I just recently killed some people. I'm not exactly scared of armed robbers."

The two boys scramble away, running down the road. It's still raining hard. Beebe flips raindrops out of his eyes. "Hey. Glad you came along," he tells Louisa. He brushes off his jeans from where he fell.

"I'm on my way to the memorial service," she says. "Maybe you could give me a ride, and we could watch the ceremony from your van. Where'd you get this, anyhow? What happened to the car and the trailer?"

"I sold 'em. This is more practical. It burns a lotta oil, though. I made up the name Tito to sound Mexican. I got the tamale recipe at the library. I was just over there, at that thing they're having."

"Why were you trying to make money at a service for your own family?"

"They'da been proud of me. I made money till the police kicked me out. And I got to be there without the press swarming all over me. Nobody notices a food seller. I didn't want to be up on the platform pitching flowers onto the water." Beebe holds open the van door for her, and she steps inside. It's warm as toast. He hands her a tamale wrapped in greasy paper, and she downs it in two bites. It's only slightly burned.

Beebe climbs into the driver's seat. His gray hair hangs over the steering wheel as he laughs. "My first customer today bought ten tamales. He just stood by the van and ate 'em. I did make money today."

They come out of a shortcut beside the woods and there's the lake: thronged. The rain gives everything a glossy look, like watching through clear jelly. TV crews are there, shoving microphones in people's faces. A trio of singers is performing a hymn on a high, covered platform.

"You can get out anywhere you want," Beebe says. "If I stick around, I'll get arrested."

"Look at all the flowers," Louisa says. Everybody, it seems, has an armload of blossoms, roses on long stems, bouquets slung into the crooks of elbows, wreaths looped lei-fashion around necks. "I guess they'll toss 'em in the lake, the way they put wreaths on roadsides to mark where accidents have been." She doesn't recognize anybody. "These must be relatives of all those people that drowned. Do you have any relatives down in Arab or anywhere else? Grandparents or aunts or . . . ?"

"Look, I got to get out of here. Are you getting out or not?"

Across the lake, Katelynn's glass house glows beautifully, like a lantern in the rain. Cars are parked all around the house, too close. Their wheels will crush Glo's flowerbeds to mud.

"I'm gunna count to three," says Beebe.

A rising wind is turning the lake choppy, furious. In all her tours, in all her years, it never looked quite like this. It's mourning. The only thing keeping her going is her love for her lost baby. Urgent as hunger, as panic, it floods her, a love equal to the grief she feels for all those deaths.

A plan comes to her.

"One. Two," says the boy, glancing at her.

"I'd like you to drive me a ways," she says, "kind of a long ways, but I'll pay you. We have to leave right now."

"Is this, like, a carjacking? Uh-oh—a cop's coming." Beebe floors the van, parting the crowd, and in a moment they're back on the road, where it's so empty, Louisa can hardly believe the scene they just left.

She says, "Boston. I want you to drive me to Boston." She's got only a few dollars in her wallet, but she doesn't tell him that. She'll figure something out. She will find her son.

She expects him to refuse. He has every right to hate her.

"I kind of wanted to go to the party. Katelynn's, you know, party." Beebe pauses, staring through the rain-splattered windshield as if at some far, fascinating speck. "This is a crossroads of life. Do I go to Boston, or do I go to the party?"

The far-off fascinating speck apparently provides an answer, for he gazes a moment longer, then steers the van in the direction of the highway.

"NOT THAT WAY. You're putting on too much. Go like this," Katelynn instructs Dora, elbowing her away from the mirror to demonstrate proper eyeliner technique. Party sounds press at the door of Katelynn's room, so that the relative quiet and the privacy feel unreal, vacuumlike. In the midst of the party, which is too loud, too chaotic, she'd spied this ugly girl, this Dora, hanging back by the table of desserts, furtive, looking like she expected somebody to slap her hand if she tried to eat. Katelynn had offered the girl something to drink, and Dora asked for Kool-Aid. Katelynn said, "Isn't that just for kids?" and the girl scowled.

The makeover was Katelynn's idea. The girl is a challenge: mustache, pitted skin, lank hair, sallow cheeks. Katelynn and Jenelle used to spend hours doing makeovers on each other and on friends of theirs. Katelynn can hardly believe that she used to go to sleepover parties, used to give them, used to have half a dozen girls in here, giggling and gossiping, brushing their long hair and smoking until the air was murky. Jenelle used to describe the sex she had with Harvey, but in a way that made everybody laugh, somehow making it funny when she'd say, *Then I went down on him, and he came, and then I got on top, and I came,* and Katelynn had laughed, too, her heart sore. She is still a virgin, for she saved herself for him. Oh, she'd had boyfriends, because she was second prettiest. Guys who hung around Jenelle were glad to settle for Katelynn. She's glad she saved herself, if only because it makes her different.

"You thought I meant kids' type Kool-Aid," Dora says, spitting on a mascara wand, leaning toward the mirror and clumsily applying mascara to her eyelashes. "I meant a special type alcoholic drink I bet you've never had. I dropped out of school a long time ago," she adds.

"Never use spit with makeup," Katelynn says. "You've ruined it." She'll have to give Dora anything Dora touches. Dora's hands are filthy, and her T-shirt and jeans are splotched with grease. She is far more ferocious than the fat girls Katelynn knew at school, who were neat and clean and usually prissy, whose harshest criticism was to refer to obnoxious behavior as "being anal." This one looks like she could rip you apart.

"I've quit wearing makeup," Katelynn says, "so you may as well have it." Dora picks up a brush and runs it through her limp, staticky hair. Katelynn's own hair, the lamb's-ear hair, doesn't need a brush anymore, but someday it might be long again. She might care how she looks again. Cares a little bit already, because of Harvey.

"Look, a blue lipstick," Dora says. "Who wants blue lips?"

"Take it."

Dora puts it on. "Hey, it's turning pink. I never saw anything like this." She jams the lipstick in her jeans pocket. "They're arguing about God out there."

"I guess it's not a very good party."

"It ain't. It's just a funeral. What's this green stuff?" Dora asks, holding up a tube of concealer and squeezing some out onto a grubby finger.

"You use it when your skin's too red. It blends in. No, don't put it under your eyes. You'll need something else for those dark circles." Katelynn sinks down in the chair beside her vanity, out of breath. She had thought she could last through the party. She wants to help her mother. What is this gathering, really? Not a party, not a funeral, but she can't do it, she can't be out there in the throng. Last she looked, there was cake smeared on the pale carpet where the plastic sheets didn't quite meet, wine stains on the white tablecloth; the barber's widow was sobbing in the kitchen, honking into her handkerchief loud as a goose. Katelynn reminds herself that the caterers are here, that they can help her mother, and that Mr. Stiles has offered to shut down the whole party if it gets out of hand. She'll catch her breath and then go out and find Harvey.

A thin layer of dust covers the top of her vanity and the containers of makeup where Dora is uncapping bottles and shaking foundation and powder into her hands. All these months Katelynn has been sick, Glo's maid has come in, yet she must not have dusted the vanity. The dust there is the proof. Katelynn has lain in bed dozing while the maid went through her chores, vacuuming, Windexing the glass walls, yet not dusting. There's dust on the temple maiden statue, light as frost. "I hadn't noticed," she says out loud.

"Well, somebody oughta tell you," Dora says, as if they are arguing. "You're white as a snowman. Makeup won't help you. Even your mom's boyfriend is worried about you. I can tell." She covers the dark hole of her mouth with her palm. "Uh-oh," she says, and Katelynn reads mockery in the ugly face.

Katelynn freezes. "That's okay." She makes her voice pleasant. So she's been right about Glo having a lover. She's got to find out who it is. "How do you know him?"

"He's my boss. I clean houses for him." Dora grinds blusher across her cheek, wipes it off with a Kleenex, and looks at the stain as if it's her own blood.

"You're in love with him too, aren't you?" Katelynn's only guessing. She tries to sound light and teasing.

"That was his house. Where the party was, the one where that bitch on the ladder talked about getting shot. Spilling her damn chicken nuggets."

Katelynn laughs, craning her neck against the shortness of her breath. "But she didn't get shot. I didn't see you there."

"I put out the fire." Dora draws herself up proudly. "My sisters and me, we put out the fire. He knows it, too. Jerry knows it was me."

Katelynn's mind reaches out to the information and grasps it. "I can't remember real well now," she says, delighted now that she has the name. "Here, use these tweezers on your eyebrows. It only hurts a little, and it'll open up your eyes."

Tweezers in hand, Dora pauses. "Do you have a puppy? I thought I heard one barking."

"I just got him. Peppy. He's great."

Dora puts the tweezers down. "What does he look like?"

"He's got big feet, and his fur is a weird color, sort of caramel with splotches in it. Want to see him?"

"He's mine," Dora says. "Was mine. My dog, you hear? You can keep him, but you better take care of him."

Somebody raps on the door. "Katelynn? You hiding in here?" It's Harvey. He's in her room now. Katelynn realizes she lost a moment or two, for Dora is sitting at Katelynn's desk leafing through the world's fair book from Mr. Stiles, and Harvey is gesturing toward the lake, saying, "Look, water-skiers. In the rain."

Two skiers slice through the water, towed by a fast white boat. It's a silent scene of water and movement, of spray and slanting rain.

Happiness rushes wavelike over Katelynn. She goes to Harvey, throws her arms around his neck, and whispers, "Marry me."

His thin chest rocks as he holds her. Is he laughing or crying? She says, "Harvey. Oh, Harvey. I'll never love anybody the way I love you."

Dora turns a page. The water-skiers bank against their own wake. Dora looks up from the book and gazes at them with her dark-circled eyes. Katelynn thinks, *Everything that happens to me now happens in my room.* Dora reaches in her pocket and holds up the blue lipstick. "Can I really have this? It's all I want."

"Sure," Katelynn says.

"This is, like, a miracle," Dora says, "that this stuff changes color when you put it on."

Then Dora's gone and Katelynn's alone with Harvey, and the house is quiet. She must have slept. Of the last hour, she remembers only Dora gabbling some nonsense about the dog. All the visitors are gone, and Glo too. Harvey's sitting on the end of her bed, watching her.

"Where's Alissa?" Katelynn asks.

"You scared her off," says Harvey. His face looks the way it did when he held his pole, just before running toward the vault.

"Really? Is she gone for good?" Katelynn sits up in her bed, reaches out, and hugs him.

"She never meant to stay in Hawk Lake. She'll keep on making new friends and telling her story. It's what she's good at," Harvey says.

"Let's eat." Katelynn's only a little shaky when she stands up. She leads Harvey through the wrecked, empty house, the silent air electric with the recent havoc. Weren't the caterers supposed to stay and clean up? They didn't. Nothing is put away. The doors are wide open to the damp darkness outside. The rain has slowed to a soft, companionable drip, sounding like a cat licking its fur. She shuts the doors. In the laundry room, she finds Peppy asleep. He wakes up and nuzzles her hand.

Together, Katelynn and Harvey pluck grapes from lukewarm fruit displays, fold limp slices of meat and cheese into rolls, and feed each other big bites. She's hungrier than she's been in months. She feeds Peppy too, whatever he wants.

"This is rich-person food," says Harvey, "but you've always seemed so down-to-earth."

She holds on to the compliment. It is a compliment, isn't it? It's wonderful to see him eat. As she eats, too, she knows they'll make love. At last, as they glide toward her bed, her breath is a tiny, rustling creature, far away from her. Harvey's mouth moves, and she leans close to hear him say, "Take my heart away."

"To MAKE HER feel better," Jerry says, swinging the keys around his finger, "and because I've missed seeing the *Arkansas Belle*. It was all part of what my dad wanted. His plan for the lake. I'll give her this boat to replace the gone one."

"She wasn't at the party. And she wasn't home?" Glo asks, snuggling close to him, drained, the raucous party still a throbbing menace in her brain. She hadn't locked her door, had driven along the shore road to his house, right out in the open, not bothering to try to hide.

"I heard her phone ringing, but she never picked up, even though her car was there. She might've been at the memorial service. I stuck a note in her door."

"What does the new boat look like?"

"It's a beauty. Got pontoons and a nice wide deck, a forward cabin, a railing all around it. It's big enough to hold lots of passengers, but it's compact. You'll have to look at it in daylight. It's out there, on the lake."

Glo says, "It's a regular boat, then. Not a duck boat."

"Not a duck boat," says Jerry, setting the shiny new ignition keys on the floor beside the bed. "They don't make those anymore."

As THEY'RE ROCKETING up the road in the tamale van, Louisa's memory rushes at her faster than the eighteen-wheelers. "There was a family tragedy at a valentine factory," she tells Beebe. "My great-grandmother worked in one, my mother's grandmother. This was up in New England, oh, about a hundred years ago. The story was that she worked in the factory painting cupids and silk and satin flowers on fancy valentines. She used to lick the tip of her brush before she painted. When she was still young, with young kids, she died from the lead in the paint."

How is it that this boy's profile is so mild, whereas when you look at him full-face, he looks so different? He says, "So the factory owner killed her, sure as if he'd shot her. Don't just about everybody kill somebody, if they live long enough? You don't have to take a gun to their head to do it."

"Like I did."

He makes an expansive motion with his hand. "I pulled a fire alarm at school when I was eight. I mighta killed people, the way they trompled all over each other getting out. All that happened was one kid got a skinned knee."

They're crossing the Mississippi. The sun's out and the river shines beneath them so broad and glorious that Louisa's heart lifts and soars like the red-tailed hawk that veers close to the van and then rights itself in an updraft. The image of her great-grandmother in the valentine factory is so clear she could put out her hand and touch the frilly lace and satin flowers on the cards. The way that woman had bent over those cards for hours each day, dipping her brush into the pots of paint and touching the brush to her lips: Louisa's life, too, has been a series of repetitive motions. Pulling the bus up to the dock, rolling into the water, flipping a little switch to retract the wheels, front first, then rear. Land-self to sea-self, bus to boat. Telling the stories of the houses, the big houses along the lake and the people in them, sending her words into all those ears, all those years. Soft, unsuspecting ears; devious, willful ears; ears hard of hearing and ears uncaring. Telling the stories most of all to herself, not knowing then that she was living a big story, not knowing how it would all end.

"What I really liked," she tells Beebe, "was the way people would say, *Ohhh,* whenever the bus turned into a boat. Day after day, they'd say, *Ohhh,* no matter who they were or how old. You'd have to take it into the water real slow, 'cuz it was so heavy. My *Belle* was always more boat than bus." She adds proudly, "Weighed seven and a half tons. Displaced that much water."

"Bus to boat. So it was a transformer," Beebe says, "like my brother's toys. They could be a dinosaur and then turn into a truck. Be a bug and turn into a bird. They were still in the trailer when I sold it. Everything was. No use keepin' 'em."

There's the Memphis skyline. Louisa feels so high on the bridge, high over the water and into the sky, that she expects them to sail right over the city, which looks big and brown and silver.

"Did she get paid with money, your great-grandma?" Beebe asks. "Or did they pay her the way they do in Russia? Whatever kind of factory you work in over there, that's how they pay you. If you work in a match factory, you get paid in matches. Underwear makers get paid in underwear. I read about that."

"Don't make fun of her."

"I ain't," says Beebe. The last part of the bridge feels rickety, and they cross it with a clatter. "How come we're going to Boston?"

"To look up my son. The baby I gave up a long time ago."

"Will there be TV cameras waiting, to film a reunion? How old's your son?"

"There won't be any TV people. I have to find him first." Louisa rests her head against the window. After a while, she says, "There was a woman on board who called eagles 'iggles.' Your mama said she was hungry and that iggle lady gave her a sandwich, and your mama was so—so gracious about it."

Beebe nods. "That sounds like her."

"That iggle lady put some lake water in a jar in her jacket just before we started the tour. To think she died with that little bitty jar of water wrapped up close to her."

"Them that's superstitious might say she tempted fate. I bet the sailors of old, the Greeks and Phoenicians, woulda known better than to carry the seven seas on board with 'em."

"Your little brother Bobby laughed at the way that gal said *iggles*. He was a fine little boy. I liked him."

Beebe is silent for a long time and then says, "He tempted fate, too, by falling into the pit at Jiffy Lube. His time, I guess, was come."

RENÉ OR CLOUD? says a sign on a pink-foil-covered box in a new teacher's classroom. Mr. Stiles explains, "That's Mrs. Harper's project. She's the new math teacher. She's letting her students vote on the name of her baby."

"You ever getting married, Coach?" Harvey asks, cuffing Mr. Stiles on the shoulder. Katelynn laughs with joy. She can't help hanging all over Harvey, clutching his arm, squeezing his hand in both her hands the way she used to long to do, the way Jenelle used to do. Her laughter echoes down the empty halls of the school. How is it that Mr. Stiles and Harvey never got enough of high school? She got enough in three and a half years to last forever. She touches the pink foil box. It's beautiful. Taking a handful of paper scraps, she votes for Cloud three times. "What if it's a boy?" she asks.

"It *is* a boy. She had a sonogram, so she already knows. We should keep our voices down," Mr. Stiles warns, "even though the master calendar's empty for today. I always check it, but you never know who might be around. Of course, my standard response is always: I'm here doing lesson plans. I've been surprised a couple of times, once by a kid coming in with his mother to get something out of his locker, the other time by the vice principal."

"Do the guys still lock him in the boys' room when he comes in after the smokers?" Harvey says. "What an idiot."

Mr. Stiles smiles with calm complicity. Katelynn thinks, *He feels popular with us.* With Harvey, she feels magical, as if the two of them make magic for those around them, never mind that Mr. Stiles was the one who found out Harvey's secret, who confronted him, all those months ago, with the musty yearbook from Benton County.

Harvey says earnestly, "I'd like to do what you do, Coach. Work with the track team and teach. I was never any good at history, like you are, but I could teach something else."

Mr. Stiles coughs and says, "There's that little matter of sorting out your past and your future, Harvey. You'll have to either go to college or find some kind of gainful employment. You can't exactly enroll in high school for the third time. Katelynn here is studying to get her credits and get her diploma. I'm so sorry about your friend Jenelle."

Jenelle's name does it. Katelynn blurts, "We're getting married. We've decided."

Mr. Stiles rests his fingertips on the pink foil box. Katelynn holds her breath. She adds, "We'd like you to be our witness, at the court-house." She swallows, her throat dry and tight. He's in love with her, and here she is, rubbing it in that she's chosen somebody else. But he's so much older than she is, and he looks like a turtle, and he must have known she would want a young man. He might have known all along that she loved Harvey.

Mr. Stiles blinks at her. "Have you heard the news around here? The seniors are making a time capsule. It'll be buried right next to the flag-pole in the front yard. They've asked me to put something in it, but I can't decide what. Everything seems important these days. I could put so much stuff in there that there'd be no room for anybody else's ideas."

Katelynn glances up at Harvey. He looks as tense as he did before a vault, his ears pricked up, ready to race a hole through the wind. "When will they dig it up, Coach?" he asks.

"Maybe in twenty years, or fifty," says Mr. Stiles. "They want to dig it up themselves, not let some future generation do it."

"Did you hear me, Mr. Stiles? Harvey and I want to get married," Katelynn says. "We want you to stand up with us. You know, be a witness."

"And not long ago, you wanted to go to the world's fair," says Mr. Stiles.

"So?" asks Katelynn. "We thought you'd feel honored, that we're asking you."

"You both know lots of people," he says. "You can find somebody else."

THEY RUN OUT of money fast, even though they sleep in the van. In Virginia, they start selling tamales. It's a good thing, Louisa reckons, that it's October, carnival time. Beebe has a knack for finding fairs. He homes in on Apple Festivals, Homecomings, Autumn Harvest Days. They find grocery stores, where they buy meat, onions, and cornmeal. Then they fire up the stove in the van and get busy. Louisa could slap tamales together in her sleep, if she had to. It's a marvel, the way they'll be cooking in an empty parking lot, and people will come out of thin air, hungry, stretching out their hands full of money, drawn by the smell of the fresh tamales. She and Beebe sell tamales at church hayrides and high school football games. They work the Virginia countryside.

They fight about the money.

"It's my van, so I should get the profits," Beebe says.

"Put me out anytime you want," Louisa says. "I'll pay you when I get home. I left without my checkbook. I'll get to Boston one way or another."

He doesn't put her out. She keeps track of the money, tying it up in an old towel, counting out what they need for the day.

"We don't have a license," Beebe says. "No peddler's license or food-fixing license or whatever. If we get arrested, I'm a hop out and run."

"Fine," Louisa says, pillowing her head on the towel full of folding money, hunkering down for the night in the back of the van. They're parked in a forest, having spent a profitable evening selling tamales to families in a picnic area.

Beebe sprawls on the front seat, and soon he's snoring. Louisa can't sleep. Is it the biting cold? The van's windows are barely cracked. The woods smell of oaks and sharp, clean air. She twists and turns, trying to get warm. This is the coldest it has been. Back in Roanoke, she bought a blanket, a knit cap, and a change of clothes, but she should have bought long underwear and a winter coat. The blanket claimed it would keep you warm anywhere, that astronauts use this type of material in outer space. She pulls it over her head but still shivers.

She keeps thinking of Beebe that first day she saw him, back there at the campground, opening and closing his legs like hinges, showing off the holes in his jeans. She's disgusted with herself. She is old enough to be his granny.

His snoring keeps her awake. Thank goodness she never got married. But there was never anybody that she would've wanted to marry, except that boy at the Ozark pie supper or Sam Moon. She'd said to Sam Moon, bold as brass, "I love your voice," and she'd meant it. If he had asked her to run away with him, she would have gotten up from that table, taken off with him, and called her mother later.

After a long time, Beebe quits snoring, as clean as if somebody snapped off a radio, and then there's just the vast, complicated silence of the forest. If she listens closely enough, will she hear an owl? She opens her eyes and closes them, and the darkness is so complete, she can't see any difference whether they're open or shut—just as the lake water, sixty feet down, was so black, those people wouldn't have known if they were going up, down, or sideways. They might have kicked and pushed through that cold water with all their might, only to hit the bottom and realize they'd gone the wrong way and it was too late, no air left in their lungs.

The moon set a long time ago. She hears a tiny sound, somewhere between a chirp and a sigh, and, just as she'd remembered her father when she was underwater, she remembers him again.

She was how old—six, seven—and excited because her father had brought home a Christmas tree that he chopped down in the woods. Her mother was happy, so happy that she hummed as they all decorated the tree. And that night, after they'd gone to bed and the house was quiet, Louisa heard a high, wild call that her father identified the next morning as a tree frog's cry. Three times more, the sound came, sweet and hollow and alive.

"That little fellow must've froze in that tree while he was hibernating, and now he's thawed out," her father said.

Louisa took all the ornaments and tinsel off the tree, searching for the frog, reaching out to any little critter that had frozen and then revived, calling out. As her son, now, must be calling out to her, in some high-frequency cry that she hears with her heart.

"They're real tiny, tree frogs," her father said. "You won't find 'im." He laughed and said, "If you do, put 'im out! I don't want us gettin' warts."

She fixed up a shoebox with rags and lettuce leaves—a nest, all ready. She searched the tree branch by branch, but she didn't find the tree frog.

Now, years later, the tree frog calls; her son calls. She's too keyed up to sleep. If she ever does sleep, it'll be a bad night for leg cramps. What is she doing, selling tamales at country fairs, whiling her days away, when up North, her son is waiting? She's sure he's up North, hemmed in by crowds, waiting for her to come and get him and bring him home.

The hearing: has she missed the hearing that the lawyer had told her about? She has lost track of the days.

She sits up, nudges Beebe, and says, "Trade places with me. I'll drive." It's the middle of the night. She'll make good time out on the road.

"YOU HAVEN'T CHANGED your mind, have you?" Harvey asks as they step out of the school into the sunshine. He puts his arm around her the way a husband would, around her shoulders, so that she has to lean her head back to look into his eyes.

"Of course not. I feel like I'm dreaming. We're being so old-fashioned." She feels shy. Early this morning, when he said the words "Katelynn, will you marry me?" she said, "I asked you first, didn't I? Just yesterday. Say it again," and he did, and she said, "Yes," and she thought, *Now my life is starting.*

He stops and turns her toward him. He's so much taller than she is that she has to stand on tiptoe, and he has to bend down to kiss her. "Don't worry about Coach Stiles," he says. "Listen. We're going to live a long time, so we might have, like, eighty years together. Will that be enough?"

"Yes. I mean, no." She laughs. It's a real laugh. What if she's pregnant? She pictures a tiny silver embryo, fused cells slicked in mercury. She doubts she's pregnant. Harvey had condoms, and they used them.

Harvey says, "Jenelle and I were going to get married in college. I was going to tell my real age and go with her, 'cause by then it didn't matter anymore. Her goal was to live in married student housing. I always thought that sounded pretty rotten, but I'd've done it for her. She used to get hot every time she talked about married student housing."

"Don't talk about her. I feel like she's mad at me, even though she's gone," Katelynn says. Her lungs are steaming kettles, and she's suddenly pressurized with resentment—toward Jenelle? Harvey? She pokes a finger into Harvey's chest. "Don't even say her name."

"You mean like never talk about her? I can't do that, Katelynn."

They get back in Katelynn's car and sit for a moment, silent. She feels dizzy but chalks it up to excitement. They are on their way to get their marriage license. She freezes the moment in time, pasting it into her mental scrapbook. If only she weren't so tired. Alissa is out of the picture, and Jenelle is gone. But two things are bothering her, and she has to get them out in the open, has to clear the air.

"Harvey," she says. "You're not going to keep on with those parties, are you, once we're married? The ones in the empty houses?"

"No," he says. "That was just for then. Just for a while."

"And you're going to do your community service, aren't you? It's bad if we don't do it."

"Don't be so anxious," he says, pulling her to him. "I don't think we really have to do that. Your dad paid those fines already. I'll be busy enough, earning a living and supporting us. I don't want to live off your money, Katelynn."

Jenelle's furious voice rings in her head: *Drop it. If you want him, you have got to get along with him.* She can't fight them both. "Well," she says after a moment. "René or Cloud?" she asks him, and when his thin face cracks into lines, she thinks how handsome he'll be even when he's old, when she has ironed his shirts a million times and they've got grandchildren.

BUT OH, just one more fair, this one a carnival that's folding its tents in the dawn, looking for all the world like a mirage. Louisa's on Route 11, the old road that parallels 81. It's got fewer trucks. She looks through the rising mist into a hollow, and there's a little carnival with its ant-people taking down, packing up. She could join it and nobody need ever know who she is.

She's heard that lots of circus people have done awful things, that the circus gives them a way to hide. Murderers, arsonists, kooks, thieves, all on parade, entertaining the public in costume, their secrets concealed, and nobody asking questions of anybody else, because every one of them's got a past.

"Where are we? Why're we pulling over?" Beebe mumbles.

"I want a corn dog."

A very old man is sitting at a portable desk beside the grounds. Louisa parks the van between a station wagon and a horse trailer, gets out, and approaches him, feeling cold mist swirling up the legs of her jeans. What if these are the Pearly Gates, and he is Saint Peter? The old man wears a light strapped onto his head with an elastic band, like a surgeon, and he's working on something. When she gets close, she sees that he's focusing on something beneath a big magnifying glass.

"Shh," the old man says, and she stops close beside him. After a moment, he sighs and says, "There. You want it?" He moves the magnifying glass away, and with thumb and forefinger, he picks up something minuscule from the top of the desk. Louisa holds out her hand, and he drops something into it: a grain of rice.

"Rice?" she says.

The old man could easily be a hundred and twenty. He's all veins and knobs, and his scalp has the oily sheen that you see on the heads of babies and geriatrics.

"Read what it says," he says, "if you can."

Louisa squints at it. It's just a piece of raw rice.

"Bring it here, under the glass," the old man says. She puts the grain under the magnifying glass, which makes the rice look as big as an ice cube, and she makes out words, etched as if in crystal.

"It says *I love you*," she reads aloud.

"I engraved it. I can write the Lord's Prayer on the back of a stamp," the old man says. "I sell the stamps for a dollar each and the rice for a nickel. Haven't changed my prices in fifty years. That's a present for you. If you want to travel with us, lady, you'll have to wait till spring. We're folding up for the season. Going to Florida."

"Oh, I'm just stopping by for some breakfast." What's this sudden lightness in her heart?

"I see you got your grandson with you. Son, if you want to work for a carnival, you have got to learn a trade."

There's Beebe, rubbing his eyes, strolling toward them.

"I got a tamale van," Beebe says. "I'm set for life."

"Come spring, we'll need somebody to work the throwing alleys," the old man says, reaching up to the light on his head and switching it off. "Need somebody to work the rides, too. I never could do that. Makes me sick to watch them wheels spinning round."

Louisa reaches under the magnifying glass, picks up the grain of rice, and puts it in the pocket of her blouse. "How'd you learn how to do that, with rice and stamps?"

"I just squint and concentrate real hard. You can't breathe when you're doing it. You add up all the time I've held my breath, I bet it's twenty years, engraving. I don't have to use the glass for regular stuff, engraving watches and rings. I just use my eyes for that. That's what I'll be doing in Florida, this time next week, engraving watches for rich folks."

"You got horses," Beebe says, waving toward the packing-up crowd. There's dust now, rising to mix with the mist, and the sun's up.

The horses look wild, and to Louisa they make a sort of slow-moving rodeo, dancing away and backing up from the men trying to lure them into trucks.

"Come 'ere!" says a dark-skinned little man who looks like an Indian. He makes a chirring noise in his throat, reaching out to a pony. "I'll never catch that spotted one," he calls out to the old man, who is putting his desk and his magnifying glass away, folding them into themselves so that they make a wooden box no bigger than a suitcase.

"Naw, you never will," the old man calls back.

Ponies, dust, sunrise. The lightness in Louisa's heart spreads all the way down to her feet, so that she feels like cartwheeling. "Here, hold this," she says and pushes her pocketbook into Beebe's hands. "If I can catch that horse," she says, and in her mind, she adds, *Then everything will work out.*

The men have got all the horses except the one into the trailers. The spotted pony trots fast in a circle, tail held high. Louisa takes a deep breath, and next time he spins past her, she falls into step with him, chugging along, keeping up. The pony's wild eye rolls toward her, taking her in. He lifts his thick lip in a grin, showing corn-colored teeth. Louisa runs, and it feels good. She runs in the circle the little horse creates, and people stand back and murmur. She can tell when she passes the old man, because the light on his head shines like a star. The sun strikes the metal and he is a beacon. Not since she was sixteen and dancing the reels and jigs at the Ozark pie supper has she felt so light. Why, that music of fiddles and flutes had a meaning more than anything her experience could allow her to know back then. Only now, when she has nearly drowned, when she has run away, can she begin to understand those songs. The music comes back to her and lends wings to her feet, and she thinks even the pony knows it.

She speaks to the pony, but she's speaking to herself, too, and to her lost son: "You'll come home. You know me, and you'll come home."

And it does. It comes to her, rubs its big head against her hand, lets her wave it into the van, while the carnival people clap and cheer and whistle, and for a moment, she's triumphant. A woman who's sure of herself.

BUT KATELYNN IS so tired, she has to rest, if only for a little while. "I'll be all right in a minute," she says. Then they can go to the courthouse and get their marriage license.

"Here," says Harvey, opening the back door of the car, "lie down on the backseat."

She does, but she can't stand the motion of the car. "Take me home," she tells him, and her stomach's rolling too, rebelling against the rich food she ate last night, meat and cake when she has eaten lightly for so long. She presses her hands to her mouth and tries to think of clean mountain air and sweet clover. But her guts bubble and surge. She sees the boat tilting upward, sliding down into the water. Her symptoms had started like this, back in the spring, with nausea, but there had been pain in her back then, too, where she later learned her kidneys were. Lying on the backseat, she's hearing "The Night Has a Thousand Eyes"—a song from her mother's era, no, earlier than that, a song about telling white lies, about being watched and judged and found wanting.

"Turn the radio off," she says.

"It *is* off," says Harvey. "Hey, hey," he says, reaching back from the driver's seat to touch her. "No tears, honey, okay?"

Honey. She loves it. Say it again, she wants to tell him, but she can't get the words out. Forever won't be long enough, because the world will end. Didn't she read that in the paper, not long ago? The sun's getting hotter all the time. Eventually, it'll grow so hot that the seas will boil and evaporate, and by then all the living creatures will be dead and the land and trees and cities scorched away. There will be a last child and a last cat, last bird. Will people pray, up to the end? Well, she wouldn't. She won't. God could step in and stop it, but He won't. He could have saved the people on the boat, but He didn't. He could have saved Jenelle, but Katelynn was supposed to do that. When the silver drop fell from Jenelle's hand, it would have been the easiest thing to reach out and break its fall.

The car stops, and Harvey reaches back and touches her face. "Jeez, you're burning up."

"The world will burn up," she says. "The oceans will get so hot, they'll turn to steam. I can't bear it. Don't say it won't be for a billion years so not to worry about it. Because that won't make it not happen. We've all been set up to die. Harvey, what did you do during all those years in between when you were in school? You've got to tell me."

"It wasn't so long," he says.

"It was years. Four or five years," she says. "That's a long time."

"I'm not old, honey," he says and laughs.

The car stops, and through the window, she sees her own house. Harvey says, "I was assistant manager of a tuxedo-rental store, the only one in Benton County."

"That's not so bad, is it? Why keep that a secret?"

"Don't try to talk anymore right now," he says, and his voice is buzzing like the wasps her mother killed, long ago. His hand is on her forehead again, and she grabs his wrist.

"How many times would you rent out a suit before you threw it away?"

"Lots and lots," he says, "unless a guy really ruined it."

"That's a career you can go right back into, isn't it?" she says, meaning, *once we're married.*

"Can you walk?" Harvey says. "Here comes your mom. She doesn't like me, does she?"

She hears her mother's voice, not words, just shrillness, and she hears Harvey answering her mother, while Peppy yips and yaps, springing into the car to be with her, but she's too weak to cuddle him. She wants to tell her mother and Harvey she'll be all right. If she can just stop thinking about the boiling seas and the exploding sun. But she can't stand up, and Harvey has to drag her off the backseat of the car, pulling her toward him by her ankles. Lifting her up, he carries her to her room, through the shrapnel of her mother's voice.

When she wakes up, Harvey is gone, and Dr. McKellar is speaking to her mother. He is furious. "Tootsie Rolls and candy corn? Pepsi? No wonder she's not getting any better."

"I can't do anything with her," says Glo.

"I ate last night," Katelynn says, as the doctor listens to her heart. "Meat, grapes, lots of good stuff." The thought of food makes her sick.

Her mother and Dr. McKellar don't answer her. They are conferring. Glo says, "What can they do for her in the hospital that can't be done for her here? I can hire nurses. I haven't been paying enough attention to her. I should have hired somebody long ago."

Dr. McKellar says, "This is just old-fashioned heatstroke, is all, but I'm putting her into the hospital anyway, for observation."

Glo lowers her voice and says, "She was doing better till that boat sank and that con artist came back, the one who'd already graduated from high school and then reenrolled. He left, didn't he? Yep, I hear his car." Glo cocks her head. They're behaving as if Katelynn's not even there.

"Oh yes, I remember him," Dr. McKellar says. "The pole-vaulter. He was right much of a hotshot, wasn't he?"

Katelynn laughs then, sharp hard hoots, because she's crying. Her mother and the doctor look at her as if they still don't understand, just don't get it. Peppy comes in and whines, knowing exactly how she feels.

"Funny-looking varmint," says Dr. McKellar.

THE ANSWER IS in the lake. This comes to her during one of the half-lit, plastic-smelling nights in the hospital. These nurses are vampires, taking her blood. Whenever she needs to pee, she has to call one of them so they can help her go in a bottle, to measure it.

"The answer is in the lake," she tells a nurse, a big blonde with metallic pink makeup.

"You want what, sweetie? Did you lose something? I swear, I think I'm going deaf, but I asked the doctor and he said it's just my sinuses backed up from this cold I had so long."

"I'm getting married," Katelynn says. "Has Harvey come by? He's my boyfriend. Fiancé."

"No, nobody's come by for you," says the nurse in a pretend-innocent way that infuriates Katelynn. "Hold still, now. I'm having trouble getting a vein in your arm. We'll have to use your hand."

It's sickening to have blood drawn from the back of her hand. Katelynn turns away as the needle slides in. Where's Harvey? He didn't stick around after he took her home. Maybe it's too much for him, that she's so sick. She's been in the hospital for two days, and there's been no word from him.

Somebody's knocking on the door. Katelynn looks up to see a man in the doorway.

"You must be Harvey," the nurse says, smiling toward the man, a stretched smile, all for show. "I'll leave you two alone." She finishes drawing blood, tucks her equipment into a little kit, and bustles away.

It's not Harvey, it's Jerry, with a vase of flowers. Katelynn blinks, her vision just blurred enough that she can't read his expression. It's the first time she's seen him since the day the boat sank, when he'd just pulled Louisa up onto the grass in Katelynn's yard.

"Hi, Katelynn," he says. "I'm Jerry Fiveash. I'm a friend of your mother's. We kind of met the day of, you know, the day of the boat." His face rumples up as if he's about to sneeze, and he holds the flowers away from him.

"You can put those anywhere. Thanks," she says, and he sets the flowers on the table by her bed—chrysanthemums, dyed Technicolor, exuding a rusty, dusty scent. Jerry does sneeze, a huge *raaatch* that makes Katelynn want to laugh.

"You can sit down," she says, gesturing to a chair, and he does. "I remember you," she says. "Do you know where Louisa is? I can't reach her on the phone. We got to be friends after you saved her."

"I got a phone call from her today. She'd been trying to reach you. She's on a trip. She's fine. Said she's gone to Boston to look for somebody—she said that you would know who."

"Oh, wow!" says Katelynn. "So she's okay."

Jerry nods. He doesn't press her to say who Louisa's gone looking for, and she likes him for that. "She's a fine lady. She took care of my granddad till he died." He pauses. "It's an awful thing. I wish I could have saved more of those people."

"I used to be a lifeguard, but I never saved anybody's life."

"You want anything, Katelynn? Another blanket or something?"

"I'm fine." She isn't. Her heart is racing, and a big welt has risen on the back of her hand, from the needle. This is her chance to talk with Jerry. "Is Mom going to run off with you? Because if she does, it's okay. Dad is never home. When I find Myanmar on the map, I can't believe how far away it is. He gets mad if you call it Burma. The capital used to be called Rangoon. Now it's called something else, I forget what." She sits up, and the bed rises up with her, buckling, making the humming, scolding sound it makes whenever she moves. "I figured it out about you and Mom. And then Dora said something about it. This doesn't mean I don't love my dad."

Jerry's laugh surprises her; it sounds relaxed. "Just where do people run off to, from Hawk Lake? I've lived here all my life. I've always wondered where people go, when they leave."

"Well, Burma," she says. "Anywhere." Sweat springs out on her face, hot and beady. "I was just thinking, the answer to all of this is in the lake itself. I don't mean it's something like a message in a bottle that we have to find. I don't know quite what I mean."

"You sound like my grandfather," Jerry says. "He kept working on the lake, building around it, but he wanted more than he found here." Jerry pauses. "He was a painter."

"And you identify with him," Katelynn says, guessing.

Jerry nods.

"Do you paint, too?"

He nods again.

"What do you want?" she asks. "To be with my mom? And what else?"

"To dream."

Katelynn waits for him to laugh, to be embarrassed, to deny having said this, the way most people would do, but he doesn't.

"THERE'S, LIKE, a black market for things that came off that boat," says Dora, "at yard sales. My sister Sharon bought a life jacket. You can buy stuff that came off the people. A friend of Sharon's bought the fat guy's belt. At least, he says it was off him. If they'd a been wearing the life jackets, they wouldn't a died."

They're collecting sticks and debris in the yard of the abandoned house. She works as hard as Jerry does, sweats as hard as he does in the warm October sun, gathering litter in the high grass while grasshoppers spring back and forth and bright clouds of gnats glitter just above them. "How does your sister know that life jacket's not from some other boat?" Jerry says.

"'Cuz it says *Arkansas Belle* on it. And it's all beat up and water-logged. You can buy little bits of wood and metal and rope, like buying pieces of the cross Jesus died on. Them divers, Coast Guard guys, they thought they got it all, but they didn't. Other people got stuff, too, junk that floated up. I've seen a clipboard with a duck on it that must've come from there, and a camera that was all messed up. I told Sharon not to get that life jacket. It's bad luck."

Jerry takes a gallon of water from his truck, swigs from it, and offers it to Dora. There's still no water out here, no electricity, no cars going by on the graveled road. This is where he would come if he ran off from Hawk Lake. With Glo. This is the end of the earth. They'd dig a new well and live by candlelight.

Dora drinks deeply from the plastic jug, her eyes closed. How can anybody so young have such dark circles under their eyes?

"Till I met you," she says, "there was something I was gunna do. I was planning to blow up a casino. I was gunna make a bomb and go to Tunica and blow one up. They're bad places, and they're all fake. They claim they're boats, but they ain't, they're just big buildings in ditches. It's some law, they got to say they float."

"Where'd you learn how to make bombs?"

She grins, showing a bad tooth. "I know plenty guys who know how. I was gunna plant it under a blackjack table and wait outside for the boom. Watch all them sinners come running out. People go down there and gamble their food money and rent money away. They let their kids wander through them places all night long and don't give a damn." She drinks from the jug again, then wipes her mouth and hands it back to him. If he didn't know she was only eighteen, he would think she was thirty-five. The smell of her sweat carries like gasoline. "But I love you, Jerry, so I changed my mind."

"You're too smart to love me, Dora." He bends down and fools with the pile of brush so he won't have to look at her face. She *is* smart. He could teach her how to search a title and confirm property in court. He pictures her years from now at a tax sale, hard-faced and clear-headed with a property list and calculator on her lap, joshing with the farmers, outbidding the real-estate ladies and company reps, making her career in the battered county courthouses where fortunes rise and fall. Her eyes are meant for measuring acreage, her arms for wielding posthole diggers. He could paint her that way, but he wouldn't want her to know it.

"I've never done nothing worse than put sugar in a guy's gas tank that I was mad at," Dora says, plucking a twist-tie from between her teeth and tying up a plastic sack of trash and brush. "Man, I think about us, if we lived out here, living an old way of life." She turns to the sagging little house as if it's a castle.

"RIGHT ABOUT HERE," Louisa says, and Beebe pulls the van to the curb. "Yes. I remember I could see that park out my hospital window. It was a right nice hospital."

"I don't see any hospital."

"It's gone," she answers.

Fashionable shops cover the block instead: a sporting goods store, an Ethiopian restaurant, an art gallery, a bookstore, and a pizza parlor. The sidewalks teem with people. Two sleek young Oriental women strut by, and Beebe flips his gray hair off his forehead, preening.

She does remember the park and the statue in it, a bronze sculpture of a war hero. Aunt Patsy had said how lucky she was, said usually girls in her situation had to give birth in a kind of barracks in the basement of the hospital, that the doctors and nurses must have taken a liking to Louisa by letting her have a semiprivate room with a view of the famous park.

"Why couldn't Aunt Patsy have taken the baby?" Louisa asks. "Why didn't anybody think of that? We weren't thinking, not any of us. Turns out Aunt Patsy couldn't have any babies. She married one of those guys she used to dish it back to, and they wanted kids but could never have any. They ended up getting dogs, one poodle after another. Aunt Patsy gave up nursing, dyed her hair red, and went to cocktail parties all the time, and her husband stayed home with the poodles. And years went by, and then they died."

"I'm cold," says Beebe, shivering. How is it that his neck has grown longer during the trip? Why, because he's young and still growing. She keeps forgetting how young he is.

"Here," she says, handing him her knit cap. He tugs it over his ears and stops shivering.

She gazes at the park and the statue. There's been a light snow. She'd given birth in late February, and there had been snow then, too, ragged and stained on the sidewalks but crisp and clean in the park. It all comes back to her, the lunch she ate ravenously a few hours after the birth, a tray of pork chops and gravy, mashed potatoes, and canned applesauce. Why, she'd always heard hospital food was terrible, but that had been delicious.

Her roommate had kept talking about Louisa's accent. "Say *onion*," the woman would say. "Say *water*." Louisa had played along until she got fed up and changed the subject. She got the woman talking about places she had traveled. Montreal: the woman had been to Montreal, where, she said, people put butter on their radishes. This absorbed her for some moments, an oddity outstripping even Louisa's accent. The long-ago roommate had been only a little older than Louisa, but she had a husband, whom she talked about incessantly, rubbing it in. Her husband had been the one to notice the buttered radishes, on their trip to Montreal. He'd insisted that she try them, and they were "quite good, actually," she said, turning the wedding ring on her hand. She'd have seen that Louisa didn't have a ring on. Women can be so mean that way. Maybe that's why Louisa has spent her whole life working instead of making friends. Why, she's put so little effort into making friends, it's a wonder even Barbie bothers with her. She's lucky Barbie thought enough of her to come over the night of the sinking, Barbie and the other neighbors who dropped by and brought food. She has to thank them for all that food, has to dig out the casserole dishes from her cupboard and figure out who they belong to and return them, the pie plates and stewpots and Tupperware.

She's just never taken the time with people. She worked at the old folks' home and then spent all those years with Mr. Fiveash, and then that phase of her life led to the duck boat. She'd talked to passengers all day. That was as good as having friends, wasn't it? And now, she has Katelynn, the best friend she's ever had. She and her hospital roommate, in their beds overlooking the snowy park, had been rivals, locked in some competition Louisa had not understood, and the roommate had won, had presumably gone on with her comfortable, ordinary life, taking her baby home to her husband. Louisa remembers the blonde at the Shore Club, the girl in the black cashmere sweater who came up to Sam Moon to get his autograph. That girl had looked at her with envy, because she, Louisa, had been sitting with Sam Moon. What happens to people, Louisa wonders, to all the people you bump up against in life?

She stares out the window of the van at the street scene in front of her—Boston, early in the twenty-first century. Another planet, another century from her life in Hawk Lake. At least two hundred years from her life in Yellville. Cheesy, doughy pizza smells reach her even through the windows. A panhandler begs from a black man in a leather jacket, and the man gives him money. Two huge Dalmatians strain their leashes, while their owner, a rich-looking woman in a fur coat—Louisa doesn't know when she's seen a fur coat—leans backward against the dogs' strength and weight. They pass close enough to the van that Louisa can see that the woman's perfectly straight teeth have coffee stains.

She's lost them all, every one, parents and baby, Aunt Patsy and Sam Moon, cashmere girl, hospital roommate. Lost them or shaken them off, however you look at it. Her mother's dream of Teddy Shatford as a prince had died an awful death. When Louisa got home after the prom, her mother took one look at her face and the ruined ruffly dress and covered her mouth with both hands, her eyes stretching so wide that Louisa thought of a rabbit being shaken in a dog's jaws. She can still hear the cries her mother made behind her hands.

"I can't track down everybody," Louisa says.

"Naw, you can't," says Beebe.

She could go all the way to Maine. She could stride into Teddy Shatford's old metal-sided garage, for that is surely where he is, he and his father both leaning over the dirty lobster pound watching the critters eat each other up. She could walk in there, bold as day, and grab hold of him by the hair, say, "Damn you, I had your baby." He'd given her picture to *People* magazine, wielding scissors, snipping out his own face and leaving Louisa alone in the picture. How long would she have to thump his head against those metal walls before he begged for the forgiveness of the girl in the ruffle-necked dress that he raped after the prom? She would open her mouth and Sam Moon's songs would come out, while Teddy Shatford's father, if he is still alive, would rush at her with tongs and knives, mallets and forks, weapons for spearing long-dead, raggedy-tailed lobsters from the kettle, for fending off the likes of her. But Teddy must be old by now, a stooped-over geezer gone sweet with his years, that's what she can't get over, that all these years have passed, and her own grown baby is the age her father was, back then. Teddy Shatford—still tiny-featured with that little bitty chip of a nose, but wrinkled as a basset hound now— nods and grins, lifts a lid, pokes his crazed lobsters back into the pot, and the water boils over, drips onto the dirt floor of the garage. He would not understand, no matter how she might yell. He would cup a quivery hand around a hairy, big-lobed ear, he would shake his head, and she could never make him understand how it was to linger in that hallway, back at school in Yellville, while the other students swirled around her and she filled up with love for the baby, love that's still waiting.

There'd been no milk to speak of, no milk in her breasts when her baby was born, as if her body knew she could not keep what it had grown. A nurse had noticed this and commented on it, telling her she was lucky.

Her memory is a pile of dirty, heavy, lumpy sacks that she will not put down. Old Mr. Fiveash used to claim he could recall when the churning Mississippi River created Hawk Lake, gouging out the oxbow and gushing into it, filling it up, after a storm, he said. But he was wrong. The river was never so far west, and the lake was formed long ago, way before the days of Indians. The old man's imagination seized on the river and the lake, making a story out of them that was his own. Whereas she can try and try to remember her baby, but memory will never take her beyond the roommate, the park, the snow.

The face of Barbie's young child appears before her, the sweet twin casting her that look of forgiveness after she cut its hair. She didn't deserve the understanding the child gave her and yet it was granted to her, offered as a little valley for the river of her grief to flow into.

Beebe's stomach growls loud as a thunderclap. He turns to her, and his voice is quiet. "So what does it add up to, Louisa? This trip? You don't know where he is. Everything's different than what you remember."

It adds up to the grain of rice. *I love you,* written so small you wouldn't know it's there. "What it means is, I love him. I love my child. I can say that now," she says.

She opens her door and gets out of the van. They've come all this way. They can get pizza anytime. She scans the restaurants lined up on the block. "Hey, Beebe," she says. "If you want Ethiopian food for lunch, you better come on."

GLO HIRES THE metallic-faced blond nurse to take care of Katelynn at home. "I've never seen anybody with mercury poisoning," the nurse says brightly, "but Dr. McKellar told me all about it. You must be a very special young lady. The doctor told me he'll come by anytime you need him. We'll take *good* care of you!"

Katelynn's heart sinks. She wishes Glo had consulted her. She doesn't like this nurse, and now the woman is installed in her room like a spy, armed with stethoscope, thermometer, pills, and bags of liquid.

"I'm hungry," Katelynn says. She once read an article about a woman in a nursing home who vowed to get out and did. The woman had been sick, bedridden, and almost dead, but she exercised and got out of the nursing home. "Bring me some meat," Katelynn orders the nurse, "and rolls and butter. Milk, too. And vitamins."

The nurse scurries out, tripping over Peppy. Glo has also hired a registered dietitian, who probably expects to do nothing but serve the Tootsie Rolls and candy corn that Katelynn has heard the nurse laugh about with the dietitian. But oh, no. Katelynn gives up her candy. She'll keep the dietitian busy, will make her cook all day. She feels purified and full of purpose, the way she did the day she stood up in class and said, "I died." You could say it only once. There's a line of Emily Dickinson's poetry she likes, from the same book that contained the poem by Walter de la Mare. *"Hope" is the thing with feathers—/That perches in the soul—*

The tail-wagging puppy clambers onto the bed, and Katelynn wraps her arms around him. She looks out to the lake, the calm beautiful blue wall of water, and sees a wide, sturdy boat drawing near her house, a new, dazzlingly white boat. The light hurts her eyes. She needs her dark glasses, but she's too tired to reach for them. People are waving to her from the deck of the boat, waving hard, and the memory of the sinking washes over her so that she feels sick, seeing the tilting, vertical *Arkansas Belle* sliding beneath the surface. She blinks, hauls herself out of bed, and goes to the glass wall for a better look. The boat veers close to the grassy point, to the very spot where the *Belle* sank. She holds her breath. This boat will sink too, or it'll plow right through her walls, bringing the whole lake with it, a cold tidal wave smashing through her house. *I died,* she'd said to her homeroom class, and this is what it means.

But it's Jerry and Dora on the boat, saluting her, as if it's a real boat, as if they're happy. She smells meat cooking in the kitchen, and her stomach turns. It's a darkish, fatty smell that makes her think *mutton,* even though she knows it isn't. She'll eat it. She waves back.

•   •   •

THE MIRACLE IS that he finishes writing the card, though he can't find the pen he was using last week, two weeks ago, whenever it was when he smudged the word "Dear," and so he uses different ink. The card will have a crazy look, with red ink, then green ink, his finger-prints blotted all over it. At least it's an actual Burmese postcard, bought at a tiny shop that sells flowers, candy, athletic socks, fake Rolex watches, packets of English tea, and small golden lizards. This card has a photograph of a temple. She will stare at it, holding it close to her eyes, which always look sun-strained to him, older than her years, not the eyes of a cheerleader–lifeguard–homecoming queen runner-up but the eyes of an explorer caught in a sandstorm. He's never been sure the mercury was her trouble. Maybe the mercury is what's holding his daughter together, keeping her from leaking out of her own pores, unzipping her own scalp. He doesn't blame them for playing with it, bathing their arms in it, dipping cigarettes in it, even pouring it on the ground. What else would you do with a whole glori-ous vat of the stuff, like a zillion melted dimes? He's proud of her, really, for loving the stuff, for making hay with it. Only young people know how to deal with mercury. As for smoking it, well, wouldn't he have done the same as a kid, and Glo too? Maybe Katelynn inherited his own love of risk.

Oh, he remembers Jenelle, the girl who died: a heavy smoker, always at the house, so sturdy with her cheerleader's legs. He hadn't liked her smile, the way her upper lip rolled back from her teeth. Her bovine kind of beauty wouldn't have lasted through her twenties, and that long, coal-black hair would have coarsened and turned gray in stripes and streaks, like the hair of Plains Indians in old pictures. She might have been part Indian, that girl. A century ago, she'd have plaited weasels' tails in her hair.

The vapors were what got them into trouble. If they'd just swal-lowed some of it, just dipped their hands in it, they wouldn't have got-ten so sick. He remembers the swift elusive pearls of mercury that fled from his hands when he was a child chasing the liquid from a broken thermometer. The beads rolled across the floorboards, disappearing. Is that a memory shared by everybody of a certain generation? Since his daughter's diagnosis, he has read all he can about mercury poisoning. He knows that dentists have sometimes been sickened by drops of loose mercury caught in the cracks of old floors. All spring, whenever Katelynn smiled at him, he examined her teeth for gingivitis, looseness, a blue line along the gums. Her teeth seemed to be all right.

He finishes the card and searches in a carved wooden box for a stamp. No stamps, just a scrap of soap, a coin, a pebble. Glo's image forms on the inner screen of his eyelids: her new, madwoman haircut, her dazed, combative stance, her stubborn silences. Before they were married, when they had lived together, he'd been amazed by how much she slept, usually with a cat on her head. Then she gave her cat away and quit sleeping, as far as he could tell. For months, years, whenever he has woken up in the night, she'll be sitting up against her pillows, silent, tense, as if she is on the brink of figuring out something, in a silence so profound, so interior, that he has not intruded. He'd wanted more children. For Glo, Katelynn was enough. A tug-of-war between Glo and Katelynn developed after the mercury poisoning. It wore him out, never mind that that's how mothers and daughters are. He grew up with a sister. He remembers their mother's sharp words and tears, his sister's rebellion.

If it hadn't been for the mercury, Katelynn would be in college, and what then for Glo? Had she planned to cut loose, leave him, get a job, get an advanced degree? How fierce she has grown with him. She has that right. He was home two months, this last time, and she only turned to him once, abandoning her silent sleepless watch. Even in the dark, he could read her expression with his fingertips—that stubbornness on her face. He had touched her face lightly, feeling heat like fever on her skin. Maybe something had happened that day to make her happy. It had been the day the magazine people visited, taking pictures of her beloved house.

"So boat sank," the woman says, the woman he adores. "Boat sank, and she saw."

He lies down beside her, laying his hand on her belly. Her hair is black, too, blacker than the cheerleader's but not so long. She keeps asking for ice. He'll get her ice. He'll buy her a refrigerator, which hardly anybody has. Nor telephones, nor televisions, except for a very few. They make them last forever, improvising rabbit ears, condensers, making do with old, brittle wire. Hasn't he heard that bicycle parts are harvested for use in medical equipment? This woman is a widow. Through pantomime and broken English, she has explained that she does not miss her husband, that the man not only beat her but had a habit of rolling onto his stomach every night and delivering farts of extraordinary volume and lasting offense. She'd mourned the fact that they had no children, and now—she pats her belly—that dream's in the making.

Oh, he should leave this country, leave this woman, right this instant. He'll leave tomorrow, or next week, allowing himself just a lit-tle longer to stay in the spell of the place. He tells the woman the story as he sees it, of the plunging boat, the glass walls showing everything, his daughter distraught.

He will go to a café where you can get on the Internet, where they sell the American papers. You can do that here, can skip from the nineteenth century to the twenty-first just by pushing open the door of a café. Someday, these cafés will be as quaint as rickshaws or Victrolas.

The woman he loves doesn't mind when he goes out without her. She'll sew baby clothes while he is out, working the treadle of an ancient French-made sewing machine that smells pleasantly of oil, holding up some tiny garment and shaking the loose threads from it. Then she'll lie on her back with her eyes shining at the ceiling, dream-ing of ice. She will fix a supper of garlic and seafood, and he'll glory in the scent and the taste when he comes back.

This country is not safe. In villages not so far away, slaughters are being carried out by order of military generals who, on weekends, play golf on verdant courses, picking through the woods and irons in their supple leather bags, sighing over which to choose. It's a challenging game. One must get everything right: the stance, the grip, the swing. But it's a good way to do business with those foreigners who have money and bring it in, tiresome as they are, oh, you can shade your eyes and scan the fairway while they go on and on.

In refugee camps along the Thai border, children whose limbs have been hacked off in ambushes are learning to use toothbrushes for the first time. The medics hand them out. Such quiet children, brushing their teeth. What can you say to them, except how important it is to brush your teeth? Of course, you can say whatever you want. You can talk about the proxy parliament and the democracy opposition and the resolutions they have made, and the children will go on brushing their teeth, in the direction in which they grow, as they have learned.

He might go back to the woman's apartment at any time and find her gone, dragged out by thugs, jailed or shot. She is safer here in Yangon than she would be in a village, surrounded by the jungle. She grew up in such a place; she has described its crumbling pagoda, which by now must be ruined. He imagines vines snaking through the windows and up through the stone floors. Monkeys leap on the looted altars and swing screeching through the gaps in the broken walls. The sacred urns are smashed, the priests are dead. Shedding feathers, blackbirds pick at the bodies, at the bones, and at night, big animals come out. Silently, a jungle cat steps over a gun that a rebel left behind.

She misses her home, she says. Will he go with her to the village, take her back to visit her parents, her grandparents? They must go visit when the baby comes, she insists. Not with the war on, he says, not with the risk of capture, torture, forced labor. Don't be crazy. *Shh,* she tells him, as if it would be easy, as if a road to the mountains is laid out just for them.

For now, he'll sip espresso and read about the sinking, and his daughter's laughter will raise the hair on the back of his neck, it's so hearty.

PART II

*S*HE DIALS LOUISA'S NUMBER ALL
evening. No answer—so Louisa is still on her trip. Katelynn orders a
large supper from the dietitian and eats every morsel. Fried liver. She
actually eats fried liver. Jenelle would gag at that.

"Somebody's feeling stronger," says the nurse doubtfully. "You're
not going into the bathroom and bringing it all up again, are you?"

"No," says Katelynn. "Why don't you take the evening off and go to
a movie or something?"

"Oh, I couldn't." The nurse turns to the vanity mirror and picks at
her high, stiff blond hair.

"Sure you can. My mom's out for the evening. She'll never know."
She guesses that Glo is at Jerry's.

"Who's that fellow who came to visit you in the hospital?"

"A friend."

"Popular gal," the nurse says. "I used to stack my dates when I was your age. Do girls still do that? I'd say to one guy, I have to be home by eight, I have to study, and then I'd have another guy pick me up at eight-thirty and bring me home at ten-thirty, and then I'd have my late date, who was my real sweetie—"

The dietitian knocks on the door and opens it, leaning in to say, "I'm heading home now. Night, Teena," she says to the nurse.

Though Teena, the nurse, is irritating, the dietitian can be kind. Katelynn almost likes her. The dietitian just picks up Teena's ways when they're together.

"You both go," says Katelynn, making her voice gentler than she feels. "You've had a long day."

"I'm supposed to stay here," says Teena, wavering.

Katelynn picks up the world's fair book. "Go ahead," she says.

"If you're coming, Teena, come on," says the dietitian.

"You promise me you'll take your medicine," the nurse says.

"I promise," says Katelynn into her book.

At last, they're gone. In truth, she feels bloated and swollen from all she has eaten. She dials Louisa's number again.

She dials Harvey's number—his uncle's number—but it just rings and rings. Once more, he has vanished. She had really believed, for the space of a morning, that he would marry her. Maybe, if she hadn't had that sick spell, he would have gone through with it, and then where would they be?

Glo is home. Katelynn hears her bumbling through the dark living room, sighing as she knocks into furniture. Katelynn drags herself out of bed and goes into the hallway. "You can turn on a light," she says. "I'm awake. I sent those people away."

"You can't do that. They're my employees, not yours." Glo's face is red and sore-looking. Katelynn feels a dart of envy. It's Katelynn's face that should be beard-burned. She's supposed to be on a honeymoon with Harvey. She'll get well. She'll use her own money so they can go away together, set up a tuxedo-rental business and prosper. Pageantry: her ostrich-cart great-grandparents would be proud. She sinks down on the sofa.

"Mom." How to say *I know about Jerry*? "The cat's out of the bag."

"You mean about Harvey breaking off with you?" Glo peels off her jacket and throws it on the sofa. "Oh, Katelynn, couldn't you tell about him? He's the kind who wants drama, but when it comes to any real trouble in his life, he runs off like a rabbit."

"I'm not talking about Harvey. Besides, just because I don't hear from him for a few days doesn't mean anything," Katelynn says, so smoothly she almost convinces herself. "Quit making things out like they're worse than they are, Mom, just 'cuz you never liked him."

"Katelynn, I'm sorry. I had no idea you really loved him."

"I did and I do. I do love him."

"Okay, what did you mean at first?" says Glo levelly. "What cat is out of what bag?"

Katelynn can't bring herself to say it. Her mother looks so tired that Katelynn's anger drains away.

Glo's eyes meet hers. "So you know about Jerry. He told me he visited you in the hospital. I gave him hell about that. I didn't know he was going to."

"It's okay, Mom. He's cool. I don't blame you." This is the most unreal moment in her whole life, this conversation, with her voice sounding calm about her mother's having a boyfriend. She feels a rush of gratitude to Jerry for loving her mother, for saving Louisa. She hasn't even thanked him for the flowers.

"Your father." Glo says and stops. "I still love him."

"He called when you were in New Orleans. I told him about the puppy. He gave me his number, but I couldn't write it all down."

"It's all right." Glo motions for Katelynn to slide down to the end of the sofa. Glo stretches out full length, toeing off her shoes. "I think I'll sleep right here. I'm too tired to move. There was the strangest girl at Jerry's house tonight, a sort of awful person he's hired to clean out old houses, a big mean-looking girl. I think she was here at the memorial reception."

"Dora! I know her."

"She kept talking about casinos, how she hates them. She does have a point. I hate all that artificial light the casinos make, and all those billboards they've put up on the highway. I talked with her about that for a long time."

Katelynn can't imagine her mother and Dora talking about anything.

Glo says, "Well, she was frying catfish and wouldn't go home. My hair smells like fish." She sits up and holds a fistful to Katelynn's nose. The silky red hair reeks. Glo lies down again. "And you know what? He took her out on the new boat today, the boat he bought for Louisa. I didn't want to go. They both got sunburned, though she's so dark already, you could hardly tell."

"I saw them out there, Mom. She's in love with him, too."

"I could see that, and it doesn't worry me, Katelynn. He thinks I'm the bee's knees." Glo's head is turned sideways, and she seems to be already falling asleep.

"Why do you and Dad fight about the littlest things?" Katelynn says, but Glo doesn't stir. "Once you fussed at him for getting the wrong plates out of the cupboard." Katelynn is terrified, thinking it could happen to her—rage against a husband about something that would never matter, and then he disappears on you.

Glo is not asleep. "I can't live here much longer, Katelynn. I keep seeing that boat, sinking. I keep seeing a ghost of it, with all those people on board. Don't you?"

"You saw it sink, Mom? Why didn't you tell me before?"

"Oh, Katelynn. I see it in the daytime and at night too. I see it each time I look at the lake. And every time, they die."

GONE SO LONG, *the 'lectric company cut off my lights.* That's what Louisa's daddy said when he got home from the last handyman job he would ever do. He sounded so satisfied to be home in his trailer with candles burning, home safe in Yellville. Louisa liked that trailer, an old one twined with trumpet vine, jewelweed, and birds' nests. He'd moved there after her mama died and lived there how long by himself? Ten, twelve years? She can't remember.

She hasn't been gone from her own house that long. It just feels that way, after the days on the road, the fairs, the few hours in Boston, and the trip home, with a few thousand tamales in between. She turns the key in the lock, pushes open the door, and goes inside, with Beebe following her. They have no luggage, of course, and most of the money they made selling tamales on the trip north went to cover expenses for their return home.

The sofa is still made up with sheets from when Louisa slept on it, the night after the boat sank, when Barbie and her twins had taken over Louisa's room. "You can sleep there," she tells Beebe. "Don't you dare have that woman over here, you hear me? I don't want to find her on the sofa with you."

"What woman?"

"That Mrs. Testa."

Beebe's gray head hangs low with exhaustion, and she's ashamed of herself. "It's two in the morning," he says, as if she doesn't know it.

"Tomorrow's a school day," she says. "You planning to go? I can drive you over."

"I dropped out already. I ain't going back."

While she puts things away in her bedroom, she hears him scrabbling around in the kitchen like a big mouse. Except for the night Barbie and her twins stayed here, there has never been an overnight guest. What a solitary life she's led. Beebe had wanted to go back to the campground and sleep there, but she told him it was too cold, and now it's raining, too. Tomorrow spreads out blankly in front of her. How has she spent the off-season the last twenty or so years? Working on the *Belle,* when it was housed in her garage. She'd paint it and wax it and get it all nice. She'd researched duck boat history, piecing together what she thought was the tale of the *Belle*'s life: the boat had been to Italy, to Leyte. She and the boat were about the same age. She'd even written a booklet about duck boat history, illustrating it with photos of the *Belle* and selling photocopies of it for a dollar until she ran out. Oh, and she'd kept up with her training and certification and all of that, going to CPR classes at the high school and getting her boating and commercial-vehicle licenses renewed. Once she'd gone to a tourism seminar at the local Holiday Inn, paying an outrageous amount to attend programs with the words *marketing* or *leisure* in the titles. The presenters were eager, confident young people who spoke fast and laughed a lot at the beginning and end of their talks. In the middle, they were deadly earnest and passed out glossy notebooks with charts and favors inside: a bookmark, a pencil eraser. Seventy-five bucks for a bookmark and doughnuts and coffee and all the gab. Some of the advice about marketing was useful, though. She'd had brochures printed up, with a color picture of the *Belle* on the front, and she took them to restaurants and motels where tourists would see them.

Far more fun than that seminar was an actual duck boat convention she'd attended one time in Wisconsin, a duck boat hotbed. Operators from all over the country shared tips, stories, and advice. They swapped photos, anecdotes, and superstitions ("Never have thirteen on your boat"). A Coast Guard officer gave a slide show. A photography teacher from a local university spoke about how to take better pictures of your passengers when they handed you their camera. Louisa paid attention. Always have the sun behind you. Tell a joke or a riddle just before you press the button, to make them relax and laugh. *Why do gorillas have big fingers? 'Cuz they've got big nostrils.* Click!

She has taken thousands of photos of strangers, those happy vacationers with the lake as their background, maybe a child or two in front of them, sunglasses dark above their grins, their hair rakish from Hawk Lake's breezes.

Beebe's little brother, Bobby, had a camera. This comes back to her as she sits on her bed, too tired to undress. Bobby was the only passenger who ever took a picture of *her*. He did it after she explained about the hawk and the elusive king rail.

At the convention, Louisa had bragged about the *Belle,* flipped open her wallet to show pictures, listened to the other operators' stories, and had a wonderful time. That was where she'd bought the red cap that became her trademark on the water. You could get the name of your duck boat embroidered on the crown of the cap for only a few dollars extra, so she'd done that, watching the words *Arkansas Belle* appear in script on the vendor's machine. For a few years, Christmas cards had come from people she'd met there. Do they know what happened to her? Nobody talked about sinking and drowning at the convention. Of course she has thought about the possibility of it, all these years, the thoughts besieging her when she was grieving first for her mother, then Mr. Fiveash, then her father. Her feet would be firmly on the deck and she would imagine the boards giving way, swamping.

Yet she did not wear a life jacket. They were cumbersome. You could never get one to fit right. She never wore one. She felt safe on her *Belle.*

In a few days, Beebe will leave, and then she'll have to fight an endless off-season the rest of her life, without a boat in the garage to paint, without the return of spring to launch a new year of tours. Already, she's low on money. Except for a thousand dollars set aside for emergencies, she was never more than a few weeks' groceries ahead, anyway.

The thousand dollars should go to Beebe, for taking her to Boston. She can't bear to think what he has lost. She writes out a check and goes into the kitchen, where he's eating crackers.

"Here," she says.

He stares at it. "I can't take that."

"Please take it," she says, and he does. "Thank you for what you did for me. What'll you do back in Arab?"

"I might work for that lady who takes care of The Candles, the ones that sing."

"Who's been looking after your house down there?"

"I 'magine it's been let to other people by now. We owed right much back rent."

"Beebe," she says, "stay here at least till you get rested up. Stay as long as you want."

"Oh. Okay." He peers into the empty sleeve of crackers, palms the crumbs, and pops them into his mouth.

THE MAN LOOKS like a hunter, and that is what Katelynn wants. He has a hunter's rangy legs and back and the kind of squint you'd use to stare down the barrel of a gun. He just listens to her. She says, "Like I told you on the phone, this is for a friend—to help her find her baby."

"I understand," he says.

Katelynn is delighted. She got him out of the Yellow Pages, and he has driven here from Memphis, in a gray Oldsmobile parked outside her glass walls, the kind of car you'd never notice, a detective's invisible car. "I just picked out your name," she says. "I decided I couldn't find the baby on my own. The hospital where Louisa had it is gone. She never saw the child. That's how they did things back then." She speaks quietly. The nurse and the dietitian are close by, whispering in the kitchen. She will not let them know who he is. She made them bring her two breakfasts today: bacon, buckwheat pancakes, oatmeal, and orange slices. She ate it all and enjoyed it.

He just listens, doesn't write anything down. She likes his cowboy boots. She points out the window, at the lake. "You heard about the duck boat that sank. She was the captain. It was later that day, after she'd been underwater and almost drowned, that she decided to find her son."

"I understand," he says.

"You really do, don't you?" she says. "This is important to me, to help her, to balance out what happened. I've promised to help her look for him, but she doesn't know I've called you." She started to say "hired you," but is afraid that would somehow offend him.

The detective is listening, watching her face. Occasionally he glances beyond her, through the glass wall of the living room to the lake. She doesn't tell him she woke up in the middle of the night and never got back to sleep, from excitement, from a certainty that this man will find Louisa's son, that the son will love Louisa, that he will make up for the accident.

She wants him to find Harvey for her, too, to find him and ask him if he loves her. The silence from Harvey, his absence for more than a week, frightens her.

She has to focus on Louisa now, though, Louisa and the lost baby. She goes on, "I'll need proof, to know that it's not just anybody, that it really is her son. How much do I pay you, right now?"

He names a figure. It's the biggest check she's ever written, but she expected it would be. She signs her name and tears it from the checkbook. It feels good to be generous for Louisa's sake. "How long will it take?"

"No telling. Could be a few years," he says.

"That's too long." Her hand with the check hovers in the air like a Frisbee she's not ready to throw. "I can't—it's just . . ." Nobody has years to wait, but that would sound spoiled, and she's already aware of creating an impression: a rich young woman in a glass house, an odd-looking puppy slobbering at her feet. Giving in to panic, to temper, might scare him away. And if she dies, she dies. He must wonder what's wrong with her. He might have figured it out already, might have read her pallor and short hair and thinness like a banner headline about mercury poisoning. She is transparent, without secrets.

The man says, "He might not want to be found. He'd have an easier time of it, from his end, finding *her* if he wanted to, and he doesn't seem to have wanted to. He might not know he's adopted. Being contacted might cause disruption in his life that he doesn't exactly welcome. He might be a sort of person your friend'll wish she'd never found."

"I know." There's no sarcasm in his outdoors face with its hunter's eyes. She hands him the check. The thought of disrupting a stranger's life is so thrilling, she can hardly wait. She already knows from TV she might not see this detective or hear from him, for months. He might go underground (whatever that means) for weeks at a time, calling her at night from pay phones, talking behind a cupped hand. Her money will buy him coffee, eggs, and sausage at truck stops, it will pay the rent on a one-room office with a manual typewriter, a black rotary phone, and a single, unshaded bulb overhead, an office where he'll never be. Years from now, a stranger might fall into step with her on some dark, foreign street, and it will be this man.

His fingers brush hers as he takes the check: big, dry fingers, warm as paws, not like Harvey's wide, thin hands, webbed almost with string and muscle. He might know all about her. Let him, so she will never have to explain. That would be love: to have him come to her with the whole story already, so she'd never have to go through the telling. How as soon as Harvey poured it on the ground, she knew. No, sooner: go back to the silver drop falling onto the back of Jenelle's hand, back to the kiss they shared while she talked about Walter de la Mare.

"How did you start doing this?" she asks him. She has to lean back against the sofa cushions and speak slowly, hoarding her breath. "You must have been a cop. I mean a policeman." She knows that from TV, too. Or a bail bondsman, whatever that is—always, in the movies, detectives and bail bondsmen are just this side of the law, yet righteous. She tries to memorize his face. He might have to search forever, the money she gave him giving out.

"How'd I start doing this? I answered an ad in the paper," he says. She laughs a little, taking this for a joke—as if a man like this would flirt, as if he would flirt with her.

"There's something else," she says, "something for me, a place I'd like you to take me."

"What about . . . ?" He gestures toward the kitchen, where she knows the nurse and the dietitian are eavesdropping. But she ate two breakfasts today; she can outrun them if she has to, or she could if she could only catch her breath. "I know you've been sick," he says.

"We won't be gone long," she says.

For the first time, he smiles. "That always sounds like a lie."

LOUISA HAS NOT missed the hearing; she's just in time. Her lawyer says, "It's a Coast Guard board of inquiry. The National Transportation Safety Board will have reps here too. It's a hearing, not a trial, Louisa."

But what's the difference? Louisa will be accused, found guilty, probably sentenced right here in the Holiday Inn, the same place she came for that tourism seminar, years ago. The lawyer looks just the way Louisa imagined her, trim in a navy blue suit, a Yankee to the core, pronouncing all her final g's. She has a habit of nibbling at the inside of her lips, and she smells of wintergreen gum, though Louisa can't catch her actually chewing it.

"What do you call that bunch of men," Louisa asks, "the soldiers that stand in a line and shoot somebody?"

"Firing squad," the lawyer says.

"That's it."

"Louisa, listen to me: all you have to do is tell what happened. You're not charged with anything. Oh, they'll be tough with their questions. We went over that," the lawyer says, shoving her glasses up her short, wide little nose. She looks hardly older than Katelynn.

"Can I go see the boat?"

"It's impounded. I've already been to see it, while you were out of town." The lawyer glares. "I was allowed to look at it, but not touch it. It's a wreck, Louisa."

This is unbearable. "I still want to see it."

"It has been examined by the Coast Guard's own expert. He'll be here today, I imagine. I got an affidavit from that sick girl who said she's a friend of yours, the one who saw the sinking."

"Oh! Katelynn. I'd hoped she would be here."

"No need. Also I got a statement from Jerry Fiveash, who pulled you out of the water. Now, follow me."

Meekly, Louisa follows while the lawyer pokes her head into this conference room and that one, searching for the one where the hearings will be. Why, there's a cosmetics convention going on. A banner behind the speaker says so. Women in brilliantly colored silk suits are pumping their fists in the air and cheering, and the air smells of lipstick and perfume. Wouldn't this be the perfect career for Barbie? Louisa makes a mental note to suggest it, next time she sees her. "Well, not this room," her lawyer says, as if Louisa might be wondering.

Rugs are for sale in the next one, piles of Orientals that are probably way overpriced, judging from the cocksure expression on the salesman's face. "Help you, ladies?" he calls. There are no customers. Louisa's lawyer turns on her heel so fast she bumps into Louisa, saying in an offended voice, "They're fakes."

In the next conference room, the biggest of all, there's a sale of sewing machines. Louisa steps past the lawyer to stand inside the room and listen to the hum, the *ziggety, ziggety* sound of all the fancy machines. Women are going from one display to another, their husbands in tow. "Look how many men are here," Louisa says. She has to shout over the noise. "They realize this is an investment." She remembers the vendor at the duck boat convention who stitched *Arkansas Belle* on her red cap, the needle flashing in and out of the spongy red cloth, spelling out the words with white floss. "Look, a raffle," she says to her lawyer, and stoops over a table to fill out a ticket. She might win a Singer sewing machine that can do everything, according to the sign in front of it, even buttonholes. But aren't buttonholes old news? Her own mother, eventually, got a machine that could do buttonholes, long after the prom dress with the ruffled neckline. That dress had a side zipper, which her mother said was elegant. Why, there's Violet's voice, high and sweet, somehow reaching her through the din in the room: *Oh, Louisa, this dress will flatter your figure,* and Louisa hears the hope in her voice, that maddening hope that always made her want to cry— as if Louisa ever had a figure, as if a side zipper would change anybody's life. Teddy Shatford hadn't bothered with the zipper. He just yanked up the dress while the zipper bit into Louisa's skin.

The woman in charge of the raffle table says, "This machine can do featherstitching, hon, can hem velvet and velour. You need to get you one of these! Crunch up your ticket real good before you put it in the box. I always do that to make my ticket bigger."

Velvet and velour: even Louisa knows velvet and velour are hard to work with. "My mother said velvet was the worst thing to sew," Louisa tells the woman. "We didn't know about velour, back then."

The woman cries, "I can't live without velour, can you? Half the clothes in my closet's made out of velour." Louisa writes her name and address big and clear. She wants this machine. Wants to win. Without the boat, she'll have to fill up her days, and by golly, she'll be productive. She'll learn to sew—curtains, slacks? But somebody's jostling her so much she can't write.

"Come on, Louisa, we're late," the lawyer says, pulling her along. They leave the sewing-machine sale and step into the hallway, which feels almost like somebody's bedroom, it's such a narrow hallway, with pictures of flowers on the walls and a smell of talcum powder in the air.

"We must be in here," the lawyer says, pushing open a door into another huge conference room, but she's wrong again, and Louisa bursts out laughing, for they have walked into a cat show. There are kitties loose and kitties in cages, with judges holding cats up high, stretching them out to measure the tails, handing blue and red ribbons to the owners. The air is stingingly scented with cat urine and kitty shampoo.

"God," says the lawyer, "let me out of here. I can't breathe."

Louisa is delighted. She can't wait to tell Katelynn: *The air was all full of fur, and people were using litter boxes as ashtrays, stubbing out their cigarettes in 'em.*

At a line of booths, people are selling flea powder, brushes, scratching posts, hairball remedies, and fancy collars. "Need a teaser?"

asks a man with a falsetto voice. He holds up a wand with a feather on one end and drags the feather across the tip of his nose. "Kitties love these," he says knowingly. "It's only a dollar."

"I'll take it," Louisa says, paying, and the man beams at her. She stuffs the teaser in her pocket.

The lawyer shakes her head and turns on her heel, and all Louisa can do is follow her. They're back in the hall again, closing the door on the jollity of the cat show so that Louisa wonders if it's really behind that door after all, or if, when she opened it again, the room would be empty, just a silent, gray-carpeted cavern with fluorescent lights hanging from the ceiling.

"We must be in the wrong place," she says hopefully. "The hearing must've been canceled."

"Here we are," the lawyer says, pushing her glasses up her nose in front of a door bearing a sign that says COAST GUARD MEETING. She sails in without looking back. Louisa could run, she could bribe the rug salesman to roll her up in a carpet and hide her until it gets dark. But she follows her lawyer to a long table with a maroon-colored fabric skirt hanging from it and pitchers of ice water and bowls of mints on top, as if this is sort of a party, a cold, nervous party where you have to stay in your seat. She and her lawyer are the only women. Several men sit at another table, with their own supply of ice water and peppermints. She recognizes the uniform of the Coast Guard, but she does not know any of the men. Her stomach drops and she shivers, wishing she'd worn a sweater over her dress.

The bilge pump, the bilge alarm. Is that what she should talk about? She can't remember what the lawyer said. The lawyer showed up yesterday, the first morning Louisa was back, all business suit and black briefcase, took one look at Beebe sleeping on Louisa's sofa and shook her head, asking, "What's this? What's all this?" and Louisa tried to explain about wanting to find her son, about going to Boston. When Beebe woke up and she introduced him as the son of a survivor, the lawyer hustled Louisa into her car and out to the little store, where they sat in a corner, drinking coffee out of Styrofoam cups while the cashier, round-shouldered with excitement, sniffing suspense in the air, hovered over them with the coffeepot. The lawyer said, "You shouldn't be talking to that boy or having anything to do with him. Forget charity, for God's sake," and Louisa had said, "I like Beebe." She burned her tongue on the coffee, thinking there was almost nothing at home for Beebe to eat. She'll have to go shopping. The food the neighbors had brought, right after the sinking: what had happened to all those casseroles and cakes? That's what she tried to remember while the lawyer went over things with her. Some of the food she and Katelynn had taken to Beebe in the woods. Some of it had been eaten by Barbie and the twins. One of the twins had gouged a hole in a blackberry pie. Trying hard to follow the lawyer's words—*liability, negligence,* and *culpability*—she could only think about that pie.

If she's supposed to tell the truth, then she'll have to tell what happened when she was underwater, how she heard her father's voice say, "G'awn up that ladder," and she'd climbed up, up into the air, where Jerry saved her, Jerry whom she hadn't even recognized at first, for it had been some years since she'd seen him, and his hair was all wet. Should she tell, too, about Mr. Fiveash and his turtle and parrot, and Jerry the tiny grandbaby blinking in the sunshine of that sunroom, where the turtle and parrot vied to outlive each other among their melon rinds and seeds? For it all has bearing. The whole truth would take longer than life to tell. She'll have to tell all the stories that she told about the big lakeside houses where the rich people live, about all that she held back, the not-telling: *I didn't tell when they were on vacation. I was afraid they would get burgled. That girl in the glass house's father, Katelynn's father, he's hardly ever home. I never said that. Rich people go away a lot. I knew that woman and that girl were there by theirselves, and I didn't want anything happening to 'em.* That should matter to the Coast Guard, that she knew better than to tell. It won't make up for the deaths. Nothing will. They'll put her in the strongest jail so she won't break out and run off to Boston again. *I put a horse in a truck when nobody else could do it. There was this little carnival packing up to leave, and it was morning.* She'll have to tell about deciding to find her son. That hadn't happened underwater. It was later that day, in the evening, when Barbie and the sheriff were talking and eating cake in the kitchen. She'll tell about that, about how mad she was that they assumed she was alone in the world. She'll say: *You have to believe me when I say there were times I hardly thought about that baby all those years, and then all of a sudden, I wanted him. The wanting has taken over my life, that and the drownings are all tied up together.* Oh, there were moments in these long years when she thought of him. There used to be a TV commercial for cotton swabs that showed a mother swabbing bubbles out of a smiling baby's ear, the part of the ear that curls. That commercial was enough to silence her the rest of the day. Every Halloween, when children dressed as astronauts and goblins came trick-or-treating at her door, she wondered if her son might be under one of those masks, flipping a cape, happy with his sack of candy. It's hard not to think of him as little, even after all this time. It just took this life-altering event to activate the wanting that had been there all along.

What if she does find him, and he's the spitting image of Teddy Shatford?

She shakes her head, shaking that thought away. *Uh-uh.*

If she has to, she'll go all the way back to the prom. *I wanted my mother to be happy. That meant I had to go out with Teddy Shatford.*

"What baby, Louisa? There was no baby on the boat," her lawyer whispers, frowning. "What are you talking to yourself about?"

"My own baby," Louisa says. She's ready to talk. She could stand up behind the maroon-skirted table and talk all day.

"Oh, dear," the lawyer says, and Louisa wants to smack her. "Here we go," the lawyer says, as a man in the white uniform of the Coast Guard stands up and gestures to a flip chart.

The chart shows diagrams of duck boats. Louisa glances from the chart to the officer to the other men seated at the long table, thinking they look too pale. They need to get out in the sun. Do they have to work in offices all the time, instead of getting out on boats? The air is stale, the room has no windows, and the men won't look at her directly, only in sidelong glances. Accusation and awfulness are present in the room. Is there no place for love? She has loved so much since the sinking: that should count for something. She has loved not just the given-up baby and the lost *Belle,* but those drowned passengers, the fat man sinking so intently he might have meant to. Why didn't she call Katelynn and Jerry and beg them to come today, affidavits or no? Why didn't she bring Beebe? Maybe, as Katelynn watched Louisa's last moments on the deck of the *Belle,* or as Jerry rescued her in the cold water, they saw that Louisa Shepherd is able to love. If they were here today, in this freezing, hostile motel, they would say so.

She has loved, in retrospect, her whole life: her innocent mother, her hammering daddy, old Mr. Fiveash and his turtle and parrot, Jerry as a baby in the sunroom with his kindhearted, joyful parents, almost phantoms now in her memory. What had Mr. Fiveash seen in her the day he hired her? She was just a tired young woman, bumpy-haired and plain, who'd walked a long way from the bus station on a Saturday after tending nursing-home patients all week. She didn't have any halo of goodness around her head. Was she the only person to answer his ad? If no ad, then no *Belle,* for the events had progressed just that way.

Predestination, the preacher used to say, the Presbyterian preacher in the little church her parents took her to, with an echo in his voice of how grand and how terrible predestination was, so mixed together that you could not ever sort it out. Predestination: the preacher must have known something of it himself, to draw the word out in the air the way he did. It means you sin, and are forgiven. You sin, and you are damned. God picked her to be the woman who gloried in an old war boat, who got a career of many years out of it, only to come to this—freezing air-conditioning, mints. She'd rather the bodies were laid out in front of her, all honest and plain, for that's what this is about, isn't it?

That preacher loved baseball. Clear as a bell, she hears him say, in his ringing voice with hills and valleys in it, silence and softness and bellows, "You've got the Trinity on your side! Why, you're on the pitcher's mound all your life, and you got the Father, the Son, and the Holy Ghost at first, second, and third base, their love all around you, ready to do battle for you, a low-down ol' sinner! And who steps up to bat . . . but the devil. You got to strike out the devil." Here he drew back his arm and flung an imaginary ball to the congregation.

"I've got to strike out the devil," she tells her lawyer.

The young woman's head whips around. Her eyes bore into Louisa's. "I don't think I'd tell the Coast Guard that," she says.

The lawyer snaps open her briefcase and lifts out a box of Kleenex, the tiny size for children or travelers. The tissues inside will be the harsh, small kind that will burn your nose. The lawyer places the box near Louisa, rips out its cardboard center, and fluffs up a tissue— ready for Louisa to cry. Louisa imagines telling Katelynn: "I felt just plain paralyzed." Yes, she'll tell Katelynn about this. She'll live through it, even though right now she can't make sense of the words spoken by a bearded officer. His mouth moves but the words are just a jumble, as if his beard and mustache are trying to talk to each other. Katelynn will ask about her trip. It will matter to Katelynn about the tamales that Louisa learned to make, the carnivals they went to, the park up in Boston and the shops across from the park. She'll ask what Louisa and Beebe ate, the day they had lunch in Boston. It will matter to Katelynn that the Ethiopian food, though it looked funny, turned out to be terrific—a big soft pancake topped with dollops of eggplant, carrots, chicken, and lentils, which Louisa had never known could be a side dish and not just soup. Plus stewed onions, which tasted as good as the meat. *Unnn-yun,* that mean hospital roommate had said, way back then, testing out the word in her Massachusetts mouth, mocking Louisa. What kind of mother had that woman turned out to be? Would that be brought out today? Well, it should, Louisa wants to say.

Raggedy Andy is here. He steps through the door with his jumpy little walk, and he's wearing a gray suit with oversized shoulder pads, looking miserable. He should be back in his repair shop down at the lake, in his coveralls. He looks over at her and raises a hand as if to wave, but the hand doesn't make it that far. His stitched-on mouth quavers between a smile and tears. Hasn't she loved him, too, and doesn't that count for something, loved him the way a girl loves her little brother? He should not have to spend his day like this. His red hair needs combing. He didn't think of that, even though he is wearing a suit. He finds a seat at the long table. She knows he has never been to a place like this in his life, for any reason, not for a fancy hotel dinner nor a dance nor to look at Oriental rugs or sewing machines for sale, and certainly not for a Coast Guard hearing. The wide tie on his thin chest sports a sailboat. A boat. Raggedy Andy, what were you thinking? Is that your only tie? Oh, how Katelynn's face will work, how she'll laugh and gasp for breath, when she hears about the tie. Laugh until you cry—the saying was made for that poor girl. Louisa will tell this panel about that, if the Coast Guard men, so stern in their white uniforms, will let her. Raggedy Andy will let her. He will understand. His eyes seek hers so sweet, so scared.

And somebody else is coming in, with a flurry and a bustle: the fat man's wife. For a moment, Louisa feels sorry for her, because she looks uncertain about where to sit. Louisa felt that way every single day in high school at lunchtime, going into the lunchroom and wondering where to sit. That was how it was in Arkansas and again up in Maine, at Teddy Shatford's school—a lunchroom where every day she felt there was no right place for her and nobody to sit with. But Truman Testa's widow just sits herself down alone at a fresh long table and unwraps a peppermint. When her eyes meet Louisa's, they spit such fire that Louisa remembers the experience of sticking a fork into a toaster when she was a child. She expects the woman to run over and pummel her face again.

"Louisa," her lawyer hisses into her ear. "Louisa, go ahead."

The Coast Guard officer has stopped speaking. He's waiting for her to answer. They're all waiting. The box of rough Kleenex is wait-ing. Her lawyer clears her throat and says something, but Louisa is paralyzed.

There was a game they played when she was a kid: how to paralyze your arm. A friend would slap your palm, hard as she could, then roll up your fingers over the sting and squeeze your rolled fingers, count slowly to ten, and let go. Only then were you allowed to uncurl your fingers, which were stiff and gnarled, while your friend stroked the underside of your wrist—cold, by then, numb yet prickly—with her fingernails, asking with a sly, eager smile, "Well? Are you paralyzed? Now do me. It's my turn!"

It had almost worked.

THE DETECTIVE UNLOCKS the padlock with a key, explaining that this kind of key can open many locks. He goes in first, though not with gun drawn, as she had pictured. In fact, he doesn't have a gun, not vis-ibly, just a flashlight. What she notices first is how dark the warehouse is. The windows are overgrown with vines, and the air is heavy and stuffy. Mud daubers have built nests high in the corners, and they swoop and drone, disturbed.

"This is different from how it was," she says, "because it was March then, and the vines had died back. There was plenty of light to see by. I read 'mercury' on the side of that can. Harvey already knew it was there. He'd planned it."

The detective plays the flashlight over corners, ceiling, shelves. He makes a slow spinning motion with his arm, and she understands he's furling a cobweb.

"I was supposed to be somewhere else," she says, "because I'd won an essay contest. I was supposed to be at a dinner given by the D.A.R. Harvey pried the lid off the vat of mercury, and we started playing with it. Look—you can see where that vat was, that round place in the mid-dle of the dust."

Here's the exact spot where she sat, to dip her cigarette into the silver liquid, right here on this low table. She remembers brushing away a half-moon of dust before sitting down, lighting her cigarette and wishing Harvey would do that for her, the way men light her mother's cigarettes, but Harvey and Jenelle were kissing, leaning over the vat. She was thinking she could still get to the D.A.R. dinner if she rushed home, changed clothes, and drove fast as hell. The mercury-coated cigarette blazed in her lips as if she were eating a flare. She'd pictured the old ladies chewing baked chicken, corn-bread dressing, soft rice, and spiced apple rings on lettuce leaves. They would be furious at her, taking her absence as proof positive of young people's sinfulness, sloth, and rudeness; this would put an end to the essay contest for all future generations.

"That was when Harvey told me about his real life," she says, "that he'd already graduated from another high school and was older than everybody thought."

Where is he, the detective? The beam of his flashlight skews over rows of boxes, lumpy cartons that must contain neon-making equipment, but she can't see him until he's right beside her, like a shadow, like the outline of all the wayward people he's been able to locate.

"Who are you?" she says.

"Just somebody you hired to find a missing person."

"I want to know how you find people."

"Mostly I just listen."

"There has to be more to it than that."

"Sure there is, Katelynn. I deal in paper trails and family trees, debts and crimes and old bones. I have to figure people out. That's the challenge," he says. "We don't own this building. We should leave."

"That's how I've felt all my life," she says, her voice rising, the sound bouncing off the walls the way the drops of mercury did, when Harvey flung out his arms. "I think my father has left Mom and me," she says. "He's always making business trips to Myanmar, but this time, it just feels different. I wonder if he's coming back."

"Would you like me to find out for you?"

He is serious. He's not laughing at her.

"No," she says. "It makes me feel bad. I know Mom feels terrible."

"He might've been drawn to whatever is over there, in Burma. In Myanmar. He might not have been getting away so much as going to someplace else."

"Somebody else," she says, "some woman, you mean." This warehouse is a crystal ball and she's inside it with this savant. "Oh," she says, as the likelihood of her father's leaving sinks in and hurts. She wonders if the detective felt a vacuum as soon as he walked into her house.

"Katelynn," the detective says, "what do you want to accomplish right now, in this building? What did you want to come out here for?"

"Because the mercury changed my life. I can't undo that. I just wanted to go back to the beginning."

He doesn't say, "You have to move forward," and she likes him for that.

"I miss Jenelle. She died from mercury poisoning," she says.

He takes her arm and leads her to the door. Aware of his health and wholeness, she picks up his scent—denim and tangerines. She lets him lead her out the door.

Burma, meaning: a grass window in a glass house. Myanmar: I can erase myself. Land of bullocks, elephants, rain like spear points in your eyes. Or modern, with enough neon and noise and hashish to knock you over. She has read that restaurants in China have all the food on display for you to choose and eat, and it's all live: fish, jellyfish, snakes, cats, rats, and dogs. Barbarity. Burma is no different. And that's where her father is. What he chose.

"THIS DETECTIVE I've hired says he'll find your son. Louisa? Are you there?" Katelynn says into the phone. She's scared for Louisa, who bolted out of town and came back and faced that hearing. It was in the paper. The article gave Louisa's age: older than Katelynn knew.

"We can go out in the boat, Katelynn. Want to?" Louisa says, and Katelynn feels the hair on the back of her neck rise.

"But Louisa, your boat is gone."

"Honey, I know that. I mean the new one Jerry bought. He gave it to me. Can you believe how kind he is? That boat must've cost thousands, and he just handed me the keys and the papers. He's keeping it over at his house, for now."

"That boat! I saw it," says Katelynn, remembering Jerry and Dora on board, like giddy pirates.

"What else happened, while I was gone?" Louisa asks.

"That's exactly what Harvey asked me, when he came back," Katelynn says. "I told him about the boy who found that diamond last summer." She's telling Louisa all about Mr. Stiles and the time capsule when she looks up and sees Harvey lounging outside her glass walls, hands in his pockets.

"I BET I CALLED your number about a thousand times," the woman says, carting a box of record albums into Louisa's living room and setting it down on the coffee table with a loud sigh. "My granddaughter told me 'bout you. I always knew there was other Sam Moon fans out there besides me."

"I've been on a trip," Louisa says. "This is Beebe." The boy waves from the sofa.

"Like I told you on the phone, I won't sell these, no matter what my granddaughter told you. I'll just loan 'em to you. I know 'em all by heart." The woman's white pageboy hair has a touch of yellow, and Louisa imagines she's the cashmere blonde from the Shore Club, that long-ago northern beauty, who turned out to be the homespun type after all.

"I met him," Louisa says.

"So did I." The woman nods vigorously. "Some of these here covers got his autograph on 'em. Lord, what am I doing?"

"Thank you," says Louisa, thinking she herself wouldn't be this generous. "I'll be real careful with them. Whatever became of him?"

"Why, girl, he was on TV just last week, didn't you see him? He was on some special with that gal that does the talk show. *She* can't sing worth beans, but he's better than ever."

After the woman leaves, Louisa goes through the box, album by album. She doesn't own a record player, but as she holds the records in her hands and stares at the rapturous face on the cardboard covers, she can already hear his voice.

She digs money out of her pocketbook and hands it to Beebe. "Would you go buy me a record player? Not a new one. You can probably find one at a pawn shop."

"We had one in the trailer, an old crank-up kind," he says, but Louisa hardly hears him.

"WAS IT MY MOTHER, Harvey? Did she scare you off?"

"No," he says.

"Was it because I felt sick that day? I'm better. I really am."

"No."

"Then what, Harvey? Do you love me or not?"

They're lying on her bed, having made love. She knows it's the last time. As they kissed and rolled and explored, she'd thought of mercury droplets rolling into corners of the warehouse, lodging there, the rivulets running into all the shallow places in the dusty road, under the trees.

She rises up on her elbow and looks down at his face. "Why did you come here?"

"You're a sweet, sweet woman," he says, touching her hair. "I just loved Jenelle more. I ought never to have talked about us getting married. I got carried away."

"We're not ready," she agrees, fighting to stay calm. "We need to just spend days together, take our time. Maybe in a year or so—"

"No, Katelynn." Sitting up, he reaches for his shirt. "You're too good for me. I loved the way Jenelle was so damn bad. So mysterious."

"She wasn't! She was just mean, and she didn't care about anybody but herself."

"See, I liked that about her. You'd be after me all the time to be better than I am."

"Then why did we just . . . ?" She indicates the rumpled bed, their naked selves.

"Because I knew you wanted to," he says. "Look, Katelynn. I've got a job at this new formal-wear store that opened up, same kind of work I did before. Seeing people getting all hopeful about marriage, you can't help but think about it yourself. I would've married Jenelle and done the married student housing bit, for her."

"I thought you meant it, with me. I thought you loved me."

"I did, for a little while. I want to work on my career for now and, well, play the field. The lady who owns the store, I think she likes me. It makes me nervous."

They're silent for a long time. He says, "You knew it wouldn't work, Katelynn. Didn't you? We were just kinda playing."

"I wasn't."

While he dresses, she stares at the little temple maiden statuette. Take her ghost with you, she wants to say, take Jenelle's ghost out of here. It won't be so bad, if you just do that.

Louisa runs the feather end of the teaser along her arm, across her lips, and sneezes. Sam Moon is singing about heaven. She has the record player turned up as loud as it will go, so that Sam Moon's voice echoes through her bones. *Heaven, I'm in heaven . . .* Now she understands how kids can't get their music loud enough. What is heaven like? Isn't that the ultimate question. Will she go there?

"Probably not," she says, addressing the teaser, which looks just like a long pencil with a spring and a feather attached to one end.

A memory comes back. She's sixteen years old in Maine, at her grandmother's house, and her mother is telling her in a stifled half whisper about a terrifying phone call she received years earlier, before she met the man she would marry. A strange man had called for Violet by name and muttered obscene suggestions. Violet was upstairs, alone in the house. "Finally I said, 'I think you have the wrong Violet,' and I hung up on him," her mother said. "The war had just started, and you can't imagine . . ." Violet's eyes widened with fear, remembering the war, the phone call, the man's voice.

But Louisa can't be remembering right. There was no telephone in the house when she was there. Maybe her mother and grandmother used to have a phone, a big, heavy black one that would have sat on the dresser in the upstairs hallway, but gave it up. Louisa lays the teaser down on the coffee table, disturbed by the thought of her mother alone with an obscene phone call. She wishes she could go back to that time and say something to comfort Violet.

MR. STILES IS HERE, but he won't come in, just talks with her in her doorway, businesslike and swift. He has an offer for her, he says. She can forget the oral exam. If she makes a presentation to his senior class, it will count as a final. "Topic of your choosing," he says, "but if it's autobiographical, you must not in any way glamorize what you did. The incident with the mercury. You know how kids are. They'll look up to you for the wrong reasons."

"Not the boat, then, either."

"I'm doing you a favor, turning over my class to you for the entire period," he says, holding his cap in his hand in a way that reminds her of old-timey newsboys. There, leaning against the glass wall of her house, is his bicycle. It's evening, but the last of the sun is dark and hot on her cheeks, and it casts a slice of shadow across Mr. Stiles's face. She doesn't have to do a presentation for him. Colleges will take anybody these days, diploma or no. Probably all she needs to do is write her application essay about the mercury episode and the boat sinking, and some admissions committee, somewhere, will let her in. Maybe she should go directly to the backpacking-in-Europe stage that in the normal scheme of things would have followed her college years. That trip would have to be lengthy and somehow menial. It wears her out just to imagine it. You can't just fly everywhere and stay at hotels. That is uncool. Her money is a strike against her. She learned from Jenelle, who had older friends who'd been to Europe, that it's more authentic, more hip, to travel by oxcart or freight train and stay at the lowliest places until your money runs out.

The only traveling she has ever done was with her mother, to New York a few times. They went to plays, shopped, ate at wonderful restaurants, visited art galleries, and stayed at expensive hotels.

If she ever does get to Europe, maybe then she can get to Asia, to Myanmar. She'll show her father's picture to everyone she meets until she finds him: Have you seen this man?

Mr. Stiles waits in her doorway. Beneath the fur triangles of eyebrows, his eyes look so tired, and he still has to bicycle back to the school.

Throw your heart over the bar . . . Peppy leans against her legs. She picks him up and kisses the top of his warm head. He's heavier. How can he have grown so much in these few days? "So you're afraid I'll be a bad example to young, impressionable minds?" she says.

"I'm afraid of wasting time. My time," Mr. Stiles snaps. "You can do the presentation or not, Katelynn."

"I'll do it. Thank you," she says, meaning it. "Could I read my essay? The one I wrote for the D.A.R. contest?"

"Write me something new."

"DERN CHIGGERS." Sitting in her underwear, Dora dabs Chigarid on the welts on her skin. The potion smells like nail polish and menthol and leaves shiny circles over the red marks on her ankles, torso, and waist. "They even got my boobs." She peels off her bra and tosses it on the pile that includes her shoes, jeans, and T-shirt. Jerry turns away from her. This was a bad idea, his plan to camp overnight at this house with her and thus get more work done. They've worked all day, mowing high grass, cutting brush, pulling creeper off the sides of the house, pruning bushes. It's been hot and dry again, with no wind. Crop dusters have flown all day across the fields, looming low and loud out of nowhere, skimming over the neighboring acres, barely avoiding the power lines. They are dusting the county's fertile acres, crisscrossing the farmland on every side of Jerry's patch of land. They are known to die young, those pilots, for it's a dangerous job.

Now it's evening. In the back of his truck, he has two small tents and four plastic jugs of water. "We're going back. Staying out here would be stupid," he says, without looking at her. "Come on."

"What if I don't? It's great here, being able to strip naked in the front yard. Here, put some of this Chigarid on my back. I can't reach all the bites."

"Dora," he says and faces her. Methodically, she applies the medicine to her thighs and the tops of her feet. Jerry looks at her levelly and says, "Dora, I don't want to get involved with you. If you don't get dressed, you're fired."

A patch of ruined skin, like a jellyfish clinging to one of her shoulders, catches his eye. She pats it and says, "That happened the first time I got drunk. I fell asleep against a radiator. A person usually has to be older to be that dumb. That was the last time I ever got that drunk." She puts the stopper back in the bottle and turns the cap, her big breasts bouncing on her knees as she leans forward. She scratches her knees, then scratches the brick-colored nipples on her huge, droopy breasts, and claws at her scaly ankles. Jerry feels a sharp itch beneath the waistband of his jeans.

"Damn," he says. "I got 'em too. How'd that happen? We used Off."

Dora laughs and holds out the bottle of medicine. Another crop duster flies over. Dora cocks her head, listening, staring up at it, and then she stands up and runs out to the dirt road, waving at the plane, arching her back and waving at the sky.

"Hey, hey! What are you . . ." says Jerry. He can't get over her. The pilot will see a naked woman flagging him down and think she's in some kind of trouble. "Dora!"

Just as suddenly, the plane is gone. Dora sighs and strolls back to the house. "I think he waved back at me," she says. "He's the last one. The others musta all went home." She puts her clothes back on.

He takes her to a steak restaurant for dinner. Why? Why not just cart her on back to Hawk Lake? Glo has a yoga class that goes late. He can be home in time if she calls. The restaurant is in an old cotton town near his property. It faces the railroad tracks. The ceiling is made of pressed tin. On the walls hang photos from past decades—there's a sepia picture of the town in its heyday, with bales of cotton waiting to be loaded on railroad cars, and horses and wagons lined up right outside this very building, which was a feed-and-seed store back then. A black-and-white photo shows members of the local Ruritan Club from fifty and sixty years ago: young men and middle-aged men, but their features are of some species that aged faster, so that they all somehow look old and dignified, bearing the burdens of hard work, prosperity, reputation. All are white. A few black people do appear in the cotton photo, rawboned and raggedy, men hefting bales, a woman in head scarf and apron standing half in shadow beneath the awning of the store, a barefoot child at her side.

Scratching her thighs through her jeans, Dora picks at the polyurethane varnish on the oak surface of their table. The waitress brings a crock of port-wine cheese and a basket of crackers. The air-conditioning is much too cold, but at least it ices down the fiery chigger bites on his skin. A hornet got him, too, on one hand, which is so swollen you can't see the bones, knuckles, or veins on the back of that hand. Dora is silent, and he wishes he hadn't done any of this, not the plan of the overnight trip, which to her would have seemed a promise of sex, nor this meal at a restaurant that might, somehow, embarrass her, for the steaks are expensive. At a table in the corner sits a group of out-of-towners, from the looks of their black shirts and black jeans.

The other diners are farmers, hunters, and the Young Turks of the tiny town—lawyers, doctors, and their debutante wives, boisterous at long tables. Blondes and brunettes outfitted in clothes and jewelry worth comfortable stock portfolios, the wives laugh through rosy, perfect lips. Do they ever stop laughing? Jerry knows their story as surely as if it were spelled out on the walls. They all went to Arkansas or Ole Miss, belonged to the best sororities, competed in beauty pageants, found husbands among the planters' sons who still rule the campus, patrician boys and the occasional bumpkin who might outrank the genteel ones. The men at the table are of both types, the handsome, high-cheeked aristocrats and the heavy-browed, lumpier sort who is no less courtly toward women, who might be seen by the girls' mothers as a good catch, a family man, "a boy with possibilities."

Glo is more beautiful than any of these women. When she dresses up, she wears flowered dresses, high heels, no hose. The flowered dresses are sexy because they're almost dowdy, they're loose and made of cotton.

Two of the women rise from their table and brush against the back of Jerry's chair on their way to the ladies' room. He catches their lilting, flirtatious apologies and a flurried scent of cologne.

Dora glances at them and says scornfully, "They went to college for their M.R.S. degree."

"Not so loud," he says. He remembers his father telling him how much money there is in this town, never mind that the population is only two or three thousand. It's old money, cotton money invested a century and a half ago and compounded into gazillions. Studying the menu, he wonders: *Who am I? Just a small-town hippie who might or might not be mistaken for a musician, who has not done anything except fix up a few old houses and sell them for a small profit.* He has enough money to do something great, greater than just the purchase of the new boat for Louisa. He must be a lazy man, or a wicked one, that he has never done anything truly worthwhile with it. He loves to watch other people working. Of course, he enjoys work himself. It's just that the sight of others toiling, laboring, has always delighted him. That's what's inspiring about Dora. Those women at the next table—do they work or spend their lives shopping, planning dinner parties, painting their nails for evenings such as this?

"Y'all ready to order?" the waitress asks. "What do you want on your baked potato, hon?" she asks Dora.

"I want it loaded," says Dora, her eyes on Jerry's.

The two beautiful wives come out of the restroom and sashay back to their table. Jerry watches their hips. He can't help it. But they're not Glo. She has some quality they'll never have, some desperation that draws him. That's what he noticed the first time he saw her, carrying groceries to her car at the lakeside convenience store, her head down, like someone in the throes of an awful decision, gathering her resolve. He asked her, "Is there any chance you'd go out with me sometime?" Her head snapped up, her hand with its wedding ring flying to her mouth, but then she smiled.

One of the women pauses by Jerry and Dora's table and leans down, her cranberry dress tight across her breasts, her long curls brushing Jerry's arm. Her smile is meant for fashion runways. He smells olives on her breath. She points an enameled fingernail toward the black-clad people at the corner table and confides, "Y'all know who they are? Movie folks! They're shooting a movie right here in our town. If you want to be in it, just go talk to 'em. Mary Grace and I got little bit parts. They've rented out my mother-in-law's house and they're paying her a *mint*." She slips back to her seat, leaving a cloud of her perfume around his head.

Dora's brow beetles as she stabs at her salad. He guesses this is not good news, and that movies are as bad as casinos.

"I TALKED ABOUT that tree frog," Louisa says. "They musta thought I'd lost my mind. Every time I tried to talk about the boat, I went back to that frog I heard in the Christmas tree when I was a little girl, the way it musta been hibernating and woke up in the warm room, cheep-cheep-cheeping."

"It says here," Katelynn says, thumping the newspaper, "that a seal over the boat's drive shaft was found to be dislocated on a rear axle. I can't picture that. But the paper says that was how water got into the hull. It says this came out at the hearing." Katelynn holds the paper close to her face to read. "And part of the bilge-pump hose had separated, so it couldn't operate efficiently."

"That's what the inspectors found out. I learned all that for the first time at the hearing. Raggedy Andy pointed at a big diagram of the boat. He cried. My lawyer was horrible to him. I fired her. Have I told you about Andy, Katelynn? My mechanic. He's so sweet, and he's blaming himself."

"But there's more about a pump," Katelynn says, squinting through her dark glasses, clutching the paper with her thin white hands. "There was no alarm connected to the bilge pump like there should have been. The Coast Guard said the alarm did not need their approval before being installed. Instead, it says here, you planned to install it the next time the boat was in the repair shop. Oh, Louisa, for want of a nail, the kingdom was lost."

Louisa says, "What kingdom? Heaven?" She stares at the blind-looking girl in front of her, who is chewing a Tootsie Roll and petting her funny-looking puppy with all-different-colored fur. "I was mistaken about that alarm needing to be okayed before it was installed. I told Andy not to hook it up till they'd approved it."

Katelynn sighs. "Whether or not that alarm thing was hooked up wouldn't have made that much difference. The boat had more than one fatal flaw. It took on water fast and sank in about thirty seconds. I saw it happen, remember? You didn't have a chance, Louisa. Now everybody knows that."

"Oh, I don't know." Louisa is exhausted. She hopes Katelynn won't insist that she, Louisa, did nothing wrong. That would take more energy than Louisa has. The *Belle* was like a human body. You can look after all your parts and pieces and think you're A-OK, and then something quits or comes loose, and you're done for.

Katelynn won't stop. "The Coast Guard said the mechanic was at fault. Sounds like it was more his fault than yours."

"It wasn't Andy's fault. I said so at the hearing. Besides, he never had a repair manual for the *Belle*. They haven't printed them for fifty years." It hurts Louisa to think that the *Belle* was old. Her lawyer had used that word. *An old, antiquated vessel.* She has too much on her mind. She needs to think about the man who sold her the teaser, or the Swede she read about in the paper who ate an electric drill. Her toes curl, her foot tingles, her calf muscle tightens in the old, familiar way, and she's not even lying in bed, she's sitting on the little bench in front of Katelynn's vanity, staring out at the lake that she navigated for so many years. "Leg cramp," she gasps, as the pain seizes her whole leg.

"That means you have a potassium shortage," says Katelynn. "Hang on, I'll get you a banana. That'll cure it."

The pain is easing by the time Katelynn gets back, and Louisa is massaging her leg, weak, washed out. She bites into the banana. She should have known about the drive shaft and the bilge pump the second there was trouble. The duck boat was an extension of her own self, and it was not supposed to have mysteries, to falter. Dr. Morton, the psychiatrist, had showed up at the hearing and read his report about the hypnosis session, a bunch of technical-sounding gibberish that nonetheless seemed to count in her favor. She still has a wrongful-death suit against her, filed by Truman Testa's widow, and there may be more to come. The lawyer warned her of that. Raggedy Andy not only blamed himself, he cried. Next to the deaths, that's the worst part.

What would her father say, he who spoke to her underwater and made her climb up that ladder? She was with him when he died, in that old trailer. He'd never had much. Toward the end, he didn't want much, just his cats and a glass of cool water. A county nurse would come around every so often, but mostly it was Louisa he relied on. She drove over to Yellville once a week and stayed two or three days, never mind that it meant canceling tours in the middle of the season. He was proud, wouldn't talk about his illness or how he was feeling, didn't want her making doctor appointments for him and taking him to clinics or hospitals. The visiting nurse brought a portable oxygen tank, but he wouldn't use it. From Louisa's own nursing background, she knew he didn't have much time left.

He hated the word *cancer* and refused to say it. "They can dang well say I died of old age," he said, meaning doctors, or the newspaper.

"You're not that old," she said.

"I miss your mother. My Violet."

"I miss her too." Tears stung Louisa's eyes, and she turned away, for it seemed her mother appeared before her, her face dreamy, her fingers fluffing the ruffles of the abominable dress. Once, when Louisa was grown, Violet had told her, "I've always found it so easy to love you and your father," and Louisa took the remark as a criticism, knowing she had failed the test of wifehood and motherhood. Now she thinks how many years have gone by since Violet died of heart failure, and the pure sweetness of her mother's remark strikes shame into her, for she knows it was true: her mother loved easily, all her life.

Louisa's leg cramp is gone. She finishes the banana and throws the peel in a wastebasket. She wants to ask Katelynn about that little Oriental statue, but Katelynn slips out of the room. Louisa is free to gaze out the glass wall to the lake and remember.

Her father had never been a cat person when Louisa was growing up, but toward the end of his life, he took in two sly little strays and loved them probably as much as he'd ever loved anyone or anything. The cats slept on the bed with him, the narrow bed in the trailer that was hardly bigger than a closet and smelled of kerosene, coffee, and worn-out clothes in need of washing. On the last day of his life, the sun shone through the ruby-streaked flowers of the trumpet vine that wound in through the window, and Louisa smelled paint from the cans stacked outside the trailer, paint he'd used on his handyman jobs. She let the cats outside to do their business. Her father's hands picked and patted at the coverlet on his bed, and she realized he was searching for the warm furry bodies. Stepping outside, she called, but they didn't come. They were off hunting in the tall, whispery grass. Red-winged blackbirds dipped over the meadow, crying, *Kong-ka-ree!* The trailer seemed so dim when she went back inside, so quiet and full of waiting. It was morning. She was stiff from sleeping in a sleeping bag on the floor.

"It's so hot, the devil musta just run through here," her father complained, kicking off his covers with surprising strength.

It wasn't that hot, but she found an electric fan, plugged it in, and turned it so the breeze blew on his face. He closed his eyes. She knew he had about five minutes left in this world. She leaned over the bed and cradled his hard old whiskery head in her arms.

He said, "I'm so sorry that happened to you, Louisa," as if they'd been talking, all these years, about Teddy Shatford and the baby.

"S'all right," she said. She wondered if he still thought about his dead son, the little boy who had rolled down the Ozark ravine.

His hands picked at the covers, searching for cats. His last words were "Where are they, anyway?"

THE CANDLES ARE COMING, the anorexic gospel-rock singers who are cared for, managed, and promoted by Beebe's neighbor-lady back in Arab, Alabama. For Beebe's sake, they'll perform at Hawk Lake High School, will sing hymns about healing and deliverance, their manager is quoted in the paper as saying: ". . . so that the sorrow of the sunken duck boat will be expunged. The Candles will throw a party for God." The manager will not be coming, because she has broken her toe. The Candles will travel to Hawk Lake by themselves, and Beebe will be in charge. Their performance will be a benefit concert for him.

Katelynn helps by selling tickets to Mr. Stiles's classes. Mr. Stiles lets her come in and sit on his desk. He even helps her sell the tickets, fast, faster, the boys and girls pressing cash into his hands and Katelynn's hands. Everybody wants to go to the concert, which will be recorded live and sold on CD. The Candles are sought after, beloved. The papers say that men and women have forsaken their families to follow them. Admirers have been known to mob their front lawn in Arab, holding aloft Mason jars full of fireflies, The Candles' emblem.

"I love The Candles. I love it when they sing about the end of the world," a girl with tattooed fingers announces, tears coursing down her face, pushing her way through the crowd to the desk where Katelynn and Mr. Stiles sit. "I've waited all my life to see them. My mom, the bitch, won't let me go anywhere. It's like an answer to a prayer, that they're coming to me."

"I'm all out of tickets," Katelynn says, spreading her empty hands. "Just sold the last one."

"Me too," says Mr. Stiles.

The girl's mouth pops open. This is the senior class, and Katelynn should remember these kids, but she does not. The girl says, "But I have to have a ticket." The kids behind her clamor, "We're coming anyway." They press toward Katelynn, their faces avid, hostile. "It's an outdoor concert. Why don't you have more tickets?"

"Sorry," Katelynn says, shrinking from them, scooting back on the desk.

"Limited tickets equal more mystique for The Candles," says Mr. Stiles, sounding amused.

"Fuck the tickets," the girl says.

The last bell of the day rings. The girl stomps her foot and wails, but she leaves, and the others follow. For ten minutes, kids stampede through the hallways. Lockers clang so much louder than Katelynn remembers. This is a rougher bunch of kids than her class ever was. Even the silence they leave, when the rush in the hallway is over, is harsher, more temporary. She and Mr. Stiles are alone. He erases the chalkboard, sneezing from the dust.

"I was supposed to get one of those dry-erase boards this year, the white kind you use with Magic Markers," he says. "It didn't happen."

"I was never like that. Like them," she says, gesturing toward the hallway. "And even if I'd been around in the sixties, and the Beatles came to town, I wouldn't have screamed and fainted for them."

"Who would you scream for? There has to be somebody."

He dusts off his hands. In a couple of hours, he'll be sitting in the home ec suite, laying the table for one, cooking his supper. She says, "You can't go on like this, living here, hiding away from the world."

"Where's Harvey these days? Did you and Harvey decide not to tie the knot after all, Katelynn? Maybe he'll turn up in next year's freshman class."

"I love somebody else now," she says, stung. "A private eye." Saying it makes it true, though she can't picture his face, only his arms like slow windmills in the warehouse, as he moved through cobwebs.

Energetically, Mr. Stiles gathers up all the money, tens and twenties, ones and fives, into a big, soft-looking green pile in his arms and climbs onto the top of the desk. "Watch this," he says and throws the money up toward the ceiling. The bills float down softly, landing on his head, Katelynn's shoulders, the floor, and the long air-conditioning unit along the wall, where cool rising air keeps a few of them aloft and spinning.

"I have to go," says Katelynn, but she doesn't move. The dancing, airborne bills are mesmerizing. "My mother drove me here. She's waiting in the car."

She turns and scoops up the bills, peeling them off the floor.

"Not enough of this money was earned," Mr. Stiles says. "Most of this is just allowance. When I was their age, I had a paper route. I had aspirations. When grown-ups asked me what I wanted to be, I used to say, 'a dignitary.' Here." He hands her a wad of the money, and she stuffs it in her jeans.

"This money's for that boy that's staying with Louisa. Did you know that? Beebe, the one whose family drowned. He doesn't have anything," she says. One bill is still caught in the updraft of the air conditioner. She goes and plucks it out of the air.

"It doesn't get any easier, Katelynn," says Mr. Stiles.

"Don't say that," she says, turning and walking out the door.

• • •

GRATING A CARROT onto a bowl of lettuce for a salad, Louisa thinks, *I should have done this for him, my baby: carrots to make his eyes bright.* Putting a load of laundry in the washing machine, she thinks, *I should have washed his diapers and his little clothes. He's had a lifetime of shirts and pants and sheets by now, none washed by his mother.* Tears come then, in a peppery flood, tears for the apartness, and she blots her eyes with a corner of a pillowcase. Why has her family had such a hard time holding on to their little boys? First her brother and then her own son.

"Louisa? Where are you?" Barbie has let herself in and is yoo-hooing through the house. Louisa closes the lid on the washing machine and hurries into the living room.

"What's this?" Barbie asks, picking up the teaser from Louisa's coffee table and running the feather over her hand. "Never mind," she says and tosses the teaser away from her. "I just came by to get my Tupperware. From, you know, that day it happened. I brought you potato salad, remember, in a Tupperware bowl. I want it back."

Louisa leads Barbie into the kitchen and opens the cupboards wide. She wants only to think about the baby and listen to the Sam Moon records. She doesn't recognize the jumble of greasy containers in her cupboard.

"It's in here somewhere. Barbie, I'm sorry about getting out of your car the day of that memorial service." The day comes back to Louisa in bits and pieces—the bowl haircuts she gave the twins, the issue of *People* with her prom picture in it. She must have hurt Barbie's feelings. "Where are the twins?"

"I have a new friend. She's baby-sitting the kids for me. She knows friendship is a two-way street." Barbie buries her head in the kitchen cabinet and burrows through stacks of containers, emerging with a blue plastic bowl. "Here it is. It's all sticky. Didn't you even wash this stuff?"

"I thought I did. I don't remember."

"That's exactly what Stella said you would say, that you don't remember a thing. Very convenient." She holds the Tupperware bowl in front of her breasts like a squirrel gripping a prize nut.

"Who is Stella?"

Barbie exhales in disgust. "You don't even recognize her name, do you? Stella Testa, whose husband died on the boat. The one you told to move over."

"Oh! Her. The one who beat me up."

"She's moving here. She sold their house in Tenafly, New Jersey," says Barbie, in the tone of someone who has won an argument so completely, they wonder why they're bothering to keep on talking. "She got her husband's life insurance money, and she's opened up a wedding-gown store right here in Hawk Lake."

"Is she sure she can make a go of something like that?"

"I'm helping her. I'm working at the store."

"Why did she say I wouldn't remember whether I washed the dishes?"

"Forget the dishes, Louisa," Barbie says, and Louisa realizes Barbie's storing this up to tell Stella. "She said you claimed you'd told all those people about life jackets, but she can swear you didn't. You should go to jail, Stella says. If you could only see her pain, Louisa. If you had done something, anything!"

"I told her I was sorry at the hearing," Louisa says. "I can't begin to say how sorry I am. Some people have lots of words. I don't, but I have feelings." She pictures Stella at the hearing, a severe presence gliding toward a bowl of peppermints, and right after the sinking, hysterical, striking Louisa's face over and over. Barbie's cheeks are red in the center, white at the edges, as if she too will hit Louisa.

"Sorry isn't enough. This has changed me, Louisa." Barbie clutches the Tupperware bowl so hard Louisa expects her fingers to puncture it. She strides into the living room. Louisa follows her. Barbie says, "I teach my children lessons every day that I've learned about this, about you. I was going along, just a happy, modern wife and mother, taking everything for granted, thinking the best of people, going out of my way for everybody, just a little Pollyanna, and now I see how dark the world is, how full of evil." Barbie's glance falls on the stack of Sam Moon albums. "Evil happens when people don't do enough, when they don't warn people on boats to put on life jackets, for Pete's sake, even when there's kids on board, and then they just go on with their lives, listening to records, collecting little pencils with feathers on the end."

"That's from a cat show. It's not a pencil. And the music, well, a long time ago, I met that singer."

"I'm teaching Sunday school now," Barbie says. "Every Sunday, the kids in my class want to talk about you. This has shaken up what they know about right and wrong. Don't say it was just an accident."

"Then what was it?" Louisa's gaze falls on the keys on her coffee table, the keys Jerry Fiveash gave her: keys to the new boat. She could pick them up, hand them to Barbie, say: *For Stella,* and maybe Barbie would forgive her. But she doesn't.

Barbie shakes her head and looks around the room. "Where's that weird boy? Beebe?"

"We ran out of crackers. He went to buy some."

"Stella kinda likes him," Barbie says. A playful expression, naughty and impish, flashes across her face. "Her life will work out," she says. "Who's the strongest person you've ever known, Louisa?"

"Well, my daddy was real strong, and my mama. In different ways. And Jerry, who saved my life and then saved your friend. And that girl—Katelynn Troy. Do you know her, Barbie? She's strong. You might not think so, to look at her."

"I know *about* her, about the mercury. I have no interest in getting to know any juvenile delinquents." Barbie belches so softly it's almost a whisper. "Stella and I talk about God all the time. We wonder, if He saved her by lifting her out of the water, like she says He did, then does that mean He held her husband down?"

"I saw a ladder underwater, Barbie, but it seemed like my daddy put it there. I wasn't thinking about God," Louisa says.

"You jumped out of the car before we got to the memorial service, and you missed the party that Glo Troy gave," Barbie says. "That's where everybody was talking about this. Talking about God. I can't stop thinking about it; God was reaching down with his arms that day, pulling some up and pushing others down in the water. It was Judgment Day, Louisa."

"Then why did I get out?"

Barbie is looking past her, her eyes full of fear and something else, like glory. "Stella's already been through Judgment Day, and we talk about what it'll be like for me, when my time comes. Her shop is beautiful. She's hired a guy who knows the business. He used to sell tuxedos."

AFTER BARBIE LEAVES, a memory comes back to Louisa, or maybe it's just a dream. She's four or five years old and her father has taken her hunting with him, only because she begged and teased to go. They're in a stand of flooded timber, waiting for ducks. She's perched up in a cypress tree at shoulder level with him. He's in his hip waders with the gun in his arms, and it's early morning, still dark out, and she understands that all they have to do is wait, that the ducks will come. She must have slept while he brought her here, holding her above the water to keep her dry. The tea-colored water looks deep and still, between the tall trees. Her father stands so still she thinks he must be sleeping, with the gun in his arms.

She blinks, breathes, and smells the swampy water, scented by a million years' fallen leaves.

She figures it out, then, figures out that they have come to kill birds. She must have known this before, but she didn't understand it. Now she does. Her father has talked about a trip he took to Louisiana with a cousin of his, a trip that involved something called white-rag hunting. He and the cousin put white rags out in a flat field at dawn to lure the geese, for the rags would look like geese, and the men lay down and waited for real geese to come. Louisa and her mother had listened to this, and Louisa had laughed. It struck her as funny, her daddy and another grown man putting white rags on the ground.

Violet disapproved, because the trip cost money they didn't have. The geese the men had shot had all been eaten in Louisiana. "They was good, Violet," her father said with a chuckle. *Violent.*

Shot, killed, dead, eaten. She puts it all together then and wonders why she'd laughed. She loves birds, all animals. She has got to tell the birds to stay away.

In her tree perch, she opens her mouth and draws air in, packs it in deep in her lungs, picturing a woman who sings in church, a pigeon-breasted soloist with fancy high hair and a red dress, who packs air in and lets it out in song. Louisa tilts her head back and screams. She screams and knows they hear her, the great flocks of ducks winging their way through the darkness, teal and mallard, black duck and redhead; they hear her and they turn back. Her father cries, "Louisa, Louisa!" And pulls her out of the tree, asking what was it, did a snake bite her.

She's at home, now, in her own kitchen, staring into the cabinets, her throat sore from the very memory of that scream, her heart knocking, beating hard as a window slamming down, over and over.

Louisa would do it again. Scream and warn the birds away.

HE HAS DREAMED of this—showing Glo the house. She walks through it gingerly, as if afraid of brushing the walls or door frames with her shoulder. Now and then, she touches something with her fingertip. "It won't pass any white-glove test," he tells her.

"It's not like I expected," she says, slipping out of his arms when he reaches for her.

"There's the grass," he says, "outside. We brought a blanket, remember?"

He feels like a truant, a bad influence on her. He had suggested they bring Katelynn, but Glo refused with an are-you-crazy look.

He leads her outside, seeing the property through her eyes: derelict, isolated, lost. From far off, a rooster crows. Cotton shines whitely in the field beside them, hot in the late fall sun. There was that heavy rain the day of the memorial service. Even with that, he can't remember a longer, hotter autumn, the grass burned to thistles all over the Delta.

"Glo," he says. "Your daughter's almost grown, and she's almost well. Your husband doesn't seem to want to be around very much. You're at a point where you can decide what you want to do. Be with me."

"I am with you," she snaps, staring across the cottonfield as if it's a battlefield or a storm at sea. She turns to him. They've had sex exactly once since the boat sank.

"Glo, it wouldn't be impossible to track your husband down in Burma or wherever the hell he is, and have it out with him. I could go with you."

"Katelynn misses him, but I don't. I'm still waiting for all that quiet to end, all the quiet in my marriage."

"What about me, Glo?" When she doesn't answer, he says, "Do you want me to take you home and not bother you anymore?"

"All I want to do is read." She climbs into the bed of the truck, spreads the blanket, and lies down with a book.

He sighs and heads to the barn for a lawn mower he stores there. Amazing how fast grass grows here, even with the sun beating it down into straw. He should insist Glo go somewhere with him. The weekend in New Orleans wasn't enough. Glo went to Europe after college. He's never been overseas, just down to the Gulf Coast a few times, to California once, and he was glad to get home.

"Hey, mister. Mister, wait, I got to talk to you," a man is calling.

Jerry looks up. A man is loping toward him across the cottonfield, a young man with his face tanned the dark orange of sweet-potato flesh beneath a billed cap. He holds his arms straight out from his sides and says, "This is me, most of the time. Birdman!"

A crazy, but Jerry puts out his hand, and the man shakes it, catching his breath.

"That woman," the man says. "That woman you were with. Who is she? She your wife?"

Over the man's shoulder, Jerry sees Glo's head rise above the truck bed. The man goes on, "Because I have to meet that woman. The way she ran out, nekkid, when I was flying my plane over here. I 'bout crashed when I saw her. I can't get her out of my mind. I live over there." He jerks his thumb behind him. "Behind the old school. My truck's broke down today, so when I saw you drive by, I just set out after you. Hope you don't mind. If she's your wife, you've got a mighty pretty one."

"That was Dora," Jerry says. Glo's head vanishes. "She works for me."

"The day I saw her was the day I quit dusting," the man says. "Nobody lives real long in that line of work. I saw her, and it changed my life." He pauses. "She's not your wife? Not your girlfriend?"

"No. Dora's—a neighbor, and she helps me out."

The man is young, but young like the tired gravediggers in the old black-and-white picture in the album Jerry found. "Is she comin' back anytime soon?" he says. "I'd like to meet her, proper, if you wouldn't mind."

"I don't mind." If Glo starts laughing, over there in the truck, he'll never forgive her. "She'll be out here again. She lives up at Hawk Lake."

The man is digging in his pockets. He pulls out a pen and a scrap of paper and scrawls a few words on it. "Would you give her this for me?"

Jerry reads the paper. Hoyt Landry. A phone number, and the words "Marry me."

"I don't know that Dora's ready to marry anybody just yet. She's only eighteen," Jerry says.

"And got loads of guys after her, I'm sure," the man says. "She's not just gorgeous, she's interesting. I can tell. Even that thing wrong with her, that burn or whatever it is on her shoulder, that's special. She's got a mind on her."

"What'll you do now that you quit your job?"

"Wouldn'ta been much work till springtime, anyhow," the man says, "so I'll do what I always done. Farm a little, help out my brother.

Help the other dusters fix their planes. Plant the winter wheat." He gazes over the cottonfield. "This land ain't mine. There's some rich folks around here, but I ain't one of 'em."

After the man leaves, Jerry goes to the back of his truck and finds Glo with her book facedown on her chest. She sits up when she sees him.

"I'm not going back to Hawk Lake," she says. "I'm staying here, but I want to be by myself for a while. Just so I can quit seeing that boat sink."

"Want me to get Katelynn to pack up some clothes for you?"

"No." She stares across the field where the man went. "It'll be really, truly dark out here at night, won't it." She is silent for a moment. "The happiest I ever was, was when I was a teenager and just starting to go out on dates. I'd be upstairs, and I'd know my date was down-stairs, and those were the best moments of my life. Nothing has come close to that, not being married or having a child."

"What about me?"

"You *are* the closest thing, Jerry." She frowns at him steadily, as if seeing him for the first time in a long while.

Across the field, Hoyt Landry is a retreating doll, a blown leaf. Jerry won't give up. "I'll go into town and bring you some groceries," he says. "Just how long do you think you'll want to stay? Don't you think you'll want company, after a day or two? There's no phone out here, Glo. No water, no electricity. I'll call Katelynn from town and have her drive your car down here, then I'll take her back in the truck. You've got to have a car."

"She's still not supposed to drive, and I don't need a car. Just bring me some bottled water and some good things to eat."

"This place has that effect on people," Jerry says. "I didn't think you'd like it quite this much, though. At first, I didn't think you liked it at all. Glo, it's not real safe for you to stay out here by yourself, at night. Anything could happen."

"We passed a barbecue place on the way out here," she says. "Bring me some of that."

•   •   •

KATELYNN HAS REACHED a milestone: Dr. McKellar says it's okay for her to drive again. She drives to Louisa's house, where The Candles are staying. She's eager to meet them. Louisa has given them her room. All five of The Candles are gathered in the bedroom, but one is sick. They insist on staying together, even though it means sleeping on the floor. The sick one lies in Louisa's bed moaning, while Beebe says, "Katelynn, they need a sub to fill in. This is your chance. You can be a Candle," and the other Candles chime in, "Do it, babe! He's right. Your hair's already short."

One of the Candles leans over and runs her hand through Katelynn's hair and says, "Just a little bit of bleach. You can use what we use. Pure peroxide."

"I can't," says Katelynn, panic bubbling inside her chest. "Maybe your friend'll be okay. Maybe she's just got stage fright."

"Honey, we don't get stage fright," says another Candle. Katelynn can't figure out their ages. They are all so thin and pale, with their bleached short hair. "We aren't afraid of anything in this world, except maybe ice cream." The others laugh. Their laughter sounds like dogs baying. "You've got to help us out."

She asks the sick woman in the bed, "Would you like for me to call a doctor?" She can call Dr. McKellar. He'll come if she asks him to. She wishes Louisa were here, but Louisa is out returning pots and pans and Tupperware to neighbors. Katelynn helped her wash all the containers and put them in her car.

The woman raises her head off the pillow and says in a tone somehow ironic, "No," and this makes the other Candles guffaw.

Katelynn gives in. To the others, she says, "It's time we got you to the school. It's a sell-out crowd. I sold the tickets myself. My history teacher helped me."

"History teachers love us," one woman says. Katelynn is beginning to be able to tell them apart. This one's roots are showing dark at her scalp, and she has a faint green tattoo on one cheek. She might be Glo's age, or she might be twenty-two.

"Honey, you've just got to help us," says the woman with the green tattoo. "You don't have to sing, just stand there. We won't shine the light on you. You'll just lip-sync. Don't you want to?"

"Lemme do it. Who says a guy can't be a Candle?" Beebe says.

"Do you want anything to eat before we go?" Katelynn says, and The Candles bay again. They collapse on the bed, laughing, jostling the sick woman.

"Honey, we don't eat nothing," says the green tattoo. "Ask Beebe. We sing and we pray, and we work out. We might drink some white grape juice, if you've got that, and put a little gin in it. I ate some serviceberry pie, oh, about a year ago."

The sick woman in the bed says, "Is your history teacher going to be there? There's a whole special fan club just for history teachers."

"Mr. Stiles? I don't know if he's coming," Katelynn says. She pictures him hunkered down in the school, trying to sleep in the nurse's office, wishing the music would stop.

The woman with the green tattoo shoots a look at Beebe and all of the other Candles, except the woman in the bed, and they leave the room, as quietly as a hush, so that only Katelynn, the sick woman, and the green tattoo are left behind. Katelynn hears Beebe and the three women out in Louisa's yard, their voices light as rain falling.

"We'll make so much money tonight," the green tattoo says. "The money you gave us already, the money you got from the tickets, well that's a drop in the bucket. People come up to us all the time at our concerts and just give us money. They throw it on the stage. They put it down the backs of our gowns. They slip jewels to us in their mouths when they kiss us. This'll make Beebe a rich young guy. He'll be taken care of forever."

Katelynn looks out the window. In the dusk, Beebe and The Candles are playing flashlight tag, light stippling the grass and their bodies as they chase each other.

The sick woman moves her head on the pillow and says, "I'm from Minnesota. Our manager stole me out of the hospital. She paid some guy to dress up like a doctor and come in and wheel me out of there in a wheelchair he found in a hallway. I haven't spoken to my parents since then. They don't know where I am, and I intend to keep it that way. When I saw my manager for the first time, at the airstrip in Alabama, I cried, because I was seeing unselfish, unconditional love for the first time."

"Tell about the helicopter. That's the best part," says the green tattoo.

The sick woman coughs. "There was a helicopter waiting for me on the roof of the hospital. The guy who was dressed like a doctor, he was the one who flew it. He did everything. He put me into the helicopter and just left that wheelchair on the roof, and then we took off. I was scared, but I loved it. I wish that would happen to me all over again."

The green tattoo pushes Katelynn toward Louisa's bathroom, her fingers sharp as knitting needles on Katelynn's back. She's never been in Louisa's bathroom before. There's a cheerful nautical theme: sailboats on the shower curtain, a chipped boat-shaped soap dish on the sink. The woman says, "Take this peroxide and put it on your hair with a little bit of shampoo. When you come out, we'll get you dressed."

"Wearing what?" Katelynn says. The Candles are too much for her. She can't resist.

"Wings. A tiara. Whatever you want, as long as it's long and white. We travel light, but we have extra gowns," the woman says. "Aren't you surprised we don't have three or four trailers with makeup artists and stuff? All we need is a guy to work the lights, and our guitarists. They're already over there, at the school."

Katelynn pauses inside the bathroom. For these strangers, will she ruin what is left of her hair? She says, "My best friend wanted to sell her eggs, and now she's dead."

"You mean the doctors messed her up? I'd sue. You let 'em open you up, you don't know what they take out. Watch out, girl," trumpets the woman with the green tattoo, which stretches across her outraged cheek like a second face.

"She didn't have time to actually sell them. I just never forgave her for wanting to. I'm too judgmental."

"I've never forgiven anybody for anything," says the woman on the pillow. "Too much trouble."

"I'm Amber," says the woman with the green tattoo. She points to the woman in the bed. "She's Amy. The others are Anya, Adelaide, and Apple. Our manager named us."

"I won't change my name," Katelynn says.

"You won't have to. You're just a sub. Go do your hair," the woman says.

KATELYNN UNCAPS THE bottle of peroxide, sniffs it, and caps it again. She can't bring herself to bleach her hair, but she stays in the shower for a long time. The warm water and soap feel wonderful. Bits of adhesive tape still cling to her skin from the IVs the hospital used. She scrubs herself with a clean, rough washcloth and steps out of the shower onto Louisa's nautical-themed bath mat. She'll encourage Louisa to get rid of all these boat things and buy almost anything else.

Wrapped in a towel, she pushes open the bathroom door, calling out, "I'll sing with you, but I didn't do my hair." Maybe it won't matter. They said they wouldn't shine a light on her. She'll go with them and sing a few songs with them, and then she'll go home, snuggle with her puppy, and sleep.

Louisa's bedroom is dark and silent. Where did they go? Katelynn's toes curl up on the carpet, expecting the green tattoo to jump out of the shadows at her. She yells, "Boo!" at whoever might be here, hiding. Here she is, doing these women a favor, and they just cut off the lights. Was she in the shower that long, that they forgot about her or gave up on her?

"Boo," she says again, in a whisper.

No answer. It's as dark inside as it is outside. The Candles and Beebe must have left without her, and Louisa still hasn't come home. Katelynn fumbles with the wall switch, and the overhead light comes on, shining harshly on the woman in the bed, who lies as still as if she is dead.

Katelynn will call Dr. McKellar and ask him to come over and tend to this person. Right away. She should have called him even when the woman refused. Sick people don't know their own needs.

She *is* dead.

Katelynn knows this even as she walks around the bed and gazes at the woman's face, a face as pale and translucent as the plain kind of Halloween masks. What is this stranger's name? One of those A names, but she can't remember. The woman's head is turned to the side on the pillow, and her arms lie askew on top of the turquoise chenille bedspread. Her mouth is slightly open, and Katelynn smells a caked-blood odor, though she doesn't see any blood. This woman is older than Katelynn had first believed her to be, at least thirty, and her cheeks show a caved-in hollowness, as if she has few teeth. Her face appears to be sinking and growing cobwebs or flakes or ashes even as Katelynn stands over her, clutching the bath towel closed under one arm, holding her breath.

The doorbell rings, and somebody knocks loudly.

The floor feels gritty as Katelynn crosses the hallway and the living room, barefoot. She turns on a lamp by the door and pulls it open to find a man peering through the screen door, an old man.

"I'm looking for Miss Louisa Shepherd," he says. "Is this her house? Is she here? Are you her daughter? Granddaughter?"

"Louisa's not here. I'm a friend," Katelynn says. "Please come in. I need you."

"Oh, no, I can't," he says, looking away from her. "You're not dressed. I'll come back another time."

"No," she says. "I mean, help. Help me. There's this woman in Louisa's bedroom, a stranger, who I think just died. She's a member of this singing group that's here in town, and she was alive when I went into the shower, and I just came out and found her."

"Goodness," he says and steps inside. The screen door bangs shut behind him. "Are you sure she's dead?"

"Yes. Absolutely. Come this way." Katelynn leads him to the bedroom. She can't bear to look at the woman's face again and permits herself only a glimpse of the arms, thin as twist-ties on top of the bedspread, and the strange little cap of hair, not the peroxide blond of the other Candles but a kind of pinkish gray.

The old man wears a new-looking, well-cut suit, a fresh white shirt, and gold cuff links. "Let's try and get some help," he says, reaching for the phone on the night table. Katelynn feels appalled for Louisa: a house of death. While the man is on the phone, Katelynn goes into the bathroom and puts on her clothes, and when she comes out, rubbing a corner of a towel through her hair, he is hanging up the receiver.

"This poor lady," he says, bending to the woman in the bed, lifting an arm, feeling for a pulse. He shakes his head and lays the arm down gently.

"She was telling me about a helicopter ride she took," Katelynn says. She puts out a hand to him, thinking it can't be good manners to shake hands across a corpse, but it's too late, she's already reaching toward him. "My name is Katelynn Troy."

His grip is firm and friendly. "Sam Moon," he says.

LOUISA HAS TO PARK way far away from the school, because that's the only space available. Cars are parked in people's front yards and double-parked on the lane leading up to the school itself, which is all lit up for the concert—more cars than there are people in Hawk Lake. Lots of the vehicles have out-of-state license plates.

Louisa is exhausted, but relieved. She has returned every container to its owner, making the rounds of the neighborhood and thanking all those who brought her food on that dreadful day. She wants only to go home, but those gals—she can't quite bring herself to call them The Candles, or even to think of them that way—are house-guests of hers, and Beebe gave her a ticket, so she has to attend. She should have given the ticket away to somebody.

She'll stay for just one song, and then she'll go home.

A large stage has been set up in front of the school, flooded by lights, with a great milling flock of people in front of it. The stage is empty. Louisa guesses The Candles like to make a grand entrance. Aren't they lucky it's a nice night, still summery and warm. If the darned lights around that stage weren't so bright, you could see the stars.

Why, they've got this place roped off tight as a jail, with security guards stationed every ten feet along a portable fence. "Ticket, ma'am?" asks a guard, and she fishes it out of her pocket.

"T-shirt? You wanna buy a genu-wine Candles T-shirt?" yells a boy with a souvenir cart. "Get 'em here! Candles, matches, cigarettes, bottled water."

She should have thought to bring the tamale van. She could have made a fortune tonight and given the money to Beebe. Maybe Beebe thought of the van already. She searches, but she'll never find him in this crowd. Who are all these people, anyway, whooping and hollering and in general causing a commotion worse than the crowd at the memorial service. She smells dope. She's never smelled it before, but she knows by instinct that the ropy, sly odor riding the balmy currents must be exactly that, even though she doesn't see anybody smoking it.

It's thrilling, that smell. If somebody offers her a puff, she'll take it. Just one.

And that must be recording equipment up on the stage, those huge amplifiers with a zillion wires. Beebe has explained that The Candles' performance will be turned into an album, a CD that he will get money from, and she's glad for him.

I'm just a kid, she thinks as she stares out over the flaring sea of heads and bodies, all strangers to her. I've stayed a kid in my heart, never mind that I've gotten old.

The T-shirt seller sells out. People strip down right in front of everybody and put on the T-shirts, which are silk-screened with pictures of The Candles' faces. All around her is a roar and a ruckus, and then somebody steps up on the stage, and a hush falls.

But it's not a Candle. The man is saying something over the vast sound system: "Patience, patience." He kneels down on the stage and uncoils some heavy wires.

A woman near Louisa cries, "We've waited already! We been waiting all this time! Where are they?"

"We want The Candles!" a man yells, and those around him pick it up in a chant that consumes the crowd: "We-want-The-Candles."

Louisa makes her way around the edge of the crowd and through the packed throng closest to the stage. She will get to the bottom of this. She has a right. They are her houseguests, after all. To the man uncoiling wires on the stage, she says, "Have you heard from 'em? Are they coming?"

"They've never been this late before. We're about to have a riot on our hands," he says. "I'm just a sound guy. These other guys"—he waves toward shapes on the corner of the stage, in the dark—"they're the guitarists. They won't play without The Candles. We tried it one time, when they were late for a gig in Atlanta, and the crowd 'bout tore us apart."

"They have to come. This is a benefit concert, for a friend of mine."

"Yeah, I heard about that," the man says. "For that guy whose family died on the duck boat. He ain't here either. You got any ideas?"

"Well," she says, catching another drift of that sweet, punky smoke. She can see how you'd love it, even if it made you sick. "Give me the mike," she says, and from the coil of wires, he unloops a microphone on a black cord and hands it to her. "How do I get up there?" she asks him, searching for steps. He reaches out a hand on the longest arm she's ever seen and pulls her up on the stage. In that one motion, she loses her breath, and on the platform, with the lights in her eyes, she is blinded.

"You a comedian or something?" asks the man, holding a bundle of wires between his teeth while his hands braid and sort, twist and wrap them. "I seen you somewhere before. Was it last week, in L.A.? Warm 'em up, lady. Stall for time."

"Is this thing on?" Louisa asks, tapping the microphone, and her voice booms out over the crowd.

"We want The Candles," yells the crowd, holding up Mason jars full of lights. Could they have found lightning bugs this late in the year?

Louisa blinks. "We are here to help a motherless, fatherless, brotherless boy," she says into the mike, which amplifies her words. "The Candles are coming. They'll be along real soon. Does anybody have a hat?"

"Here," says the man who is working on the wires. He takes off his cap and tosses it to her.

"We will pass this hat," Louisa says, and her voice falls into the cadence of the Presbyterian preacher in Yellville who talked about pre-destination. "We will pass this hat, and we will be generous for the sake of Beebe Usry."

From her wallet, she takes money and puts it into the cap, which feels warm in her hands. "The Candles want you to be generous." She passes the hat to the helpful man. He puts money in it and passes it to an outstretched hand on the edge of the crowd.

"What you gonna do next?" he asks her. "We gotta entertain 'em somehow."

She's not herself tonight. She's some quick-witted stage presence, for she has remembered something Katelynn told her and she has thought of what to do. "Is Mr. Stiles here?" she says into the mike, which makes words loud and stretched out, dreamlike, so that they must reach the stars. "Coach Stiles, could you come to the stage, please, and bring the time capsule?" And she says, "Keep passing that hat, now."

"LOUISA WAS ABOUT your age, back then," Sam Moon says, while the paramedics are draping the body with a sheet and placing it on a gurney. He speaks softly, no doubt distracted, as Katelynn is, by this scene. The medics have tried to restart the Candle's heart with electric paddles, without success. "I met her at her prom, and she's always been the height of innocence and loveliness to me, never mind that we only talked for a little while."

Two police officers, a man and a woman, are writing on small tablets. They have already interviewed Katelynn and Sam Moon; they have located and examined the half dozen clear-plastic suitcases and dress bags that make up The Candles' luggage.

"Are you the singer?" Katelynn asks Sam Moon. "You must have sung at so many dances and met so many people," she says, watching the paramedics. Which Candle is it? Amy, Amber? No, Amber has the green tattoo. She and the old man are superfluous in this drama, hovering in the doorway of Louisa's bedroom, yet they are somehow guilty, suspect. "Louisa has your records," Katelynn whispers to Sam Moon. "She doesn't listen to anything else."

"I've met lots of people, lots of women, but she just stood out from all the others. If it weren't for *People* magazine, I'd never have found her," he says quietly. "I used to look up the name Louisa Shepherd in the phone books of towns where I sang. She was just beautiful, the night I met her, and she was with this oaf. I've always remembered the way he hauled her out of there. I almost climbed down off the stage to go after her. But I was in the middle of a song." His voice trails off. "She didn't deserve to have her boat sink and people die."

"She blames herself," Katelynn says.

The head paramedic takes a stethoscope from around his neck, stuffs it into the pocket of his white jacket, and says, "You say this woman was talking to you just a little while ago?"

"She talked about a helicopter ride," Katelynn says, expecting to be handcuffed and taken to jail. Was she really in the shower, or was she out here holding a pillow over this stranger's face, snuffing out her breath? While this person was dying, she herself was thinking only of her hair, about whether or not to bleach it. She has learned nothing.

Sam Moon says to the paramedic, "Entertainers who are on the road a lot often die while away from home. It's a risk we take. This lady probably knew that."

Sam Moon and Katelynn stand back from the doorway as the medics roll the gurney through the narrow doorway, bumping it against the wall.

"My husband is at that Candles concert this very minute," the policewoman says. Her face is a collie's, all pointed nose and shaggy long ears of hair. "I'd have gone too, but I had to work. If the press calls here, tell 'em to call me. Here's my card. Although I won't tell 'em anything till we notify the next of kin." Katelynn takes the card and puts it in the pocket of her jeans. Her hair is still wet. She's glad she left a note at home for her mother so Glo won't wonder where she is.

"You okay, sir? And you, hon?" The policewoman's collie face shows sudden, friendly concern. "It'll be a long night for me, with that concert. People go nuts," she says on her way out the door.

GLO IS NOWHERE in the house. Jerry searches, but she isn't in the musty living room or the bedroom with the lumpy bed or the kitchen with its neat jars of ancient spices like desert sand. She is not in the yard, where the air is sweet with the smell of fall grass and holds that single, high note of insects' cries, a sound that Jerry thinks of as glistening. The dawn sky shows a dark golden glow at its edges.

He has brought two cups of coffee, cool now in their Styrofoam cups, and a bag containing jalapeño bagels, bananas, and canned orange juice. The only sign that Glo has been here at all is the flattened, empty bag that contained the barbecue he brought her the other day, and the book she was reading, about world's fairs, lying facedown on the scarred coffee table.

Maybe Katelynn came and took her home. Maybe after two whole days, Glo was ready to go back. She might have walked to a farmhouse, used the phone. He sits down on the front steps. Here's the bottle of Chigarid Dora used, empty and uncapped, still smelling of menthol and glue.

Flummoxed. It's a word his mother used. He's flummoxed, with no idea what to do except to unwrap a bagel, sip some coffee, and try to keep his heart from pounding. He should never have left her here by herself.

The insects' hum deepens. It's the sound of a guitar string, plucked and resonating. But it's too loud for bugs, and it's coming from the sky. He gets to his feet and goes to the road.

It's a small plane coming in for a landing, just like the crop duster that Dora ran after naked. While he watches, the plane coasts over woods and brush, above the road where he stands and over the yard of the little house, and lands smoothly in the field next door, where shreds of cotton cling to the dried plants. The engine cuts off, and the windless air is silent, the bugs stilled. Then Jerry hears a laugh: Glo's laugh.

The hatch of the plane pops open, and her head appears, red as a woodpecker's. There's a man with her, climbing out of the cockpit: Dora's crop duster, Hoyt Landry. When they look up and see Jerry, they wave.

"What did you think of that landing? That was all mine. Did you bring breakfast?" Glo calls cheerfully, striding toward him. She kisses his cheek, and in the kiss, he knows it's over.

Hoyt Landry shakes Jerry's hand and says, "She's the best pupil I ever had. Well, the only one, but I can't imagine anybody learning any quicker. She's been ready to fly all her life."

She wants to get her pilot's license, Glo says. She will never go back to Hawk Lake, not back to that house, at least, she says, not to live there anymore. She will get her license, and she will fly.

"What about Katelynn?" Jerry says.

"I saw the river from the air," she says. "I saw it, and I knew Katelynn would be well."

"Glo knows what she's doing," says Landry. "She flew all by herself, this time. We were up in the air almost all day, the last couple days, and some at night too."

Jerry starts to ask if she'll take him up, but he can't bear the answer, whether yes or no. Glo finds the bag of food and digs into it hungrily.

"When we flew last night, I saw the stars," she says. "I was in the stars."

AT DAWN, Louisa comes home to find Katelynn's BMW in the driveway, the house unlocked, and Katelynn asleep on the sofa. "Wake up, hon, and look at this," Louisa says, nudging Katelynn's shoulder. "Look at all the money I collected for Beebe. Why, that crowd must've filled this hat ten times over. We kept dumping it into this shopping bag. I bet there's thousands of dollars here. Maybe as much as ten thousand. The Candles were late getting there. You know what we did while we were waitin' for 'em? We buried that time capsule. Your teacher was there. Mr. Stiles. He went into the school and got that thing and a shovel, and we shined the big lights on it and dug a hole. The time capsule looked just like a big Thermos to me, a silver one. The Candles showed up just in the nick of time, when Mr. Stiles was flinging dirt on that time capsule."

Louisa sets the bag of money down and looks proudly at Katelynn, who seems to be awake now. Something's not right, but Louisa doesn't know what. She goes on, "Beebe's bringing The Candles back here. They oughta be along any minute. You know what their music makes me think of? Rayon. Rayon and static, isn't that funny? They sing pretty good, though."

Katelynn takes a deep breath, as if remembering something that startles her. "Something bad happened, Louisa. One of them died, the one that was in your bed. She's been taken away," she says.

"Dying? What? Who died?" Louisa cries. It's then that she catches sight of another person in the room, a man asleep in her easy chair, and she covers her mouth and points to him. Is he an intruder who has broken in and, like Goldilocks, fallen asleep? Does Katelynn even realize he is here? Why is Katelynn beaming, when she was just talking about somebody dying?

The man's about her age—no, older. His eyes open and he blinks. When he focuses on Louisa, he gets to his feet. "It's been a long night," he says. "I've been worried about you, Louisa. You won't remember me. We met one time, briefly, a long time ago."

That voice. Recognition comes to her slowly while she looks from Katelynn's radiant face to the old man's expectant smile. The two of them wait. It's his voice, echoing in her very own living room. The voice gives shape and substance to the face with its fine features, the proudly tilted head, the easy slope to arms and shoulders accustomed to a stage, the hands that have held so many microphones. His eyes are like a sailor's; he has gazed out over seas of dancers. At last she whispers, "Sam Moon?"

She has always pictured him as the young man he was when she met him, crowned with that jet-black hair. Her memories of the real person are all mixed up with the memories of the cardboard Sam from the motel where she used to work, the cardboard Sam with musical notes around his head. This man looks thin as a chicken breast eaten down to the bones, but his voice could still fill the Shore Club. She puts out her hand to him. He is holding out both his arms, as if he will hug her or ask her to dance.

"Do you remember when we met, Louisa?" he says. "It was at your prom."

She nods, unable to speak.

Sam Moon looks at his watch. "Do you normally stay out all night?"

"If I'd known you were here, I'da been home sooner."

He does hug her then, gently, and she stands in the circle his arms make, thinking this is the way a cat lets you hug it, not hugging back. She is as stunned as if she's discovered a talking kangaroo in her living room. "I just always remembered you, Louisa," he says. "I read about what happened to you and your passengers on that boat, and I just had to see you. I didn't think you'd remember me. It's nice to see you've got my albums."

"They're not mine. A gal whose granddaughter I met in a record store, she loaned 'em to me," Louisa says. Over Sam's shoulder, she sees a crowd barge through her front door: Beebe and The Candles, laughing.

"We went out on the boat before the concert," Beebe says, "your new boat, Louisa. I took my family's ashes and we threw 'em in the water. I decided that was the right thing to do. We lost track of time. I'm starving. I think even these skinny women are hungry, after sailin' and singin' all night. How's our pal in the sick bay?"

Silence, while Louisa thinks she'll never be able to speak again.

Katelynn takes charge. "Sam, could you tell everybody what happened? I'll fix us some breakfast," she says and disappears into the kitchen.

"TAKE YOUR PICK," says Stella, gesturing to a row of gowns. "Let me make some suggestions." She chooses three or four dresses and hangs them on a hook. "Nothing too bulky or floaty, I'd say. The column styles are slimming."

"I never thought . . . ," Louisa says, fingering a tulle overskirt.

"Did Sam get down on bended knee? It's so romantic," Stella says, "even at your age. Especially at your age. He really came out of nowhere, after you've been dreaming of him all these years?"

"I can't believe it," Louisa says, amazed not only by what has happened but by how fast the news traveled, about Sam showing up and wanting to marry her. Stella's face looks eager for more information, so Louisa volunteers, "He's not even going back to close up his apartment in New York. He's just getting his things sent to him." The dresses shine like cake frosting, just like the seven-minute icing her mother used to put on birthday cakes, and they smell like the icing, too, sweet and airy. They're for young gals like Katelynn or Stella, not for her.

"These are more expensive than I can afford. I should just be married in my everyday clothes."

"Like what, the lion sweatshirt you wore to the memorial service? I saw you in Beebe's van. That was a hoot," Stella says. "This is a present." Stella loops her hair behind one ear and then the other. "I want to give you a wedding gown. When I hit you across the face, I hated you, but you know what, Louisa?" She lifts a sleeve of one of the elaborate dresses. The cuff is decorated with a little white satin dove. "I was awake for the first time in years. Getting dumped out of that boat, seeing my husband sink right past me, that woke up my soul." She yanks the dove-dress from the rack. "This'll fit you if we let out the seams a little. Go put it on."

Louisa's head spins. She thinks of a top, spinning, or a dust devil, or the little eddies of autumn leaves that twirl and lift in country roads. Sam Moon did propose on one knee. After Beebe and The Candles had gone out in the yard and Katelynn cleared away the breakfast dishes and went home, Sam and Louisa sat in the living room and talked all day, all night, until the sun came up again. She realized she had been up for two whole days. Then Sam asked her to marry him. He's getting up in years; his grin turned to a grimace as he bent down, and he murmured something about arthritis. When he kissed her, his lips felt like the songs she had listened to for so many days, and she knew then that she was waiting for something, that whatever it was, it was drawing closer, but she has to wait for it, beckon it.

She said, "Yes, I'll marry you," exactly as if speaking words in a play, but she was waiting for something, and Sam was a big part of it, but only a part. She told Sam, "I've never kissed anybody since that prom date, and that turned into something awful. He raped me." Sam was quiet for a long time, and then he said, "You've lived your old age first, and now you can be young with me."

Stella is holding the dress tightly, clutching it to her waist, her head bent, her long hair falling over her chest. Louisa asks, "Stella? Are you all right?"

Stella's head snaps up. "I'm suing you, remember. But we can still have fun, right? You're getting married, and I'm wider awake than I've ever been. You should really have a train with this dress, and a long veil. How about a tiara? Tiaras are in. And have you seen the great fake orange blossoms up by the cash register? Go grab a bunch, and I'll twine them in your hair."

JERRY LOSES A LOT, fast. He is wasting money and time. He should be home, painting, or out at another property, making repairs, cutting grass. The cards in his hand feel sticky; the air reeks with cigarette smoke.

The woman next to him rises from the blackjack table and says, "Want to join me for breakfast? They've got a great buffet."

"No thanks." He hasn't lost enough yet. He keeps hearing Glo's bubbly laugh as she climbed out of the little plane. She never used to have a bubbly laugh. Her laughter was more like rapid sniffing.

The woman touches his arm. "Who are you so mad at?"

He looks at her then: a lady about the age his mother would be if she were still alive, sweet-faced, her eyes a little puffy, her lipstick feathered, a turquoise scarf tied haphazardly into her hair. She says, "The buffet's the best thing they got here, that and that automatic card shuffler. I might buy one of those. I used to play cards all the time, growing up. Go Fish and War and Old Maid. This blackjack stuff, it's not for me." She laughs a little. "You can tell I'm not winning. How long have you been here, anyway? More than twenty-four hours, solid. I've been watching you. You got dumped, didn't you? Who is she?"

"Ma'am," he says and her smile stiffens a little; she thinks he's freezing her. "I'm going to keep on playing awhile." Who is it she reminds him of, or what? She holds her head jauntily. Her nose is just this side of beaky, her skin chalky. His mother would not have befriended this woman.

The woman touches his arm and says, "These places will eat you alive."

"I have a friend who wanted to blow one up. Maybe she oughta," says Jerry.

"You'll lose your shirt," she says and leaves him then.

KATELYNN AND GLO fight on the phone. "I can drive now. I'm allowed to. I'll just throw your stuff in the car and bring it," Katelynn says, but Glo says no.

"Just ship it," she says. "It's an hour's drive over here. That's too far for you, just yet, no matter what Dr. McKellar says."

"If I'm so sick, then why are you going off like this?" Katelynn says.

"You're much better," says Glo. "It's just the driving that worries me."

Katelynn gives up. She drags the biggest box she can find to her mother's closet and throws in the things Glo has asked her to send: all her jeans, her leather jacket, a stack of T-shirts, socks, nightgowns, bathrobe. Katelynn checks the things off a list. Her mother had explained about learning to fly. She has directed her to send the box to the old house owned by Jerry. Katelynn recognizes the address.

"Is Jerry there with you?" Katelynn asked, straining to understand. The idea of her mother flying a plane is terrifying. She imagines Glo in goggles, dogfighting in the air: a ghastly cartoon.

"No," Glo said. "I can't talk long. I'm using a friend's phone—Hoyt's phone. He's giving me the flying lessons. I'm going to buy that house from Jerry."

"I was there one time, for a party," Katelynn said. "Mom, how long are you going to stay there?"

"Honestly, I don't know," Glo said. "Would you put some sweaters in that box? It gets cold up in the air. See if you can find my earplugs in the medicine cabinet. Flying's noisy."

"Okay, I will. But Mom."

"What?"

"I love you," Katelynn said.

"I love you, too," said Glo.

"What about Dad?"

"That is such a good question," Glo said, in a hearty tone Katelynn hardly recognized. "That's what I think about while I fly. What about him? I think about it so hard, I can forget about it."

Katelynn finds the earplugs and tosses them into the box, tapes it shut using extra tape at the corners, calls the delivery service, and lugs the box outside, into the driveway. The day is warm enough that the slight exertion makes her sweat. She walks around to the lake, which is empty, its horizon edged in pewter. Hasn't she wanted to live alone, to have this house all to herself? The nurse and the dietitian are gone. She paid them herself and sent them away. There was no time to tell Glo about the Candle who died at Louisa's house, or about Sam Moon showing up and proposing to Louisa.

Was it only a few months ago that the photographers from *Southern Living* were here? How is it that the house and the yard have gone to seed, before her very eyes? Surveying Glo's beloved flower gardens, she notices weeds, crabgrass, and, apart from one late-blooming crape myrtle, an utter lack of flowers. What has happened to Glo's prized Autumn Joy sedum, the famous antique mums, and the almost-year-round rosebushes? Did they bloom already, and did Katelynn not notice? Wandering back inside, she realizes how dusty the house is, its windows and glass walls not so much smudged as filmed over, and a stale smell lingers, an odor like that of burned toast.

She is alone. She stands very still in her foyer, listening, hearing nothing.

She feels in her pockets, finds a few pieces of lint-ridden candy corn, and chews them, remembering this is the day she's supposed to speak to Mr. Stiles's class. Where is the world's fair book? She intended to use that as the basis for a presentation. She'd started making notes from it, but now the book is gone. Mr. Stiles disapproved of her personal topics. It must be his way of showing her how self-centered she is. He knows her own life is all she has to talk about. She'll have to come up with something else.

• • •

THE CANDLES ARE climbing into Beebe's tamale van, settling their sheer white dresses around their thin legs, singing a low song that must be a dirge, a word Louisa doesn't know how she knows. Louisa hands Beebe a basket full of food. He will drive The Candles back to Alabama, where they will sing at the funeral of the woman who died. "This has happened to them before," he tells Louisa. "Losing one among 'em, I mean."

"And they just keep on singing and finding replacements?" Louisa says.

"I reckon," says Beebe. He flips his hair off his forehead and starts for the door, holding the basket of food.

"Wait," says Louisa. "Beebe, I haven't done anything for you. Not really."

He sets the basket down. "Oh, but you have," he says. "You've given me a lot."

He holds out his arms and hugs her.

"You drive careful," she says. She lets him go and stands at her window to watch his van peel out of the driveway.

She has not slept in her bed since the woman died in it. The couch has been her bed, and Sam has slept on the floor these last few nights. Beebe and The Candles have slept on the boat, that new boat that Jerry bought for her, that she has never set foot on yet. Her bed will have to go. It should be hauled to the dump and replaced with a new bed, one big enough for her and Sam.

Her house is a shrine for the dead Candle. People come up and leave bouquets of flowers on the steps and in the tiny front yard: bouquets tied with ribbons of black or pastel, many with tearstained notes or with stuffed animals. Black candles are stuck in the ground; she has seen them burning at night. Piled on top of each other, the bouquets and baskets grow crisp in the hot fall sun and lose their color. Fans roll up in cars or arrive on foot, as if her yard is public land, and they deposit their flowers, kneel or linger for a while, wiping their eyes. The surviving Candles, when Katelynn told them what had happened, gave a single unanimous cry, then went out in the yard, sat down in a circle, joined hands, and remained that way all morning. Katelynn took them breakfast food on a tray, and they ate it all. Beebe stayed with them. By evening, they were playing flashlight tag again, yipping like a pack of beagles.

She surveys her yard. It reminds her of a birthday party gone wrong, as if guests have played havoc with flowers and gifts of stuffed animals. She doesn't dare clean up or haul the mementos away, not yet, even though the floral scent is turning sickly and the foot traffic is wearing her grass thin.

She watches Beebe's van rattle away from her house and is startled when somebody comes up behind her and drapes an arm around her waist: Sam. Why does he want an old maid like her? He has told her he was married to a beautiful brunette who left him ten years ago to run a sanctuary for exotic felines, tigers and lions and cheetahs that people acquired as cubs and then didn't know what to do with when they got big and scary. No children, he has said. "But I have a son," she has said, and she has told him everything.

She lifts his hand from her waist and turns to him.

"It's been half a century, Sam. We talked for a few minutes, all those years ago," she says. "We didn't know each other then, and we don't now."

"Yes, we do," he says. "We always have. You're the sweetest one. I always trust my first impressions."

"I'm not sweet," she says, and he laughs.

"You were delightful, that night we met," he says. "You said the most wonderful things, such kind things, and you were nothing like the others. I wanted to ask if I could take you out, but I was too old for you then."

"But I didn't say anything unusual," she blurts, thinking: *He's remembering somebody else, like the blonde in the cashmere sweater.* "And you weren't too old."

"I like to jaywalk, count money, and pet strange dogs. I grew up in a rough part of Boston, where people referred to dollars, in all seriousness, as clams. When I was about six, I discovered I could sing. It gave me a way out. What more do you need to know?"

"We're going to stay here, right?" she says, for this has to be settled. She doesn't want to leave her house.

"Don't you want to get away from the accident, and from this?" He gestures to the piles of flowers in the yard. "You can do that, with me. We can go anywhere."

She shakes her head. "This is the only place for me."

WHEN JERRY CAN'T find the exit, he figures that's intentional. The longer they keep you here, the more money they make. Well, they've got plenty of his. His ATM card is about worn out, thanks to the first sizable dent he has put into the fortune his parents left him.

Down one corridor, up another, around a corner, across yet another low-lit chamber where slumped shapes push coins into pulsing, chiming machines. He's trapped. Where the hell is the exit? He could ask one of the cocktail waitresses hurrying by with drinks on trays, but he feels incapable of speech. If he opens his mouth, he'll bellow. Like a hospital or an airport, this is a sealed-in world, creating its own stale atmosphere. He turns another corner and runs smack into a door marked EMERGENCY EXIT. He pushes it, but it's locked. What if there were a fire in this place? He won't think about that.

What had he hoped for with Glo? Everything. A family. She is not too old. An only child, he was always fascinated by the siblings he knew when he was little, by their intimacy, by the emotions that brewed in big families, by the kids' nicknames bestowed on them by their parents or by one another, and the way they would reject those nicknames in moments of rage, an emotional growth spurt put to song: *"Don't* call me Peanut anymore!" "My name is *not* Tiny!" He'd imagined a long life with Glo, children and grandchildren inheriting her stubborn, far-off gaze, inexplicable ways, and beautiful hair. Thinking of her flying a plane, he shudders. That Landry guy must have a death wish.

Wandering past an elaborate bar and a gift shop with windows full of mugs and cheap watches, he locates an elevator, presses a button, and in a moment finds himself in what is evidently the basement, a dim, humid corral of mops and barrels of cleaning fluid, the low ceiling crisscrossed with pipes. What a coincidence: stepping out of the very next elevator is the woman in the turquoise scarf, from the black-jack table. There's a man with her, a large young man with black-framed glasses and voluminous hair jutting out in a triangle from his head.

"Hey. Are you lost, too? How was the buffet?" Jerry asks the woman.

She doesn't answer. Her lipstick-feathered lips twitch toward the man with her, who whips something from behind his back and swings it toward Jerry's ear. Jerry ducks, flinging out an arm, his hand encountering the surprising softness of the jutting hair. Then the man tackles him, and he feels the sharp, sure strike of metal against his skull.

"WHERE IS EVERYBODY?" Katelynn asks Mr. Stiles. "It's the last period of the day. This is when you said to be here."

He stands up from his chair and steps around the desk. "There's a pep rally going on. Class was preempted. I'm surprised you didn't hear them all down in the gym, cheering their little hearts out. When I was your age, I managed to almost never attend a pep rally. I despised them. So much for school spirit."

"I've written a report on Andrew Jackson. Should I come back another time?"

He holds out his hand, takes the report from her, writes "A" on it, and gives it back. "I've been fired. The other night, when those damn Candles were late for their concert and your buddy Louisa demanded I come out and bring the time capsule, well, kids were running amok through the school. Finally, I thought they'd all gone home, but I was wrong. Some of them were still here, and early in the morning, they found me asleep in the nurse's office, on the cot, and they ran home and ratted me out to their parents, who of course told the principal, the superintendent, and the school board. At first, I bluffed. I tried to say I'd gotten here early that day and just lay down for a snooze, but they soon got the whole truth out of me." He speaks bitterly, waving his hands. Katelynn stares at him. He goes on: "While I dug the hole for the capsule, there was this Fleetwood Mac tape playing on the sound system—that foolish *murmuring* that passes for music. I can't get it out of my head."

Katelynn gasps, but it comes out a laugh. "I'm sorry! I really am. But it wasn't good for you, living here. It was not a life."

"But it was a real job," he says mockingly. "Ever had one to lose?"

"I'm sorry, Mr. Stiles."

"Oh, call me Oscar." He opens the closet, pulls out a jacket, and kicks the door shut. "I'll turn in your grade as I pass the office, on my way out of this damn place."

"Is this really your last day? Where will you work now? Where will you live?"

"This is it, Katelynn. I don't know what I'll do. They did give me a little bit of severance pay, but you can bet they won't give me a job reference. They think I'm a nut, and they're mad that I fooled them for so long, living here. Let them wonder how it was. I told them how loud that falling pencil sounded in the middle of the night, rolling off a desk, like a bowling ball. It was wonderful, I said. I've had the whole place to myself, night after night. I've gone sliding up and down the hallways in my sock feet, something most people only dream of doing."

He has lost weight, Katelynn notices. Angry as he is, he looks younger and more vigorous, awake and alert.

He goes on, "Would you believe, the school nurse quit because of this. When she found out I'd been sleeping on the cot in her office, she pitched a fit and gave notice. I don't know why she got so worked up. I used my own pillow, after all, one that I keep in a locker."

Katelynn is staggered by all of this. She can't imagine how he must feel, but the image of Beebe comes to mind, of what he said in the woods after his whole family died, that he felt awful but so free. "Do you feel free, Mr. Stiles? Oscar?"

He throws her a withering look. "What a stupid question." He slides his arms into his jacket, saying, "That stuff in the lockers. I could go get it. But what the hell, it's just a few clothes." He sighs. "I told them everything. How I've sat naked in this very classroom in the middle of the night, smoking cigarettes. I've broken all the rules. But don't the rules apply only during working hours? What bad thing, really, have I done? Nothing. When I saw it was curtains, I wanted to shock them. You could tell they were all wondering what it was like, living here, keeping that secret all this time."

"Are you taking anything with you? What about your bicycle?"

"I guess I'll get on it and ride away." He goes to the open window, raises his arms as if to close it, then doesn't. Gusts of sweet air blow in. "I love that this school is old," he says. "They're going to remodel next year. I'm glad I won't be around to see that. A new blackboard was all the renovation I ever wanted."

Katelynn steps to the window, breathes in the fresh air, and tries to think of some way to cheer him up. "Can you think of this as graduating? Could it be a good thing, in some way you don't see now?"

"Oh, let me think that over. The big silver lining must be right under my nose, and here I am, focusing on the little things of no consequence, aren't I."

"Would you like"—she can hardly believe she is asking him this—"would you like to stay at my house for a while? My father's in Burma. He might not come back for a long time. My mother is, well, on a vacation. It's a big house. I won't bother you." She has never seen a more startled face than his, at this moment. "You can put your bike in my car."

He stares at her, and she has to turn away from the amazement, the joy, in his face. She says, "What was in that time capsule?"

His Adam's apple moves as he gulps. "Ordinary things. Pictures. Letters. Snippets of people's hair, their favorite CDs and T-shirts, a digital watch, the same stuff you'd find in any landfill. The results of some election the students just had, student council or something. Trite little sayings people wrote to sound wise, all buried with the great solemnity of putting away the Dead Sea Scrolls. My arms are still sore from digging that hole." He pauses. "I won a student election once, to be a librarian's helper in the fourth grade. That was one of the happiest times of my whole life, it really was. I'm not trying to be melodramatic or pitiful. I'm, as your contemporaries would say, like so way past that. And you won't believe what else was a truly grand moment for me."

She steps out into the hallway. He switches off the lights and follows her. They leave the window open. "So what else, Oscar?"

"One time in junior high, I dropped a tray in the cafeteria, and everybody clapped. I stood there for the longest time, loving it, even with gravy all over my shoes."

JERRY COMES TO with a bucket on his head, a puddle of dirty water around him, and a mop handle balanced across his shoulders. He'd blacked out when the man hit him, then come back to consciousness for just a moment while they rummaged through his pockets. Groggily, he remembers the frisky way their hands felt, as if they were tickling him. His wallet, with its credit cards, was pay dirt. The mop and bucket must be their idea of a joke. They took his watch, too, so he has no idea what time it is. Even through his fog, the irony registers on him: he used to think robbers followed you only if you won.

His swollen head buzzes and thrums as if stuffed with cicadas. As he pushes the bucket and mop away and hoists himself up, the woman's sweetness comes back to him, the kind, down-home way she was when she invited him to eat with her. Maybe she really was sweet, until she hooked up with the jutting hair. No, that could not be. If he'd eaten a meal with her, she'd have spiked his drink with poison, sprinkled broken glass in his food.

The parrot. With the turquoise scarf in her hair and the jaunty angle of her head, that's what she reminded him of, the clumsy plaster statue of the parrot that once stood beside the lake and now hunkers in his garage. Not the real parrot, beloved by his grandfather and hated by the tortoise, that actual creature he barely remembers, only its crude double with its chipped, saucy aqua head. So the thing got out of his garage and sought him out. If he can get himself out of here and get home, he will find only the plaster tortoise crouching in his garage.

He crawls out of the water, drags himself on his knees and elbows over to a cinder-block wall, and hunches against it. The cement floor feels gritty, and the clammy air smells rusty, dank as a drain. Where did this blood on his shirt come from? His mind is all cicadas, droning and whirring. *Don't fall asleep. Don't dream, or you will die.* Even this is not enough to win back Glo. This would not compel her.

He remembers the photo he found at the abandoned house, the picture of the gravediggers' strong, busy arms, the beautiful light reflecting on the shovels in their hands, and he thinks: *Nobody would believe it, unless they saw it.*

What was it his father wanted him to do? *Keep on reaping,* as if the lake were an endless field of grain. What has Jerry done at the lake? He rescued a puppy. He saved Louisa. Painting is what he has left, so he'll paint the lake and its people and the gallery of faces that he has imagined from his tax-sale properties, people whose stories are unknown, buried. He tries to focus on the faces in his mind, but he keeps going into semiconscious glides.

I'd have found somebody else to love, his mother said.

MR. STILES MAKES Katelynn laugh. They lie back on chaise longues and eat warmed-up canned beef stew on trays at the edge of the lake, while thin red shadows of sunset creep across the water. She finds him one of her father's beers in the refrigerator and he accepts it with delight, popping it open and drinking deeply. He talks about his career, about things students and administrators and other teachers have done, goofy things. She has only to mention somebody and he's off on a story about that person. He's making her school more vivid to her than it ever was when she attended it, when her looks and her popularity were all that mattered. He's ugly; he's been mocked and disregarded so long by students, and yet there were those who revered him—the guys on the track team that he coached. *Throw your heart over the bar . . .*

"Harvey was the best of them," he says. "Olympic material. He could still do it, if he would practice, but he won't. I hear he's clerking in that formal-wear store."

He is goading her, and she knows better than to respond. Instead, she gazes across the lake, now dark, and realizes she can live in this house her whole life. Nobody will make her leave. She does not have to go to college or get married, or even work unless she chooses to. She has money of her own. She is almost well. She feels other people's expectations fall away from her like dead leaves or dirty old fur that she is shedding.

"I'm free, Oscar," she says, and Mr. Stiles frowns, looking concerned. She sets her plate down on the grass. It's dark now. "I have survived this," she says, sudden happiness sending chills up and down her spine, like icy, racing fingers. Jenelle's ghost is really gone, the curled lip and the toss of that long black hair. Adventure is as close as the lake itself. She doesn't need Harvey or her father to bring mystery to her life. They're gone, into whatever is mundane or exotic, and she is here—a young woman getting well, sitting beside a lake, talking with a friend.

"I have many friends that I write to, out of state," says Mr. Stiles, "and I mean actual letters, not e-mails. My friends all know about Katelynn Troy by now, and they want news of you, any news. What shall I tell them next?"

"Whatever it is, I'll have to live it before you write it," she says.

SAM IS STRONG. He dismantles Louisa's bed. "We can pick out a new bed together," he says. "How about a king-sized brass one, Louisa?"

"If you throw your lot in with me, won't you get sued too, and lose everything you have?"

"I'm not worried about that," he says.

He hauls the bed out onto the sidewalk, mattress, sheets, pillows, and all, and pays one of Louisa's neighbors to carry it off in a truck, to the dump. It was Louisa's bed from childhood, the same bed her own mother had slept in when she, too, was young, and Louisa loved it, never mind that it was rough-hewn, that the springs were going bad. She stands in the yard, fighting tears as her neighbor carts it off. This is wasteful, and she hates waste. She should have scoured the bed and given it to somebody who needs it.

Suddenly she wants Sam to have a place of his own, not forever, just until they are married. She has had no time to think. One moment, he was a cardboard cutout in her memory, a record on her turntable, and the next, he was flesh and blood, opinions and suggestions, in her own house. He will have to go to one of the places in town, the Hawk Lake Chalet or the Hummingbird Inn or even the Super 8 out on the highway. She can almost hear her mother's voice— "Don't send him away, Louisa!"—and that convinces her that she will. For now.

Sam is gathering puffs of feathers that fell out of the pillows when the bed was loaded onto the truck. Why does he bother? Her yard's a mess. She doesn't worry that the bed carried plague. The Candle who died there died of being so thin that her heart gave out. That was in the paper; that was what the coroner said, though he used different words. Autopsy: the word makes her think *topsy-turvy, start at the top and get to the bottom of it all*. Still, she will scrub the spot where the bed stood. Maybe then she can cry for the young woman whose heart gave out, who could not eat to save herself, cry for all who died in the water and the one who died in her bed.

Bending over, Sam reveals a bald spot on his head, a tiredness in his shoulders. Among the sheaves of roses, gladioli, iris, mums, and teddy bears, elaborate funeral wreaths have appeared, wreaths as tall as Louisa is, shaped like hearts and featuring white candles as thick as coffee cans. Here and there is a musical instrument—a guitar, a child's plastic flute. She feels sick, so heavy she could lie right down on the prickly bouquets. She has not known this kind of exhaustion before. She used to give tours all day, on land, on water, never minding the sun, and she'd come home tired out, but not like this.

A picture of her flower-strewn lawn is in today's paper, the caption reminding everyone, just in case they've forgotten, that Louisa Shepherd, who lives in the house where the Candle died, was the captain of a certain ill-fated duck boat.

Feathers blow out of Sam's grasp and waft over the carnage of flowers.

"Sing to me, Sam," she says as he crosses the yard, his hands full of feathers.

KATELYNN BLINKS into the sun, waking up, so stiff in her chaise longue she might be made of wood. Her heart gears up and races. She is late for school. How is it that she slept outside, and who put this afghan over her? Then she remembers everything, and she turns to the side, to the other chaise longue, to see if Mr. Stiles slept outside too. Oscar. She'll have to practice calling him that.

In his place is a stranger. She sits up, gasping. No, it's the man she hired, the detective, perched gingerly on the chaise longue as if he can stay only a moment.

"Easy," the man says. "You can go back to sleep if you want. This can wait."

"Did you find him?" she asks, over the chaos that is her heartbeat, her breathing. May she never wake this way again. It's as bad as a phone call in the middle of the night. Who was it she told that she loved this man? Mr. Stiles. Oscar. She told him she loved this detective, said it to save her pride. You would have to be brave to love this man. He must have fifty women in love with him. She says, "He's dead, isn't he. That's why you're here in person."

He opens his mouth, but she holds up her hand, certain the baby was stillborn, that he died as an infant, without ever leaving the hospital. She says, "Did he die young? Like, at birth or in an institution, when he was a child, or a teenager? Long time ago?" So long ago, that maybe Louisa's grief will be blunted, her sorrow will spend itself fast, like a thunderstorm.

The detective's smile rearranges his face, laying bare the intelligence, the skepticism that lie beneath his skin. "He's fine. Better than fine, I'd have to say. He's a banker up in Boston, with a wife and four kids."

"Are you sure it's the right person?"

"I'm sure."

"Have you told him? Does he know he was given up and adopted? Has he ever tried to find his mother?"

"He was adopted by a working-class couple. I don't know what they told him. Of course I haven't spoken to him. You only asked me to find him. Both his adoptive parents have died."

She picks at the puffy plastic cushion of the chaise longue, awake now, even in her confusion feeling embarrassed, as if he has walked into her bedroom and found her in her nightgown. "So what next? What do I tell Louisa?"

Producing a manila folder, he brings out a newsprint photo clipped from the society pages of a Boston paper—a handsome couple at a table, both smiling, wearing funny hats for New Year's Eve.

"Can you prove this?" she says, holding the picture up to the sunlight. Looking beyond the man's smooth good looks, she finds the proof for herself: there in his hairline is Louisa's ragged widow's peak. And his eyes tilt down at the corners, just as Louisa's do. Katelynn says, "How come you found him, when I couldn't?"

"What had you done, type in Louisa's name on the Internet a few times?" He shakes his head, and she thinks: *chameleon.* Her fourth-grade teacher kept a chameleon in the classroom, a creature both proud and mysterious. When Katelynn picked it up and held it against her pale-blue blouse, it lightened to a shade like the sky. "He's not in Boston right this minute," the detective says. "He's on vacation out west, at a highfalutin little place called the Ponderosa Canyon Ranch and Spa. My guess is, he's got the kids out on a sunrise trail ride right now, and the wife's in the steam room with cucumber slices over her eyes. I happen to know he takes his cell phone everywhere he goes. Here's the number." He holds a slip of paper toward her, tiny as the fortune from a Chinese cookie, and she plucks it from his fingers with a shiver. "There's more. It's all here," he says, laying the folder beside her feet at the end of the chaise longue. "More photos, of him as a child and on up through the years."

"Well," she says. "I'll get your money." But she doesn't move. Should she pay him and watch him melt away? In ten years, she will know what she should have done. She wonders if Mr. Stiles is watching from the house. She'll wait until she's alone to examine the New Year's Eve party clipping and to look at the photos in the folder. She will not let anybody else see them before Louisa does.

The man waits. The sun rises higher behind him, making a flaming silhouette of his head.

THE HOSPITAL in Tunica is brand-new, with the same low fluorescent lights as in the casino. Dora pushes Jerry's wheelchair out to the curb, and a nurse waits with him while Dora brings his truck around. He makes a mental note to reimburse her for the bus fare. She took a Greyhound from Hawk Lake, came here, got his keys, went back to the casino, fetched the truck. Painfully, he wobbles up from the wheelchair, crawls into the seat beside Dora, and buckles his seat belt.

"Keep icing that head, you hear?" the nurse chirps through the open window. "You are so lucky, Mr. Fiveash." Her eyes flicker over to Dora at the wheel.

On the road, the motion makes Jerry feel sick at his stomach. Dora faces straight ahead, not looking at him, silent. Jerry closes his eyes.

When they're halfway home, she bursts out, "What did you expect, Jerry, going to one of those places? Only fuckin' idiots go to casinos."

"What." Groggy, he can't wake up fast enough to keep up with her.

He had no idea she'd been seething. "Don't blow 'em up, Dora. Don't blow up those casinos."

"I told you I'm not gunna do that. Anyhow, that's not why I'm mad." She steers the truck skillfully through highway traffic. "Jerry, do you realize you've never asked me anything about myself? My life? Why I ended up at Hawk Lake? I could be an ax murderer, and you wouldn't know it, 'cuz you're too wrapped up in yourself to ask anybody anything."

The "Marry me" note from Hoyt Landry—he'd forgotten about that. It was wrong of him not to give it to her. "Dora, there's this guy," he says, "this pilot, the one that saw you naked that day. He wants to, uh, marry you. He came running over one day and asked me about you."

Dora pulls the truck to the side of the road so fast Jerry hangs halfway out of his seat belt. She stops the truck at the shoulder.

"Look at me," she says.

Through his swollen eye, and past the corner of the big gauze patch taped to his forehead, he meets her flinty gaze. He says, "Dora, I've wondered about you, but I didn't want to be nosy. Okay. How did you come to be in Hawk Lake?"

"I don't believe you've wondered about me for one second," she says. She makes him wait, and then says at last, "A tornado hit the trailer where my whole family and me was living. Well, my dad had already left, before that. The tornado tore up the whole trailer, just carried it off and smashed it into some trees."

"You survived a tornado?" Somehow, he should have known she'd ridden the shrieking winds of a funnel cloud, been blown to hell and back.

"No, stupid. I wasn't home. None of us was. Thank God we picked that night to go honky-tonkin'."

Passing traffic rocks the truck. He is ashamed. She's right. He never gave much thought to her life, what experiences she might have had. "So you got back and there was nothing left."

"Just a bunch of sticks and trash. We stayed at a shelter for a while, and my mom saved up money. I worked, and my sisters did too, waitin' tables and cleaning houses till we had enough to move. When I made a down payment on my ATV, I thought I was in heaven. Them dogs you saw eatin' on the sofa, they just came to us, strays same as us."

He takes this in, picturing her and her mother and sisters counting their money, shoring up their hopes. "I'm glad things got better for you, Dora."

When she doesn't answer, he's afraid he sounded patronizing. His head aches.

He asks, "What about the crop duster? You want me to introduce you to him? He seemed like a nice guy."

She raises her hand as if to slap him, but stops. "If you wasn't already hurt so bad," she says. "Jerry, you just don't get it." She starts up the truck again, peers out the window, and eases into the road.

He has got to help her. Through his sickness, he has a vision of her: prelaw at the University of Arkansas. They'll never have seen anything like her. He'll pay her way, if she'll let him. Meanwhile, he hopes she'll keep on working for him. He'll feel better if he can only get back to work. After all, he still has his tax-sale properties and his art. He can make repairs during the day and come home at night and paint.

"I'll be up and around in a few days," he says after a while. "Want to plan on doing some work, say, by the end of the week?"

"I don't think so," says Dora. "In fact, I quit."

Okay, he thinks. That's it. What I've been waiting for, and didn't even know it. The Game is really over. He'll just have to dream harder, paint better. He hopes Dora will let him pay for college, but he'll wait a good long while before he brings that up.

THE HUMMINGBIRD INN lives up to its name. Scores of the tiny birds buzz across the wide porch, rising up and down around feeders of scarlet sugar water, all motion, all whirring. Louisa was inside the inn only once before, when she brought the *Belle* brochures over to Mary Griffin, the woman who runs the inn. There weren't as many hummingbirds then. She wants to hold one, to touch it, but their wings spin so fast, she can't get near. Passengers used to praise the inn and the birds.

"This is the latest they've ever been here," says Mary Griffin, who doesn't seem to recognize Louisa. "Global warming, I guess. They're supposed to be gone to South America by now, or wherever they go. Every summer, when they come back, I feel my heart turn over."

"Amazing," says Sam, reaching toward a bird as if to touch a soap bubble. "I've never seen one before, only in pictures."

"Grab me that feeder, that one," says Mary Griffin, gesturing with her chin. She's about ten years younger than Louisa, Louisa guesses. Her gray-blond braids are coiled over her head. "They aren't eatin' from that feeder. That means it's gone bad. Fermented. I have to put fresh sugar water in all of 'em, every couple days. When I was younger, I had five or six dogs, and you know what? These little birdies keep me every bit as busy as those dogs did."

Sam unhooks the feeder from its chain and hands it to the woman. She pours the liquid over the porch railing onto the grass, and a sticky, vinegary scent floats up. "Room for two?" she says, looking at them with a smile, leading the way inside to the reception desk, the old-fashioned kind with a cuckoo clock and keys on hooks on the wall behind the desk. On one end of the desk are stacks of brochures for local attractions—including ones for the *Belle*. Louisa stares at them. "Honeymooners?" Mary Griffin asks. Her gaze, flat and perceptive as a cat's, discomfits Louisa in a way that the stare of thousands, at the would-be Candles concert, had not.

"Just me," says Sam.

"But you're not far off. Soon we'll be married," Louisa says. She clears her throat. "Mary, I'm Louisa Shepherd. We've met."

"Oh, yes, I remember now," says Mary Griffin, holding up Sam's credit card to read the name and then running it through the machine. "Complimentary tea, coffee, and pastries in the morning, Mr. Moon," she says. "If you want eggs and bacon, I can fix 'em for a small extra charge. Lunch and supper, too, for that matter. The season's winding down, except for the hummers out there. You get the best room, high up in the treetops. You can see a little bit of Hawk Lake from the window."

Sam leans down to pick up his bag, his shoulders slumping crookedly the way they had when he scooped feathers from the yard. Louisa wants to say, "Have lunch and supper with me, Sam! Breakfast, too," but she can't, not in front of Mary Griffin. Should she go up to the room with him? She has no idea what to do. Sam looks so forlorn, like a child sent off to summer camp. Should she kiss him? Go upstairs and climb into the bed with him? How will she ever know what to do in bed, she who has had no practice in her whole long life? Teddy Shatford took that away from her—the physical longings she used to feel as a girl, the joy she'd felt at the pie supper when the Ozark boy led her outside the schoolhouse into the fine sleet and kissed her. After she had the baby, she might as well have been made of plaster, like yesteryear's lakeside statues of the parrot and the turtle, for all the desire she'd felt.

"It's not supposed to be this way," she says. Mary Griffin and Sam blink at her. "I just never got over it," she says.

Above them, the cuckoo bursts out of its clock and screams at the three of them. They freeze, transfixed by it, until the bird vanishes into its tiny house, the doors slamming shut behind it.

Mary Griffin says, "I guess I oughta toss these, right, Louisa?" as she sweeps the brochures off the desk and into a trash can.

BRIEFLY, IN THE WEEK before the mercury episodes, Katelynn had started stealing, and that time it was different from her thefts at the academy. Jenelle had been stealing for years. In the dressing room of a discount store just days before the mercury discovery, Katelynn had watched with scorn as Jenelle stuffed a package of hose into her pocketbook, then tried on a bra and wore it out of the dressing room and right out of the store. Katelynn had given up trying to talk Jenelle out of stealing, but she worried, as always, that if Jenelle were caught, she too would be accused. Because she *was* guilty. She knew.

Following Jenelle out of the double doors to the parking lot, Katelynn's thought had been *Those things will never really belong to Jenelle.* Jenelle's thefts were anonymous, not personal. Wasn't it more dangerous to cadge something from somebody you knew? Not a gardener's rake or a stranger's backpack, but an object with meaning.

So she had an electric week of it. A frosty nubbin of Jenelle's lipstick, the tip scoured off from use. A new pale green sweater belonging to her mother. Glo searched the house, when all along the sweater was scrunched up in Katelynn's bottom drawer. A tie clip from Mr. Stiles, in the shape of a golf club, which she found in his desk drawer, between classes, when the room was empty for five sweet seconds.

Everybody around her trailed objects with them, after them, comets' tails of belongings ready to be traded, sold, spirited away, handed over. In the hallways at school, at games while she cheered, at parties where she forced herself to drink the beer she hated, she saw how stealing could take over, how close were the world's pockets for any clever picker.

It took getting sick to see how stupid the stealing was, yet the temptations lingered. Wasn't Dr. McKellar's stethoscope, bulging from his coat pocket, just dying to leap into her fingers? But she didn't take it.

A lipstick, a sweater, a tie clip. Small lightweight things, yet how heavy they lie on her heart. If she hadn't played with mercury, what then? How much would she have stolen and from whom? Jenelle didn't know Katelynn stole, didn't know how much better Katelynn was. Anybody could take stuff from a store. You had to be better to do what Katelynn did. At the end of Katelynn's electric week, a parable played itself out. A member of the Hawk Lake town council was caught stealing key rings from the convenience store and was forced to resign. How foolish and petty the councilwoman had seemed, newly nicknamed "Key Ring," a pretentious face and a mop of dyed hair on the front page of the newspaper. Katelynn's parents laughed about Key Ring, and Katelynn joined in, sick at heart.

The lipstick, the sweater, and the tie clip were enough. Even now, they're in her room, the very embodiments of guilt. The rake she stole from the boxwood garden at the academy was worse: she'd learned that the aged gardener got a tongue-whipping for its disappearance.

A breeze from the lake sweeps over her, and she's glad for the afghan, pulling it to her chin. Mr. Stiles must have put it over her while she slept. Her mouth tastes stale and metallic. Where did the detective wake up this morning? Did he drive all night to bring her this news? With the sun behind him, she can't see his face.

So Louisa's son is a banker. A thrill runs over her like the thrill of standing up in her black dress at school and announcing "I died," an excitement as profound as if she, Katelynn, is responsible for his success.

"I'll get your money," she tells the detective, but she doesn't stir. She should get up and move out of this hard morning sun, go inside, find something to eat, and feed Peppy. She must return the stolen tie clip to Mr. Stiles. Oscar. But she feels as weak and giddy as she did in the walled boxwood garden at the academy. She has reached the center of the maze. She's found the sundial once again. None of those other girls ever talked about it. Is she the only one who knew about it, sought it out?

The slip of paper with the phone number is in her hand. The folder of pictures is at her feet. The detective sees her glance at it, then says, "Don't worry. He doesn't know anything about this. He never saw me."

He sighs, leans back on the chaise longue and puts his feet up. What if she doesn't pay him? Will he kill her? His sunglasses slide out of his pocket and onto the grass, but he makes no move to retrieve them. He's testing her, for he knows all about her. Green-black, like beetles, the plastic lenses shine from the grass.

She reaches across to him, her fingers lightly brushing his arm. His fingers lace through hers.

"That folder will change her life," he says. "You don't have to give it to her. You can put it away for years and years. Put it away forever, if you want. You can throw it in the lake. It's up to you. You don't have to decide today, Katelynn."

"But I do," she says. "I've put off everything, all my life. This is different. This is the most important thing I've ever done for anybody. Even if it had taken you ten years to find him, it would still be urgent. This is the day I tell her."

He moves his hand so their palms are pressed together. Can desire be learned in an instant? This is leagues beyond what she felt for Harvey. She is not imagining this. Or: she is imagining all of it, but she won't stop.

The sun's behind his head, and she's in his shadow. She guesses they have been here for hours, with the sun and clouds moving over the lake.

"I don't know how to talk to you," she says.

"You're doing fine," he says.

WITH SAM OVER at the Hummingbird Inn, Louisa cleans up her yard, raking all the flower arrangements into a pile and dumping them into trash bins, wheeling the bins to the street. There are far too many bouquets to fit inside, and the wreaths are much too large. The flowers just plain stink. She piles them on top of each other, the slick, decaying petals wetting her hands and leaving brownish smears on her blouse. Some of the dried-out leaves have sharp points that stab the skin on her hands and wrists, as if the mourners, raging with her, are exacting a scanty revenge. What about the stuffed animals? It seems heartless to throw them away, with their blank furry faces and shoe-button eyes. She separates them into their own pile so that they nestle beside a trash bin. Maybe a child will come along and spirit them away. She should take them to the Salvation Army or bring them inside. Maybe later on, but now there's much to do.

The damp, balmy air feels unhealthy, as if full of yellow fever germs. She buttons her denim blouse to her chin. Her hands sweat on the handle of the rake. She has got to finish cleaning up the yard, ridding it of all the symbols of death and mourning, and then she'll call Sam at the Hummingbird Inn, to see if he's doing all right.

She misses him, not the way all her life she has missed the suave young celebrity who deigned to speak to her, but misses the old man who bolted from his real life to chase the dream of a girl in a ruffle-necked dress who once talked to him about music made from jaw-bones.

The work wears her out. She leaves the rake outside, goes in, and lies down on the sofa, but she's too tired to relax or fall asleep or even doze. The *Belle* is gone. The *Belle* sank. Those people, all those people. Again she feels the weight of the cold water all around her. It was like pushing against heavy doors.

She sees faces, the passengers' faces, forming around her so vividly that she gives in and thinks: *Okay, come on in. I'll have you over. It's time we talked.*

They visit her; their souls do. First Bobby, Beebe's little brother, saying nothing, just tilting his head from one side to another as if she is blocking his view of a hawk. Then the Hedgepeth woman and her sister, clutching stuffed animals, and Louisa wants to say, "Help yourself to the ones out front, all those stuffed animals people brought for that poor Candle," but her teeth are glued shut and her heart is racing. Beebe's hungry mother hesitates at the end of Louisa's sofa and then glides past the others into the kitchen. In a moment, she's rustling around in the cabinets and opening the refrigerator. The iggle-watcher sits cross-legged on the floor, squinting as she pours liquid from one test tube into another. Little Bobby goes over to watch. Bobby's father leans against the wall, yawning, tapping his chest with his fingers, hooking his thumbs through the belt loops in his jeans.

They have materialized.

So this is what ghosts are like: restless, not unfriendly, neutral almost, just dropping by to tarry awhile, but she senses they are waiting. This is her chance. She tries to rise up from the sofa, but something pushes her back—the heaviness of her own heart, beating so hard she can only flop back down on the cushions.

"I'm sorry," she says. "I want to apologize to all of you. I would do anything for you to be alive again. I feel so bad for the ones who love you, for their broken hearts. Beebe, who has every reason to not be able to abide me, was nice enough to drive me all the way to Boston—to help me try and find somebody."

Do they hear her? The hungry woman returns with two jars pressed against her chest, dipping peanut butter from one and jam from another, licking her fingers, her expression gentle, yet distant. Can you be hungry in the afterlife? Apparently, yes. The stale marshmallows in the cupboard would seem more suitable food for ghosts. Louisa opens her mouth to tell her, "There's spoons in the far right-hand drawer and bread on the counter, didn't you see it?" but she can't find her voice.

Then the fat man appears.

Did he have this dignity when he was on the boat? He is in charge here, Truman Testa, the barber, reversing the injustice she did him on the boat—making him move. He hasn't lost an ounce. Drawn to his full height, his arms at his sides, he surveys the others in the room, taking in one after the other as if checking their names off a list. His hair looks wet at the tips, and a smell emanates from him, not the odor of mud and fish and lake water that she would expect, but the smell of fresh-cut summer grass and beer, as if he has just cut his backyard lawn on some ordinary evening and is relaxing with a Budweiser. Louisa's heart thrashes, not beating anymore but just sloshing, as if bilgewater is moving through its chambers. The blood pressing in her ears makes a distant spinning sound. Yet even now, here, she takes mental notes to report all this to Sam and Katelynn: *I couldn't see through them, exactly, but they weren't like real live people.* Katelynn will ask: *Did they throw shadows on the wall?* And Louisa will answer: *Not so's you'd notice. They were here, yet not here.*

"I went all the way to the bottom," Truman Testa says, speaking first to the other passengers, then turning to Louisa, "and I saw the turtle shell, the giant one from way back. You told us about it on the tour. You talked about wanting to see a certain type of marsh bird, a king rail, but mostly you talked about the turtle."

"I did?" She does not remember ever telling anybody about the turtle on any tour she ever gave. She always just thought about it, as they passed over the spot where she and the long-ago boys pushed the turtle overboard.

The people nod, and Truman Testa says, "You told us how you pushed it over the side of the boat, with the help of some neighbor kids, and you'd always wondered what happened to it."

She tries to say, I knew it was down there all along. I knew I hadn't heard the last of it, but her breath catches and no words come.

"The shell's lying on its side like a turned-over saucer, empty except for some mud," he says, cupping his hand to demonstrate, "and it's rough to the touch, all encrusted. That must have been some turtle. It reminded me of my first car, a Volkswagen Beetle, with those rounded fenders. How I saw it, I don't know, because there's no light that deep in the lake. It was very dark." He pronounces very "vurry," and she remembers that he's from New Jersey; she tucks this pronunciation away to tell Katelynn and Sam. He goes on, "At the bottom, I gathered all my strength and pushed with my feet, trying to come up again, but it was too mucky, and of course I was just too far down."

"Was there anybody else on the boat? Anybody not accounted for?" Louisa asks, raising her head from the sofa and addressing the whole group. The effort exhausts her. "I have to know."

They shake their heads no, looking puzzled. So this much at least she knows. The psychiatrist, Dr. Morton, had merrily declared, *You made him up.* Yet her heart sinks as if these visitors had answered yes, for their presence is overwhelming, and she can't separate one loss from another. Did she interrupt Truman Testa? Has she offended him?

Wetting her lips, she manages to say, "You-all are greatly mourned." To Truman, she says, "Your wife lived. Stella. She has a store."

The man nods but seems scarcely interested, as if something else is preoccupying him. Beebe's hungry mother stops eating; the iggle woman quits playing with the test tubes of water. The two sisters exchange glances, nodding. Beebe's father flips his hair off his forehead in that gesture she's seen Beebe make. Motionless, silent, they all regard Truman Testa and Louisa. The word *attend* crosses her mind. They are attending to him.

To her.

She realizes then: she must be dying. Her fall through the lake was a prelude to this, the nearness of these souls, of these risen dead. In the lake, she'd found that ladder, but now, in her familiar living room, there is no ladder, only these quiet shapes and her own flooding chest.

The man nods toward the little boy, Bobby, Beebe's younger brother, Bobby who had doubted that the bird he saw was really a hawk, Bobby who had taken her picture with his camera.

"Your brother," Louisa says to the child. "Your brother, Beebe, did a marvelous thing for me." She's running out of breath, but she has got to tell him about the trip to Boston, about the fairs and carnivals, about Beebe's kindness in sticking by her, when he could have ditched her and driven away at any time. Grasping at some way to tell all of this, she can only wheeze, "Tamales."

Stiffly, as if the word were a cue, the child gets to his feet and approaches the sofa, his eyes holding hers. Such depth in those smart, skeptical eyes, like she has seen in faded photos of Civil War drummer boys, Civil War fighters; they are eyes older than her own. He was robbed of a long life of hawk doubting, of staring into the sky and watching the wheeling birds. Compared with this child, this Bobby, she knows almost nothing.

He stretches out his hands, holding his palms toward her, and moves closer, until he places his hands on her neck, around her throat. Vanquished, she closes her eyes, unable to bat away the child's thin, cold fingers. He will stop the ragged ribbon of breath still feeding into her lungs. His fingers are sticky, as if from syrup or melted candy. She bets he'd like sorghum the way her grandparents made it, dense and pure. She smells its sweet smokiness with that undercurrent of green cane in it, smells it cooking in big cast-iron pots in the yard of her grandparents' cabin. Cooked long enough, it'll thicken and turn into molasses. Spoon it on a biscuit, pour it into a glass of well water, ask Granny to make gingerbread with black walnuts. *I'll crack them myself.* The scent deepens, and she sees the mule turning the creaking sweep of the roller mill, pressing the juice out of the stalks. Tossed to the side is a pile of used-up canes, "pummies." She hasn't thought about pummies in years. She will die breathless, thinking of a word nobody uses or even knows anymore. Her grandparents tended their canefield like it was a rose garden, but it stayed wild, for that was a wild place. Her grandfather used to say, "If you hear somethin' a-comin' through the cane, it's sure to be a bear or a preacher," and she, as a child, used to laugh, but the old man didn't, for bears and preachers were serious business.

She wants to tell her son that. She can't die, for she hasn't found him. She has to tell him about pummies and about how her grandfather always preferred mules to horses, because mules are stronger and not as like to scare. It was always a flappy-eared mule that powered the sorghum mill, plodding round and round, while her grandmother tended the boiling pots and Louisa's mouth watered for syrup. What were the mule's thoughts as it circled the mill, the landscape of cabin and ravine and old woman stirring pots repeating over and over in its view? An ox is even better than a mule, an ox is worth twenty horses. *Hit's the truth . . .*

The child's sticky thumbs press against her neck. He will hold down her windpipe and grind away, the way the mill crushes the thin, sweet juice out of the stalks of cane, turning her neck into a pummy.

The little boy's hands rustle at the collar of her blouse. All he does is unfasten the straining button at her neck, so she can breathe easier, the air whooshing into her tight lungs just as it did when she climbed that ladder through the lake and burst up to the surface. She inhales deeply, breathes past a pain in her chest, and opens her eyes.

They're gone.

A cricket chirps just outside her window, a raspy hitch. The light has changed, as if it's late in the day.

She wishes she'd asked after her father, her mother, Mr. Fiveash. Her grandparents and Aunt Patsy and the brother she never knew. The Candle who died in her bed. Asked them if they've met her baby, if he is up there, or out there, with them.

She has to wait and keep on waiting to see them again, and she has already waited so long to see the people she loves.

PART III

"**Y**ou're swelling, Maddy. Hold on, hon, I've got Cortaid around here somewhere," Louisa says, fumbling in a drawer.

"It itches like crazy," says Madison, clawing the rising red welt on her upper arm.

"Don't scratch. That'll just make it worse." Louisa rattles things in the drawer.

Maddy knows exactly what's in the drawer: Band-Aids, Bactine, Q-tips, head-lice shampoo, and sample sizes of toothpaste. She's had time to examine the contents of every drawer and cabinet in the nurse's office during the lunch breaks she spends here, after Louisa administers the twice-a-week allergy shots: every Tuesday, her right arm gets a shot; every Friday, the left one. One day, she even found the secret stuff, the sanitary pads and Tampax the older girls get. She can't wait for whatever event it is that requires these cottony, clean-smelling supplies. Her mom has explained the mystery in stiff, dull phrases that don't make sense. Then her mom launches into how babies are made, but that's even more confusing. Maddy can't follow what the egg is doing and what the "visitors" sent by a man have to do with it. Her mom's weird drawings of little fish attacking a big circle just make Maddy crack up.

Fairley's lucky. He has nothing more than an occasional sniffle, whereas she, Maddy, has been known to sneeze forty times in a row. Fairley keeps count, egging her on, swiping his hand through the air each time like he's waving a flag to help her win the Indy 500. He wants to be a race-car driver. The shots are slowly helping. Maddy's eyes aren't as red, her nose doesn't stream all the time, and the back of her throat has quit aching so much. The chapped skin between her lips and her nose is finally healing. Still, she keeps Kleenex in every pocket.

The time with Louisa is worth the trouble of the shots. Dr. McKellar has declared that she must get these shots for at least five years. Didn't he notice how that pleased her? Twice a week for five years is wonderful, because she and Louisa have fun. They talk about all kinds of things. Maybe Maddy can get her mom to take her to Louisa's house in the summertime. Her mom probably won't. She'll take her to the clinic, where the air-conditioning's too cold and the magazines are always the same boring ones with pictures of houses.

Until Maddy knew Louisa would be giving the shots, she dreaded them. She hates shots. Fairley practiced on her to get her used to the idea. He spit on his finger and rubbed the spit on her bare arm. That was the dab of alcohol. Sometimes he blew on it, to make it cold, like the real thing. Then he'd take a corner of his fingernail and twist it ever so lightly into her skin, not puncturing. It made her sick at her stomach. She'd slap his hand away while he fell back laughing. Thank goodness Dr. McKellar told her mom that these days, any school nurse could give the shots; no sense coming all the way to his office in the middle of the school day. At first, Barbie hesitated. She'd never quite forgiven Louisa, she said, for being so—so—Barbie would frown, concentrate, and belch softly. Maddy could only figure that her mom was jealous of Louisa being famous, even if it's for a bad reason—that boat.

Yet people seem to have forgotten. How can they? She is amazed by the shortness of people's memories. Maybe she's entirely wrong, though, and they think about it all the time.

"Here we go. A little bit's left in this tube." Louisa presses the bottom of the crumpled tube, and a white blob of Cortaid bubbles over the top. Maddy rubs it on her skin, but this is a bad itch, to her joy. The swelling is the size of a quarter. It can get bigger, but not too much bigger. One time it got to be Ping-Pong-ball-sized, and she had to go to the hospital, which was awful. A quarter-sized swelling is perfect. It won't last long, anyway.

Louisa asks, "Ice pack? We're out of the fancy blue kind, but I've got regular ice."

Delighted, Maddy nods. Until the after-lunch crowd comes in, the really nutty kids who need Ritalin twice a day, she has Louisa all to herself. She can probably wheedle ice in a cup, too, and a can of cold ginger ale from the compact refrigerator where her serum is kept. She loves the word *serum,* such a sleek, grown-up sound. Her serum is packed with invisible bits of all the things she's not supposed to be around: dog hair, cat fur, pollen. These shots, she has announced to Fairley, are nothing, not even as bad as mosquito bites, 'cuz the needle's real thin. Keep your old fingernails to yourself, she says.

Having allergies isn't like being sick. She's never been sick the way Louisa was sick, when she had a heart attack two and a half years ago and had to spend a whole week in the hospital. She'd been sort of dreaming, Louisa said, about the people who had died on her boat, and then her chest got all tight.

"What were the people doing? Was it a bad dream?" Maddy had

asked, a dumb question she decided, since Louisa looked so upset. In the special language Maddy and Fairley invented, a long time ago, there was a word for that look. Maddy figures Louisa had seen Aunt Stella's husband in that dream, her first husband who drowned.

"Here you go," says Louisa, handing Maddy an ice cube wrapped in a clean towel.

Stella is not really Maddy's aunt, of course. Her mom just wants the twins to call her that, because her mom and Stella are best friends. Her mom works at the store. Business is so good that her mom says Stella's getting rich. Maddy's never been able to warm up to Stella the way her mom wants her to. The same goes for Stella's husband, Uncle Harvey. Maddy loves playing dress-up in the flower-girl gowns, though. "Bring all your little friends. Have a party," Stella will say, and then Maddy knows it's time to change back into her regular clothes and hang up the flower-girl gown, fluffing the plastic wrap back over it, because, except for Fairley and Louisa, she doesn't really have any friends.

The best part about dressing up is the basket you get to carry, after choosing from all the different baskets in the store. The baskets are lined with satin so the rose petals won't get bruised. If she's ever going to be in a wedding, she'll have to practice tossing the rose petals. When she watches herself in the three-way mirror, her arms look jerky, all sharp elbows and floppy wrists. If she had petals to practice with, she could get it right.

If she's not asked to be a flower girl soon, her chances will be over forever. Stella made a remark about the gowns looking too short on her. It was just a mild remark, as Stella pinned up the hem on a lady's bridesmaid gown. Maddy went on practicing the petal-tossing movements, but Stella's words stung. Maddy's growing, and a lot faster than Fairley. He's jealous, but it's not the kind of jealous she can enjoy, like the times she takes longer to finish her half of a Klondike bar and he begs for the last bite.

Louisa leans down to inspect the swelling on Maddy's arm. "Keep that ice on it," she says. Without Maddy even having to ask, Louisa takes a plastic cup from the cabinet and lifts the ice tray and a can of ginger ale from the refrigerator. "Think I'll have some too," she says, pouring. "I'll just drink out of the can."

Maddy sips her ginger ale delicately, pretending it's champagne, which she has never tasted, but according to books is bubbly and fantastic. She watches Louisa bustle around the tiny office, adjusting the eye chart on the wall, weighing herself on the big scales, sighing.

"You're not feeling tight in your chest, are you? Trouble breathing?" Louisa asks.

"No." Maddy felt the tightness the time she had the Ping-Pong-ball-sized swelling and had to go to the hospital. Dr. McKellar said it just meant she needed less serum per dose. It wasn't as bad as the times before she started the shots, when she'd have an asthma attack and wheeze and gasp for breath. She had to go to the emergency room twice for that.

She will never forget how awful it was to have trouble breathing.

Her mom makes her clean her room all the time now, dusting under the bed, wiping down the floors every Saturday with wet rags. She hates the cleaning and the dumb way the allergies make her face look, like she's always on the verge of sneezing, which she usually is. Fairley never has to clean his room. His toy race cars clutter the floor; his racing posters hang at crazy angles on the walls. Once, Maddy opened up the vacuum cleaner bag, stuck her hand in, grabbed a handful of lint, and made him sniff it. He still didn't sneeze.

He won't do their secret words anymore, and she's sure that he has forgotten the language, on purpose at first and now just from not using it. They'd invented it together and used it till Fairley wouldn't anymore, starting about a year ago. Oh, they understood regular words too, all along. Understood perfectly, though it could be useful to pretend they didn't, like when Mom and Dad were fighting. Maddy misses the language. She and Fairley used to make up dozens of new words every day. Now Maddy is forgetting it, too, and that makes her sad in a way she can't tell anybody about, not even Fairley. She'll form sentences in her head, but they slip away. The language had a pretty sound. Lots of the words were said louder in the middle, and there were rules about not sounding singsongy. Fairley could speak it faster than she could. Now when she tries to start a conversation in the old talk, Fairley cuts her off with, "Stick with regular words, Mad. Or work on Spanish." They've had Spanish since first grade. It's old hat. You can learn it from TV, where those silly kids' shows teach you how to say *hola!*

Once, she taught a little neighbor boy a few words of the secret language, and he latched on to it immediately, picked it up like she was handing him candy. She had to stop teaching him, though, because it hurt Fairley's feelings. Fairley actually cried when she told him the little boy understood the secret talk. It's a shame that Fairley won't talk it anymore, yet he doesn't want anybody else to learn it. Maddy just loves words. She's practicing reading backward. She can hold up a greeting card to the mirror and puzzle out the message, if she takes her time.

It's not the same as the secret language.

Someday, she realizes as she sits in the nurse's office, she and Fairley will have forgotten the language entirely, every word. Someday, Fairley might live far away from her, and he'll forget a lot of things that are important now, and so will she, and they'll be like so many other people, who don't know how important it is to remember.

People still ask them twin-type questions. She and Fairley are used to it. Do you feel each other's aches and pains? Are you identical? They say yes because it makes people happy. Maddy and Fairley can feel each other's pain because they tell each other about it. Does your mother belong to a twins' support group? *She used to.* She still has their double-wide stroller that somebody in the support group gave her, back when they were babies. She predicts Stella and Harvey will have twins, too, and then she'll pass the stroller on to them. That makes Aunt Stella turn red, and she'll say, *Barbie! Don't wish that on me,* which makes Maddy want to say, *What's so bad about it?* But she just watches all the feelings race across Stella's face.

From watching the ranges of expression on people's faces, Maddy and Fairley had invented phrases for a zillion different feelings. No face ever looks the same for more than a few seconds in a row. You just have to watch close.

Her mom always says, about Louisa getting the job as school nurse: *They were desperate.* Louisa first worked at the high school, because the nurse there had quit. Then the job opened up here at the elementary school, and Louisa says she likes this better, because she gets to work with the little kids. *But I'm not a little kid,* Maddy always says. And Louisa's a wonderful nurse, the best. The school was not desperate. *They're lucky to have her,* Maddy thinks.

With both hands, Louisa takes the drawer with everything in it and lifts it out of the cabinet, then sits down in the chair beside Maddy's, balances the drawer on her lap, and drags the trash can over beside her. "I got to go through here and clean house," she says, but not like she minds. *Thunk,* and a bottle of aspirin flies into the trash can. "Why, I could go to jail for giving a kid aspirin, did you know that, Maddy? Unless there's a note from a doctor. Not just a parent, a doctor. Same with Tums and cough medicine. Lotsa this stuff's expired anyway." She tosses sticky jars and packets into the trash can. "Here. Want an emery board?"

It's a cute yellow one with hearts on it. Maddy puts it in her pocket. Next, Louisa finds a stub of a lipstick—it's the exact pinkish-orange of Maddy's favorite shade of construction paper. Without even looking in the mirror that hangs over the sink, Louisa runs the lipstick over her lips, plucks a tissue from the box, and presses it against her mouth.

"There," she says, holding up the Kleenex with the kissprint on it, a little bit smeared. "A Mexican fortune-teller could look at this and predict my future. That's how they do it. A lady—a lady on my boat told me that, one time."

"What else is in there?" Maddy asks, peering into the drawer. "Any condoms? Do you give those out?" She's fishing, hoping to find out what they are. Fairley says they're nasty. She guesses he doesn't really know, either.

Louisa doesn't act the least bit surprised about condoms. "I gave 'em out by the handful when I worked at the high school." She crumples up the Kleenex with the kissprint and throws it away. "Better they use 'em than not use 'em."

Maddy sips her ginger ale, thinking, *champagne*. Champagne and serum and condoms. "What are condoms?"

"Just a little piece of rubber the boy puts on his self to keep from making babies for the girl."

"Oh."

She has known Louisa for such a long time, since the night of the day the boat sank. She still remembers what her mom fixed for supper at Louisa's house, her favorite meal back then: fish sticks and Tater Tots. She remembers the day of the memorial service, when Louisa cut her hair and Fairley's. The botched bowl haircuts lasted for months, because she and Fairley have the kind of hair that never grows. As they drove toward the lake, as her mom and Louisa went on about *People* magazine, all Maddy's emotions rushed together—guilt about gouging the middle out of a blackberry pie at Louisa's house, the dizzy way she felt when she looked at the appliquéd lion on Louisa's black sweatshirt, and her shame about her mom's burping. All the feelings boiled around in her stomach. Before she knew it, she'd crapped her pants right there in the car. Talk about embarrassing. Who could blame Louisa for hopping out on the side of the road?

Yet that saved her from having to go to the funeral, or the memorial service, or whatever it was. Even as her mom drove home, fussing all the way, Fairley whispered to Maddy, "Better not try that again, just 'cuz you want to get out of something," and they laughed and laughed, making their mom angrier than ever.

"Mom eats grit," Maddy volunteers to Louisa, "this orangy-smelling stuff she stirs up in a glass of water. It looks like fish food. It's supposed to help her digestion."

"That reminds me. Katelynn's husband got us some fish," Louisa says, "in a nice big aquarium. Did I tell you? Tropical ones, all different colors. They're not supposed to get too much food, or the water turns cloudy. We watch 'em for hours. Come see 'em."

"Can I?" She's ready to jump up right then and go. She's been to Katelynn's house a few times, when Louisa has baby-sat her and Fairley. Louisa lives at Katelynn's house. There's never enough time to see everything, and Maddy knows better than to run around opening all the closets and picking everything up. But when she's at Katelynn's house, she holds her eyes open extra wide, to take everything in, and she tucks away the sounds and the smells to think about later.

Louisa slides the drawer back into the cabinet and checks Maddy's arm. "More ice?"

"Yes," says Maddy, to keep the excitement going. She doesn't want to go back to the classroom, where the teacher fussed at her yesterday for reading *The Hound of the Baskervilles* during arithmetic, not understanding that Maddy was through with the problems. She's the fastest person in class, so fast she has to try to make herself slow down. She has worked ahead three chapters in the arithmetic book. She misses Fairley. This is the first year they're not in the same room.

The Hound of the Baskervilles is scary, but in a good way, not scary like the last book she read, which was written by a long-ago girl who was captured by Indians when she was almost nine, the exact age Maddy is now, and who then grew up and wrote the book. The Indians had killed the girl's parents, sisters, and brothers. Yet, the girl wrote, as she grew up, she began to love the Indians, to see how kind they were, and she almost forgot, sometimes, that they'd killed her family. Don't, Maddy wanted to tell her. Don't love them. Yet the author, as if arguing with Maddy, wrote of how the Indians had been hurt by white soldiers, how their land was stolen from them.

After that, *The Hound of the Baskervilles* is a relief.

She takes fresh ice cubes from Louisa and wraps them in the cold towel. They stick to the terry cloth. She's supposed to stay here exactly thirty minutes after her shot, then go to the cafeteria for fifteen minutes, but she's found that if she distracts Louisa, she can usually get to spend her whole lunch period right here.

"Who's cooking tonight, at your house? And what?" she asks. It's a favorite question. Everybody who lives at Louisa's house—Katelynn's house—is famous. Maddy can't imagine a town with more famous people than Hawk Lake. Famous, yet they still eat supper.

"Lemme think," says Louisa, leaning against the built-in sink, as if it's the most ordinary thing in the world to live in a glass house with a bunch of your friends and take turns cooking every night. "It's Oscar's turn. He likes those store-bought biscuits that come in a pop-open can. He'll put a slice of apple and a piece of cheese on each one, then pour syrup over that and bake 'em. They're right rich, but real good."

"What kind of cheese? Cheddar cheese?" *Cheddar* is another wonderful word.

"Velveeta, which I love, but I'm not supposed to eat too much cheese or butter, 'cuz of that heart attack."

"That biscuit stuff sounds like dessert. Or breakfast food," says Maddy critically, but she memorizes the biscuit-apple-cheese recipe to try at home. It sounds delicious.

"Sometimes he does fix breakfast food for supper—bacon and eggs. Katelynn won't eat meat. She gives her bacon to the dog."

Even Katelynn's dog, Peppy, is famous, because of the way he looks, not like any other dog: funny and spooky at the same time, with big feet and a big neck like a horse's, but skinny in between, with a high ridge on his back and a crazy-colored coat. Whenever Peppy gets loose, which is a lot, you can hear Katelynn calling him, her voice echoing across the lake. If you put glow-in-the-dark paint on the dog's pointy nose and sent him out at night to scare people, he would make an awesome hound of the Baskervilles.

Louisa goes on, "I used to eat bear bacon, when I was a child. My grandma, the one who lived up in the mountains, she used to fry it up in her iron skillet."

Bear bacon? Maddy's alert. She loves to hear Louisa talk about her childhood. She's learned when to ask questions and when to be quiet, to let Louisa just go on. This time, though, Louisa doesn't go on. She just stands against the sink, her hands clasped. "I'd love to go back there," she says at last, "and find that old cabin. But it's all gone, bound to be. I wouldn't even know where to look."

"Katelynn's husband could find it, I bet," Maddy says. Katelynn's husband is practically a magician. Most of the people he finds are either dead or have done bad things, Maddy knows that much. *A person who solves crimes, who searches for perpetrators of crime, or their victims.* She read that in her encyclopedia when she looked up *detective.* She has seen him only a few times, because he's out of town a lot on mysterious business, but she knows the story by heart, about how they all ended up at the glass house. Mr. Stiles got fired for living at the school, and Katelynn invited him over and he just never left. Together, he and Katelynn wrote a book about the history of Hawk Lake, so now they're officially Authors. That fascinates Maddy.

And Louisa ended up at Katelynn's house too. Louisa lost her own house in the lawsuits, not just Stella's but other suits filed by other relatives of people who died on the boat. Maddy pictures an avalanche, a huge sliding mass of house, yard, furniture, dishes, all slipping down a hillside: that's what it means to lose your house. The lawsuits cleaned Louisa out, though she still owns a boat she hardly ever uses. Other people live in her house now.

Louisa could have gotten married. Sam, the love of her life, showed up out of the blue and proposed, and Louisa said yes and then changed her mind, but they're still friends. Maddy has heard Aunt Stella say, "Stupid, if you ask me." Maddy doesn't think Louisa was stupid not to marry him, even though he's so nice. It's almost more romantic to have him around as a friend.

And Katelynn's husband-detective, well, that's the most wonderful story of all, Maddy thinks, except that she knows so little about him. Details, she wants more details. She knows Katelynn hired him for some reason that no one will talk about, and then they fell in love.

"Do y'all say the blessing before you eat?" she asks Louisa, who nods slowly, as if she's still thinking about bear bacon. "Do you hold hands while you say it? And take turns saying it?"

"Most of the time, I say it. We don't hold hands."

"How does Katelynn collect rent from everybody?" Maddy asks. "Does she make you line up and hand over the money?"

Louisa looks surprised, as if she'd gone back to the cabin in her mind and forgotten all about Maddy. "Well, there's only two of us she collects from, me and Oscar. Her husband doesn't pay rent, of course. I just leave the money in an envelope on her dresser, first of every month. So does Oscar. She's gotten real neat, now that she's grown up. We put the money underneath this little statue on her dresser, a statue of a little Oriental girl."

"Oh, I want to see it!"

Louisa warms to her subject. "Katelynn took us in, Oscar and then me. She never has charged us nearly as much as she ought to, but she's got a few house rules. No smoking, but that's not a problem except for her husband. He has to go outside in the yard to smoke his cigarettes. All the shades have to be down and the curtains drawn before dark, so nobody can see her moving around inside the house. Funny, sometimes I almost forget it's glass. I tease Katelynn, tell her she's the old woman in the shoe, taking care of all of us."

"What if you quit paying rent? Would she kick you out?"

"I always pay. So does Oscar."

"But what if."

"Well, I guess she'd have to kick us out eventually," Louisa says and laughs. "You can't let people just sponge off you."

Of all the famous people in the glass house, Katelynn is the most famous. She has done so many amazing things. Long ago, she ate mercury or smoked it, Maddy has never quite gotten that straight, but what it meant was that Katelynn got sick, never finished high school, and had to take a special test instead. Her dad ran away to the other side of the world, where he married another woman before he even divorced Katelynn's mother, and they have a daughter. Maddy wonders if the Oriental statue on Katelynn's dresser could look like that child. Katelynn's mother ran off too, to Mississippi, to a little house in the middle of a cotton field, where she flies a plane. Louisa has said that Katelynn and her dad send e-mail back and forth, that she hears from him more than she hears from her mother. *I got sick of living in a glass house,* Katelynn says her mother said, as if that sentence means lots of things.

Maddy and Fairley talked about the duck boat for years in their secret language, mapping out survival strategies should they ever find themselves on board a sinking, canvas-topped tour boat, with or without a fat man. The fat man was a wildly comic figure in their early lives. To Maddy, he's stopped being funny. The sinking wasn't his fault at all. She knows the rest of the story, about the bad seals and something about an alarm not being there, that would have sounded when water starting coming in. Plus, some kind of hose came apart. When Maddy has trouble getting to sleep, she tries to picture seals, alarm, and hose, and then she drifts off.

The duck boat's sinking haunts her and Fairley both. Just last night, Fairley said he can tell as soon as he meets somebody if that person would try to save your life or not. "It's all that matters," he said. Then he lay back on his bed, looking the way he does when he's figuring out an arithmetic problem. Maddy is way ahead of him in arithmetic.

"What about Mom?" Maddy asked Fairley. "Would she save people?"

He was quiet for a while. "I've thought about that a lot. She'd save us, but only 'cuz she knows us. She'd save Aunt Stella, too. But that's all. She wouldn't take an oar and knock people out of a lifeboat, but she wouldn't, you know, really help."

Maddy knew he was right. "Would she save Dad?"

"Before they got divorced, she might've. Now, no way," Fairley said.

Now she asks Louisa, "Did you ever think it would sink?"

"I never did," says Louisa, not at all surprised. "Not once, in all those years. Sometimes when I wake up, it's still a few seconds till I remember."

Suddenly, Maddy is frightened. To sink, to almost drown, means not being able to breathe. It means being underwater and choking. That happened to Louisa. It's too awful to think about. To change the subject, fast, she offers Louisa her latest secret.

"I have a cat."

Louisa, who is now rearranging things in the little refrigerator, says over her shoulder, "With your allergies, hon? You ought not to."

"I know."

"What color is it?"

"Orange. He's not really mine, but when I go out on the back porch, he comes up after a little while." She stops. She can't tell Louisa about speaking the secret language to the cat. She has to hold that back because of promising Fairley she won't speak the language to anybody else. That probably means other people, but she still won't tell.

"Where does the kitty come from?" asks Louisa.

"I never see. All of a sudden, he's just there," she says, "and sometimes he leaves stuff for me, like feathers. One time he left a mole. They're presents." When her mom finds the things on the back steps, she kicks them into the bushes, saying, *Ick,* a word she's picked up from Stella.

"Aren't you getting hungry? It's lunchtime," Louisa says, smiling. "Onion rings with hamburger patties today."

Maddy's hungry, but she'll put off going to lunch as long as she can. Onion rings, though, are hard to resist. Onion rings are what her mom puts on top of everything when she wants food to be fancy— onion rings on pork chops, onion rings on the green-bean casserole.

"Lemme see that arm," Louisa says.

When Maddy peels the wet towel away, she sees her skin's back to normal, flat and pale, with just the tiniest dot to show where the needle went in.

"Good. You're all set," says Louisa. She takes Maddy's empty cup, throws it into the trash, and tosses the wet towel into a laundry hamper. "Now scoot."

Maddy sighs. She imagines the printed words *She sighed,* and the phrase is thrilling, almost tragic. When she gets home, she'll get her mom's lipstick, kiss a Kleenex, and figure out her own fortune. "Okay," she tells Louisa. "Bye."

As she hurries down the hallway, toward the smell of onion rings, she can hardly wait until Tuesday, to find out what Louisa does over the weekend.

TOMORROW, KATELYNN WILL be busy. Cleaners are coming with power hoses to wash the glass walls outside. She'll be driving to Memphis for lunch. Malcolm, her husband, will be here, and they'll spend time together, maybe have dinner at a new restaurant where people rave over the shrimp scampi. She's done nothing but read all day, and now she has to rush to do the housework, the chores she sets for herself: putting out clean towels, walking the dog.

She finds the picture in the linen closet, the laminated newsprint photo of Walt, Louisa's son, the one taken at a New Year's Eve party, and she bursts out laughing. You never know where it'll turn up. When she'd finally told Louisa she'd located him—that the detective had found him—it got to be all she and Louisa talked about. That was before the detective, Malcolm, became her husband. Katelynn and Louisa told Oscar Stiles about the discovery, and then the three of them talked about it all the time, until Louisa said it wasn't fair, that they knew about her son and he didn't know a thing, didn't know he'd been found and that any day she might call him or write him or just go up there and who knows, just knock on his door. Would everybody please quit talking about him behind his back?

And no, she couldn't decide whether she would call him or not, or write to him or not. A hundred times, she confessed, she'd had her hand on the phone, but then she couldn't do it. She'd feel so strongly one way, then the other way. I will never figure this out, she said.

Katelynn had told Louisa, "Maybe if you see him here, then see him there, if he just pops up in front of you, and if you keep track of how you feel, then you can decide. You need to explore your feelings." Katelynn felt old and wise, saying that.

Louisa shook her head. "See him here and there? What do you mean?"

So Katelynn started this. She laminated the Walt picture with see-through tape and put it in the closet, balanced on top of Louisa's coat. She didn't hear or see Louisa find it. It was Louisa who turned this into a game. Katelynn heard Oscar say, "Oh, my goodness. *Walt!*" Oscar's louder and more confident than he used to be. Waving the picture, he'd raced into the living room, where Katelynn and Louisa sat, and said, "Who put this on my pillow?" and Louisa had chortled, a real belly laugh. That surprised Katelynn, that laugh.

So Oscar had the picture then. He sneaked in and put it on Katelynn's dresser, with his rent check. Katelynn propped it up in the cabinet where Louisa keeps her jar of instant coffee. She heard Louisa find it, early one morning, with a little gasp. *There he is. Here he is.*

Louisa is getting used to Walt. They all are. This is what it takes. They don't talk about this game. That's the only rule—that nobody mention the photo circulating throughout the house. Walt might pop up in a drawer that's not opened very often, or on top of the TV set, or high up on a curtain rod, his party-hatted head inclined toward you in perpetual celebration, the newsprint eyes fixed just beyond your own. He might go underground and not be seen for a week or two, and then, all of a sudden, there he is on the bathroom mirror or on Katelynn's mouse pad. You're not allowed to fold, spindle, or mutilate him.

Just a few days ago, Katelynn had the best idea of all: she propped him behind the aquarium, so that air bubbles trailed through his New Year's Eve party, and fish glided to and fro across his smile. All three of them—Katelynn, Louisa, and Oscar—leaned down and stared at him, as if at any minute, he'd speak. It was as good as a movie.

The aquarium was one of Malcolm's best ideas. It has just the right amount of stuff in it—a little submarine, a miniature diver in goggles and helmet, a mermaid with green plastic hair, real live plants, and beautiful fish in jelly-bean colors, their tails and fins waving like scarves.

The Walt picture is at the bottom of a stack of fresh towels. Katelynn lifts it down and holds it to the light, wondering for the thousandth time what else, besides the widow's peak and the down-turning eyes, he has inherited from Louisa. She bets the knowledge that he's adopted would knock that party hat right off his head. Walt's one of those glossy movie-star types, but who's to say he might not be nice, and his wife, too? His wife looks chubby and friendly, if pampered, with wide cheeks blossoming in a heart shape around her lipsticked lips. She would remember the names of his colleagues' wives and remember to send thank-you notes after they go to dinner parties. She's the one who deals with sitters, caterers, yardmen, repairmen, and maids, sees to Walt's dry cleaning, takes the pets to the vet and the kids to the doctor, orthodontist, child psychiatrist, country club, ballet class, stable, soccer field, and birthday parties where bored youngsters, heirs to billions, ride on rented elephants and go on treasure hunts for hidden trinkets like mini–laptop computers, Rolex watches, and bejeweled purses in the shapes of animals and fruit. That's Walt's wife's whole life, what she does daily, sighing, smiling, martyred.

Katelynn hates them both, hates their kids too.

She argues with herself. She has money, maybe more than Walt. What's the difference between her own mother and Walt's wife? Didn't Glo lead the rich-lady life, meeting with the people from the house-and-garden magazine, calling in caterers whenever she felt like it? Yes, but Glo has left all that. Left it, in fact, to an alarming degree, and now lives on the little farm she bought from Jerry as if it's eighty years ago and she's dependent on her chickens and her crops. Jerry sold Glo the house for a song.

Glo never asks about Jerry, but Katelynn makes sure Glo knows how successful Jerry has become with his paintings: big canvases, visions of the lake in mist, in storms, paintings on display at the ice-cream parlor and the museum. And paintings of people he must know or used to know, faces that aren't quite Glo's or Dora's or the cashier's at the convenience store, but faces that make you think of them for an instant, as if he has painted the feelings beneath the faces. Katelynn bought Jerry's painting of the boy who found the diamond at the diamond mine a few years ago. The child's expression isn't the joyful, giddy one that appeared in newspaper photos, but rather is reflective, with a blaze in the eye that stops Katelynn in her tracks. That painting is a small oil, unframed, which she keeps in her bedroom, the room she shares with her husband.

When she cowrote the book about Hawk Lake, collaborating with Oscar, she got to meet the diamond boy. By herself, she drove to Joliet, Illinois, and interviewed the boy at his kitchen table. He'd grown a lot since he'd found the diamond, but his sunshine-and-buckteeth face looked familiar as she sat there with her tape recorder and notebook. "Soon's I pulled it out of the rock, I knew it was real," he said. He wore braces by then, and he had on a Chicago Bears sweatshirt. Schoolbooks were stacked on the table. His mother offered Katelynn doughnuts and milk. "What did you do with the diamond?" Katelynn asked him. He'd sold it, of course. "Money for college," he said, biting into a doughnut. Outside the kitchen window, snow was falling, and Katelynn felt so cozy and warm, she wanted to stay in that kitchen for a long time. The boy's mother announced that their whole family had learned about investing, that her son had already figured out how much he would need not only for college, but for retirement. "But Mom," the boy said, "she wants to know about the diamond." To Katelynn, he said, "It didn't sparkle that much, but it was real pretty. Nobody but me thought so." Katelynn kept looking past the boy to the window, in hopes the snow was still falling, and it was. During the boy's vacation at Hawk Lake, he and his parents and his little sister had been out on the *Belle,* he said. He'd heard about what happened. It was terrible, he said.

The trip was partly a test Katelynn had set for herself, to prove she was well, to see if she could make the journey alone. That was before she was married. Just before she set out, Malcolm had asked her to marry him, and she'd said she would let him know. Oscar and Louisa insisted she call them every night to tell them where she was on the road. She did just fine.

She came back and wrote up the interview as part of the book about Hawk Lake's history, but she doesn't think she got it right. Oh, the facts are there—diamond, discovery, fame and fortune—but there was more in the boy's face and in the snow outside the window, more than she could put into words. There are so many more questions she should have asked that boy. *What other differences has the diamond made in your life? Describe the mine, how it smelled and how the dirt felt under your hands, the exact color of the stone. Tell me what you had for breakfast that day and what was the first thing you ate after you found the diamond. Tell me everything.* His life changed overnight, just as hers did, though as she sat at his kitchen table and watched snowflakes tumbling against the window and smelled the sugary doughnuts, she was glad she didn't have to tell him about mercury poisoning or seeing the *Belle* sink. She could think about those things, but she didn't have to say them.

She has tried to explain all of this to Malcolm, Oscar, and Louisa, but she's not sure they understand. Does Peppy? She's talked more about it to him than to anybody else.

Peppy goes wild when she takes him to Mississippi to visit Glo. He runs loose in the fields, lolloping through the brush, chasing rabbits and scaring up quail.

Sometimes, Hoyt Landry is at the house visiting Glo, but Glo has made it clear to Katelynn that he's just a friend. Glo shuffles around in an apron she found in the old kitchen and seems to be having a grand time planting her own sweet potatoes and flying her own plane whenever she takes a notion.

It's been two and a half years since Glo moved out there. "How long do you plan to stay down here, Mom?" Katelynn asked her mother, as Glo wrung out clothes in an old-fashioned wringer, a terrifying-looking contraption that could eat her alive.

"Forever," said Glo. "This is it for me, Katelynn. It's the part of my life I skipped and am making up for."

She does have her flying license, and Katelynn's proud of that. Glo has invited her to go up in the little plane sometime, but Katelynn isn't ready. Not yet.

Despite the chickens, Glo's still rich, drawing money from her bottomless bank account whenever she wants. It's just that she doesn't seem to want much anymore. She's grown freckly and age-spotted, her red hair shot through with gray streaks and hanging limp and long over her shoulders. Yet she's developed a new, careless, sloppy beauty that she never had back when she took aerobics classes and worried about wrinkles. It's all a rebellion against her father, Katelynn thinks. They didn't officially divorce until a few months ago, but Katelynn kept their room ready at the glass house, just in case.

"You can get another boarder. Rent that room out, Katelynn," Glo said, pulling a pair of jeans out of the wringer.

"Well!" said Katelynn. That's all she seems to say to her mother these days, so shocked is she by Glo's choices. "I like things the way they are."

"So do I," said Glo. "I like being alone, out here. Sometimes at night, I take a sleeping bag outside and just sleep under the stars."

The world's fair book was on the kitchen table, but Katelynn didn't have the heart to ask for it back. Beside it was a copy of the book by Oscar and Katelynn. It was Katelynn's idea. Oscar did most of the writing. The book was open to the photos of the ostrich carts. Katelynn stood in Glo's kitchen, which still has a faint skunky undercurrent, and she remembered the costume party there, which seemed like a million years ago. There isn't much of her old mom in this new Glo, except the love that will always be there, beneath the skin of distraction and impatience. "You're looking good," Glo said, bringing in a load of dry clothes, stiff from the clothesline. "That mercury. You'll never know how scared I was, that you would die."

"Dr. McKellar wrote me up in a medical journal. Oscar showed me a copy. Not by name. In the article, I'm just 'a female adolescent' who inhaled mercury vapors." Seeing the article, recognizing herself, had startled her. Waving the thick, scholarly periodical, Oscar had said indignantly, "He's made a career off you," but Katelynn defended him: "He made me well. He can write about it, if he wants."

Glo just smiled about the article. "Pregnant yet?"

"Mom!" Katelynn wailed. "Give us a little time. We don't even know each other that well, yet." We never will, she thought proudly. We'll never fall into that deadly married habit of not talking, or just concurring.

"You mean you don't have sex?"

"Mom!" Katelynn's cheeks burned. "That's not what I mean." She knows her husband is surprised by how eager she is in bed, and that it delights him. She meant, literally, that they don't know each other all that well in terms of all the other ways people know each other. Their years ahead are like a deep well, waiting.

Glo shrugged. "Just wondering. How's the Famous Author?"

That's how she refers to Oscar.

"He's fine," Katelynn said.

Glo tilted her head and blew smoke on a diagonal, the way Jenelle used to do. It made Katelynn nervous, seeing that. "If you get any more ideas like that, don't share them. Do the whole project yourself," said Glo.

"Without him, it wouldn't be nearly as good a book," Katelynn said, but Glo shrugged, and Katelynn realized that her mother was ready for her to leave, that the visit was over.

Standing in the open linen closet, inhaling the scent of the lavender sachets that she put there herself, Katelynn lifts out two sets of fresh towels and tucks the Walt picture back where she found it. Her husband is due home tonight, late. That's another unspoken rule of this silent game: she and Louisa and Oscar don't play it when Malcolm is home. Walt's picture will wait in its hiding place until Malcolm takes off again. *My husband.* She's almost used to the word. My husband, Malcolm Scott Lee.

So many men have a jack-in-the-box quality. There's the sudden, demanding drama of their presence, and then what? Silence, while they wait to be entertained, to be stuffed back into the box, to leap out again. Boys she knew in high school, so many of them, were like that.

Malcolm is twenty-nine. He grew up in Las Vegas. His father and mother were both electricians, the live-wire Lees, he likes to say. In the old warehouse—the abandoned neon factory—he'd felt right at home. He must have learned his watchful ways from his parents. He's always detecting, always alert. How is it that he blends into any crowd, yet by himself he's so attractive? She has tried to analyze the appeal of his terry-cloth-short hair, his chive-green eyes, his trip-wire attention to the world. He never watches TV, his favorite fruit is dates, and he'd be happy to wear a white shirt every day of his life. As a kid, he was a ham radio operator, staying up half the night, thrilling to messages from Singapore or Saskatchewan, "so much better than the Internet," he says. A few months ago, he moved his office from Memphis to Hawk Lake, renting a small suite in a building with dentists' offices and a pet store, the place he bought the aquarium.

Being able to blend in with a crowd is a skill, he said when she asked him about that. It took him a long time to learn how. You hold your breath, he said, and you disappear.

Harvey was a jack-in-the-box.

Harvey married the wedding-gown lady. She must be a good fifteen years older than he is, but when Katelynn sees them together, they seem settled and content. Occasionally, from the corner of her eye, Katelynn spots Harvey crossing a street or pumping gas into his car. When she waves, he lifts his arm, his face registering a complex, puzzled squint, as if she's a pole vault he can't quite focus on. She can hardly believe he's the person she once wanted to tell everything to.

I listen to people, Malcolm told her back in the mercury warehouse, when she'd asked him how he did his job. She's trying to do that herself, to listen better to Louisa and Oscar and to Malcolm himself, to listen to her mother and father and yes, to listen more closely to Peppy, who has so many different barks and whines and cries, he ought to be in the opera.

Ever since she and Malcolm got married, a year ago, she has enjoyed a full eight hours' sleep every night. Whether or not he's home, she feels peaceful, whole, and well. She is used to him in bed—his compact strength, his smell of clean denim and tangerines.

Not every night, but often, she has a dream that pleases her, a long, unfurling adventure in which she finds extra rooms in her house, rooms she didn't know existed. Sometimes they contain only sunlight and quiet. Other times, they're chock-full of furniture, old chests of drawers and bedsteads stacked against the wall, one room of treasures leading into another, through French doors and down hallways that she follows, in that familiar way of dreams, to more forgotten rooms. *Oh yes, it's been so long since I was here.*

The mercury has left her body. Maybe the dream is the form its farewell takes. She can't say exactly when she got well, when she lost her sense of contamination and regained her well-being, just as Dr. McKellar said she would. Even though she's well, she pictures the quicksilver still in her body, as if she's a human thermometer, all pulse and response. When, by accident, she cuts herself with a kitchen knife, she's surprised to see blood.

Her hair has grown back. She wears it in a scant puff tucked behind her ears, and along with gaining back the weight she'd lost to the mercury, she surprised herself by growing an inch taller. When she catches sight of herself in a mirror—even now, when she closes the glass door to the linen closet and sees her reflection in the pane—she looks like a girl in a photograph she remembers from her French text-book, a breezy girl wearing a kerchief, straddling a bike, and shading her eyes against the sun, with the caption "I'll meet you at the pool." *À la piscine.*

She spent a lot of time at the pool last summer, giving swimming lessons to kids—her community service, long delayed. It was so much better than lifeguarding. She gave the lessons in the morning, before the sun was too hot. To prepare, she had to brush up on her own skills, review levels 6 and 7 of her Red Cross training. The chlorinated water burned her nose worse than it ever had before, and she couldn't hold her breath as long underwater. On the grass, the children pushed each other and shivered. In the water, they behaved better. When fall came and the kids went back to school, she missed them.

The old woman in a shoe, Louisa calls her. How well the role of landlady suits her. She pictures herself forty years from now, still laying out fresh linen for her husband, for their boarders, saying, *I just fell into it.* But of course, Oscar and Louisa are not just tenants. They are her best friends.

They've got to stay, to live here forever.

At first, she'd tried to get Oscar to give tours. She went out on the lake with him on the boat that Jerry gave Louisa. Oscar was terrified. Katelynn learned how to operate the boat so that she could teach him, but he was an awful pupil. She made him talk with Louisa to create a script. "It's not hard, Oscar," Louisa snapped when Oscar flubbed the lines. Louisa reported to Katelynn that Oscar's mouth was so dry from fear that his lips actually stuck to his teeth.

Katelynn was outdone with him too. "You used to teach. You taught for fifteen years. What's the difference?"

"Everything. It's like selling, plus I'll worry about doing something wrong to the boat."

Miserable, he hung the keys to the boat on a hook beside the door and refused to try again. "I like the history," he said. "I'm just not ready to face whole bunches of people. And I don't like being out on that water. I can't swim real well. If the new boat were a duck boat, and part of the tour were on land, I might feel different."

So the beautiful white boat stayed tied up at the dock. It's there still. They go out on it occasionally. Katelynn will never get used to seeing it, tied up in the water or, in wintertime, pulled up on the grass and steadied on blocks, where it has a beached look. "I don't know what to do with it," Louisa says.

Then Katelynn got the idea for a book about Hawk Lake. She dug out her photos of the ostrich cart, and Oscar paid attention when she described the book. Together, they outlined its chapters. There's a chapter on the early days of the warm springs, back to the days of the Indians, another chapter on the Fiveash family, and of course one on the *Belle*—they interviewed Louisa for that. They spent hours at the library doing research. They talked with old-timers and put an ad in the paper asking people to loan their photos for the book. Pictures poured in. Katelynn loved going through them. It was her idea to bring the book into modern times; Oscar had planned only a retrospective. So she was the one who got to interview the diamond boy. In the end, it was Oscar who put it all together and found a publisher. Oh, they've earned a little bit from the book, not very much. The book's cover shows an aerial photo of Hawk Lake, shaped like a wide, crooked smile.

Oscar's current occupation—tutoring a few very smart kids—is something he hit on himself. Each term, he accepts only two or three promising students whose parents can afford to hire him. Officially, he teaches history, English, and writing. Unofficially, he coaches one or two students in track, if he believes they have a gift. There'll never be another Harvey, he sometimes says, just to make Katelynn mad. His mentored students go on to the best schools: Yale, Princeton, William and Mary.

She has missed all that. Or: just skipped it. Now and then, Malcolm suggests that she apply. "But where?" she'll ask.

"Anywhere you want. You could get into a great school. You'll be through before you know it."

"What about you? And the house, and Oscar and Louisa?"

"What would it take for you to leave this place?" Malcolm asked her, the last time they had the college discussion. It was a cool, rainy evening. He was outside smoking a cigarette, so they had to talk through the screen door. "I like this lakefront mansion, Katelynn. I'm just wondering what it would take for you to make a change."

"I made a change when I married you." She thought but didn't say: If Louisa and Oscar moved out, I might go. If you ever left me, I would leave, too. She's glad that when he exhales smoke, it's matter-of-fact, nothing like Jenelle's way.

He said, "If you go to college, I'll move to wherever you are. And this house isn't going anywhere. Those two could stay, or maybe it's time they moved on."

When she sputtered, he finished his cigarette and tossed it into the wet grass. "Don't get me wrong. I like 'em both."

"How can you be a detective and smoke? Can't people smell you?" *All poisonous,* she thought, *like the mercury vapors were. We all poison ourselves.*

"I'm quitting," he said. "That was my last cigarette ever."

"I'm too old to go to college. The others would seem like babies." She held the door open so he could step inside. She believed him about the last cigarette. He doesn't joke about things like that. The rainy air smelled of hyacinths.

He clasped her shoulders. "You're twenty-one, Katelynn. You're not too old."

"I just don't want to."

At that, he laughed. "Then don't."

Yet she tells herself, I will. College applications sit on her desk. Month by month, she puts them off. Surely a moment will come when she'll be all in a rush to leave for college right that instant; she'll want to pack a trunk with plaid clothes and freshly sharpened pencils. She imagines stepping out of a classroom building into falling leaves, while earnest students hurry beneath stone archways.

She loves her life in the glass house. She's not really expected to do anything at all. She doesn't have to get a job or entertain Malcolm's clients. His clients don't want to come forth and be noticed.

With Malcolm gone so often, so long, he's a kind of sea captain out on his voyages. She savors waiting for him, thinking her thoughts. Last week, during the first warm spell of the year, she was seized with longing for an old-fashioned, handheld fan. She found one in the little antique shop that is part of Mary Griffin's Hummingbird Inn, a treasure chest of a store filled with crocheted doilies, gold thimbles, lace parasols, rose potpourri, and painted teacups. Opening a glass case and lifting the fan carefully from a shelf, Mary Griffith explained that it was made of swans' feathers: "See how they're strung? All the feathers on this side came from the right wing, and on the other side, from the left wing." The dense feathers were pure white, tinged with ivory where they were attached to the handle.

Katelynn felt sick. "So they killed the swan to make the fan?"

"Oh, no! You can pluck the feathers. They might not like it, but they have plenty to spare."

Stroking the feathers, Katelynn envisioned the summer ahead: whole days of lying on her chaise longue out by the lake, shaded by a wide straw hat and a beach umbrella, fanning herself, with Oscar and Louisa for company. She would fan them, too, while they closed their eyes and leaned into the breeze of the swans' feathers. They will talk and read the paper, play cards and sip Coca-Cola and toss stones in the water for Peppy to chase, and when the sun says noon, they'll draw straws for who will fix lunch, then bring their sandwiches outside and sit until the sun goes down, and finally Katelynn will snap her fan shut and they'll go inside.

It will be wonderful.

The swans' feathers sweep through the air in such a wide, windy, graceful arc that you would think angels were fanning you.

The day she bought the fan, Sam Moon was getting ready to make a recording. A permanent resident of the Hummingbird Inn, he goes out on tour for a few months every year. He's up at Branson, Missouri, a lot, but Hawk Lake is his home. In fact, the Hummingbird Inn had a sign out front for a while, advertising itself as the home of Sam Moon and the Mountaineers, until Sam asked Mary Griffin to take it down. Too many autograph-seekers were hanging around outside. He insisted on a quieter place to hang his hat.

With the fan in a pink plastic bag, Katelynn had stepped from the antique shop into the living room, where all the sound equipment was set up. Sam was sipping from a thick mug, and his musicians were warming up—fiddlers, a banjoist, pipe players. He raised the mug toward her and said, "For my throat. Catnip tea. Mary makes it."

The tea gave off a green, grassy scent. Katelynn told Sam, "Louisa said to tell you she's on her way." Louisa plays the spoons in Sam's band, but only when she feels like it. Katelynn admires this, the way they have stayed friends even after Louisa decided she couldn't marry him; her heart wasn't in it.

Sam nodded. "She plays the hell out of those spoons."

He's having a second career, a big one, as a neo-Ozarker: Sam Moon and the Mountaineers. Now that his voice has aged, its reediness lends itself to the Scotch-Irish ballads he has learned to sing. You wouldn't know he's over seventy. He has sworn off what he calls "that lethal cocktail lounge music."

"Isn't it strange," he said as Katelynn stood there holding the bag with the fan in it. His eyes, with their thick white brows, held hers as he drank from the mug. She's always wondered if he were one of those singers, like Sinatra, who had gangsters for friends back home, in the Northeast, but she doubts it. "Everything, these last few years, so strange."

"Yes," she said. "I often think so."

He gestured toward the foyer, with its rosewood furniture, hurricane lamps, and stone fireplace. "You could turn your house into an inn, Katelynn. Have you ever thought of that? Innkeeping's hard work, but you get to be home a lot. You'd be good at it."

Swinging the bag with the fan, she gazed around the room. Too many knickknacks. She'd like to take those tacky sun catchers out of the window and put some of the perfumed candles and bric-a-brac away. Outside, the day was bright with springtime, too early for hummingbirds. Hydrangeas bloomed in the yard, a deep purple-blue like the blue lights on a Christmas tree that look always like they belong in snow. The cuckoo clock at the reception desk tick-tocked. In some of Sam's recordings, the clock chimes and the cuckoo crows in the background. In other recordings, the Mountaineers chat, swap jokes, and reminisce about possum hunts and 'simmon trees, so that the music is flavored with the sounds of their voices.

"I'm an innkeeper already," Katelynn told Sam. "The old woman in the shoe, Louisa says." It was then that she thought, *The boat. That's what I want to do. It'll be even better than giving swimming lessons. Why have I waited so long? I'll have the fan and the boat tours, too.* She realized these were not activities that would involve Malcolm. And yet, she loves him.

What the boat will give her is the voyage itself, the exoticism of not knowing whose life will brush up against her own. She will buy the boat from Louisa.

Louisa had hurried into the inn then, with those twins in tow. Katelynn can't stand their mother, Barbie, Louisa's old neighbor. Katelynn has trouble remembering the children's names. Madison and Fairley. The girl was carrying Louisa's spoons, rattling them so that they sounded like woodpeckers. When she saw Katelynn, she gave such a sweet smile that Katelynn was ashamed of herself for thinking critical thoughts.

Sam looked at the children and said, "Louisa, I don't think—"

Louisa interrupted. "Oh, Sam. They'll be quiet as mice. You always say you do better with an audience, anyway."

The fiddlers were tuning up, the pipe player pursing his lips, the banjoist strumming and adjusting his strings. Sam set his mug down on a table. The girl twin sniffed the dregs of tea in the mug and sneezed. Her brother took that opportunity to snatch the spoons from her and clack them against his knee. Louisa was speaking to one of the musicians, a wild-looking, steeped-in-tobacco-juice man, and they were laughing. Katelynn stepped back, watching them, telling herself: *Remember this.*

They'd forgotten she was there. *All of it, so strange.*

Now, as she hangs the fresh towels in the bathroom, she plans for tomorrow.

Tomorrow she will see her father.

It won't be the first time. He's been back several times, has even visited here at the house. Katelynn owns it now, which seems incredible. Her parents signed papers at a lawyer's office, during their divorce settlement, to make her the owner. When her father visits, he can't sit still. When he asks her to meet him in Memphis, because he has business there, she agrees.

So Memphis it will be: lunch at The Peabody.

Always she worries that something will go wrong. She will oversleep; she'll get into an accident on the way over; her car will flip off the bridge. She'll mistake a stranger for her father, will chase him down the street, will hire one of those horse-drawn tourist carriages to follow the fleeing man as he flings himself through alleys, careening through traffic and barbecue smoke. He will elude her, and he won't even be her father—her father, who taps his fingers on the polished table back at the hotel restaurant, wondering where she is.

She arranges washcloths over the tidy towels, replaces the damp bath mat with a clean one, and puts a fresh bar of soap in the shower. Glo had wanted heated towel racks, had actually planned to have those installed, saying, *Then I'll know we've really made it.*

All of us were heating up, Katelynn thinks, Mom and Dad and me, like pots heating to the boiling point on separate burners, with nobody minding the stove.

The towel racks are plain stainless steel ones, but the faucets on the sink and on the whirlpool bath are shaped like golden pineapples. The room is immaculate, for Katelynn cleans it herself, plus she has kept the maid. She thinks, *I could do this all my life. I'll do this and I'll give tours on the boat, and it will be enough.*

A savory scent rises from the kitchen: Oscar's invention of biscuits topped with apples and cheese, one of her favorite meals. Usually, he serves canned peaches on the side, or heats up some cream of mushroom soup.

My husband is coming home tonight, and tomorrow I'll see my father.

The first time her father came back was a few weeks after Glo moved to Mississippi. The doorbell chimed, and Oscar answered it. Spotting her father over Oscar's shoulder, Katelynn started screaming at him: "Get out! Get out of here!" She pushed Oscar out of the way and shoved her father so hard his knees buckled, right there on the doorstep. He was taller and more stooped than she remembered. How had she ever compared him to a newly hatched chick? This man was lean as a starved wolf in his black clothes, and he smelled of stale, starchy airport food.

The next-door neighbors, the Johnsons, came rushing over to see what was wrong. Katelynn kept on yelling at her father, hearing herself occasionally: *Didn't love. Walked out. Think now you can just . . .* Pressure in her head made the whole scene spin. It was early evening, dark, chilly out, and Christmas lights dotted the neighborhood, colored lights strung on shrubs and hedges outside and visible through windows on trees inside, in radiant family rooms. Lights spun, and Katelynn screamed at her father. In the dark yard, the colored lights reflected on his face. His cheeks looked as pale as stomped-on snow. Katelynn hoped she was scaring him.

The Johnsons said hello to her father as if nothing were the matter, as if he were just getting home from work, and they scurried back into their house. In a little while, Mr. Johnson came back with a plate of Christmas cookies, the cheap ones that Katelynn has always liked, plain cookies topped with red and green sugar. "Just making sure you're all okay," he said to Katelynn and her father both, who answered the door together that time, and she said, "Thank you. I think we are," thinking how people see so much more than you think they do, and that Mr. Johnson was the sort of person you needed in a crisis. Mr. Johnson would not take sides; he would just bring cookies and take a truly good look at both her and her father, to decide if he needed to call the cops or just go home and pray.

She and her father took the cookies back to the living room, where she lambasted him for deserting her and her mother. Chewing the

Christmas cookies and tongue-whipping her father, she tried to explain. "It's like you threw ice at us," she said. "Once when I was a lifeguard, kids at the pool did that. They knew ice couldn't be seen in the water. It just flies through the air and hurts you." When he looked puzzled, she said, "You don't know about that. You were probably on the other side of the world when it happened."

"Well, Katelynn, you were the lifeguard—what did you do?" he asked. Peppy ran into the room just then, as if Oscar and Louisa had been holding him back somewhere in the house and he'd gotten loose. Peppy planted himself on the rug, leaning against her father's knees and gazing up at him with an expression that said, "There you are. I've been waiting for you." Her father rested his hand on Peppy's head.

"What did I do with kids who were throwing ice and hurting people? I kicked them out. I got in trouble for that, because the manager thought I should just have warned them. I kicked them out, and I'm still glad of it." She'd hurled herself at those kids, flying at them in a fury that surprised her, scattering them and their treacherous plastic cups of ice chips. One minute, they were sitting smugly on the grass, tossing their little spears of ice, laughing as people in the pool yelped in pain. The next minute, she'd grabbed them by the backs of their necks and harried them out, two boys and a girl, old enough to know better. She ran them out through the gate and threw their beach towels over the metal fence.

"And how are you, Katelynn?" her father asked quietly, the question she'd wanted him to ask for so long.

So she told him, and they kept talking, staying up for hours into the night. After a year—no, more like two years of his occasional visits—she felt for the ice in her heart that had her father's name carved into it and found that the ice had melted. She has asked him if he will bring his wife and daughter to the States, and he always says he's trying, that it's hard to get them out, that he has paid bribes to officials with no result, and then his face looks as if he's disappeared inside himself, and she lets the subject drop.

Tomorrow, they'll talk while they eat, and he'll insist on buying her something in the gift shop, and then he'll walk her to her car. She always orders the same lunch at The Peabody, the same food she ate as a child when she lunched there with her parents. Tomato aspic, chicken salad, and fresh asparagus: a perfect meal, arranged on a gold-rimmed plate.

She piles laundry into a basket and pads downstairs in her bedroom slippers, passing through the kitchen, where Oscar perches on a high wooden stool at the butcher-block counter, correcting a student's essay.

"Is Louisa home yet?" she asks him.

"She came in, and I sent her out for milk and paper towels," he says, writing something on the paper. He has taken to wearing half-moon reading glasses, which, Louisa and Katelynn have agreed, make him look distinguished.

"You should let me do the shopping. That's my role," says Katelynn. "When do we eat?"

"Soon as she's back," he says, returning to the essay. He has taken the biscuits from the oven and arranged them on a platter. They're perfect. A pan of soup is warming on the stove. With her fingertip, Katelynn swipes a bit of syrup from the platter and licks it off her finger. Impulsively, she hugs Oscar's back, wrapping her arms around him from behind.

He jumps, nearly falling off the wooden stool, his half-moon glasses clattering to the butcher-block counter. "Sorry," she says, laughing. "I'm just so happy you're here."

When he picks up his glasses and puts them back on, she notices that his hands are shaking. "What's wrong, Oscar?"

"Nothing," he says. "Where did you live before you moved here, Katelynn? I've always wondered."

"In a split-level that was out on the highway back then, but now there's more development around it. It wasn't anything special." She can hardly remember it. What was she like back then, moving around in that forgotten house?

"I'll always think of you here," he says.

"Think of me here? But you live here. We *are* here."

Then he tells her he has news—that he's been offered a teaching job in Helena, that it's time he moved on, got back in the classroom, picked up his career again, that he will miss her.

LOUISA IS RELIEVED that Oscar sent her on the errand. What is it she's supposed to get? Eggs? Milk. Yes, whole milk for Katelynn, skim for herself and Oscar. At the lakeside convenience store, she finds herself beside the cash register, staring at the maps. *Get the milk, Louisa,* she tells herself, but all she can think about is the fact that if she leaves Hawk Lake right now, she can be up in the hills in, oh, three or four hours. By then, it'll be dark.

It's Friday night. She's not due back at school till Monday morning. She can sleep in her car, wake up at sunrise, and go hunting for her grandparents' cabin. Ever since she talked about bear bacon to Maddy this morning, she's been on fire. To get back. To see it again.

"You're a mountain gal at heart. Did you ever used to go owling?" the lead fiddler in Sam's mountain orchestra asked her last week, the day she went to the Hummingbird Inn to play the spoons.

"Owling?" she asked.

The fiddler turned a charming, lopsided grin on her. "You know, go out in the woods at dawn and make a bunch of crow sounds, like crows do when they catch an owl in the daylight, when it can't see so good." The man took a deep breath, cupped his hands around his mouth, and emitted a guttural cry that sounded exactly like a crow cawing. "Other crows hear you and come flying in, wanting a chance to beat up on their old enemy, the hoot owl, to fuss at 'im when he's stayed out too late. Kinda like my ex-wife used to do me." He threw back his head and laughed through a tobacco-stained beard. She urged him to caw again, to teach her how to do it. Maddy and Fairley clamored to learn, too, but the sounds they and Louisa made through their cupped hands were just plain comical, and then they were all laughing.

It was the day she gave up Walt. His picture had appeared behind the aquarium, and she and Katelynn and Oscar had watched the fish moving, the bubbles floating, and the ferns waving underwater, and she came to the end of wondering what to do about him. She will not do anything, for it is enough to know that when he smiles, his eyes crinkle at the corners, showing it's a real smile and not just for the camera. Enough to know he has a beautiful wife, laying her hand on his tuxedoed arm.

If they are ever to meet, he'll have to come to her, and she doesn't believe he will.

Her heart reached out and fastened on Walt, on the face beneath the pointy, glittery party hat. What have Teddy Shatford and his dead lobsters got to do with this man? Almost nothing, but they're still there, a small part, if you uncover them. She can't go to Walt and tell him only a little bit of the story. It would all tumble out. What if she arranged to run into him, say, on the Sunrise Trail while he's on his next vacation? "Oh hi, I'm your mother, I was raped at age sixteen and gave you up for adoption." And: "Oh yes, seven people died on a tour boat I used to run. So let's get caught up on your entire life."

It's enough to send love out to him like a song.

Fish the color of Katelynn's candy corn swam to and fro across Walt's face, as if they were guests at the same fancy-dress party where he and his wife waited, beaming, at their table. In the time it took for an angelfish to cross paths with a few of those little neon kinds, in the moment that a moonfish voyaged from the edge of the photo to the corner of one of Walt's eyes—glimmering eyes despite the graininess of a black-and-white newsprint photo—she gave him up.

"Anybody want popcorn?" she asked Katelynn and Oscar, with her face turned away from them—she's sure they didn't know anything was wrong—and they said okay, so she went to the kitchen and fixed it, crying while it popped.

Later that day, she lifted the Walt picture out from behind the aquarium and put it away. Where? Oh yes, the linen closet, under the towels. She should put it in her dresser drawer, put it away for good. Her other photos of him are in her dresser drawer, the other pictures that were in the folder that Malcolm gave to Katelynn. Malcolm had certainly tracked him down. There are elementary school pictures of Walt with a crewcut and a bow tie, his little face so gentle, so open, as if he's thinking about a pet kitten. The party picture she can look at; she has held it up to the light and examined it for any resemblance to herself or Teddy Shatford. The little-boy pictures she can't bear to inspect.

If she had the *Belle* back, how different her tours would be now. She would say, *Look, everybody, here's Hawk Lake, the town, with its churches and fire station, the library and the warm-springs spa and the old-fashioned ice-cream parlor. Here's an ordinary street corner where one fine summer day, I all of a sudden wondered who taught my little boy to tie his shoes. Here's the lake, where deep down I heard my daddy tell me to climb a ladder. And that house is where Barbie lives, Barbie who's kind and maddening all at once, who was in my kitchen slicing cake when I decided I had to find my son. There's the school where I work as the nurse, where I get to take care of Barbie's daughter, Maddy, who gets allergy shots, and I guess I got a child after all, because I love that little girl and her brother too, Fairley, who thinks about things so hard you just have to hug him and tell him it'll be all right.*

She is ready for a change. She's old enough to retire. Not yet. Because she loves her job, she'll probably work as long as they'll let her. She misses having her own house, even though it's fun to live with the others, to be part of their daily dramas. Could she leave the glass house? Yes. It's not good for a young couple to be cooped up with other people crowding into their lives. Katelynn has needed Louisa and Oscar, but now, Louisa believes, Katelynn and Malcolm should have the place to themselves.

She has cried at the side of the lake, has lost her house, and packed it up. How could she still hurt when a fish's swiveling little fins floated across the picture of that stranger, her son, propped behind the aquarium? The popcorn popping in the pan that day sounded like the fireworks she felt in her heart, like short bitter sobs or tiny fists pounding the metal of the pan. She went back into the living room and handed the bowl of popcorn to Oscar and Katelynn without a word, then went to her room and lay down on the bed. Hours later, after she'd cried herself dry, she went to Barbie's house and picked up the twins, because she'd promised Barbie she'd watch them that day.

She hadn't planned on getting so tickled by a story about owls and crows. Her eyes felt raw and sore, yet she was laughing.

Sam had looked at them—her and the fiddler, Madison and Fairley—and said to the fiddler, "Throw in some of those crow calls at the end of our first tune," but Sam was annoyed, his voice edgy. Yet she had the sudden feeling that he was really seeing her, not with the dreamy look he used to have, which only reminded her of how old they were and of how he'd pined all those years for her young-girl self, which was long since lost. No, the expression on his face, as she laughed about owling, was new.

She used to look at her passengers like that. You had to size them up to see if they were drunk or disorderly or confused or sick. That hardly ever happened. Only two or three times in all those years did she decide somebody ought not to get on the boat—in each case drunk—and she'd left them at the bandstand. And once a shaking old man had started to climb aboard, only to have a middle-aged woman appear, out of breath as if from chasing him, saying, "Paw-paw, come on, let's go home," and to Louisa, "I'm sorry, he has a habit of wandering off."

Yes, Louisa had learned to look at people closely, if only in the moment before they boarded. At first she'd felt like a spy, checking them out, but she learned how to look at them so they hardly noticed. She was, after all, guarding them.

Eventually, the *Belle* probably went to a scrapyard. Louisa got that prediction out of the bearded Coast Guard officer at the first hearing. She pictures the *Belle* on top of a heap of junked cars, riding high, but she knows it was probably torn apart and melted down—as if that would settle anything, as if it would ever be over.

Owling. In the convenience store, staring at the display of maps, she strains to remember if her father's parents ever talked about that. Seems she can almost remember that they did. How is it that even when you're old, childhood doesn't seem that long ago? Next time she sees Sam, she'll tell him about the day her father took her hunting in the flooded timber, and how she bellowed to warn the birds away. She'll describe the cypress stumps sticking out of the water. How old were those stumps, and are they still there?

Her whole life has been that question, in one form or another, looping backward and forward: Is my baby still out there? And the answer, even when you have it in your hand, when you hold a photo of a man you believe is your own son, the answer is so many more questions that they just fill you up. That has to be enough.

She's been in this store long enough to buy milk about fifteen times, yet she hasn't moved toward the dairy case or reached for her wallet. The cashier arches her painted-on brows and asks, "Something I can help you with?" She pretends not to know Louisa, but Louisa is used to that—the cold, funny way some people have acted ever since the boat sank. Usually, she tries not to shop here. If this were back in the days when people were tarred and feathered, this cashier would be stirring the tar, hurling hot globs of it at Louisa's face, and shoving her into a tub full of feathers. If it would bring them back, Louisa would apply tar and feathers with her own hands.

She examines some magnets in a dish marked SALE! She picks up a bag of caramel corn and sets it down. She used to keep trinkets on board to give to honeymooners or children having birthdays. These magnets, in the shape of Arkansas, would be perfect for that, and even the bags of caramel corn. People used to be so happy to get those little things. She misses shopping for them, keeping an eye out.

She misses her mother.

Pulling an Arkansas map from the rack, she puts it on the counter.

"This is all." The cashier rings it up, still pretending that Louisa is a stranger who could not possibly be of less interest to her.

Louisa had asked the fiddler, "So then what do you do with all those crows you call over?"

"You've just got 'em, then. They're great to watch. You can never have too many crows," he'd said. "When you go owling, you end up with crows. Makes sense, don't it?"

She wants to go to the Ozarks, but not by herself. Who does she want to go with? The fiddler? It felt good to laugh with him, to think back to the old days.

But it's not the fiddler she pictures in the car with her. She wants to be with Sam—Sam, who dreamed of her all those years, who came to find her when he heard she was in trouble, who has stuck by her as a friend, giving her a place in his mountain band. When she plays the spoons, eventually the music takes over and she forgets for a minute, sometimes two minutes in a row, about the sinking. She can imagine living in the mountains with Sam, who knows his way around the back roads and the hollows, who has found the old-style musicians there. Sam is working too hard. She'll get him to relax more. They can stroll around the lake together—Hawk Lake, or another one, somewhere else—and she'll resume her search for a king rail.

Louisa tucks the map under her arm and asks the cashier, "Can I use your phone?" Silently, with pursed lips, the woman pushes the phone toward her.

She will call Sam and ask if he'd like to go out to the country with her. Instead, when she hears his voice, she says, "It's Louisa. Will you go to bed with me?"

A pause, while the cashier stares at Louisa with her mouth hanging open. At last, Sam chuckles and says, "Well, just come right on over, Louisa."

"We're going to the mountains, Sam."

"The mountains," he says. "Louisa, are you all right?"

"I'm fine. I mean it. The Ozarks, that's where we're going. There's a place I need you to help me find, Sam. My grandparents' farm."

He chuckles again. "How well do you remember how to get there?"

"Not real well. Besides, the whole place could be gone. By now, the whole area might've turned into subdivisions and shopping malls."

"We'll find it, Louisa," he says, and she pictures the two of them at the cabin where the mule pulls the sweep over the sorghum mill. With Sam, she'll stand again at the ravine where her little brother died.

Next, she'll call home, let Katelynn and Oscar know she won't be there for supper. With Sam along, she won't need the map, for he has learned the roads and back roads by heart, in his successful search for the Mountaineers. She leaves the map on the counter.

There won't be any sorghum mill, of course, or any little chair for her brother still sitting in a corner of the cabin. The coon skins probably won't hang on the walls anymore, and the cabin itself may be a grown-over tumble of ivy and sticks. If they find the old place at all, they won't stay long. An hour or two, while she putters around and collects her thoughts. She'll ask Sam to let her stand alone at the ravine for a while.

If only she could save him, her tiny, tumbling brother, run hard enough to reach the bottom and hold out her arms before he hurtles down. He fell so fast and there was no ladder and nobody waiting to fetch him back. If she'd been there, if she'd been born by then, she'd have grabbed him and carried him up again, clambering to the top out of breath with the baby heavy and warm against her neck, and she would never let their mother know about the fall. Her father saved her underwater. She'll have to catch the baby any way she can. If she reaches the ravine, she can catch him with her heart.

Sam will understand.

When she and Sam leave, the place will go on as if they were never there. Why this is all right, she doesn't know, but it is.

•   •   •

OUT ON THE BOAT, the lake breeze is colder than Katelynn expected. She should have brought a sweater. She's letting Peppy run loose on the shore. She ought not to. Malcolm would be annoyed, saying the dog could get lost, have an accident. He's right, but Peppy loves it, makes a wild time of it, stands on shore and yelps till she's out of earshot, then sprints off like a dervish. When she gets back to land, she'll have to holler for him.

Louisa called to say she and Sam are off to the mountains, so Katelynn and Oscar ate all the biscuits. Off to the mountains. Louisa will be back in a few days, but Oscar will be moving on. Katelynn feels restless, inspired to make a trip of her own, to embark.

Oh, it's extravagance, to run this big boat out on the water with only herself aboard, using up gasoline. "Don't go out there by yourself," Oscar said, but she waved that away. She has done this before. She'll be safe.

Her time doesn't count. She has plenty of time. Tomorrow, after her lunch with her father, while the cleaners scrub her glass house, she'll come out to the lake again. Maybe Malcolm will come with her. How is it she has never told him about that recurring dream, the extra rooms she finds in her house? She'll tell him tomorrow about how quiet and sunlit the dream house is, about the long hallways and the rooms that lead into each other.

They'll look back to the glass house and see its layers of grime being blasted away, and they will cheer. Antlike human figures will crawl across the glass, hosing, swiping, brushing, and bathing it. If she were one of them, she'd go ahead and strip off her clothes. Soap and ammonia would sting her skin, and she would clean with both hands, both feet, and a rag between her teeth.

For now, she'll sail in a perfect oval, avoiding the shallow marshes, staying where the water's deep. The sun has set, and a purple stain creeps across the sky. All she has to do is turn the wheel slowly to guide the boat. Faster than she expects, she reaches the middle of the lake, far from the sounds of voices, of households at suppertime, and she cuts the engine.

How did Louisa end her tours? Katelynn must ask her. What would be fitting, dramatic enough, after you showed your passengers the town, the lake, after you've shown them the stage on which your whole life plays out? "Those are they," Katelynn's sixth-grade teacher used to say after every spelling test, having pronounced the words carefully, lovingly, as if they were pearls in her mouth. "Not those are them. Those are they," the teacher would say with finality, while the sixth graders set their pencils down and passed their papers in, both humbled and haughty from having survived the quiz, oblivious to the teacher's benediction.

So what did Louisa tell them? *You-all watch your step climbing down. Where you going next? Oh, the diamond mine? A boy found a real diamond there, not so long ago. Good luck, now. Come back again.*

The currents move the boat ever so slowly in the wind. In a little while, she'll go back to her house to wait for Malcolm. The sick girl in that glass house, way far over on the shore, the girl who laughed when the passengers struggled and died, she's gone. Tomorrow, the cleaners will rub the last of her away, her breath on the glass walls, her fingerprints, strands of dusty hair with mercury inside it. One day, Katelynn will tell her children her story: *I got well. I married your father.* Her children will perceive that these events, these processes, were miraculous and hard. She will never get past some level of vanity. She understands that. *I got well so slowly.*

In Joliet, Illinois, she'd said good-bye to the diamond boy, stepped out of his house into the snow, and was shocked by the glorious, forestlike smell of it, for she'd never experienced a deep snowfall before. Cold seeped through her coat. She hadn't thought to bring gloves. It was a Saturday afternoon, getting late, in a town where nobody knew her. Far off, kids yelped and played, but she couldn't see them. Turning her face up to the whirling sky, she stood on the sidewalk so long that snow crusted on her cheeks and shoulders. She wondered if the boy or his mother might push the door open and call out to her, but they didn't. Already she was thinking of questions she wished she'd asked the boy. She debated if she should go back inside but decided it was too late. It was then that she decided to marry Malcolm.

Her boat is the only one on the lake. In the magnifying hollow of water and air, she might hear a distant telephone ring, a voice call out. Any minute now, she'll hear a car door slam, hear her husband greet the dog.

Acknowledgments

The author wishes to acknowledge the following:

These Were the Last: Ozarks Mountain Folk, by Townsend Godsey (Branson, Mo.: The Ozarks Mountaineer, 1977).

Arkansas: A Guide to the State, Writers' Program, Work Projects Administration (Scholarly Press, Inc.; originally published 1941, reissued 1977).

The author would also like to thank Linda Kay Myers, M.D., of the Health Science Center of the University of Tennessee, Memphis, and Mark Blaeuer of the National Park Service, Hot Springs, Arkansas, for providing information on the history of mercury.

About the Author

CARY HOLLADAY is the author of two collections of short stories, *The People Down South* (University of Illinois Press, 1989) and *The Palace of Wasted Footsteps* (University of Missouri Press, 1998). Holladay is the recipient of a 1999 O. Henry Award and numerous prestigious fellowships. She lives in Memphis, Tennessee.